For As Long As But A Hundred Of Us Remain Alive

British Espionage and the Rise of the Scottish Independence Movement

A novel based upon fact-based historical fiction.

Ron Culley

www.ronculley.com
author@ronculley.com

Edited by John McManus

Grosvenor House
Publishing Limited

This book is published by
Grosvenor House Publishing Ltd
Link House
140 The Broadway, Tolworth, Surrey, KT6 7HT.
www.grosvenorhousepublishing.co.uk

A CIP record for this book
is available from the British Library

ISBN 978-1-83615-086-2
eBook ISBN 978-1-83615-087-9

Previous books by Ron Culley

The New Guards/The Kaibab Resolution.
Kennedy & Boyd 2010.
I Belong To Glasgow (foreword by Sir Alex Ferguson)
The Grimsay Press, 2011.
A Confusion of Mandarins Grosvenor House. 2011.
Glasgow Belongs To Me Grosvenor House
(electronic media only) 2012.
The Patriot Game. Grosvenor House 2013.
Shoeshine Man A one-act play. SCDA. 2014.
One Year. Grosvenor House 2015.
Alba: Who Shot Willie McRae? Grosvenor House 2016.
The Last Colony Grosvenor House 2017.
The Never Ending Story (Editor) Downie Allison Downie 2018.
Odyssey Grosvenor House 2018.
The Bootlace Saga (Editor) Downie Allison Downie 2019.
Rebellious Scots To Crush Grosvenor House 2020.
The Odyssean Companion Downie Allison Downie 2021.
Dalriada Grosvenor House 2022.
Firebrand Grosvenor House 2022.

Web address
www.ronculley.com

A 'trilogy' of four books dealing with Scottish independence.

'Alba: Who Shot Willie McRae?'

'A brilliant book. You won't be able to stop reading'.
Donaidh Foirbeis.
'A great read'. Annette Davidson.
'A controversial story brilliantly told.' John Alder.
'Fast moving, gripping and a must, must read.' Iain Allan.
'One of the best books I have read.' Graham Baker.

'The Last Colony'

'A superb piece of work.' Craig MacInnes.
'Just finished 'The Last Colony'. Recommended.'
Catherine Campbell.
'A very important read for those interested in the
independence of Scotland'. John Alder.
'An exciting tale of the battle for a small country's
freedom.' Roddy Martin.
'Excellent plot line, well written. A good read!'
Deirdre Boyd.
"Brilliant! When is your next book published?
I'll be sure to order it!" Jordan Jindsay.

'Rebellious Scots To Crush'

'Completely believable and partly based on a true story.'
J. McManus.
'This is a scary premise. Brilliantly written.'
Allan Thomson.
'This story requires to be told. A great read.'
George Cuthbert.
'A marvellous Scots story of political intrigue.
Donald John Morrison follows dark money to its corrupt
destination - undermining a nation.' Grousebeater.

'Dalriada'

'Culley tells a fine tale.' Ray Hendry
'Ron Culley follows in the hallowed footsteps of
fellow Scot Alistair MacLean.' Alan Murray.
'Another taut Scottish political thriller from Ron Culley.'
Simon Ki
'Reading this book made me want to march on London!'
Jim Pirrie

For As Long As But A Hundred Of Us Remain Alive

'Quia quamdiu Centum ex nobis viui remanserint, nuncquam Anglorum dominio aliquatenus volumus subiugari.'

Ron Culleg

Inspired By Actual Events

This book aims to use the techniques of historical fiction to tell the tale of the emergence of Scottish Nationalism and the interest taken in it by British Security Services in the twentieth century. The characters appearing in this book all existed other than those invented by the author for purposes of the narrative. A number of the events depicted occurred at least in some form in real life. Essentially, in order to turn historical events and characters into a novel format, the author has been obliged to simplify, dramatise and invent details that allows the narrative to flow in an interesting and entertaining way. Some events have been truncated in time, again to allow the smooth flow of narrative. All photographs used are of real people. Certain of them are utilised to portray fictitious characters.

There is no way to give each year its allotted weight and in consequence, much will have been omitted - again in the interests of narrative.

And before we kick a ba', readers who imagine that there's too much whisky consumed in the narrative...well apparently you don't have the kind of friends that I have!

'For as long as but a hundred of us remain alive, never will we on any conditions be brought under English rule. It is in truth not for glory, nor riches, nor honours that we are fighting, but for freedom – for that alone, which no honest man gives up but with life itself.'

Declaration of Arbroath, 1320

Acknowledgements

For my sins, I have found myself included on the pages of Who's Who for many years now. I confess I played somewhat fast and loose with their 'Hobbies' section, designed to have contributors describe their fascination with trout fishing, train-spotting or hill walking. I set out quite a few pastimes but the 'hobby' that gave me most pleasure was that of 'contumaciousness'; the wilful disobedience of authority. Perhaps not a hobby, but it aptly describes an aspect of my personality, certainly according to my wife.

So it was then, that when advised that one cannot write in both the first person and the third person in the same work, I decided to do just that; a style referred to as *diegesis*, from the Greek, 'to narrate' a method of storytelling in which the author presents the actions and thoughts of the characters to the readers. It will be for you, dear reader, to decide whether the advice I was given should have been better regarded.

As ever, my grateful thanks go to my beloved family members who are my north, my south, my east and my west, and to my dear friends, especially my friend of *circa* fifty years, John McManus who yet again has edited one of my books. His contribution, as ever, is much appreciated but any mistakes made within these pages remain mine. In writing the book, I may not always have recorded that which is true...it is a fact-based novel after all, but I have not written that which I know to be false. Where I do depart from *l'actualité,* I 'fess up in the Notes section at the end of the book.

Special mention must also be given to my wonderful friends, George Cuthbert from Bonnybridge and Jim Coll from Dunnet who each shared their knowledge of the earlier days of the movement and of life in rural Scotland. In addition, George's friend, Iain. S. Johnston presented me with a clutch of annotated copies of Wendy Wood's monthly magazine, *'The Patriot'* which allowed me to quote her directly. He also supplied copies of Major Frederick Boothby's occasional publication, *'Sgian Dubh'*. Donald John Morrison, he of Benbecula, also supplied text of considerable value. Without their helpful notes, I'd have made some serious mistakes. The lovely Lorna Hutchison gave freely of her time to discuss the role played by her father, Robert at the time of the formation of the Scottish National Party. It was most enlightening and much appreciated. Last but by no means least, the admirable Donald Anderson has been extremely helpful as he knew many of those cited herein personally and gave unstintingly of his time to have me educated.

My genuine thanks goes to each one of them - but as earlier, all mistakes are mine.

Ron Culley

Ron Culleg

For As Long As But A Hundred Of Us Remain Alive

Contents

Chapter One

1945. DRESDEN, GERMANY

My given name is Manus, my surname is Canning and I come from the age of steam. I write these words at the end of the second millennium, which seems as good a vantage point as any from which to tell my story.

I hail from a windswept and damp croft on the Isle of Lewis where my family eked a living from the land for generations and from where, in 1943, aged eighteen, I left to fight Hitler.

I am old now, slightly doddery and I've served time in prison as a Scottish patriot because while a long life brings many things, a blameless life is seldom among them. War changed me. When I caught the ferry from the island to the mainland harbour of Ullapool, the khaki uniform and the dark green, white and red kilt  of the Highland Light Infantry, I was excited. My teachers thought me bright and in other times, an education in one of Scotland's great universities would have lain before me as it had other scholars from the island. Instead, I shot and killed other men. I survived due to my then belief that the small Gaelic Bible, forced into my top left uniform pocket would protect me from a kill-shot. Other Western Islanders had testified to its efficacy in this regard. Mind you, they were mostly talking having first spoken with John Barleycorn.

At the time I felt no remorse as soldiers of the Axis forces would surely have killed me had they been able, and all around were engaged in that same ghastliness. I even received a field promotion

1

aged only twenty-one to sergeant and confess that at the time I believed it well-deserved as I was popular, brave and had the respect of my fellow soldiers. But, as I say, war changed me as it changed everyone. Gradually my feelings towards my adversaries altered and I came to believe that they were mostly young men who were trapped in a nightmare as was I. As the war drew to an end, my heart was no longer prepared to kill for Queen and Country so it was something of a relief when, in 1945, after the Battle of the Reichswald and the final advance into Germany, I was given a detail of six squaddies and told to escort an eejit General called Ernest. E. Clutterbuck - and honestly, that was his real name - who was sent south-east to Dresden in order to hold talks with the Russians about Christ knows what. The First Armoured Guard Army of the Soviet Army and the Seventh Panzer Division of the National People's Army had been stationed in and around Dresden as the great powers began carving up Germany.

Clutterbuck was not untypical of many of the officers under whom I served. With the squaddies he was brusque and spoke to us monosyllabically as much as possible in order to issue instructions but when meeting other officers of similar social standing as he saw it he'd become almost garrulous and always make it plain that he was one of the Hampshire Clutterbucks and they'd nod knowingly. When speaking with those he considered his equals, he was inclined to speak for long moments with his eyes closed, a trait which left me curious as to how and when he'd decided that this might be a better way of communicating. I'd shake my head imperceptibly at his sense of entitlement and mindful class-consciousness.

When we arrived, General Clutterbuck was billeted in a large mansion that had largely escaped destruction. Me and the boys were offered a nearby hay-loft on the northern bank of the Elbe. We'd become accustomed to roughing it and having a straw bed and a leaky roof over our heads was no inconvenience whatsoever. With bugger all to do while the General was conferring with the Ruskies, we took it upon ourselves to visit the city of Dresden. What I saw there scarred me.

2

Churchill had dropped untold tons of ordinance a few months earlier which set ablaze a largely wooden habitation killing thousands of innocent mothers and children. From February through April of that year, more than five hundred Lancasters dropped almost six thousand tons of bombs on the city, many of them incendiary. Over four hundred American bombers unloaded more tonnage. Some of the Russians spoke decent English and told us that cremated adults had been shrunk to the size of small children, whole families had burned to death and all the time the hot wind of the firestorm drew people back into the burning houses they were trying to escape from. It was carnage. It was unnecessary. It was blood-lust. The war had all but been won.

The lucky ones in Dresden were those who had been killed outright by the explosions and shrapnel. Many of the maimed and burned lingered painfully before surrendering to the inevitable. We spent some time helping the Russians offer some relief to those starving and injured who might make it through the end days of the war if given food, water and shelter. Russian soldiers had themselves undergone great privation and were then bent upon securing cigarettes more than the demise of Fascism when we met them, offering vodka in exchange. Americans we bumped into were loud, cocky and well-supplied. I didn't take to them but back then we were in the process of winning a war together and I tolerated their relative brashness given that quite a few of us in the HLI had our own frailties in that regard.

All of our boys were big fans of our British Prime Minister, Winston Churchill. They loved his confident "V' for Victory' gesture, his enthusiasm for appearing unannounced but with great subsequent publicity in war zones, his purported enjoyment of a glass and his speechifying. Me? I thought him a mass-murdering psychopath. I'd read of his starving the Indian population, his early enthusiasm for using poisoned gas

3

in a war zone and was aware of his proprietorial attitude to Ireland. When he firebombed Dresden, it was inhuman. He was of his age, I suppose, and was an enthusiastic racist, a steadfast royalist and a fervent colonialist. But I had to remember that Hitler was an evil adversary who had to be defeated. Still, much as I was repulsed by Churchill, I nevertheless learned at that young age that keeping my own counsel was a wise practice and it served me well in later years in Scotland when I couldn't be sure if I was speaking to a Scottish patriot or an agent of the British Government. It was also an advantage once the war ended and the British Establishment came calling.

So, as I say, I left a rural Lewis excited and optimistic but returned to an urban Glasgow hardened, bloodied and angered. I had survived the war. Many friends hadn't.

Although I didn't realise it at the time, a pig changed my life.

In our small farmyard encampment, my men were retrieving cooked potatoes from the coals of a hot fire and were tossing them from hand to hand to cool them. Russian soldiers in charge of about fifty defeated German prisoners had been chasing a domestic pig around, anxious to have it butchered for dinner that night, when its frightened evasions saw it crash unceremoniously into a bicycle whose rider careered into a group of Germans. One of them was knocked backwards and I saw him knock his head against a stone mooring bollard before he splashed unconscious into the River Elbe.

Due to attending to my ablutions, I was dressed only in pants and a vest and had lain down my battledress outside the barn to dry in the sun. My boots had also been set out to dry. I was therefore, as a consequence of this coincidence, perfectly prepared to attempt a rescue. The German, still insensible, surfaced and was immediately swept downriver by the dark, fast-flowing Elbe. Without giving any thought to the consequences of failure. I ran fast along the bank and as I came up alongside the man, dove into the swirling waters, my breath immediately being caught by the freezing temperature of waters that had but recently tumbled from the high Krkonoše Mountains on the Czech-Polish border. It took me several long strokes before I came up beside the soldier whom I grabbed roughly by the neck. Gathering him into my body, I changed to a side-stroke using only my left arm and slowly, against the flow, brought him back towards shore where several of his colleagues had now gathered. One of them waded towards us but was instantly surprised by the steep bank of the river at that point so he too, was submerged. He surfaced close enough for me to grasp his collar and now on my back, I kicked furiously, unable to use my arms for propulsion until I made shore with the two men. The Russians looked on disinterestedly, their general demeanour being one of '*Zhopa*! Let the German bastard drown'.

Strong arms lifted us from the water and rather intemperately, I pushed aside those helping and turned the still unconscious soldier onto his side in order to affect ventilation of his lungs. As my thoughts turned to additional resuscitation, the man began to recover, coughing water out of his mouth and after a few moments, had manoeuvred himself on to his knees where blood from his head-wound and water from his lungs mingled and flowed together onto the brown earth. The other soldier was only slightly the worse for wear. One of my men, Ian McMurtrie, offered him a sip of earlier stolen *schnapps* which was willingly accepted. My soldier recovered more slowly due to his more protracted immersion in the Elbe but he too rallied following some of Ian's purloined schnapps. Two Russians attempted gruffly to intervene but my harsh language stopped their commands being followed.

The German was surprised at my bullish attitude towards his guards.

"You speak English! You are English?"

I smiled. "One more insult like that and I'll throw you back in the river. I'm Scottish."

5

He returned my grin. "I think I owe you my life, Scottish."

I turned to McMurtrie who hovered beside me with a first-aid bag.

"Ian, hand me those bandages." I returned my attention to the German. "You have a bad head wound there. Hold still while I put this dressing on. It'll stop the bleeding."

A few moments passed while I tended to the man's head.

"One of my men is a better medic than me. He's away in Dresden just now but when he gets back I'll ask him to look at that cut. It'll need cleaning and better bandaging that I can offer." The German's eyes creased in smiled gratitude.

"Your Russian friends would not have been so helpful. I'm surprised they didn't shoot me in the back for trying to escape."

I eyed the group of Russian soldiers who appeared genuinely perturbed at the efforts I'd gone to, first to save, then to tend to the needs of a belligerent whom they believed was only worth the bullet they'd happily bury in his chest.

I reassured him. "They're cautious around us. They know we're here dealing with their commanders so they walk on eggshells a wee bit." I stood. "Better get those wet clothes dried. Mine and the boys' are over drying in the sunshine. Put yours on the line there and I'll get us a pretty disgusting coffee. Your pal there looks like he's none the worse after his attempts at saving you."

"*Obersoldat* Schröder tried to save me?"

"He waded into the river to help as I approached the bank. The river took him also."

The German rose cautiously to his feet and offered his hand, which was taken.

"May I know your name, Scottish?"

"Sergeant Manus Canning, Highland Light Infantry."

"I am *Stabshauptmann* Jürgen Roth of the *Kommandeur der Nachrichtenaufklärung*, what you would call our Signals Intelligence Regiment, and I am indebted to you, Sergeant Manus Canning. I have survived bullets and bombs but the river was almost the end of me."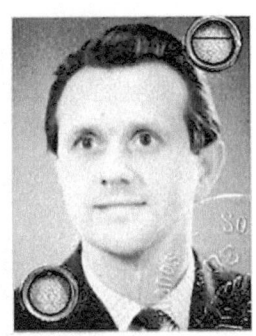

"What kind of rank is *Stabshauptmann*?

"Ah, it is an unusual one my friend. I was a specialist officer who dealt with technical army intelligence. Mostly to do with communications, the design of wireless sets, training of wireless operators and some research. I was to be promoted from Captain to Major but as this war draws to an end, I was informed that there were what they called 'administrative difficulties' so I was given this temporary half-way house. As I say, it is an unusual rank but I am the most senior officer here so our Russian friends have been giving me special attention. They believe I must know Hitler personally." He looked at me, assessing the cut of my jib. "You are young for a sergeant."

I shook my head, pretending modesty.

"All the older ones were too drunk, too stupid or too dead."

He chewed his lower lip in thought.

"I do not think so, Scottish Sergeant Manus Canning of the Highland Light Infantry. I think the British army knows your worth."

Chapter Two

AN AWAKENING

Demobbed in 1946, I returned briefly to my family home but despite my parents quite obviously failing in health, I surrendered their care to my wee brother Seumas, who worked the croft, and my sister Jean who worked as a fishwife down at the harbour in Stornoway where she would gut and cure the catches, as well as baiting lines. Nevertheless, I couldn't but help feel a pang of guilt as the ferry took me back to the mainland where I caught a MacBrayne's bus on the long trip south to Glasgow.

Seumas had been spared war service due to him being seven years younger than me but having seen life in the raw across France and Germany, I wasn't prepared to return to the Presbyterian ways of the island, the arduous discipline of croft work or the silence of the Sabbath. My sister Jean was a wonder. She worked hard hauling and cleaning fish and carrying her produce on her back in a creel to McCrimmond's old truck before returning to the croft and helping Seumas before tending to our ageing parents.

My first job in Glasgow was as a shirt manufacturer's clerk where I was responsible for the management of a shift of ladies who worked hard under poor conditions. The company was located in an old sandstone workshop in the city's Broomielaw down on the bustling banks of the Clyde. The building had poor ventilation, dim lighting and cramped work space. The ladies were underpaid but grateful for the work. Within a month, I was less so and after an argument with an indifferent owner about these conditions I left, returning two minutes later to flatten him with a single punch to loud cheers from his workforce. When in the army, I'd become known for my occasional hot temper and had a reputation of sometimes hitting people first and asking questions only when they were unconscious. So it was here.

An afternoon in the city's Horseshoe Bar drinking whisky, tending my bruised knuckles and talking through my woes with some squaddies still in uniform, left me considering re-enlisting but instead I stumbled back to my cramped lodgings in Anderston where a fellow ex-patriot islander had let me a room I could afford. I spent a week looking for work, determined this time to do something that tested me and that had the potential to be enjoyable. Few jobs of this nature were in evidence until a conversation with a friendly off-duty policeman from South Uist guided me towards a job in the civil service which involved joining a small team which reported on the conditions of the ports of Scotland. I applied and was successful. The job took me out and about, returned me to the experience of working in a group as was the case in the army and allowed me to satisfy my yearning to learn. Some of my colleagues were highly educated and were involved in the study of ocean floor depth and elevation at the entrance to the ports. Others assessed the wave climate which in Scotland is mainly influenced by conditions in the North Atlantic ocean where the fetch is long enough to establish large, regular waves. As an uneducated and inexperienced civil servant, I was tasked with measuring the fishing effort in any given port in order that cleverer people than me could assess the sustainability of fish stocks. Mostly this involved me in affable conversations with fishermen and boat owners and I enjoyed these enormously, developing a life-long respect for the arduous life these hard working people endured.

My life was nomadic and I stayed in lodgings around Scotland which were in close proximity to ports from as far north as Scrabster down to Troon in the south-west. To my great delight I was from time to time required to visit the port of Stornoway and so kept in irregular touch with my family.

I was in lodgings in St. Monan's in the East Neuk of Fife one evening, the air was still and a mist rose from the calm sea. I set off for a short walk. With nothing better to do, I strolled along the front, listening to the rattle of the small waves on the shingle and the hiss as they receded. I was attracted into a meeting in a church hall which promised some warmth. The speaker was a small man called Harry Selby. He was a barber from Govan in Glasgow and was a member of the Revolutionary Socialist League. He was all fire and brimstone and was a whirlwind of hand gestures as he stood on his tiptoes in indignation, stamping his feet and pouring scorn on the past colonial approach of the United Kingdom, traducing the Royal Family as parasites and speaking passionately about protecting workers' rights and the importance of trades unionism. He was elaborate and flowery - stopping just short of pomposity, I thought - but I was mesmerised. He was supported by Abe Moffat, a Communist and the President of the National Union of Scottish Mine Workers who spoke articulately and at length of the tribulations faced by those tasked with going underground to produce coal.

In 1950, the first general election ever to be held after a full term of a Labour Government had just taken place and the government's 1945 lead over the Conservative Party had shrunk dramatically, returning Labour to power but with an overall majority reduced from one hundred and forty-six to just five. Selby argued that this was proof positive that the Labour Party in government had sold out to capitalism and that only with a much stronger left-wing agenda might they be returned to full power. I found myself agreeing with much of what the man said but when he asked people attending to join his movement, I did nothing. Mindful, perhaps of the soldiers' code, 'never volunteer', I decided to keep to my practice of thinking things through myself and holding my opinions close to my chest, particularly when they were not fully formed.

Perhaps a week later when I was in Aberdeen, one of the men with whom I worked, Andy Forsyth, encouraged me to go with him to hear Wendy Wood speak. She was by then a weel kent face in

10

Scottish politics and must have been in her fifties when we went to see her. She was forever getting arrested in London and elsewhere for her fiery espousal of Scottish Nationalism and I was intrigued as to her take on matters as she'd just returned from a visit to New York where headlines such as 'Tartan Whirlwind Hits New York' followed her back to Scotland.

Like Harry Selby the week before, she spoke without notes and was witty, angry, incisive and commanded the stage on which she stood. She took questions and answered them all very ably, also seeing off a critic who had obviously visited the pub before jousting with her. He was dispatched with a flea in his ear following a few well-chosen remarks and retreated into silence. It was a bravura performance and she didn't hold back on her distaste for everything to do with British rule and the unfairness of a political system that she argued held Scotland back. As with Selby, I found myself in agreement with her arguments and this time allowed myself to accompany Andy when he suggested that we stop for a quick refreshment in the pub round the corner to where, he told me, Wendy Wood would repair after her speech.

Andy had met her twice before, was a supporter of her movement and using a pseudonym, had written a couple of articles printed in a monthly broadsheet called The Patriot that she edited. When she entered the pub, she recognised Andy and joined us straight away asking only for a glass of water. I intervened and asked if she'd not prefer a wee whisky after her vocal sparring but she demurred.

"I used to enjoy a glass until I realised that the cost of a bottle is mainly tax which all goes to the English Exchequer. We see very little of it up here in Scotland. So I forgo its pleasures…but that's just me. If you enjoy *uisge beatha* don't let me stop you." She changed the subject.

11

"We haven't been introduced. My name's Wendy.'

"Manus."

"Please join us."

In photographs in the newspapers she always seemed to wear a beret pulled over one eye, a large silver broach depicting a thistle propping up the high side and so it was as she sat with us. A tweed jacket with a badge on its collar denoting Scottish Patriots, the organisation she founded, completed the image.

Supplementing her rebuke over my enjoyment of whisky she expounded further on the subject, telling me that while in America she had been offered a very remunerative contract to promote a particular brand of whisky (which she wouldn't name) but rejected the offer due to her antipathy towards the British Chancellor of the Exchequer.

One of the articles Andy had written for Wendy was his about the paucity of Scottish history being taught in schools with preference given to English history such as the rule of Henry the Eighth, Trafalgar and Oliver Cromwell rather than Wallace and Bruce, the Battle of Stirling Bridge and Bannockburn. He spoke of how the achievements of Scottish statesmen, soldiers, men of science and men of letters were put down to the account of England with the result that in the eyes of the world England has all the glory. I confessed my surprise at Andy's contribution to the conversation as I had never heard him speak of these concerns before and, as we sat, Wendy asked my own experience having been educated in the Scottish islands.

I was able to tell her of my good fortune in two ways; the first being that we spoke both Scots Gaelic as well as English in Lewis, and that at home, stories were told round the evening fire in the Gaelic tongue making the point that not all learning comes from books alone. The second advantage I had was that my teacher in Carloway

Primary School for much of my childhood was Mrs. Floraidh Donaldson, a distant cousin who was most supportive of the Gaelic language. When I moved up to the big school, the Nicolson Institute in Stornoway, I was aware from other friends that some teachers in the Western Isles actively discouraged the speaking of Gaelic and that some actually punished children heard to speak it, even in the playground where it was the *lingua franca*. However, Mrs. Donaldson's sister, Mhairi taught there; they were twins, and she not only also used the language, but used it judiciously; speaking English when teaching maths but Gaelic when teaching history. We learned French and German, were taught Shakespeare but also Burns. We studied the French Revolution and Thomas Paine's, *'The Rights of Man'*, but also Robert Burns whose poem, *'The Rights of Women'* initially had us giggling at the preposterousness of the notion before coming to accept Burns' point of view due to the patient exploration of the subject by Mrs. Donaldson.

Wendy became most animated at my recollections arguing that while adults viewed history as an intellectual exercise, children were engaged emotionally when being informed of the history of their nation and that augured well for our future if only every school in Scotland could be as progressive as was mine. At one point in the conversation, she recited lines from Burn's Poem, *'Such a Parcel o' Rogues in a Nation'* leaping to her feet as she declaimed the last stanza, 'Wi' Bruce and loyal Wallace...'

As Wendy tended her single glass of water, I enjoyed a second Glenfiddich then a third was called for as our discussion continued into the night, our friendly barman closing the door to customers at the appointed hour whilst allowing us to sit and drink unmolested. Indeed, he joined us and wouldn't take payment from Wendy when she insisted on buying a round of drinks. It was evident that he, too, was a supporter of Miss Wood.

She was a formidable woman. I'm getting ahead of myself, but a decade later, as it became evident that the Labour Party intended reneging on previous leader John Smith's promise of a Scottish

13

Assembly, Wendy announced she would go on hunger strike and drink only water until Labour put the Scottish Assembly in their manifesto. The issue was raised in Westminster and only after six days, when Jim Sillars, then the MP for the pro-Scottish Home Rule, Scottish Labour Party, went on television to ask her to call it off did she agree and the 1979 referendum for a Scottish Assembly was endorsed.

We were all by now fairly giddy as Wendy summarised my evening's contribution.

"So, Manus, you would accept that you believe in women's rights, you speak of your endorsement of the left-wing views as espoused by Harry Selby and you declare your love of Scotland. By heavens, you and I agree on everything! You must join your friend Andy here, my Scottish Patriots movement and help me and your fellow Scots end English rule in Scotland."

Intoxication permitted me momentarily to view her comments as flattery. However, I had also appreciated early on in the conversation that Andy's articles submitted to Wendy and the Scottish Patriots had been enabled by his use of a *nom de guerre* and that involving myself openly in any such politics would see my job as a civil servant ended. I murmured some platitudes and said I'd mull over the evening's discussion and talk to Andy about it but I knew in my heart that I would not put my head above the parapet. I had learned many things when serving with the Highland Light Infantry; the first was that I would endure a life-long affection for Capstan full-strength cigarettes, the second, as I've mentioned, was 'never volunteer' and the third was that while it was necessary to put one's head above the parapet in order to achieve anything, it was only to be done in an emergency or when a plan of some kind was in evidence and when the timing was right.

It was to be some time before the timing would be right.

Chapter Three

RE-ENLISTMENT

In 1952, I had turned twenty-seven years old. Demobbed six years earlier, I'd spent most of my time as a civil servant and had quite enjoyed the mobility of my job, spending time in the fishing community and taking pleasure in the friendship of those with whom I worked. However, something was missing; excitement. My years in the army had whetted my appetite for something a bit more adventurous. I contemplated life in Australia or Canada where a couple of friends had settled but my restlessness couldn't quite overcome my apprehension that when I'd get there, I'd merely become a civil servant or something similar again, but in a land with more sunshine.

A lack of imagination saw me standing outside an army recruiting office in Glasgow where I was encouraged to enter by a recruiting sergeant possessed of an accent that placed his antecedents as Glaswegian. I was offered a cup of tea and was made comfortable as Sergeant Alistair Cuthbert went through a well-rehearsed routine. As it became evident that I had myself been a sergeant in the Highland Light Infantry, the private who was also staffing the office was ordered to take charge of the office and the two sergeants disappeared round the corner to the drab Old College Bar in the city's High Street.

For some time, stories of our war exploits were shared in a noisy pub midst a haze of smoke and over whiskies and cigarettes. Alistair was perhaps ten years older than me and had spent his war years in the Argyll and Sutherland Highlanders in the Western Desert of North Africa. He had seen action in Crete, Abyssinia, Sicily and in the Italian Campaign. Wounded in Sicily, lighter duties had followed along with a now barely discernible limp and the job he did presently was due in considerable measure to to his fear of 'Civvy Street' and the prospect of leaving the only employer he had known.

"Listen, Manus", he smiled, his strong Glaswegian accent now a throaty growl due to years of abusing whisky. "Normally I'd just use my considerable personal charm to lure you back into uniform but you've got a chance to make some intelligent decisions here. Now, there's thousands of our boys over in Korea. The Kosbies have some troops over there. We've got pockets of troops all over Germany but all they're doing really is babysittin' the conscripts and drinkin' *Kräuterlikör*. We're startin' tae see deployments in Cyprus because of the Greek-Cypriot revolt in favour of union with mainland Greece and that's lookin' awkward for our boys because you don't know who's for us or who's goin' to produce a gun and blow your bloody head off. The Argylls and the Gordon Highlanders are out in Malaya but so are God alone knows how many conscripts so it's another babysittin' job although this time you get shot or get malaria for your troubles."

"I kind of just assumed I'd rejoin the Highland Light Infantry."

"Of course that's your first option, Manus but take a breath and work out how you'd like to spend the next part of your soldierin' career. You've options. Take a week to think things through. Read the newspapers and check out what the army's doin' in different parts of the world and maybe choose something that interests you or else you run the risk of endin' up in some forgotten corner of the globe doing hee-haw and being bored out of your mind." He lifted his glass and drained it before continuing. "Look…if you're interested, I'll have your file sent up to Glasgow. Maybe we could meet again in a week and we could go over this with a desk in front of us instead of a bar-room table. We'd baith be in a better position to make sensible decisions. What d'you say?"

"S'pose!"

Shaking hands, the men agreed to meet in a week.

* * *

The Reading Room in the vast Mitchell Library had become a sort of home from home on many evenings as I read both eclectically and voraciously and spent time scrutinising broadsheet newspapers so as to keep up with world events and political activity nearer home. I read everything, hungry for information. It became all-consuming. I'd read the injunctions on the back of an Aspirin bottle or the information presented on the labels on beer bottles, so concerned was I to learn everything about the world I inhabited.

I read and re-read Orwell's *'Homage to Catalonia'* where he wrote of the revolutionary fervour of left-wing patriots during the Spanish Civil War and of how it had been the first time he'd seen the working class in the saddle. I began visiting Glasgow's *avant-garde* cinema, the Cosmo in Rose Street and started to listed to the music of Enrico Caruso and attended the concert in Edinburgh's Usher Hall where communist, black American singer Paul Robeson sang for Scottish Miners. I was inspired by the passage of Clause Four of the Labour Party's constitution, *'To secure for the workers by hand or by brain, the full fruits of their industry and the most equitable distribution thereof that may be possible upon the basis of the common ownership of the means of production, distribution and exchange.'* However, two shipyard workers who also sat and read beside me most evenings, both communists, were outspoken in their criticism of the Labour Party as having sold out by having joined the very Establishment they were sent to London to destroy and of offering only lip-service to their famous clause.

One night I noticed an article which told of a talk that was to be given by Hamish Henderson. I knew of his reputation as an intelligence officer in Italy, found myself whistling a pipe tune he'd employed when writing, *'The 51st (Highland) Division's Farewell to Sicily'* and had read a challenging book of his poems written in broad Scots. He was another left-wing Scot who was involved with Wendy Wood and the author Compton MacKenzie who not only had written the book and screenplay of *Whisky Galore,* but was also a founding member of the National Party of Scotland which had transmogrified into the Scottish National Party in the years before World War Two. I'd persevered with Henderson's book and decided to buy a ticket for the talk, eventually buying two and taking my friend, Andy along with me.

On the night, Partick Burgh Hall was packed. We sat at the end of the front row and I was surprised when taking the stage, Hamish Henderson as he passed, acknowledged Andy with a wave.

"You know the guy?" I asked.

"We're a wee political party at the minute, Manus. It's still like a family. Everyone knows everyone but they know not to say too much about my involvement in case our bosses in St. Andrew's House boot me out the door."

"Well, *you* have hidden depths, Andy."

"Most people have secrets, Manus. Mine is that I want Scotland to regain its independence. The people I'm dealing with are all good souls. They're kind, highly intelligent and most of the ones I mix with are all creative. Hamish there, is a poet and songwriter, Wendy writes books for children and paints in oils. Hugh MacDiarmid is a poet whose real name is Christopher Grieve. Compton MacKenzie is an author. I like to write too but I do it under a pen name like Hugh does."

Hamish Henderson was riveting. He spoke of his days with the Eighth Army in North Africa during which he wrote his poem *'Elegies For the Dead in Cyrenaica'*, and then discussed his role in May 1945, when he personally oversaw the drafting of the surrender order of Italy issued by Marshal Rodolfo Graziani.

Hilariously he told of how he'd been kicked out of Italy and condemned as a Communist because he'd translated the works of Antonio Gramsci into English. He went on to discuss his passion for collecting the songs of others and used as an example the lyrics to *'D-Day Dodgers'*, a satirical song to the tune of *'Lili Marlene'* which had achieved real popularity amongst squaddies during the war. I'd sung it often and it was a great delight hearing of its creation from Henderson (although others claimed that it was written by Lance-Sergeant Harry Pynn of the Tank Rescue Section, 19 Army Fire Brigade, who was with the 78th Infantry Division based just south of Bologna in Italy.) Hamish spoke at length of how his war experiences had had him write the lyrics to *'The 51st (Highland) Division's Farewell to Sicily'*, set to a pipe tune called *'Farewell to the Creeks'*. He had a pleasant singing voice but not one which would trouble any of the great singers of the day.

The second half of his peroration was devoted to his ambitions for Scotland and how 'Perfidious Albion', as he called England, couldn't be trusted to realise the potential of his native land. I confess that as he finished, I joined the throng of those who stood and applauded him to the rafters. In the pub afterwards there were talks on the plight of the working man, some rousing Scots' songs were sung by a trio of woollen-sweatered young men and a collection was taken in support of striking shipbuilders. I was in my element. In the space of only some days, I had begun to sculpt a set of political beliefs; home rule for Scotland, socialist principles and had also re-introduced myself to the notion that perhaps the British Establishment and its Royal overlords wasn't the perfect vehicle for the changes I now wanted to see happen.

These matters preyed on my mind in the following days and reached something of a crescendo as I walked up Glasgow's High

19

Street to meet, as agreed, with Sergeant Alistair Cuthbert to discuss a return to uniform and the service of the Crown.

I was welcomed warmly and was invited to take a seat. The private on duty was dismissed to an outer office.

I leaned forward and positioned my cigarette in proximity to Alistair's flaming match.

"Hadn'y realised you were such an accomplished celebrity, Manus," grinned Alistair.

I returned his smile and presumed a tease.

"My good looks or my ability to juggle three apples when drunk?"

"Nah...your mentions in dispatches." He opened a buff folder. "Destroyin' an enemy machine-gun post under fire, a second when, as a sergeant, you were on your own for stoppin' a riot when a troop of drunken American soldiers threatened to beat up German prisoners of war..."

I smiled. "I remember that one!"

"Only one sergeant?"

My smile widened. "Only one riot!"

Alastair continued.

"A third for leadin' French citizens through a German minefield and a fourth for saving a German officer from drownin'...that sounds like an interestin' one, eh?"

I sat forward.

"I know nothing of that last one."

"True or false?"

"Well, it's true, I suppose, but I haven't a clue how it's in my file. The only witnesses were my squad, Russians who would have preferred me to shoot the guy and other German prisoners."

"Well, it says here that a General Earnest E. Clutterbuck commended your actions."

I sat back.

"That old curmudgeon? He would be the last person I'd expect to commend my actions. He was English upper crust, or so he thought. I spent lots of time in his company and apart from him telling me what to do, there was not anything much in the way of conversation." I leaned forward again. "Am I allowed to read what it says?"

"Absolutely against the rules, I'm afraid." He stood. "But I need a piss." He closed the folder, leaving it on the table before exiting the small office.

I read the file in his absence which, in the various spidery handwriting styles of different clerks over the years, told accurately of my personal details, blood group, enlistment, deployments, promotions, my wages, my honourable discharge and, on a separate page, four commendations for valour...and the final one was indeed from that old crabbit General, Earnest E. Clutterbuck who wrote at some length about my momentary brush with German *Stabshauptmann* Jürgen Roth of the *Kommandeur der Nachrichtenaufklärung*. For some reason it tickled old Earnest but as it was dated September 1945, someone had obviously decided it wasn't worth the bother of telling me given the chaos and euphoria of the war ending.

Alistair re-entered.

21

"Hope you didn't read that file, Manus. It's beyond my pay grade to share this information with you but I *do* have to tell you that there are two men from London comin' up here today to see you. My request for your file and the notification that you might want to re-enlist has caused something of a stooshie. I've been told that two men will arrive…" He looked at his watch… "in ten minutes, to speak with you and that when they arrive I've to make myself scarce."

All notions of explaining my dilemmas to Alistair about the wisdom of serving the Crown were placed at the back of my mind as I wrestled with the information set out before me and the imminence of a meeting with two men sent to talk to me as a direct consequence of that file.

Chapter Four

THE INQUISITION

Half an hour later than arranged, Alistair left the office and after an exchange outside, opened the door. He remained in the outer office while ushering two men inside. Both were dressed in dark suits, both wore austere, black, homburg hats and each carried a briefcase. They sat on two chairs placed earlier behind the desk by Sergeant Cuthbert.

Wordlessly, they each placed their hat on the desk and both opened their briefcase, leather straps noisily being liberated from their buckles. Removing some contents and satisfied that they were organised, the taller of the two spoke in a patrician drawl. He had a long face, a heavy five-o'clock shadow and an indirect gaze.

"You are Sergeant Manus Canning of the Highland Light Infantry?"

"No."

This caused the effect I sought, having determined that I would not easily succumb to an interview that I hadn't anticipated and of whose purpose I hadn't been informed. It is also the case that I can be a contrary so-and-so when I choose. Both men sat upright as if seated on an electric cushion.

"You are not...?"

"I am Manus Canning, civil servant. *Previously* I was honoured to be a sergeant in the HLI."

The tall man kept his temper only with effort. A short silence ensued as each man regarded the other with what I assumed was disdain for my attitude. Tall leaned backwards and lifted his nose for emphasis.

"You are Manus Canning, civil servant. Previously you were a sergeant in the HLI."

"That is correct."

"You have applied to re-enlist in the service of the Crown?"

"No."

Anticipating my response as being a literal answer to his question, he quickly re-worded his query.

"You are considering the *prospect* of applying for re-enlistment?"

"Not until I know who you two are."

Tall Man's nostrils flared as if he were inhaling my challenge. The smaller man placed his hand on the arm of his taller colleague and addressed me in a conspicuous Yorkshire accent. Somewhat disconcertingly, one of his eyes was set at perhaps twenty or so degrees from its neighbour. 'Wan eye gaun for the messages and wan comin' back wi' the change' as we used to taunt similarly afflicted kids in our less thoughtful and sophisticated youth. Mind you, it did occur to me that they might at least have sent north *one* of the two with normal eyesight!

"Sergeant Canning, we 'ave considerable interest in you. You 'ave distinguished yourself when in uniform and there are aspects of your service that appeals to our strategic mission."

"Can't see this going well unless I know as much about you as you apparently do about me."

24

Small Man placed his palms on the table and tapped in frustration as he composed his response.

"Please be assured that we are completely unimportant in this matter, Sergeant Canning. We serve the Crown as did you so valiantly not so many years ago and while we are not ourselves in the armed forces as were you, we are nevertheless fully engaged in defeating and diminishing those who would attempt to frustrate the ambitions of our great nation." He hesitated. "We have travelled to Glasgow from London on the instructions of superiors...and these are very senior people...who require...who *request* your engagement in a matter of the utmost importance."

I looked evenly at the two men who seemed now to present a less superior attitude than when first they arrived.

"You still haven't answered my question."

"Your question?"

"Who the hell are you people? Presently you could easily be confused with some of the overbearing *Gauleiters* I met in Germany. I'd bet each of you could strut sitting down! I turn up for a chat with a fellow sergeant about maybe...maybe... re-enlisting and I'm met with two men in expensive suits from London who ask a lot of questions but who don't give a lot of answers."

"Listen, you!" interrupted Tall who reasserted himself before being quieted by his colleague.

"Sergeant Canning...sorry...Mister Canning...your country 'as need of your services. You 'ave a unique contribution to make and we 'ave been asked to invite you, if you so choose, to travel to London for a more formal interview where the service your nation might ask of you would be explained."

"I have a job to do up here. I can't just up and leave when I choose. I have obligations."

"Please believe, Mr. Canning, that there will be no problems should you travel to London. The people who would 'ave you speak with them are extremely powerful and a phone call would ensure that permission to travel would be automatic."

"And if I refuse?"

"You would hear no more about it but it would represent a severe blow to the ambitions of a section of government. I can't speak for the reaction in Edinburgh when the civil service discover that you have chosen not to assist."

I allowed a silence before responding.

"Well, Mr. London, I've made it a fundamental principle in life never to allow myself to be bullied so it appears that my future lies in Civvy Street. I'd considered returning to the army but from what you say, a future in either the army or the civil service seems now to be beyond me if I resist your charms - which I do. Now, Gentlemen, there is a pub round the corner and I intend spending some time there in contemplation with my alcoholic friends Mr. Johnnie Walker and Mr. Arthur Guinness. You may tell your masters your mission has not been a success."

The Tall Drawl reached into his inside jacket pocket and removed an envelope.

"We had to anticipate the possibility of a negative response Sergeant Canning, he said, again attempting to remind me of my earlier service. "Please take this envelope and when contemplating your future over a whisky, I'd be grateful if you'd take a moment to inspect its contents." He left it before him on the table. "An opportunity still exists for you to salvage this and please understand the importance of our invitation." He began to speak more heatedly, "There are monkeys and Russians in space, circling the globe..."

For the second time in our exchange, Small Man placed his hand on Tall's elbow, discouraging further information and took over the conversation.

"You may speak of this discussion to no one. We will deny having spoken with you."

Both men rose while re-buckling their briefcases and left without any normal parting pleasantries. I remained in my seat.

After a moment, I opened the door to see Sergeant Cuthbert and Private Semple seated at their desks.

"Thirsty, Sergeant?"

"Don't know what you said to these two blokes but they left with faces like thunder and growled at us never to mention their presence and under no circumstances to discuss their conversation wi' you."

"Thirsty, Sergeant?" I repeated.

Cuthbert side-eyed young Private Semple.

"Here, young Semple, you're not involved in this. I'd like you to go to the tobacconist and buy me my usual ciggies." He shoved his hand into his pocket and placed some loose change before him. "Don't be long. When you get back, if I'm not here it's because I'm away havin' a sandwich with my brother who's in town today. Take your keys. I'm lockin' up while we're both away."

With Semple gone, Cuthbert took a set of keys from a desk drawer prior to locking up.

"The Old College Bar?"

Seated at a corner table with two half-pints of Guinness and two Johnnie Walker whiskies before us, I asked the question that had troubled me since being advised of the interview.

"Who the hell were those two?"

Cuthbert shrugged. "Didn't like the look of the wee one. Too small for the polis, too big for the circus." He thought further. "Government men, obviously. Could be Army, might be Intelligence people." He thought further. "Maybe Civil Service. Maybe polis?"

I took a sip of my whisky. Alistair lifted his own glass as we both sat quietly.

"They said they weren't Army." I hesitated. "They seem to think I can offer a service to the Crown that no one else can do. They left me an envelope. Will we open it?"

He grinned. "Aye, you open it, but don't tell me its contents if it's affairs of state or anythin' that'll get me kicked out of the Army."

Returning his smile, I opened the envelope. Inside was ten crisp five pound notes, a travel voucher for a train from Glasgow to London Euston and a small card on which was written 'Friday 4th March, 08.00am. Brompton Oratory, Kensington. Bring passport'.

"Jesus! Fifty quid! exclaimed Alistair."

"I'm presently being paid five pounds, eleven shillings a week," I responded.

Alistair turned around the voucher and the small card and read them.

"Interestin' that it's not a return ticket, eh? And you've to bring your passport!"

He looked again at the note.

"What's an oratory?"

"Its a Catholic Church, I think."

"Maybe they represent the Pope?"

"They certainly seemed to see themselves as infallible."

Alistair lifted his half-pint and quaffed a good half of it.

"You goin' to go?"

I shrugged. "I have three days to make my mind up."

"Well, you said you wanted excitement. These boys seem to have no problem settlin' money on you and...to be fair...from what you say, there might be an opportunity to serve - which is what you said you were interested in doin'."

"Ah... maybe not that bit! You're right about the excitement and more cash would come in handy but I'm wrestling with the idea of service to the Crown if I'm being honest."

"You've lost me there, Manus. Service goes with the territory. But maybe you shouldn't reject the offer just because you didn't like the two boys who gave you the invitation. The time to decide is when you hear why you're so all-fired important to them and what they would have you do, eh?"

I looked at him noncommittally and lifted the ten fivers.

"Another round? It appears that I'm in the money!"

Chapter Five

A SLEW OF SIGNIFICANT BOTHERATIONS

I spent a couple of days in the Mitchell Library and read what I could about the oratory and world events that required British soldiering. I had decided that Alistair's wise counsel was sensible advice; hear them out and then decide. In consequence I'd taken the train south from Glasgow and had put myself up in a small hotel not far from the Brompton Oratory. Unusually for me I had splashed out and had taken a taxi to the Knightsbridge area of London and, after registering at the hotel, had walked the few hundred yards necessary to view my meeting place. A Latin mass was being held as I lingered in the chapel's entrance. Inside, the chapel was particularly stunning architecturally but the light was dim and the church so large I could hardly make out the religious detail on the far walls. I stood beside scores of flickering candles for a while and wondered how I was expected to meet someone in such a vast place of worship. They must have thought of that, I thought, as I turned on my heel and walked back to a pub I'd seen only a few steps from my small hotel.

The following morning before the sun took full possession of the day, I walked again to the oratory, this time carrying my suitcase. Passing the fewer morning candles burning just inside the oratory vestibule, I elected to sit four rows down on the seat nearest the aisle and set my gaze upon a small queue of penitents awaiting confession. None seemed interested in me.

Only a few moments had passed when a voice from the seat behind me said softly, "Your punctuality does you proud, Mr. Canning. Follow me, if you will."

As I was on alert, his whispered instructions did not cause me to start and calmly I collected my small suitcase and followed a man wearing a calf-length, khaki trench coat to a car which sat purring where Brompton Road becomes Thurloe Place. Wordlessly, I was invited to sit in the rear of the car where I was joined by my host.

"Pleasant journey?" he asked.

"Came down last night. Uneventful."

These were the last words spoken until only a few minutes later, the car drew up outside a sandstone building whose plate outside announced the law offices of Brainchild and Carruthers. I followed the trench coat inside and was bade sit while he disappeared into an office before returning and inviting me to follow him upstairs. We arrived at an office which was accessed by entering via a large oak door. Inside, behind a large desk covered in files of varying thicknesses, sat a small man in a dark suit. A desk lamp illuminated his work area despite daylight rendering it relatively unnecessary. He inhaled the last half inch of a cigarette as if attempting to drain the last particles of nicotine and tar from it, his face contorting as he did so. Coughing at his efforts, he waved at a table around which were four chairs. Trench coat closed the door, leaving us alone.

Closing a buff folder whose contents he had obviously been reading, he joined me as I sat.

"Mr. Canning. It's a pleasure to meet you," he said, his lazy, dismissive tone suggesting otherwise. Opening the file he shuffled through certain of its contents.

"I am very pleased that you decided to come up to London today."

"We Scots usually regard it as coming *down* to London. It looks that way on the map." My rehearsed contrariousness kicked in

31

and I started as I intended continuing. *They want me,* I'd decided. *I'll only engage on my terms.*

"We haven't been introduced. And you are?"

Removing a packet of Camel cigarettes from his pocket he opened it and offered me one. I shook my head.

"I'll have one of my own, if you don't mind."

Removing one of my Capstan Full Strength I lit up as did he.

"I am Sir Anthony Caplan. I work for Her Majesty's Government. Until recently I was responsible for Britain's Special Operations Executive but following a reorganisation I now find myself a faceless operative responsible for certain European matters within the nation's Secret Intelligence Service and, if I may say so, I have a slew of significant botherations on my desk so let's get to the point."

He placed his cigarette in an ashtray and set his yellowing fingers to the task of filleting the paperwork in front of him. After a moment he produced a piece of paper which he read over the top of his spectacles.

"You are a very interesting man, Mr. Canning. You had a good war."

"I didn't see it that way, Sir Anthony. I did as I was told and left as soon as I could. I now have a most enjoyable and rewarding job in Scotland."

"You had given thought to re-enlisting."

"Hadn't decided."

"Hmmm."

"No trouble since you were demobbed?"

"None."

"Political involvement?"

"Define involvement. I read newspapers."

"Member of any political party?"

"None," I answered honestly, deciding not to reveal my recent political education at the hands of Wendy Wood, Hamish Henderson and Harry Selby.

"Well, I would like to ask your assistance on a matter of significant importance to us. It is not without its personal dangers but before I can tell you the nature of our request, I must ask you to sign a copy of the Official Secrets Act. Signing this has no effect on which actions are legal, as the act is a law, not a contract, and individuals are bound by it whether or not they have signed the act. However, if you sign this morning it is more a reminder to you that you are under its obligation. It binds you to complete confidentiality and should you share anything of state secrets or any official information relating to national security you would suffer very severe consequences including time spent at Her Majesty's pleasure. Would you be prepared to sign?"

"I imagine so. I understand the importance of secrecy in sensitive matters. It presents me with no problems."

Despite perhaps only being around a few years older than me he seemed overly fond of his cigarettes and licked two of his saffron-stained fingers before removed a single sheet of paper which he inspected before turning it round and presenting it to me. I removed a fountain pen from my inside jacket pocket and signed. He retrieved the paperwork and placed it back inside the folder, inadvertently smudging my signature as he did so.

"Thank you." He inspected his watch. "It's very early but I could do with a snifter. Whisky?"

Surprised at his suggestion, I nevertheless found myself replying, "If you're having one."

He rose and opened a cabinet next to the table. I could see several bottles, each containing a tawny liquid.

"I find myself enjoying some of your finer malts more and more as I mature and become more depressed at the new world order we're expected to police." He poured two rather stiff measures of a twelve year old Glenkinchie and passed one to me without water. I decided not to object at this calumny.

"A much underestimated whisky in my opinion. Obscure but most enjoyable." He raised the glass to his lips. "Chin-chin!" Most of the whisky disappeared in one smooth swallow. Before I had a chance to sample my whisky he topped his own up and set it aside, returning his attention to the folder.

"You served in Germany, Mr. Canning. You speak the language."

"Schoolboy level only. Supplemented by curse words when I was out there. I'm not fluent by any means."

Caplan pursed his lips and shrugged, conveying a 'doesn't matter' signal.

"It is a nation that troubles us still. As you know, Germany has been divided into four military occupation zones; France in the Southwest, ourselves in the Northwest, the United States in the South, and the Soviet Union in the East, bounded Eastwards by the Oder-Neisse line. Berlin has a similar arrangement. You are well aware that a couple of years ago, conflicts over currency reform among other things, triggered a Soviet Union blockade of the western sectors forcing western Allies to respond with the Berlin Airlift, an unprecedented but ultimately successful operation supplying the entire city by air. Since then, matters have deteriorated. Berlin has acquired a reputation as the capital city of international espionage. It has been divided between the Soviets and the leading NATO powers. The Establishment of the German Democratic Republic in 'forty-nine has done little other than to increase tensions. Daily, residents of East Berlin flock to the better living conditions of the west and we know from our sources that this troubles the Soviets and the East German Communists very much. It can only be a short while before they devise some mechanism to keep their population forcibly in the east. Daily, they lose doctors, teachers, nurses and engineers...even soldiers and police officers. They are haemorrhaging talent."

He took another generous slug of his whisky.

"However, some of our agents have managed to convince a number of these refugees to return to the GDR and spy for us there. That said, we are well aware that the GDR is far more advanced than are we in these matters and our institutions, our security services indeed every facet of society in Berlin has been infiltrated by the *Stasi*...East Germany's secret police."

"That much I know, Sir Anthony." I sipped at my glass. "Any quality newspaper carries these details regularly."

"Indeed so," he coughed a wheezy smoker's cough. "The bloody place...even our own Labour-run political hierarchy in Parliament... is infested with agents, double-agents, spies, fellow-travellers, international socialists, committed communists, equally committed free-world capitalists. It's a bloody nightmare because knowing whom to trust is crucial...absolutely *crucial* to understanding their political and military realities and our ability to make judgements on the next moves being contemplated by the GDR and Soviet leadership. Our problem, Mr. Canning is that they have exactly the same concerns. They don't know whom to trust either and this makes it difficult for key targets over there that we'd like to see over here to know whether they can trust someone who offers them the prospect of advancement in the west. Is it a real offer - or is it a sting operation by their fellow communists? Do you see the dilemma?"

"Indeed."

"Well, that's where one Sergeant Manus Canning comes in."

Chapter Six

HOME RULE FOR SCOTLAND

The handsome blonde sandstone tenement property in Glasgow's Dumbarton Road stood cheek by jowl with a red sandstone property indicating that the former had been built before 1890 using material from the local Bishopbriggs and Giffnock quarries, as when railways connected Glasgow to Dumfries quarries, blonde sandstone became more popular and less expensive. Propping up the building at road level was the Ettrick Bar on the corner site at Crawford Street. Within, four men sat in a small back parlour, all tending pints of beer, the fourth of which they'd each consumed that evening.

"So lemme get this straight, Benji. You're sayin' that two years ago, oan Christmas morning 1950, you were involved in stealin' the Stone of Destiny frae Westminster Abbey and bringin' it back hame tae Scotland?"

Benji Henderson wiped the foam from his bushy moustache.

"You know as well as me, Cammy, that ah'm no' at liberty to discuss ma involvement in that. For aw ah know you could be the polis."

"Yer arse in parsley! It wis students that done that," countered Dougie Chalmers. "It wis in aw the papers efter they took it back tae Arbroath Abbey."

"Suit yersel'," shrugged Henderson. "Aw ah'm sayin' is that ah wis involved. Ah never says ah actually done it."

"Come clean, Benji. Ye ken fine we're no' the polis. Whit wis it ye done that helped bring back the Stone of Destiny tae Scotland?"

Henderson shuffled uncomfortably in his chair and delayed a response by quaffing a long mouthful of beer. Gradually he found his voice.

"Well, it was only a wee bit help ah gied. Efter the Stone got returned, ah mean."

"Naw! We don't know whit ye mean, Benji. Spit it oot."

Three pairs of eyes were locked on his demeanour as Henderson explained his part in the liberation of the Stone.

"Well, it was years ago, afore ah got ma job as a welder in the yards. Ah pulled up oan ma beer lorry at Tennent's Bar oan Byres Road and while ah wis inside ah noticed that three of the boys that took the Stone were in therr drinkin' beer. The lassie that wis wi' them in London wisn'y therr but their faces wis in the papers an' they wis aw right cheery. Wan o' them wis thon Ian Hamilton. So, ah went back oot tae the lorry and brought in three bottles o' whisky an' ah gied it tae them so's they could celebrate 'cos wan o' them telt me they were gaun back tae the student's union for a guid swally tae celebrate gettin' the Stone."

"And that's it?"

"Naw...when I gied them the whisky, thon Hamilton fellah invited me tae go up therr wi' them so ah phoned ma boss an' telt him that someone had stole three bottles o' whisky frae the lorry and that ah' wis waitin' oan the polis tae gie ma evidence. The daft bugger thought the story wis true and ah was away up tae the students union wi' the boys as fast as ma legs would carry me. They goat me past the guy on

the door an' ah wis up they university sterrs tae the bar like a ton o' bricks!"

The fourth member of the group, an elderly, silver-haired man with cadaverous cheekbones, didn't join in the raucous and joyful denunciation of Henderson's tortured use of simile.

Coldly, Arnold Menzies swept back his leonine head of grey hair, drew heavily on his cigarette and spat his indictment of the group in the direction of all three men.

"Your command of the English language is as poor as your commitment to the independence of our proud nation, Benji Henderson. You three should be ashamed. We agreed to meet here tonight in order to discuss how we might take action against the English imperialists and all we've heard tonight are wee boys' stories and football discussions." He placed his pint glass on the table and continued. "Only a few years ago, the fields, hedgerows and cities of Europe were in flames as scores of thousands of young Scotsmen, thousands of the physically strongest of the Scottish race met their death there in a desperate battle with a brave enemy. Working class boys who bore no malice but were forced into uniform. A very large proportion of these young Scots were born and reared in the slums and tenement houses of this city...Glasgow. These same slums that are notorious the world over for their disease and poverty. It's known that the poor of Glasgow are housed under conditions worse than those of any civilised people on God's earth. And yet we permit these colonialists in England to determine Scotland's future. Well, socialists like us in Scotland have to recognise that the future for the working class can only be realised by the people of this country seizing governance and wresting it by one means or another from the hands of the present rulers and restoring it with all its powers to the people who inhabit it and labour upon it. We are all here agreed that with self-government in Scotland, the question of the ownership and administration of our soil can and will be approached with a new determination."

Reaching into the inside pocket of the tweed coat he'd hung over the back of his chair, Menzies produced an Enfield service revolver and placed it beside his pint glass on the table to the gasps of his three colleagues.

"The British Army used these in great number during the war," mused Menzies. "They won't miss this one...or the Lee-Enfield Mark 4 rifle I have at home. British imperialists only understand one thing, boys; violence. And that's what we'll give them!"

A new and more somber attitude overtook proceedings and the evening came to a conclusion with all members agreeing that at their next gathering, a week hence, less alcohol would be consumed and that a plan of action that carried the fight to the British Establishment would be discussed.

Outside, the four men shook hands and went their separate ways, Benji and Cammy McLaughlin pairing up for the short walk to their respective homes on Dumbarton Road.

"He's good wi' words, thon Arnold. Isn't he?" suggested McLaughlin.

"Aye, but he's awfy serious sometimes. He's a lecturer. Ah think they make ye that way in university."

They walked on for some moments when Benji placed his left arm across McLaughlin's midriff, stopping him.

"Come wi me, Cammy." He disappeared into a dimly lit close-mouth, beckoning furiously with one hand, the other gesturing silence with a finger to his lips.

"Wha?..."

Reluctantly, McLaughlin followed Benji who walked quietly to the back entrance and opened the rotted wooden door that led to the back court, dragging its base across the rough floor and causing a rasping noise despite his efforts. Grimacing at the sound, Benji froze, attempting to determine whether his actions had awakened anyone in the building. Satisfied, he stepped out into the darkness.

"C'mon," he urged.

As they approached the collection of metal bins at the very rear of the back court, Benji stooped low and gestured to McLaughlin to follow suit.

"Mind what Arnold telt us a while back? Whenever we take action, we always have to have a way oot...a 'means of escape' he cried it."

McLaughlin looked at him puzzled.

"See that wee fence? We jump it and go through the close ower therr tae Kennoway Drive and then we're away!"

"Away?"

"Aye!"

So saying, Benji lifted one of the galvanised steel bins and hoisted it to his shoulder.

"Christ, it's heavy!"

Balancing himself for a moment, he began a staggering run towards the building, his momentum carrying him to within a few feet of a ground floor flat whose windows were in darkness. Heaving his bin, he crashed it through the window, occasioning cries from inside. Turning he ran towards an open-mouthed McLaughlin.

"Quick, Cammy! Ower the fence and away!"

Both men leapt the small fence, McLaughlin less successfully, tearing a small hole in his trousers as he did so, crossed the corresponding back court and emerged through the opposite close-mouth into Kennoway Drive where they continued their hurried walk, looking over their shoulder to detect any pursuit.

"What the fuck was *that*?" demanded McLaughlin.

"The guy that lives in therr...he's Grand Master in the Partick Luudge. He's a Unionist and a right bastard. He stood as a Tory Cooncillor but got beat."

"So you pit a bin through his *windy*?"

"The fight for Scottish freedom starts here, Cammy."

"A bin through his *windy*?" questioned McLaughlin, his voice now an octave higher."

"Aye...and when we meet again wi' Arnold Menzies in a few days, ah kin dae it wi' ma chest held high!"

Henderson walked on as McLaughlin stood, open-mouthed. His head shook imperceptibly as he attempted to come to terms with Benji's actions.

"His chest held high?" he murmured to himself as he increased his stride to catch up with his friend.

Chapter Seven

THE MISSION

The day had been spent being interviewed by several other people, some of whom didn't choose to identify themselves. Some of the conversations were affable discussions of my war record and subsequent employment, a health check was undertaken, some interviews were administrative so that I might receive a salary for my new responsibilities, some were more terse and focussed upon my beliefs and opinions. I answered in a bland fashion as if I was a modest but well-informed reader of the Times of London, intrigued now as to what might be asked of me. It was made clear to me that either party could bring proceedings to a halt at any time. It was late in the evening after I had eaten what they'd called a meal but was but a cup of tea and two sandwiches when I was called back in to see Sir Anthony Caplan. He sat again behind his desk, this time possessed of a slightly thicker file which I presumed had to do with the further reports he'd received on me as a consequence of my interviews. As he read silently, I took the opportunity to look around the room and noticed that the bottle of whisky, almost full that morning, had been reduced in volume by perhaps one third. I fell to wondering whether it had been shared with others or if Sir Anthony had been sipping on his own. If so, when he spoke he showed no adverse effects.

"My people think you have abilities, Mr. Canning. All very positive, although one worried that you might be prone to insolence on occasion. Chap was concerned that you might not easily acquiesce to the requirements of authority."

"I managed to do all right when I was in uniform, Sir Anthony. I prefer to speak my mind but wouldn't say I was prone to being argumentative." I crossed my fingers when relating this last piece of fiction.

"Well, as I say, all very positive. It gives me the green light to share with you a mission that is highly secret. It is of significant importance to us in the west and you seem to us to be the perfect individual to pull it off, as it were. Normally a task of this nature would only be given to a member of our organisation who had several years' experience under his belt and when we could trust his dependability. However, I intend taking the chance that you are everything we think you are and will take personal responsibility for blooding a newcomer such as you with such an important mission. Now,"... He lit another cigarette, this time without offering me one. "What I am about to tell you cannot be taken back. It is formally a government secret and were you to share this with anyone outwith those who will assist you, it will result in a serious charge being laid against you under the Official Secrets Act. I would then move heaven and earth to see you locked up for so long you would be released only in time to attend your own funeral. Am I clear?"

"Completely."

"Well, then." He lifted my file, closed it and placed it inside a drawer on his desk before standing and returning to the bottle of whisky I'd noticed on a shelf.

"Will you join me?"

"Certainly."

He poured another two stiff glasses. This time I rebuked the absence of a drop of water.

"Scotsmen prefer a wee splash of water in their whisky. It reveals the flavour."

He nodded at a closed door.

"That's a bathroom. You can use the tap."

I did so and sat, noticing again that he'd halved the amount of whisky in his glass before I'd returned and was busily engaged in replenishing it before continuing.

"I mentioned this morning that we are in something of a pickle in Berlin. The German secret police, their Ministry for State Security, or *Stasi*, was set up two years ago under the direct guidance of the Soviet Union's secret police and, in the east, is charged with suppressing what they imagine is subversive behaviour. They operate independently of the civil police, maintain local offices in major companies and universities and carry out arbitrary arrests and mass blackmails. In West Berlin, they have focussed upon the recruitment of informants in the West's political and administrative spheres and we estimate that in Berlin alone, some forty thousand people work for them. They are formidable. *Stasi* agents want to know in advance what West Germany is planning and undertaking, especially to assist negotiations between the two countries. Moreover, the East German authorities use spies to gain access to industrial research institutions, gathering information and using it in East Germany's industries without permission and save a lot of money by stealing technology. What is most distressing is that they have engendered such a fear and apprehension amongst their populace in the east that no one there knows who they can trust. Family members are reporting on each other, life-long friends offer information on each other to avoid being arrested on suspicion of being an enemy of the state."

"So far, I can't see how I'm in such a unique position to be able to assist."

Caplan paused in his peroration and took a further large slug of his whisky.

"You are a clean skin, Mr. Canning. You came to our notice quite by chance when one of our people noticed that you had

45

been mentioned in dispatches as having saved the life of one *Stabshauptmann* Jürgen Roth of the *Kommandeur der Nachrichtenaufklärung*. After the war, because he was captured in what would become East Germany, he was forced by the Communist authorities to work in German uranium mines producing the majority of the raw material of the Soviet atomic bomb project. Fortunately for him, his earlier work in radar and electronics was recognised and he was spared the fate of many of his contemporaries and didn't have to work in the mines... effectively a death sentence. Instead he was gradually introduced to the work the Soviets are doing on the atomic bomb. We don't quite know of the progress they are making, but Jürgen Roth does. Our people reckon that what they have developed is not a fully evolved thermonuclear bomb in our coetaneous sense, but may be a crucial step between pure fission bombs and the thermonuclear model. We would dearly like to find out what's going on and our people calculate that Herr Roth might be susceptible to our blandishments but that he'd be extremely cagey and would treat any overture with deep suspicion due to the all-pervading presence of the *Stasi*. However, were he to meet you, he would almost certainly conclude that you were not some kind of double agent and could be relied on as a vehicle that might see him welcomed in the west. He has no family. He has, as far as we can tell, no relationship with members of the same or opposite sex and that makes him dangerous to the authorities as he only has to look out for himself. Our people tell us that he was no Nazi and he doesn't appear to be a natural Communist. He'll be followed everywhere as he's now a very senior person in the scientific community. However, we know that he's giving a lecture in Bratislava in a couple of weeks and we thought that an opportunity might present itself for you to meet his acquaintance once again." Caplan finished his glass. "But I must inform you that this is a dangerous mission. If the *Stasi* get their hands on you, you wouldn't be treated with kid gloves and you might have to spend some considerable time in an East German Prison before some form of prisoner exchange allowed you to return to home soil." He eyed the bottle again but appeared to think better of it.

"What say you?"

I hesitated for a moment.

"What would I be expected to do?"

"Meet him! Meet him in Bratislava. Develop your relationship with him much in the way you would fry a small fish...very gently. Be honest with him. Our estimation is that he'd be very unlikely to report your overtures to the *Stasi* or the Soviets, for the very good reason that he'd calculate that they'd probably work on the basis that he'd already been compromised. At a moment you determine to be propitious, explain that you are aware of Communist discussions to close the border between east and west Germany and that you may be able to offer him a much better life in the west before he's trapped."

"And then?"

"Then we assemble a team of professionals that will whisk him across the border to safety and a new home in England, America, Canada or wherever he'd like to spend the rest of his life. We'd happily protect him and ensure his safety. He could continue working in his field of choice along with others who share his background and in technologies with which he's familiar. He speaks very good English and would feel quite at home... but free from the all-pervasive *Stasi* and in considerable comfort."

"What's my cover?"

"You're a delegate to the conference. The Iron Curtain is not yet an impenetrable divide, and contacts between east and west take place regularly and on various levels. The European tourist industry appears successfully to have transcended the ideological fault lines and the communist states attract an ever-increasing number of western tourists as they find their spending power most valuable. We'd provide you with a false passport and we'll create a back-story linking you to the electronics industry."

"And I'd earn a salary for this?"

"A good salary…and a generous bonus if he ends up in our hands."

"And that'd be it? I'd be finished with the cloak and dagger stuff if and when he comes over?"

"Yes…unless you showed talent and wanted to remain."

I smiled at Caplan and rattled the base of my empty glass on his desk.

"Shall we have a final whisky to toast my involvement?"

He returned my grin.

"I'll even fetch the water!"

Chapter Eight

THE GARE LOCH

Ever since a young man on a hill-walking holiday on the Isle of Skye, Angus Brodie had developed a considerable respect for the crests and ridges of its Black Cuillin Mountain range. When recovering of an evening he had acquired an equal respect for the local Talisker whisky which was triple distilled from the waters of *Cnoc nan Speireag* near Carbost on the banks of Loch Harport beneath the Cuillins. Over the twenty years since, he'd pay attention to each sip of the single malt appreciating its subtle flavour, eschewing all other brands except in emergency.

In Edinburgh's Victorian Café Royale, Brodie's demeanour was far from the appreciative whisky *cognoscenti* as he swallowed the entire contents of his double Talisker in one gulp, leaving some coins spinning on the bar top as he left the premises, much to the surprise of Andrew the barman who was used to the more customary urbanity of his regular patron.

Angus Brodie was a Deputy Director in the UK's Ministry of Defence, was responsible for all matters to do with ports in Scotland and had just been informed by telephone that he'd been overlooked for promotion to the position held by his boss, Joseph Powers, a steely and humourless man of Northern Ireland extraction who had himself recently been promoted to a senior post in the Cabinet Office in London.

As he hastened towards nearby Waverley Railway Station, thin wisps of Brodie's breath trailed in the stillness of a cold and dreich Edinburgh night. Now fifty-three, life had been kind to the Scot.

He'd retained a youthful figure and more than once had caught himself looking appreciatively in a mirror at his still fulsome head of hair, greying but nevertheless generous where others of his age sported receding hairlines. He was aware of his dandy reputation and indeed often encouraged it. He was a man who enjoyed looking good and on spending his salary on clothes and other fashion accoutrements. Living alone, he'd shunned the Georgian townhouses, broad avenues and open squares of Edinburgh's New Town so favoured by his contemporaries, in favour of a less expensive apartment in nearby Linlithgow. He also rented a flat in the coastal town of Helensburgh which he used when job requirements demanded it.

Brodie was also aware of his reputation as a man who marched to the beat of his own drum in matters sexual and had been a practising, if not particularly promiscuous, covert homosexual since schooldays. He'd attended Fettes College before going on to achieve a first class degree in economics from St. John's College, Oxford without much in the way of effort.

Belching smoke, the train to Glasgow applied its squealing brakes and stopped gradually at Linlithgow where Brodie disembarked. Immediately he entered the portals of the nearest pub, the Swan, where he again ordered a Talisker.

"Make it a double," he instructed, "I'll add the water."

A phone booth in the rear of the pub was accessed as the whisky lay unattended on the bar-top. Urgent fingers stabbed and pulled at the dial. Moments later his call was answered.

"Simon, they've fucking overlooked me. Seven fucking years serving the crown in a senior position and they've decided that some overblown nobody merits promotion over me; a job previously held by an equally overblown Paddy. I've to accept this slight?"

Brodie's friend, Simon was sympathetic.

"Darling, they're out of their tiny minds. You were far and away the best candidate...you simply must have been. Come over and I'll sooth your troubled brow."

"Not going to happen, Simon. I'm absolutely furious. I was due that job...but what they seem to forget is that I'm still the man responsible for all ports in Scotland. I'm transforming a sleepy fishing port at Faslane into something much more strategic and now I'm drunk, I'm angry and I have influence. It was that complete bastard Henry Greenaway who must have put the boot in. He's never liked me."

"Darling, come over."

"I fully intend to drown my sorrows in Talisker tonight, Simon. I seek oblivion. But when I surface, I shall bring the wrath of God down upon the governance of the United Kingdom. I am not to be underestimated."

"You are formidable, darling."

"Yes, I am!"

The phone was placed on the receiver and Brodie returned to his Talisker, still fuming.

* * *

Gare Loch is an open sea loch some six miles long and about a mile wide, well used for recreational boating and fishing. During the Second World War, Faslane, a small fishing village on its banks, saw its first service as a naval base with the bay turned into a marshalling yard to serve the needs of the submarines and ships stationed there. Its depth made it suitable to accommodate a large variety of naval craft and it had been widely used by the United States military forces during the war for naval landing preparations that had been deployed in North Africa as well as the

Normandy Landings. In the 1950s, the British Government used the loch to store decommissioned naval vessels and put a Civil Servant in charge of operations, liaising with the Royal Navy in order to assess its capacity to serve as a base for the heightened use of the UK submarine fleet. Angus Brodie was the man they'd selected to oversee the transformation.

* * *

A week after being advised that he'd been unsuccessful in his bid to occupy a more senior post in the Ministry of Defence, he was called to London for a debriefing with Sir Edward Bland. *Bland by name and bland by nature, I'd venture,* thought Brodie as he sat outside the office of the Second Permanent Secretary, a Civil Servant two grades higher than the one he occupied and one grade above that of Director - the position to which he'd aspired.

"Sir Edward will see you now, Mr. Brodie."

He was shown into a deep-carpeted room of substantial proportions, requiring him to take several steps to reach the empty chair that had been placed opposite the Second Permanent Secretary's desk. He sat. Bland got straight to the point.

"Must be disappointed, eh, Brodie?"

"I'm sure the better candidate got the job."

Bland nodded. "He did, actually. Impressive chap!" He continued, "Well, the service wants to reassure you that we value your work. You have responsibility for transforming a sleepy Scottish port into something that will one day host our submarine fleet. It is of crucial importance to our national interest that we have capability along with our friends and colleagues in the American Navy, to service, maintain, stock and deploy submarines which will have frightening firepower and we can't do that without Faslane being fit for purpose."

"I enjoy my work, Sir Edward but I confess that I'm also ambitious. I seek to serve in the higher reaches of the service and trust that an opportunity might arise in the future where such abilities as I hold might be put to good use."

"Perhaps." He thumbed through a few pages of the file before him. "You're fifty-three. Unmarried. Live alone and other than taking to the hills of Scotland from time to time, have few other hobbies."

"Correct, Sir Edward. My life is my work."

"Unhealthy," growled his superior. He closed the file and leaned forward on his elbows. "Frankly, Mr. Brodie, one must speak directly. You are currently in a very sensitive position. You deal with all sorts of classified information and as you climb the greasy pole of the Civil Service within the Ministry of Defence, you would be entrusted with ever-more restricted intelligence and, not beating about the bush, looking at your file, one can't help but be aware of what one might call your lifestyle."

"Lifestyle, Sir Edward?"

"A person who conducts himself as you do, Mr. Brodie might be accused of homosexuality. We both understand, I am sure, that when there exists sexual attraction between men, it brings opportunities for blackmail and all sorts of criminality, degeneracy and abnormality. One presents oneself as available for exploitation if one is a queer and frequents that culture."

Brodie found himself reddening.

"I can assure you, Sir Edward, that my lifestyle choice of living alone has nothing to do...nothing to do with homosexuality. I just haven't found the right female partner in life. I can assure you most strenuously that I am certainly not homosexual. It is an illegal and perverted practice and I abhor it as much as do you."

53

"Well, they all say that. You look like a dandy and one can't have someone in top positions who might let the side down!"

"Sir Edward, I implore you. I am a perfectly normal man and insist that my lifestyle, as you call it, does not affect my work. If anything, I am a workaholic and give my life to my duties. I very much hope that nothing deleterious is recorded in my file. It would forever blight my chances of promotion."

Bland sat back in his chair and bit his lower lip thoughtfully. He turned the conversation to operational matters on the Gare Loch and his tone lightened. However, after some time Brodie sought further comfort that Bland's remarks would not hinder the prospect of promotion.

"These verbal remarks this morning are one's own assessments, Brodie. There's nothing recorded in your file. One is quite happy to see you continue in your work in your Scottish backwater but one is toying with the idea of asking MI5 to keep an eye on you. One hates queers with a vengeance and wants no one in one's sphere of influence who's in any way a bit limp-wristed."

Bland abandoned his use of the impersonal pronoun as he gathered momentum.

"I hope I make myself clear. I must accept your denials largely because I have no actual evidence but I have my suspicions. Let's leave it at that. Thank you for coming down to London. Your work on Gare Loch is of a high standard. I hope you found this helpful."

Leaning against the marble portals of the Georgian building from which he'd emerged, Brodie attempted to compose himself. Sweating now and still flustered, he brooded on his interview.

That was that bastard Henry Greenaway. Must have been. He's a raging queer and a screaming narcissist but conceals it well.

He's always detested my looks and is jealous after Jason Williams flirted with me at the club. The bastard's still dancing on that wound. He crossed the road to a tobacconists and regarded himself in the window. *Perhaps I am too much like a dandy. Maybe I need to change my image slightly.* He looked beyond the glass at the paraphernalia on display in the shop window. *Perhaps if I smoked a pipe!* Impulsively he pushed at the door and entered.

Chapter Nine

WEST BERLIN

A week had passed since my interview with Caplan and I found myself standing in the busy concourse at Tempelhof Airport having been transported there by a Douglas DC-3 aeroplane operated by British European Airways. I'd spent the intervening days in London learning more about East/West relations, how the *Stasi* operated and the resources available to the West in respect of its espionage activities. I read more of the life and work of Jürgen Roth; his habits, hobbies and frailties.

I confess my excitement at my mission and now thought little of the relationships I'd developed back in Scotland as a Civil Servant. Now, I was an intelligence officer; a spy and was exhilarated.

I'd been told that I'd be contacted upon arrival by a man called Horst Janson and as I walked confidently towards the exit, a burly man whose face I recognised immediately from photographs I'd been shown in Knightsbridge approached me smiling widely, his open hand offered in friendship.

"*Herr* Canning?"

"*Herr* Janson!" I responded.

"You must call me Horst," he replied, shaking my hand vigorously.

He lifted my small case and placed his free hand on my back, guiding me away from the exit.

"Come with me. The *Stasi* have a man outside whose job it is to photograph everyone who exits the airport. We will leave from a side door where I have a car sitting. No one will see us."

I grinned. "I've only been in Berlin for one minute and already I'm hiding from the East's secret police."

"Oh, they will have someone in Passport Control who will provide them with details of everyone who lands here but your name will mean nothing to them. However, if they see you with me, they would take rather more of an interest."

"Your English is remarkably good, Horst."

He nodded as we approached the door that led to his car.

"In our line of work, everybody here pretty much speaks decent English. Except the Americans," he chuckled.

The journey across Berlin was uneventful although I was absorbed in conversation with Horst. It was a brilliantly sunny day and long swords of light sliced through the gaps between buildings. I became fascinated by the redevelopment works which had taken place since the war had ended. Wide boulevards had replaced many of the bombed and debris-strewn *straßenf* which had been in existence when last I'd driven through the city en-route to Dresden. Every so often, Horst would point down a side street where a sand-bagged and raised-arm sentry post denoted the ending of a western zone and the entrance to the East Berlin zone occupied now by the Soviets but whose entry points were manned by East German soldiers. At one point he stopped and gestured towards an open park area.

"Four years ago, without informing the Soviets, U.S. and British policymakers introduced the new *Deutschmark* to West Berlin. This was to wrest economic control of the city from the Soviets in order to enable the introduction of the Marshall Plan and curb the city's black market. Well, of course, the Soviet authorities responded with similar moves in their zone and issued their own currency, the *Ostmark*, then blocked all major road, rail, and canal links to West Berlin, thus starving us of electricity as well as a steady supply of essential food and coal. As you know, it resulted in the Berlin Airlift where the West supplied everything needed for Berlin to survive. At the height of the campaign, one plane was landing every forty-five seconds at Tempelhof Airport which showed that we could sustain the operation indefinitely. This open area here became famous as pilots used to parachute what the Americans called 'candy'…as they prepared to land."

"Sweets?"

"I believe that is how you call it in England…and children would gather here to enjoy the fruits of Western economics. Only German dentists didn't approve," he laughed. "But kids loved it and we now have a new generation of young Germans completely committed to freedom, to capitalism…and to sugar!"

Some thirty minutes after leaving Tempelhof, we drove into a parking bay in front of the Ellington Hotel around the corner from *Kurfurstendamm*, Berlin's main shopping street.

"Here is your home for the next week, Manus."

"Jesus…I'm not used to such luxury. It's stupendous."

"The cream of Berlin's Establishment drinks, eats and screws here, Manus. Tonight, in its ballroom, the American negro, Duke Ellington plays here with his jazz orchestra. I have taken the opportunity of buying two tickets for you and I to attend…not because it is important for the mission but because I love Duke Ellington. I argued that it would allow you and I to get to know one another…although I confess, we could have done that over a simple coffee. The hotel is not named after *Herr* Ellington, incidentally. We in Germany are not quite so broadminded."

We stepped from the car and Horst looked upwards at the edifice of the hotel. "It has a certain grandeur, don't you think? And it allows you to play the role of a senior British Civil Servant who enjoys the finer things in life."

"Duke Ellington?"

"His jazz orchestra are touring Europe and they play here in Berlin for a couple of nights. Trust me, from tomorrow you will be fully occupied but I thought you might like to recover from your journey from London over a glass or two of your favourite drink while we listen to some good music."

"Well, I could imagine a more demanding introduction to my new duties so I'm persuaded."

"Excellent, Manus. You register in the name of Florin Albescu, using this Rumanian passport." He handed me what appeared to be a very professional forgery. "A room has been reserved for the week and has been paid for by the British Civil Service. We will review what might be necessary after that. Tomorrow I will collect you and we will travel the short distance to room three-one-four on the floor below where you will be introduced to the man who will supervise and support your work here." He grinned and clapped me affably on my shoulder. "But tonight we will enjoy ourselves. I will meet you in the bar at seven-thirty? Okay?"

Right on time, both Horst and I walked into the bar from opposite ends and, at his invitation, each of us partook of a couple of glasses of *schnapps* which I found rather less to my taste now that I was faced with a gantry comprised of some of my favourite malts. *Schnapps* was acceptable during the war when nothing else was available but here in one of Berlin's most up-market hotels, I found it rather rough on my palate.

Duke Ellington was in great form although I recognised only two of the songs played by his orchestra, *'Take the 'A' Train'* and *'It*

Don't Mean a Thing' (if it ain't got that swing). After the concert we once again repaired to the bar, now smokey and full, apparently of Americans all talking excitedly about the performance.

One man with a flash camera mingled with the crowd, taking photographs.

I drew him to Horst's attention.

"Oh, he's a photographer for *'Gondel'* Magazine. It features photographs of many women in revealing swimming costumes and carries murky stories about the lives and loves of Germany's upper and theatrical classes. Still, it might be better if you turned your back when he comes round."

I gestured to a balcony above and to his left.

"And what about him?"

Behind a pillar on a vaulted gallery above us, a slim, besuited man was surreptitiously using a camera to take photographs of those drinking at the bar.

Horst grimaced. "Undoubtedly, he'll be capturing images that will end up with the *Stasi*. Again, keep your back to him."

I sipped at my *schnapps* thoughtfully.

"It seems, as you say, that the *Stasi* are everywhere."

"Indeed they are, Manus. Indeed they are."

I decided to ask the question that had been on my lips since the airport.

"And tell me, Horst. How am I meant to know if you aren't an agent of the *Stasi* yourself?"

"Horst smiled widely.

"Now you have the right attitude, Manus. You will make a terrific agent. Be suspicious of everyone. Trust only a few people. That's how you survive out here."

"Tell me about yourself, Horst. What did you do in the war?"

"I was in the Luftwaffe and was mainly involved in flying a Messerschmitt BF 110 in defence of Berlin. I was a fighter pilot and shot down six Allied planes...aerial victories which qualified me as a flying Ace and I was 'honoured', if that is the word, to be awarded the Knight's Cross of the Iron Cross from Hermann Göring himself. I was very fortunate. We German pilots flew until we were killed, captured, or too badly wounded to keep flying. My injuries were confined to having one of my great toes shot off whilst aloft and to a concussion while I was in one of your a prison camps in Belgium after the cessation of hostilities. I was then transferred to a camp at Devizes, Wiltshire before being repatriated back home to Berlin where over the years I happily put on several kilos of weight." He patted his stomach in demonstration. "I was appalled by the treatment of my fellow citizens by the Soviets and was accepted as an agent by British Intelligence so I could attempt to undo some of the harm that continues to beset my countrymen."

"So you're no Communist, Horst?"

"I think that's fair to say, Manus. I am certainly no Communist."

An affable conversation followed and I was a favoured with a return to my malted whisky which Horst also enjoyed. We parted company and I was asked to attend room three-one-four at ten o'clock the following morning.

As we parted, I realised that my packet of Capstan full-strength was almost depleted and stepped into the small shop which occupied space beside reception. Waiting to be served, I glanced disinterestedly at the trinkets and *bijouterie* that were intended to tempt customers. A window behind a newspaper stand looked back onto the bar area and my reverie was disturbed somewhat when I watched as Horst stood talking animatedly with the man who had been photographing from the upper gallery...the man he had intimated was most probably an agent of the *Stasi*. After a few moments he appeared to hand him something and they parted company.

I bought my cigarettes and headed upstairs to bed. I didn't sleep well.

Chapter Ten

THE GAMMON BOMBS

Benji Henderson sat in the back parlour of the Ettrick Bar, nonplussed at the somewhat bewildered reaction of Arnold Menzies upon hearing of his bin-throwing exploits.

"But Arnold, he's a Tory, a Unionist and he's in the Luudge!"

"And you think that throwing a bin through his window will advance the cause of Home Rule for Scotland?"

"As sure as God made toffee apples!"

Dougie Chalmers coughed a mouthful of Guinness back into his pint glass.

"Wee green apples, Benji. Do ye dae that deliberate?"

"Whit?

"Get things wrang when ye'r talkin'."

Still laughing with the others, but attempting a defence of Benji, Cammy McLaughlin was conciliatory.

"It won't do the cause any harm, Dougie. I saw it happen and it was enough to know that a big Tory Unionist was prevented from havin' a peaceful night's sleep. Naebody got hurt, naebody got caught."

Menzies was unimpressed.

"We need to raise our game boys. Bins through windows just won't cut it." He looked over at Dougie Chalmers.

"Dougie, tell the boys what you've got."

Chalmers leaned below the table and brought up a small sack which he placed at his side and opened. From within, he produced two dark-coloured fabric bags the size of a crown-green bowling ball, each of which fed into a metal cap.

"These, gentlemen, are Gammon Bombs. Used by myself and many others during the war. If you've used them you'll know that sitting on the table here, they are perfectly safe but if I unscrew the caps and throw them, they'll explode upon impact. These two are filled with 'Composition C' ... largely Torpex and TNT. Very powerful and would do a fair bit of damage in here if I used them."

"And use them is what we're going to do, boys," interrupted Menzies.

"Are ye sure they're harmless in here, Dougie?"asked McLaughlin.

"Aye! Like I said...cap off, throw, and they explode on impact. No timers involved like other grenades."

"Well, I have the very notion for their use," continued McLaughlin. "The Duke of Sutherland. His likeness has stood on the top of Ben Bhraggie, looking down over the lands where, in his name, thousands of Highlanders were evicted unceremoniously from their homes so he could graze sheep. A statue to a man who has caused untold misery to us Scots. We should blow it to smithereens!"

Arnold Menzies shook his head.

"Cammy! We have two grenades here. That statue is so tall it can be seen from several miles away. It must be a hundred feet high. Our explosives wouldn't dent it." He looked round the table. "Also...I know I'm always on about making sure you've a means of escape. The statue is in Golspie up in the Highlands. One road in, one road out. We're not locals. A phone call to Inverness, the police close the roads and we're sunk. The revolution's over."

Benji broke the silence that ensued after Menzies' assessment.

"Arnold's right, Cammy. He teaches at the university. We've no' got a qualification tae our name!"

Menzies demurred. "But Dougie is used to handling explosives, Benji. So we should defer to him in terms of the explosive potential of these bombs."

"Aye, there's no way it'd make a dent in a big statue...but I've an idea where we could make a bit of a splash in the newspapers."

"Go on," urged Menzies.

"As well ye know, last month, in February, King George died and his oldest wean Elizabeth took the throne. They're talking about a coronation next year so as tae allow a suitably dignified amount of time tae pass in mourning before the Unionists are allowed tae get jolly again. That said, in the meantime, they've took immediate steps tae call her Queen Elizabeth the Second - even though there's never been a Queen Elizabeth the *First* up here in Scotland. It's an insult. It completely ignores Scotland. The Tudor Queen, Elizabeth the First, never ruled over Scotland. She was jist an English Queen."

"What's your point, Dougie?" asked Menzies.

"In the Scotsman yesterday they were sayin' that they were gaun tae make new post boxes wi' E.II.R. oan them. Here! Up in Scotland despite it bein' an insult tae us. They're pittin' them oot soon and whit ah'm sayin' is that they two bombs are made o' fabric. If we fold them gently we can push them inside they new post boxes and blow them tae fuck!"

"But they explode on impact, you said. Wouldn't we put ourselves in danger of the blast?"

"Only if we're no' careful, Arnold. In the war I did this a few times. You just unscrew the cap, tie wan string tae the fuse inside and have another string tied tae the cap bit. Then ye lower the bomb gently inside the post box, retreat tae a safe distance then jerk the fuse string... *Boom*!"

Benji was excited.

"What would happen tae the box, Dougie?"

"They things are heavy built, Benji. Ah've seen them. They go down intae the grun' as far as they staun' above the grun'. It'd maybe blow the lid aff. It'd certainly destroy everythin' inside and might even split the thing open. There'd be a big bang but ah canny see it causin' harm tae the general public if anyone wis passin'." He paused. "But *maybe* it wid."

"An' where are they post boxes gettin' pit?" asked McLaughlin.

"A' ower the place, Cammy." He leaned over and produced a copy of the previous day's Scotsman from the inside of his coat pocket. Opening and folding it, he read. "'The first post box featuring the symbol of the new Queen will be erected at the junction of Gilmerton Road and Walter Scott Avenue in Edinburgh. Many others will follow as the Royal Mail goes into mass production. A party of senior politicians will accompany officials from the General Post Office to inaugurate this symbol of the new order.'" He refolded the newspaper. "Later oan it says that there's wan gaun up at the post office in George Squerr in Glasgow. Nae dates yet."

Menzies smiled. "Seems to me we've got a protest that might awaken Scotland, boys. What d'you say?"

There was a murmur of assent round the table.

"One bomb for Edinburgh, one for Glasgow?" suggested Cammy McLaughlin.

"Seems about right. However, do we give them notice?" pondered Menzies.

"Eh?"

"Well, do we write to them and make the position of proud Scots clear? Do we alert them to the inevitable destruction of their boxes all over Scotland if they don't see sense and put the Scottish Crown on the boxes instead?"

"Why the fuck wid we dae that, Arnold?" asked Chalmers. "It'll be tricky enough settin' aff the bombs withoot the polis lookin ower oor shoulder."

"We need to awaken Scotland, lads. Part of that is educating Scots. Letters to newspapers and threats to law enforcement and the postal service might see the controversy finding its way into the columns of newspapers. That way we maybe get a couple of weeks of propaganda before we actually take action. Then we get another round of news stories when we act. They won't know if we're serious, or where or when we'll hit. They can't have police officers standing on sentry duty at every post box. All the odds are in our favour - and as I'm always at pains to point out, if we did this in the wee sma' hours we have ample means of escape."

"And naebody gets hurt, eh, Arnold?"

"Listen boys. Last time we met I showed you my side-arm and told you of my rifle. We have to get used to the fact that there will be blood at some time in this campaign. Do you think the Republic of Ireland would be free right now if it hadn't been for the blood that was spilled at the Easter Rising?"

Chalmers was edgy.

"It's maybe somethin' we'd need to discuss, Arnold."

"Discuss all you like, Dougie but if you think for one minute that the imperialist British Crown is going to allow their colony of Scotland to become free of their control, you've another think coming. They have us where they want us. There's no political appetite right now for Home Rule. The Labour Party has betrayed its founders and have got too used to the lifestyles they've got down in Westminster. But the arithmetic is against us anyway. If every single Scottish MP wanted Home Rule, they'd just out-vote us. The only way we'll get our freedom is if we take it by the scruff of the neck and that, I'm afraid will require that we make Scotland such a troublesome sore for them that they'll be willing to address the legalities that permit Home Rule. So if we blow up these post boxes and someone gets hurt or if someone dies…it's only what we must endure if we are to succeed in our mission."

Chapter Eleven

ROMEO AND JULIET

Checking my watch, I stubbed out my cigarette, walked down the hallway and took the stairs to the floor below where I tapped gently on the door of room three-one-four. Nervously, I eyed the carpeted corridor where a small woman dressed in white overalls was pushing a trolley towards me festooned with cleaning materials and replenishments for each room. After a moment, the room door was opened by a women in her early thirties. My first reaction was one of surprise that a woman was involved - thus far I'd only ever encountered men in the espionage business. My second reaction was to acknowledge to myself that while the young woman was strikingly pretty, she was also unsmiling and appeared stern.

"Come in, Mr. Canning."

I entered the room where, in an armchair next to the window, sat a man in a grey suit with a pronounced herringbone pattern. A drooped moustache gave the impression of a Mexican bandit. The young lady introduced us.

"Mr. Canning, this is Israel Galvan. Mr. Galvan is responsible for this mission."

"Pleased to meet you." I leaned over and shook his hand before offering mine to the young lady.

"And you are?" I asked.

My name is Emilia Meyer. I am a German national and I will be working with you on this task."

Galvan gestured at me to sit. Two chairs had been set up at the foot of the bed and both of us sat as requested. He spoke in a pronounced American accent although he informed me he was as British as Lord Astor.

"Brought up in Denver but born in Weston-Super-Mare. UK Passport. Over here the last ten years. Love both countries. Get shot at less over here."

He leaned forward as he got down to business.

"The importance of this mission has been explained to you in some detail. In essence, our job is to lure Jürgen Roth to the West. One way or another, we bring him over to us. Our preference is that he comes here of his own volition and that he spends the rest of his working life assisting us both in our understanding of the Soviets' nuclear research and that he contributes to our own. However, if we have to bring him over drugged in the boot of a Mercedes, then so be it. Miss Meyer here will be your partner. For the purposes of this mission she will be less obtrusive than a male support. It will be easier to explain a woman with whom you are having a relationship whilst in the service of the Crown than another male."

"Well, so far you seem to be *au fait* with the information I received in London but I regret that I intend to be on the next plane back to Scotland."

Galvan's eyebrows disappeared somewhere close to his hairline.

"Really? And this is why?"

"First, I have no way of knowing that you two are who you say you are. Second, where is Horst Janson?"

"In reverse order…Herr Janson's job was merely to get you here safely and to ensure that you met with myself and Miss Meyer.

70

Secondly"... he removed a wallet from his inside jacket pocket and withdrew a card. "Here is my identification card. As you can see it identifies me as a Commercial Assistant within the British Embassy in Berlin. As you might imagine, I have no commercial interests or much in the way of commercial know-how. I am engaged in espionage as, now, so are you, Mr. Canning." (He pronounced it 'Kenning'.) "Miss Meyer, not to put too fine a point on it, over the past few years has been a very effective individual as she has acted for us several times as a 'Juliet'. That is, she has developed completely artificial relationships with important East German 'Romeos' and has supplied us with information gleaned. She has also persuaded three senior individuals to defect from the East."

"And on your say-so, I am to trust her?"

Galvan grimaced. "Miss Meyer comes from Kursk in Russia. Her mother was a lecturer in pharmacy in Kursk State Medical University. One day she told a joke to her students. She said, 'Don't stub your cigarettes out in the pot plants...you might damage the microphones'. She was arrested for this light-hearted comment when a pupil reported her for anti-Soviet agitation and propaganda and spent six years in a gulag. She built a railroad instead of teaching students the miracles of science. Miss Meyer is no Communist...no supporter of the Soviets. At the first opportunity, mother and daughter defected to the west, to Germany where they now have residence.

Throughout his defence of his colleague, her eyes remained locked on mine.

I nodded acknowledgement but continued my reservations.

"Last night, as I left Horst Janson in the bar, I stayed behind for a while and noticed him meeting with and handing something to someone he'd earlier described as a *Stasi* agent."

For the first time, Galvan smiled, revealing a row of white, even teeth.

"Your diligence does you proud, Mr. Canning. Unfortunately, here in West Berlin, not everything appears to be as it seems. Part of the challenge we face is that in order to achieve anything, we have to deal with those who are agents, double agents, triple agents...I confess it can be difficult to know who to trust and who not to trust. In this mission, only your people back in London, myself and Miss Meyer are knowledgeable about exactly what is being proposed. Horst Janson knows nothing other than what you look like, when you were to arrive, where you were staying and with whom you were to meet this morning."

"So last night he could have been arranging for me to be photographed so I can be identified when in a compromising location?"

"Indeed so...but more likely he was paying off the photographer for the spool from his camera or thanking him for not photographing him in your company. However, as I have said, here in West Berlin, up can be down and down can be up."

I took a moment to allow a silence while I mulled over this information. It was broken by Galvan.

"Mr. Canning, let me point out something to you. You were a soldier in the British Army. A good one, I gather. You have worked subsequently in lower order jobs in Scotland. You would not be a catch for our friends in the Eastern Bloc. With the best will in the world, you have no information they would seek. Fishing quotas? You have no contacts they would cherish. You have no real prospect of being turned by them so as to offer high-level access to information upon your return to Scotland or London. You are here because of only one reason. You will not be seen by Herr Roth as an attempt by the *Stasi* to trick him into betraying his new masters in East Germany and will thus allow us to make overtures which he can view as credible."

Our conversation continued awhile and I was shown paperwork and tickets confirming my rail journey to Bratislava and reservations in the Arcadia Hotel. These were given to Miss Myer who opened a large, expensive-looking bag and placed them within. It was explained to me that Jürgen Roth would have his whereabouts monitored very closely and that it would not be easy to enjoy more than a momentary conversation with him without it being noticed. I was advised to use my initial contact to attempt to arrange a second meeting with his connivance.

"No time like the present, Mr Canning. Your room here in Berlin is reserved. You and Miss Meyer leave immediately. We have bags packed for you and a change of clothing commensurate with your new station in life. Your passport and papers show you as Florin Albescu, a Romanian electrical engineer. The train will have you in Bratislava by this evening. Our information is that Herr Roth is already there. He too, is staying at the Hotel Arcadia. His favourite drink is *schnapps* and he is known to enjoy a refreshment at the hotel bar in the evening. He usually drinks alone but will be guarded by two NKVD agents of the People's Commissariat for Internal Affairs. They are well trained, tough and experienced. Some of them are also amenable to bribery. Good luck!"

He leaned forward and shook my hand.

"Miss Meyer is young but is an experienced operative. You can rely upon her to offer good field advice. I look forward to your safe return. Your job is merely to establish a relationship that Roth feels he can trust. It begins and ends with that. We don't need to see a defection this week or this month…merely that he has been made aware that a defection is possible if he wishes."

"I'll give it my best shot!"

∗ ∗ ∗

The train south from Berlin to Bratislava through Czechoslovakia took ten hours and was surprisingly free of much in the way of border security. A cursory check on paperwork from a stern-looking guard was the only impediment and took but a moment. Throughout the journey, Miss Meyer slept, waking only occasionally to fumble around in her large bag for her pack of cigarettes several of which she smoked in silence. I attempted conversation but her replies were monosyllabic. As she slept, I took to gazing at her beauty. She was discomfortingly attractive and I could easily see why many of those she targeted would be tempted by her looks, if not her scintillating wit and charm, although I had to presume that she had the capacity to be charming when called to fulfil a mission.

As we approached Bratislava, I leaned across and gently shook her arm.

"Emilia...Miss Meyer. We're arriving at the station."

She awoke and once more dove into her bag for a cigarette. She handed me some paperwork.

"We will need these documents as we will be challenged by border guards. Do not worry. Everything is in order. We are boyfriend and girlfriend if asked. But don't get any ideas. If I have to pretend to be affectionate, it is just that...a pretence. We have separate rooms."

I smiled defensively. "Don't worry, Miss Meyer. You're not my type!"

Her eyes wrinkled as the cigarette smoke stung and, for the first time that day, exhaling, she smiled back.

"Yes, I am!"

Chapter Twelve

FUCK OFF, SCOTTISH

After registration we each headed for our respective rooms. I showered and changed. Slightly nervous now, I looked my watch, realising I had but five minutes before I was to knock at Emilia Meyer's door before commencing my first job as a spy. I looked in the mirror, straightened my tie, swept some light detritus from my shoulders, ran my fingers through my hair...all small acts of grooming I'd never before countenanced. I lingered momentarily before the window, looking down on the street below before re-checking my watch and deciding that it was close enough to the appointed hour to leave my room.

Miss Meyer was ready as soon as I knocked at her door. She opened it and beckoned me inside.

"This is straightforward, Herr Canning. The bar area has many alcoves...many booths. If Herr Roth is there, so too will be his escorts. If so, I will engage with them while you have a few discrete words with our man. He will not want to talk with you in the presence of his guards. That is to be expected. Somehow you must arrange that he has a one-on-one conversation with you either in an alcove in the bar or preferably in your hotel room. HIs may be bugged. You may leave the two NKVD agents to me." She stubbed her cigarette in an ashtray. "Are we clear?"

I nodded as she lifted her large handbag.

"Have you all of your paperwork in your jacket pocket?"

I nodded and we left.

Walking down the stairs, Miss Meyer's personality underwent a remarkable transformation. Gone was the dour, business-like demeanour. Now she was a smiling vamp. She sashayed into the bar, me four steps behind and ordered a vodka on the rocks from a barman who couldn't takes his eyes from her décolletage. I stuttered something about a large whisky from another barman when my eyes locked on to a man drinking alone at the far end of the bar. Jürgen Roth; a few years older now, a hint of grey about the temporal region, but unmistakably the man I'd pulled from the Elbe. As I waited for my whisky, he raised his glass slowly to his lips. The barman placed my whisky before me and asked my room number. As I complied, Roth clicked his fingers noisily, calling my barman to him.

Here goes nothing, I thought, as I collected my glass and began the walk towards my mark. As he negotiated his drinks order with the barman, I side-eyed my partner-in-crime who was now laughing uproariously with two grey-besuited men who stood as she passed their table, engaging them in conversation.

I walked the twenty-odd steps to Roth's shoulder and waited as he completed his drinks transaction. Taking a deep breath I sat on the stool beside him and stared straight ahead at our reflection in the mirror behind the bar.

"Fifty *Deutschmarks* says you don't remember me!"

Roth turned his head and looked quizzically at my profile. He allowed a few seconds.

"You owe me fifty *Deutschmarks*! I have never set eyes on you before," he growled, slurring his words.

Slowly, I turned my head until we faced each other.

"Still no," he insisted.

"Last time we met I had just pulled you from the depths of the River Elbe!"

Roth started in surprise and after a gradual realisation, allowed a smile to play across his lips.

"You are Scottish! The man who saved my life!"

As he spoke, his eyes narrowed and he glanced surreptitiously to his left where the two NKVD agents were now attempting to persuade Miss Meyers to accept another drink from them despite her having only just sipped at the one she held in her hand. Reassured, he continued his conversation, now somewhat excited.

"You are Scottish! You are Scottish!"

I returned to my original position and stared hard at the mirror behind the bar.

"I am Sergeant Manus Canning, Highland Light Infantry."

Roth's smile widened.

"And I am *Stabshauptmann* Jürgen Roth of the *Kommandeur der Nachrichtenaufklärung.*"

Still staring ahead, I spoke sternly at my image in the mirror.

"These days you are Jürgen Roth, who works with the Soviets on research dealing with the atomic bomb."

Roth's glass was slowly lowered from his lips. He glanced nervously at the two NKVD agents who seemed completely oblivious to his predicament. He placed his glass on the bar and slid from the barstool.

"Fuck off, Scottish."

He started towards the exit. I continued to face forward but raised my voice sufficiently so he could hear.

"Jürgen! I am here because you will understand that I could not be a *Stasi* agent. I am Sergeant Manus Canning of the Highland Light Infantry and I have been sent here today precisely because I saved you and you know that you can trust me."

Roth stopped and continued to face the two NKVD agents at the far end of the bar who were completely oblivious to his conversation with me.

"I am to offer you a safe home in the west. An easy transfer across the border. Work you would find satisfying and a quality of life you could never experience in the east."

Roth grasped the rear of a barstool and took a moment to compose himself. Eventually he raised himself to his full height and, pulling back slightly the sleeve of the left arm of his suit, considered his watch. Facing the two still-distracted agents, he spoke without looking towards me.

"It is eight o'clock. My two friends over there have been drinking for an hour. By ten o'clock they will almost be unconscious." He glanced around at the various alcoves. "I will go to my room. One of these two will accompany me. He will then return to the bar. I will return here at ten o'clock precisely. I will buy a drink and shall retire to the large alcove at the rear of the bar. You will already be seated in the alcove. We will then have a five minute conversation on the basis that my two friends are unaware of our conversation. If all is well, you will have five minutes to persuade me that I would be in no jeopardy and you will amplify what you just said. Do not attempt to contact me in my room. It may be bugged."

Sliding his unfinished drink across the bar, he strode towards the door. As he passed the two NKVD agents, one of them stood and speaking urgently to Miss Meyer in apparent explanation, accompanied Roth upstairs from the bar.

Pleased that I'd managed to achieve the private meeting I'd been tasked with arranging, I swallowed my whisky, ordered a second and decided that despite my instinct being to position myself in the rear alcove and drink until ten o'clock, I decided to retire to my room until just before the time of my meeting. Sipping at my drink before leaving, I noticed that the remaining agent of the People's Commissariat for Internal Affairs was grasping Miss Meyer's arm affectionately and was obviously enamoured of her charms. Miss Meyer gave every indication that she was as besotted with him as he was of her. As I sat, finishing my drink, the second agent returned and placed his hand on her shoulder, massaging her neck muscles. With his other arm, he gestured at the bar staff to approach and take a further order for more alcohol. Miss Meyers, threw back her drink and inverted her glass on the table in a gleeful gesture that suggested she'd finished and was ready for another drink.

* * *

At ten minutes to ten, I returned to the bar and noticed that Miss Meyers was now attending to but one of the agents, the other having passed into unconsciousness and was slumped in his chair. She had by now removed her jacket which was draped over the chair and was now warmed only by her rather revealing, sleeveless top. I ordered a whisky and took it to the rear alcove where I sat nervously awaiting Roth.

At ten o'clock precisely, Jürgen Roth walked into the bar and caught the attention of the remaining NKVD agent. He raised his hand to his mouth and cupped it, toggling it back and forth with a smile that suggested he'd returned for a nightcap. The agent smiled conspiratorially and drunkenly raised the thumb of his right hand in a gesture that acknowledged a fellow toper.

He returned his attention immediately to Miss Meyers whose left hand was squeezing his knee.

Roth ordered a *schnapps* and, looking around to check once more on the agent, took his glass into the rear alcove. I sat in the gloom at the stern of the booth and bid Roth welcome. He sat, having checked once more that it was safe for him to do so.

"Well, Scottish…Manus…I must say you brought back memories. I remember well the day you saved me from the dark waters of the Elbe and protected me from those Russians who would dearly have loved to have seen me drowned, shot or hung from the yardarm. I confess I would not be here today were it not for you. And now you re-enter my life with another life-saving proposition."

"It is a sincere offer, Jürgen. We can remove you from the misery of the east and can offer you a position in the west that you would find rewarding. You would be safe. You would be rewarded. You would be respected as the scientist you are."

"I assume that the young lady diverting Agent Sidorov is a colleague of yours?"

"She is. She is much more experienced than me. My use is only that you would accept that I am not an agent of the *Stasi*."

Roth frowned.

"She is leaving the table."

A few moments later, Meyer approached the booth and placing her bag on the floor, took a seat beside us, first inspecting the chair as if checking to ensure it was clean enough to sit on. She spoke in businesslike fashion.

"Sorry, people. *Herr* Roth, I am a friend of *Herr* Canning."

"He explained, but won't?..."

Meyer swept aside his question.

"Boris Sidorov understands that even seasoned drinkers have to visit the ladies' room from time to time. My jacket remains on the back of my chair. He will be fairly confident that I'll return and that shortly we will be in bed together." Without turning to view her table, she posed Roth a question. "Does he look agitated, my Boris?"

Roth leaned back and considered the prospect.

"He is pouring himself another vodka. Boris enjoys his vodka. He seems relaxed."

"I thought so." Meyer leaned over and lifted her bag on to her lap. "Do you mind if I smoke?"

Roth shook his head and glanced once more at the far end of the bar.

My eyes widened as from her commodious bag, Meyer withdrew a Mp 751 Sten pistol complete with a long suppressor.

"Goodbye, *Herr* Roth!"

Two barely audible thwacks produced two scarlet stains on Jürgen Roth's forehead and he slumped backwards. Meyer leaned forward and pulled him towards me so his head rested on the table.

Still shocked beyond measure I found myself unable to ask the many questions to which I sought answers.

"We leave now. Your belongings remain in your room. There is a rear door. Go now!"

"Wha...?"

"Questions later! Leave this place."

Carefully, she stood, returning the pistol to her bag, and checked that her Boris was still preoccupied with his vodka. Taking me by the elbow, she guided me to the rear exit, along a corridor and out to the front of the hotel where a taxi sat, purring.

"In!" she instructed. She climbed in behind me.

"*Hlavna Stanica* Rail Station, driver!"

"Wha...?"

"You have your paperwork?"

I patted my chest, feeling for the slight bulge in my jacket and could only nod.

"Then we will be home in Berlin shortly. I have reserved a Pullman sleeping compartment on every train leaving Bratislava for Berlin tonight and over the next three days. We have twenty minutes." She shouted at the driver and spoke in Czech. "*Pospěšte si, řidiči. Velký tip, pokud stihneme náš vlak!* Hurry, driver. Big tip if we catch our train!"

She sat back in the seat.

"Mission accomplished. Well done, Manus!"

"Why was he shot?"

Coolly, Meyer considered her reflection in the car window as the taxi sped in darkness towards the station.

"I read your file, Manus. You received a commendation for attacking and capturing a German machine gun position."

"So?"

"You were ordered to do this?"

"Of course! But wha...?"

"Did you challenge the command? Ask for an explanation?"

"Of course not."

"This is no different."

My rational thought processes kicked in. I decided to challenge.

"My clothes remain in my room. Your fucking jacket hangs on the back of that Russian's chair!

Meyer bristled.

"And in the pockets of your spare jacket they will find a portion of a bus ticket that was purchased in Bucharest. The make of the jacket is common in Romania. Your clothes were purchased for you. They were also made in Romania. In the breast pocket of the suit in your case is a ticket to a ballet held last week in Bucharest. You are registered as a Romanian national as am I. The top Russian agent there is a Romanian called Şerban Florescu. Since I joined the Intelligence Service I have come to know many evil men. Florescu is by far the most evil. He would be no loss to the world. It is known that for whatever reason, he hates Roth with a passion. The finger of suspicion will fall on him and could easily weaken or eliminate him."

"So a good man was shot to knock out a bad man?"

Meyer shrugged, fumbled in her bag for her cigarettes and turned to face me. "You can relax, Manus. We have achieved what was asked of us and tonight we will share a comfortable bed on the train as we head back to Berlin." She placed her hand on my knee and smiled the smile she'd smiled at Boris Sidorov. "This must have been most upsetting. I must try to comfort you tonight! I have certain skills!"

I found my voice.

"You can fuck right off, hen. I don't sleep with murderers."

Chapter Thirteen

MEANWHILE BACK IN SCOTLAND...

B rodie drew a pencilled line underneath a column of figures. *Nine hundred and seventy-one pounds, ten shillings and sixpence! Fuck!* He lifted an envelope and withdrew its contents. Re-reading it brought him no consolation. By the end of the month! *There's no way,* he decided. *Nine hundred and seventy-one pounds, ten shillings and sixpence!*

He read the itemised list of expenditure, justifying every spend.

Membership of my London club? Necessary! My new Harris Tweed coat? Necessary! That case of Château Haut Brion 1950? What might my guests think if there was a more inferior wine? Not possible...necessary! My handmade Indian, Kashmir Silk rug? Do they expect me to entertain guests on linoleum? Necessary! He read through the remaining items declaring them each to be necessary. Pursing his lips in thought, he rose from the table and moved over to the settee where he poured himself a generous glass of Talisker whisky. *My brother works for a fucking London bank. He not only earns a salary but he enjoys a bonus for work well done. My lover Simon? Sells fucking boats to moneyed people. Earns a decent salary and every time he sells a fucking yacht he earns a bonus that dwarfs my fucking salary. Me? I keep this fucking nation safe and I'm offered a salary that doesn't begin to keep pace with the costs associated with my responsibilities.* He drained the glass. *Well, fuck this! I'm going to change things. It's about time I was able to keep pace with my peers without worrying about where the next nine hundred and seventy-one pounds, ten shillings and sixpence is going to come from.*

* * *

"I fuckin' hate this fuckin' station! It's like climbin' fuckin' Everest tae get tae fuckin' Princes Street!"

Benji Henderson was breathing heavily and found himself only capable of nodding his agreement as he and Cammy McLaughlin slowly climbed the precipitous and interminable Waverley Steps from its railway station's subterranean base to Edinburgh's most famous thoroughfare. At the top, McLaughlin stopped and turning his collar up against the brisk east wind, beckoned Henderson to come closer.

"Change of plan, Benji," he breathed. "On the other side of this road is one of Scotland's finest ale houses, the Guildford Arms. Ah intend tae sink a pint and recover my composure. It would not serve the cause if we were to continue our mission when we were in a state of feverish exhaustion. Are you wi' me?"

"Bloody right, Cammy. Lead on, MacDuff!"

Both men crossed the road and entered the pub just as the barman shouted, 'last orders'. McLaughlin purchased two pints of lager and they settled down at a table.

"Think we were followed, Cammy?" Henderson looked around the pub as he asked his question. "Anyone in here could be the polis."

McLaughlin removed the olive-coloured, canvas, webbed satchel from his shoulders and placed it carefully on the floor beside him.

"It's possible, Benji. But no one's come in here since we did, and no one else is breathin' as heavily as we were two minutes ago. No one here climbed those fuckin' steps along wi' us. Trust me on that, my friend." He took a long draught of his pint. "Anyway, there's a back door so we've a means of escape if they come in through the front door. But it's unlikely, eh? Arnold Menzies is a careful man. He's thorough. He's good at the plannin'." Another long swallow. "Tonight we're gaun tae blaw her imperial majesty's new post box to smithereens just as Arnold and Dougie are gauny dae in Glasgow."

Henderson clinked his pint tumbler against that of McLaughlin in acknowledgement of his assessment and made light work of his drink.

"Mind you, Cammy. We've a long walk up tae Gilmerton Road. We'd better no' keep bevvyin'."

"It was last orders, Benji. We start the walk after we finish these." He raised the remnants of his pint and for the second time, offered his glass to Benji in a toast. "Fuck the Queen, eh, Benji?"

Henderson smiled.

"Aye...fuck the Queen, Cammy!"

"Let's drink up and go...although it's just last orders. We could maybe have a quick wee *deoch-an-doris*...one for the door?"

* * *

In Glasgow, Arnold Menzies and Dougie Chalmers stood inside the external vestibule of the city's General Post Office on the south side of George Square. Menzies' gaze swept the square looking for anything untoward.

"What time's it, Dougie?"

Chalmers consulted his watch.

"Quarter past one, Arnold."

"Fifteen minutes, then we make our move." He scanned the square once more. "Benji and Cammy should be in place over by."

George Square in Glasgow's city centre can be a lively place during the day but after one o'clock on a cold Tuesday morning, any revellers had long gone home, rough sleepers had found their doorways or hostels and any police presence had retreated to the station or had found refuge in a howf or the back room of a pub where relaxation was possible.

"Time to go, Arnold," muttered Chalmers. "That's one-thirty."

"Agreed. The square's empty."

Both men stepped forward and stooped in front of the large, red postbox which proudly proclaimed the reign of Britain's new monarch, Queen Elizabeth. Carefully, Chalmers opened a webbed satchel identical to that being used by McLaughlin and Henderson in Edinburgh. Withdrawing the device, he fed it into the post box and aided by Menzies who held the cord which supported the bomb, they lowered it slowly into the void. Satisfied it had settled gently on the bottom of the box, Menzies slowly allowed the string to go slack and both men retreated to the safety of two huge sandstones pillars that stood like sentries at the door of the General Post Office. Chalmers held the second cord which was attached to the cap of the Gammon Bomb. The men exchanged glances.

"Here goes nothin'! whispered Chalmers.

Menzies scanned the square one last time.

"Do it!"

Chalmers tugged violently at the light string. Immediately an enormous blast shook the ground as the Torpex and TNT mix exploded, shattering the post box, leaving huge shards of steel exposed and its heavy red lid on the other side of the road.

Staring through the smoke, Chalmers smiled.

"Fuck me! Mission accomplished, Arnold. It's destroyed."

"Then we're off. Walk normally."

The two men walked rather more quickly than they would have done had they been walking normally despite Menzies' injunction and after one minute found their car safely parked where they'd left it in Glassford Street.

"Hope the boys were as successful in Edinburgh!" muttered Chalmers as he put the car into gear and set off.

* * *

In Edinburgh, the boys were having problems.

"C'mon, Benji! Get the fuckin' bomb intae the post box."

"It's a wee bit stuck, Cammy. Ah canny be too rough in case it blaws!"

McLaughlin looked around anxiously. Gilmerton Road was still.

"Don't blaw us up, Benji but get the fuckin' thing inside."

Moments later, Henderson retreated a few steps and knelt beside McLaughlin as he gingerly lowered the bomb into the maw of the post box.

"Right, Benji. Behind this tree!"

Together they moved backwards as McLaughlin fed the second cord through his hands. Now safely protected by a large oak tree, McLaughlin took a deep breath.

"Okay! Here goes!"

A sharp tug resulted only in the cord freeing itself from the cap and ending up before them on the pavement.

"Shite!" exclaimed McLaughlin. "The cord came loose."

"Shite!" echoed Henderson. "It'll no' blaw up noo!" A thought occurred to him. "Well, therr gauny find it. Are you sure you wore gloves a' the time when you were fixin' it?"

"There's nae prints oan the bomb, Benji. Nothin' to track it back tae us if that's yer worry."

"Then let's get tae fuck away frae here."

Both men stood and started their walk back to the centre of Edinburgh where they intended catching the early train to Glasgow.

* * *

Communications weren't as sophisticated back in 1952 as they are as I tell this tale.

In consequence, the postman who arrived at 5.00am to collect the mail and to begin his rounds had no knowledge of the Glasgow bombing and therefore had no reason to be cautious when he discovered an odd-looking bag in the bottom of the post box. Lifting it and dropping it on the ground where he knelt was his last action on earth as the Gammon Bomb did as it was primed to do and exploded, badly damaging the red post box. The impact of fragments and debris from the explosion source tore at the postman, severing limbs, carrying his remains several feet from the site and killing him instantly.

Unaware of his death, McLaughlin and Henderson boarded the early train to Glasgow.

"Hope Arnold isn'y too pissed at us for what was a bit of a damp squib, eh" growled McLaughlin. "But on the bright side, no one got hurt!"

Chapter Fourteen

BOZOV

The substantial property at Harrington House, 13 Kensington Palace Gardens, just north of the London Oratory, accommodates the interests of the Russian Federation in London.

A token knock on the door of Georgy Nikolayevich Zarubin, Ambassador Extraordinary and Plenipotentiary of the Russian Federation to the United Kingdom of Great Britain and Northern Ireland presaged the entry of Dmitri Bozov, an intelligence officer who crossed the threshold without awaiting permission so to do. Ostensibly his role was to enhance the foreign economic interests of the Russian Federation in the United Kingdom as an integral part of the Diplomatic Mission of the Russian Federation. In reality he was Russia's top espionage expert in London.

"Your Excellency, I apologise for the intrusion but this demands your early attention."

He handed a letter to Zarubin who placed his spectacles atop his nose and read.

"I don't understand, Dmitri. Is this a joke?"

"My first reaction as well, Ambassador. But I draw your attention to the first sentence of the third paragraph. You see that the author of this letter makes specific reference to the first British nuclear-powered submarine which we understand is to be called Dreadnought and refers to the fact that it is to be based around a

U.S.-built nuclear reactor. This appears to confirm intelligence reports from other sources and is known to only a few people. The letter appears amateurish in its understanding of the espionage community but is knowledgable in terms of the nuclear defence of the United Kingdom."

"But the author seeks only five thousand English pounds for this information. If it is accurate, it would command a hundred times that sum."

"Which is why I suspect that this is a genuine offer by someone who has useful information to sell but who is not involved in the business of intelligence gathering. It might be the start of a beautiful friendship."

"He wants one of us to attend at a call box at Hyde Park Corner and await his telephone call at precisely ten o'clock this evening." The Ambassador returned the letter to Bozov. "We have nothing to lose, Dmitri. Handle this personally. Provide him with the sum he seeks."

* * *

A sunny and still evening had dimmed and streetlights had begun to illuminate the pavements beneath the darkening sky. A bank of six red phone boxes stood unattended when, at ten minutes before ten o'clock, Angus Brodie emerged from the escalator taking him from the Piccadilly line at Hyde Park Corner. Biting his lower lip nervously, he crossed the road and entered the box furthest to the right, lifting the phone and holding it to his ear as if on a call. His eyes focussed upon the five empty adjoining phone boxes. At two minutes before the hour a slight man heaved strenuously at the heavy door next to him and thumbed coins into the slot in the black box before him, dialled his number and in obvious consequence of no one replying, pressed button 'B' to have his money returned before leaving.

Again the five boxes were empty. Brodie looked around and realised that no one appeared to be in close proximity awaiting his call. In two minds whether to attempt the call or abort, he decided eventually to make the call and dialled the number he'd memorised earlier. Even allowing for four empty phone boxes between him and the target box, he could still hear clearly the ring tone as his call went through. Five rings, six rings, seven... Just as he was about to place the phone on the receiver, a thickset man stepped from behind the boxes and opened the heavy metal and glass door as if it were made of balsa wood.

"May I help you?"

Brodie turned his back on the other boxes in order to disguise his call.

"Did you get my letter?"

"And what letter was that?"

"Look, I can tell from your accent that you are Russian. I am in no mood to play games. If you found the information I included in the letter to be useful, there is much more where that came from. But it'll cost money."

"Five thousand pounds?"

"To start with."

"I found it interesting. But five thousand pounds is a lot of money."

"No it is not. It is chicken feed for you. I just need an early infusion of funds. If you are interested, be back at this phone box tomorrow evening at the same time. I will call and instruct you where to go to deliver the money. We will not meet in person."

"And how on earth am I to take delivery of the information you promise in your letter?"

"That will be explained tomorrow night."

"And how am I to satisfy myself that the information you promise in your letter is not a complete fiction?"

"Trust me, I am an expert and the information I will supply is accurate and will not be known to you."

"Trust is in short supply in my business, Comrade."

"I am no Comrade, my friend."

"And presently I am no friend, my Comrade…but I would like to get to know you. We might be able to come to a profitable and mutually beneficial relationship."

"I can't allow myself to become known to Russian Intelligence. It's too dangerous. I need to find a way to provide you with information and take a fee for this without exposing myself."

"You are new to this business, eh?"

"My unfamiliarity with your practices is irrelevant. I cannot be identified."

"We can ensure your confidentiality. You can remain a secret."

"Nonetheless. My conditions are absolute. Tomorrow, same time, same place."

Brodie placed the phone on the receiver but maintained his posture, facing away from Bozov. He listened as the door of the phone box opened and allowed a few seconds to permit his contact to leave the scene, then shouldered his door and stepped outside.

A tall and heavily built man was leaning against the adjacent phone box. His hands were cupped and he was lighting a cigarette. He inhaled deeply and spoke aloud whilst gazing fixedly straight ahead at the Underground entrance.

"See you tomorrow, Comrade."

"Bbbbut how…how did…?"

Bozov turned to face an obviously frightened Brodie.

"Comrade. I have long experience in this business. I can protect you and I can pay you. You need have no concern. You are new to this and I have much experience. I watched as you placed the phone on the receiver just as the call ended. Of course it may have been coincidence but it wasn't." He took another deep draw of his cigarette. "Now, we can keep to your plan and meet again tomorrow night via the telephone or you could accompany me for a drink in the Lanesborough Hotel just ahead of us. I don't need to know your name. You are quite safe. I am the only person in the world who knows we are meeting…and, in my pocket, I have a large envelope with five thousand of your English pounds in it."

Brodie's initial reluctance first heightened, then reduced as Bozov patted his chest pocket signifying the location of the money. He looked around anxiously lest their conversation was being overheard.

"Okay! One drink. But I do the questioning."

"You're the boss!"

* * *

A short walk took the men to the Lanesborough Hotel, Brodie insisting that they repair to a lounge bar in which only one couple were engaged in deep conversation; other booths were empty. Drinks were ordered and the men sat.

"I have an envelope for you," said Bozov. Inside is five thousand pounds." He removed it from his pocket and slid it across the table.

Despite his anxiety, Brodie brought it towards him and felt its heft.

"Five thousand pounds, you say?"

Bozov nodded.

"And all because we received this letter from you." He withdrew Brodie's letter and unfolded it, placing it on the table. "You speak of Dreadnought and of its propulsion system?"

Brodie looked around nervously.

"Look, I'm new to all of this. My position is that I've given you information and you have paid me. As far as I'm concerned our bargain is concluded. I don't want to expose myself."

Bozov sighed, "We do not know each other but you have written to the Russian Federation and have already compromised yourself by providing classified information in the full knowledge that you have signed your Official Secrets Act. We were photographed meeting outside, our telephone conversation was recorded, and when you accepted that envelope you were photographed through that window behind you. As you leave you will be followed by two of my colleagues until we learn of your identity."

Brodie's already heightened anxiety now shot skywards.

"Bbbbut...I...what...what..."

"Relax, Comrade. None of that is true. But it could have been. I want us to develop a relationship based on trust. I merely wanted to point out that you have made your move. We can help you achieve your objective of raising money. You are in safe and experienced hands. Might we start by sharing our names? My name is Dmitri Bozov and I am the most experienced espionage officer in the Russian Embassy although my business card would tell you I am part of the trade delegation. I am very experienced in these matters and am proud to say that no one for whom I have had responsibility has ever fallen foul of MI5. We would never ask you to do anything that might place you in danger. You are in safe hands...so, your name?"

Brodie now had his head in his hands and stared forlornly at the table.

"I'm fucked...I am completely fucked!"

"You are not, Comrade. Your name?"

Resigned to his fate, Brodie succumbed to Bozov's solicitation. Wearily, he sat back in his chair and sipped at his Talisker.

"My name is Angus Brodie."

"From now on you will only be referred to as 'Wembley'. And how have you the knowledge you shared in your letter, Wembley?"

"I am a senior civil servant and attend meetings regularly at which Britain's future nuclear deterrent is discussed."

"And in which department do you work, Wembley."

Listlessly, Brodie paused before revealing his background.

"I work for the Ministry of Defence and am responsible for developing the port at Faslane in Scotland which will become the home of Britain's nuclear deterrent."

Bozov lifted his vodka and tapped the edge of Brodie's whisky glass before relaxing the importance he'd placed on Brodie's code name.

"Then we will have a beautiful relationship, Angus. A great friendship and a beautiful relationship!"

Chapter Fifteen

HERR SCHNEIDER

It took some time for my anger over Roth's murder to ease. I shouted at Emilia Meyer. I shouted at Israel Galvan. I shouted at Horst Janson. I was not a happy bunny and insisted upon returning to Scotland. I took a call from Sir Anthony Caplan and shouted at him. But the long and short of it was that I agreed to stay and continue my work in espionage. If I'm honest, the morality and ethics about which I shouted were subordinated to my need for excitement and a healthy wage packet.

The next several weeks were educational and Horst Janson was my teacher. I was immersed in the education of the art of spying. My earlier scepticism of Horst was soon abandoned as I began to realise just how accomplished he was.

One afternoon we repaired for a drink at Horst's suggestion. We settled on barstools at a taproom in *Kurfürstendamm*. Seated, he began to quiz me.

"I have been impressed by you, Manus. You are clearly intelligent and are obviously very brave. But you must learn to be observant. A good intelligence officer takes note of his surroundings. Do you agree?"

"Of course, Horst."

"Then without looking, tell me how many people are sitting behind us in this bar."

Flustered, I suggested a couple of tables at which groups of men were drinking.

"Perhaps eight or so?"

Horst shook his head.

"Three tables are occupied, Manus. At one table there are three men. All are aged in their late sixties. They appear inebriated and would not appear to present any problems. At a second sit four men. All are aged in their thirties. One has tattoos on his arm suggesting a military or naval background. All seem fit. One is particularly muscular. At a third table, a young couple sit deep in conversation. The young man is slurring his words but the young lady is sober and is animated. They seem absorbed with one another. She doesn't wear a wedding ring but he does."

I looked around and found his description correct in all particulars. He supped at his pilsner and asked another question.

"Is there another way out of this bar other than the way we came in?"

"I didn't look."

"Only one door. One way in, one way out." He changed the subject again. "What is the name of the barmaid?"

I laughed.

"No idea."

"It's Petra. When we were ordering she was referred to by name by a customer."

He reached over and placed his hand on my left wrist covering my timepiece.

"Your watch. How long have you had it?"

"I bought it when I was demobbed. It has served me well. What's that, perhaps seven years or so?"

Still holding his hand over my watch, he smiled.

"Seven years! Then tell me this. Is at the bottom of your watch-face a number six ? Is it a dot, a line, a Roman numeral or an Arabic numeral?"

I was flummoxed.

"Eh, it's a Roman numeral...I think."

Horst removed his hand.

"Have a look."

I looked at my watch.

"Fuck me, it's a dot!"

We both laughed.

"Tell me, Manus, how long has it been since you looked at your watch?"

I returned his grin.

"Maybe three seconds!"

"Then tell me, Mr. Intelligence Officer-in-training. Having just looked at your watch, what was the precise time on its dial when you looked?"

Both of us laughed out loud as I confessed, "I haven't a fucking clue! I was too busy looking at the dot! About half-three?"

He reached over and turned my arm so as to reveal my wrist. With his other hand he pushed up my sleeve and revealed my watch. It showed three twenty-two.

Horst laughed long and loud.

"Manus Canning, fuck off back to Scotland and look after your Scottish fish."

* * *

I learned how to follow people without being detected. I learned how to follow people in a car without being detected. I learned how to let slip those who were following me on foot. I learned how to escape those who were following me in a car. I learned the basics of questioning people...not interrogation methods involving violence, just logical questioning to establish the fundamentals. Some elementary codes were provided me. I was given a camera and taught how to use it...taught to wind elastic bands around a pistol grip to ensure a more secure grasp. Then I was tasked with a responsibility to establish whether I could handle the requirement successfully to undertake a task that trumped emotions. Importantly, I discovered an easy relationship with the administration of being a spy. Many of my colleagues chafed at the requirement routinely to note details of their activities but I was used to recording information when a civil servant and was regularly commended by my superiors for this less glamorous side of espionage.

Israel Galvan called me into his office.

"Manus! We have your first intelligence responsibility."

"Second," I corrected him. "The first was that debacle in Bratislava."

"Your next task, then."

"I'm all ears."

"Tonight you will witness an East German officer responsible for their prisons regime engage with one of our 'Juliets'. He will be filmed *in flagrante delicto* with a young lady. When he leaves her boudoir, you will challenge him, invite him into your room, and explain the new realities of life to him. I take it this doesn't offend your sensibilities?"

"It does not!"

He smiled. "Then, if I might paraphrase your William Shakespeare, 'Cry Havoc, and let slip the dogs of the cold war." Evidently pleased with his *bon mot*, he continued. "*Herr* Janson will supervise and report on your performance."

* * *

Later that evening I was escorted by Horst to an establishment called Hotel Adlon Kempinski just inside the Russian controlled Eastern Quadrant and was taken to room one-one-seven where I was seated in front of a blank television screen. Horst turned some dials and pushed some buttons. The image of an empty bed next door, in room one-one-nine, gradually flickered to life on the screen.

"Shortly, we expect to capture images that will persuade a very important East German official to abandon all thoughts he has of operating East German prisons in the interests of the motherland and will instead favour suggestions we might make from time to time. Your job is to convince him that he has little choice. In your favour is that he *thinks* he is fucking Johanna Wagner, the much-loved daughter of Hugo Wagner, Secretary of the *Deutsche Wirtschaftskomission*, the German Economic Commission who would react very badly were he to be aware that his much-loved daughter was being screwed and cheated on by a two-timing, dirty, low-life bastard called Wolfgang Schneider. In reality he will be consorting with one of our agents. The sordid images will be available immediately upon recording so you will be able to show him an excerpt should he require more convincing.

Horst removed himself and left me alone with the television. While waiting I made a few phone calls seeking information. It took half an hour before the door in the next room opened and a young lady entered pulling a middle aged man by his tie. Immediately they embraced and as they disengaged, her face was captured as she held the gaze of a camera she knew only too well was focused upon her actions. It was Emilia Meyer. Her glance lingered long enough to make the point that she was aware that her performance was being recorded before turning and disrobing both herself and Herr Schneider. For the next half hour their writhings were recorded meticulously by the most sophisticated Vision Electronic Recording Apparatus provided by the Americans. The obligatory post-coitus cigarette saw the couple gradually de-couple and dress. Miss Meyer made her excuses and left Schneider to compose himself. As he subsequently opened the door to his room to leave, I was standing in the doorway of my own room. I spoke in German.

"*Herr* Schneider! *Ich habe etwas für dich*. I have something for you."

Somewhat flustered at being called by his real name and not the pseudonym he'd used to book the room, his slack-jawed response allowed me to step into the hallway and curtly invite him to step into my room. I'd used the time they'd employed for dressing to tee up the particularly awkward moment when he'd placed his hands around her throat and applied sufficient pressure to have her gasp for breath.

"Please have a seat, *Herr* Schneider. You will find this interesting."

He sat and I pushed the play button which saw him stand upright in appalled bewilderment.

"Whaaat...bbbut..."

"*Herr* Schneider, let me speak plainly. You have been screwing Johanna Wagner, the daughter of Hugo Wagner, Secretary of the *Deutsche Wirtschaftskomission*. You knew the dangers of this when you calculated the chances of carrying on this affair without it coming to the attention of your wife Matilda or that of Johanna's husband. You also considered that somehow you'd keep it secret from her father...a very important figure in the East German Government. If he became aware that you attempted to choke his daughter during sex play, your career would not just be over, I fancy you would spend some time either in prison for attempted murder or at best would be posted to some particularly unpleasant task in Siberia. Certainly you'd never see your lovely wife Matilda or your daughter Eva ever again."

Schneider's eyes never left the screen as I spoke. I pushed the 'stop' button and bid him sit again. I sat facing him.

"Wolfgang! We don't need to trigger all of that unpleasantness. Every so often, in your job you will require to make decisions regarding those sentenced by the East German courts. You decide where prisoners will go and what kind of regime they will face once they get there. Sometimes you negotiate prisoner release with the West. From time to time, one of my colleagues or myself will contact you using the name Gottfried Semper. You will always accept that call. You will comply with the request made. It will never be so outlandish that it would call attention to you. You will never meet Miss Wagner again or attempt to make contact with her but will return to a more traditional relationship with your wife. If you comply with this, these images will never find their way to the tabloid newspaper '*Bild-Zeitung*' or to the letter box of Herr Wagner, who, as I say, is currently Secretary of the *Deutsche Wirtschaftskomission* and who is generally reckoned to be a man on the way to the top. His influence over your life, should you decide not to assist, would be ever more significant."

Schneider began to cry, his shoulders heaving as he sobbed. I placed my hand on his shoulder and gave it an encouraging squeeze.

"Come, come, *Herr* Schneider. This horror is completely avoidable. Are you agreeable to our little bargain?"

Eventually, Schneider ceased his caterwauling and adopted a more rational persona.

"Please...*Herr*...?"

"You can call me *Herr* Semper...Gottfried Semper. That name should be burned upon your consciousness. That is the name that will save your marriage and your life as a respected controller of the prison service in East Germany."

Schneider looked lost but eventually found his voice and spoke in a faltering voice.

"Then, *Herr* Semper. I agree your conditions...all of them. I promise you, I accept that my foolish actions have compromised my marital and professional life and wish to do as you suggest to ensure that this idiotic indiscretion never surfaces."

"Aye, *Herr* Schneider, it was a bit glaikit!" I said, lapsing into my own vernacular.

"Sorry?"

"Glaikit...stupid... However, while I do not wish to appear pedantic...I do not suggest your future actions...I *instruct* your future actions!"

Schneider stood and faced me as if a soldier standing at attention.

"Herr Semper, I accept your instructions. I am yours to command."

I rose and shook his hand.

"Then you may go home to Matilda and enjoy your life as a respected controller of the East German prison service. And sleep well, Wolfgang. We will never break our word on this. Your secret is safe with us. We have a bargain."

I opened the door and he left. I sat and looked at the screen which had frozen at the scene where Miss Meyer's face was contorted in pain as Schneider's fingers wrapped around her throat. As I did so, the door opened and Horst entered.

"Manus...you are a natural...that was perfection. I didn't want to tell you lest it unnerved you but I was watching you both on a camera from room one-one-five. I have to report back on your performance." He laughed. "I will be telling our superiors that in Manus Canning we have a naturally gifted operative who can be trusted to fulfil tasks much more complex than this. I was most impressed by your research. It was excellent! You knew the name of his wife, his daughter..." He stepped back and applauded. "Your only mistake was to offer him your reassurance that we would keep our end of the bargain. If at any stage it suits us to throw him to the wolves, he will be discarded as if he was so much disposable rotten meat!"

Chapter Sixteen

THE SQUARE ROOT OF VODKA

Ensconced once more in the enclosed back parlour of the Ettrick Bar, Arnold Menzies reached below the table and produced his revolver. He raised it, cocked it, and pointed it at Cammy McLaughlin before moving his arm to the right and covering Dougie Chalmers. Making his point, he slowly moved the pistol left until it pointed at Benji Henderson who evinced concern.

"Fur fuck's sake, Arnold! Stoap wavin' that gun aboot. It might go aff!"

"All for one and one for all, boys." He let the gun hammer down gently, placed the revolver on the table and lifted his pint glass, talking as the pint tumbler was paused at his lips.

"If we are to achieve anything, we must accept that spilling blood goes with the territory. That postman was unfortunate. We all read the papers. It was a shame he had a child and that his wife is now a widow. But I repeat a point I've made several times before. Would Ireland have secured its freedom without the bloody Easter Rising? Let me help you...it would not! We are now engaged in a similar struggle. We need to usurp the English invader. Do any of us think that the British imperialists would hesitate to kill and maim if it suited their struggle? No they would not! And nor should we. There will be protests in the papers in order that the Establishment might continue their colonial domination of Scotland...there will be those who will protest any kind of violence…some will argue for the likes of us to be strung up but we must be strong. We must be indefatigable…"

"Eh? asked Benji.

"Tireless, Benji…relentless…"

"Ah agree wi' Arnold," nodded McLaughlin. "We startit somethin' when we blew them post boxes up. We've had boxes defaced in Stirling and Inverness. Fires have been startit inside boxes in Selkirk, in Dumfries, in Auchterarder and in Ayr so that the mail wis destroyed. Someone even pit cement in the mooth of the box in Bonnybridge. We've certainly startit somethin', eh?"

"Look!" insisted Menzies. The only people who know we were behind these bombs are the four of us. The police have said in the papers that they are still looking into things as they have nothing to go on. I can't see there being any forensic evidence that would link us to either of the two explosions. No witnesses." He looked around the table. "My point is a simple one. If we keep our mouths shut, we stay out of prison…we stay out of jail…and most importantly we remain able to take the fight to the enemy and promote Scottish home rule. So…" He glared at the other three men. "I tell you here and now…we tell absolutely no one of our activities. The price of a mistake here exposes all of us so be aware, if anyone talks loosely, I shoot them."

"Fuck aff, Arnold," protested McLaughlin. "You're meant tae be the brains of the outfit. The university academic. And now you're talkin' about shootin' us?"

"Never been more serious, Cammy. There needs to be internal discipline in this man's army. We can't go blethering and shooting our mouths off to all and sundry. If they get one of us they get the four of us. So that can't happen. We swear an oath right now that nothing…*nothing* is ever said by any one of us. The penalty has to be severe…and if anyone is ever pulled by the police, we don't

 even give them our name. Make them work for it. If we don't open our mouths even to ask for a toilet break, they can't interrogate us and hope we slip up...so we say the square root of fuck all!"

"What's a square root?" asked Benji.

"Somethin' tae dae wi' the speed of light," responded Chalmers helpfully.

"Nah, it's a thing ah got telt doon the allotment. It's tae dae wi' spuds," ventured McLaughlin.

Menzies shook his head.

"Look...Dear Christ! It doesn't matter. What's important is that presently we have committed an act of rebellion against the state and against the Crown. We have done so successfully. We are now the only people who can fuck this up...so we don't fuck it up!"

He lifted the revolver from the table and lowered it to a shopping bag that he'd brought with him, concealing it before lifting his head to address his three friends.

"And I'm completely serious about shooting anyone who is stupid enough even to tell his wife, weans or drunk pals what we've been up to!"

Discomfited, the three men nodded agreement.

"Here's our next move, boys," suggested Menzies, as from the same shopping bag he lifted a miniature bottle of vodka.

"Ah'm merr o' a Guinness man, Arnold," laughed McLaughlin.

"Aye, well so would I be if this was my only other choice, Cammy."

"Fuckin' vodka? Who drinks fuckin' vodka?" asked Henderson.

"Let me explain, boys. I was at a university bash in the Central Hotel early last night. They've a wee shop for tourists. I was just looking around and noticed that they had a number of gifts that involved whisky miniatures. Then I saw two things. The first was a pack of three miniature bottles of vodka, attractively packaged and the second was a magazine on the rack with a story on the cover about how our Conservative and Unionist Secretary of State for Scotland, one James Stuart, the first Viscount Stuart of Findhorn, has a preference for vodka over Scotch whisky, the traitorous and tasteless bastard! I had a look at the article. This entitled dolt, whom the Tories trust to run the nation of Scotland, married Lady Rachel Cavendish, the sister of the wife of Harold Macmillan in 1923 having earlier been noted as a suitor of Lady Elizabeth Angela Marguerite Bowes-Lyon...who as we all know, married King George the sixth and who, until a couple of months ago, was Queen of England, the Dominions and the British Commonwealth. For these sins alone he should perish."

"Agreed," acknowledged Chalmers. "And is that one of the wee bottles of vodka that James Stuart likes?"

"In a manner of speaking," said Menzies. "With one significant difference. This particular miniature bottle of vodka was purchased in an anonymous Agnew's off-licence in Shettleston last night and taken this morning to the Science Faculty of the University of Glasgow where, with the door closed behind me, I introduced a measure of sulphuric acid to the mix. If this were to be consumed as it stands...well, severe lung damage would follow. It would cause burns to the mouth, throat, larynx, oesophagus and stomach and would result in vomiting, haemorrhage, vomiting blood, diarrhoea and abdominal injury. Probably septic shock."

"Aye, that's why I prefer the Guinness," laughed Cammy McLaughlin.

As the laughter died, Menzies again took up his line of thought.

"But, suitably packaged and presented, we might consider offering this wee gift to the aforementioned James Stuart, the first Viscount Stuart of Findhorn. It might have mortal effect."

"Whit's 'mortal' mean?" asked Benji.

"He'd probably wake up deid, Benji!" explained Chalmers.

"Then let's send him a wee present," suggested Benji.

"My thoughts exactly, Benji. But we do this carefully. The police would throw all of their forensics at this so the vodka pack has to be purchased in a way that the purchaser can't easily be traced, the acid has also to be introduced in a way that can't be traced, the package has to be sent to his home, not his office, so a civil servant doesn't interfere with it and it has to be accompanied by a letter that gives the good Viscount Stuart the confidence to drink the stuff."

"What do you suggest, Arnold?"

"One of us, disguised, travels to Edinburgh and buys the vodka pack. If it's in the Central Hotel shop at Glasgow Central Station, it'll also be in the North British Hotel shop at Waverley Station. I take the three bottles of vodka and strengthen their contents. We replace the three bottles. We manufacture a letter from the vodka people and we post it to him."

"Sounds dead simple, Arnold," encouraged Chalmers.

"The vodka side seems pretty straightforward, boys. But we need to find his home address, we need somehow to manufacture an authentic looking letter from the vodka people and we need to frame the letter in such a way as to encourage his sampling of the vodka quite quickly. It wouldn't do if he decided to offer it as a present to the local bowling club as a raffle prize, eh?"

"Wi' ma luck, ah'd probably win it, Arnold," chuckled Benji.

Menzies responded. "With my luck, I'd probably see you drink it but then recover, Benji."

As the laughter subsided, Menzies brought them back to the matter in hand.

"So is this a goer, boys? And remember...all for one and one for all. If we're in, we're all in and I will shoot anyone who betrays the cause."

"Fuck me, Arnold. If it comes to the bit where you intend to shoot me, just give me wan o' them voddies. I'd rather go to ma grave pissed than shot," grinned McLaughlin.

"That could be arranged, Cammy," responded Menzies grimly.

Chapter Seventeen

HOMEWARD BOUND

I remained in Berlin for seven years. During that time I became entirely comfortable in my role as an MI6 spy for Her Majesty's Government. I flatter myself that I became quite good at it and was given ever-increasing responsibilities. Annually, I was called to London to present myself in front of Sir Anthony Caplan where his rheumy but forensic eye was cast over my annual appraisal. That said, after my first two winter visits - they were always in November - so effusive were the assessments of my abilities, that Sir Anthony began to use the afternoon sessions as an excuse to open a bottle of Scotch and the two of us would demolish it in great good humour while swapping war stories. I used to leave his appraisal giddy and bouncing off the walls of the law offices of Brainchild and Carruthers where Britain's Secret Service - at least Caplan's part of it - were housed. Caplan, however, continued working as I left, to all the world, as sober as the teetotal wife of the chairman of the London and District Temperance Society.

In 1960, that changed. After a cursory trail through my year's activities and once the bottle of Glenfiddich had been opened and sampled, he turned his attention to my new duties.

"You have proven yourself, Canning. You have won the admiration of your colleagues and have been a great servant to the cause. We hold you in the highest esteem. However, it is now time to move you from Berlin and to place you where we anticipate you again might play a decisive role, particularly because of your heritage."

"My heritage, Sir Anthony?"

"You are a proud Scotsman, Canning?"

"Very much so."

"MI5 have need of your services in North Britain…in Scotland."

"I thought I was in MI6, Sir Anthony. In terms of Scotland, I was last there two months ago to visit my parents in Lewis. I'm very fond of the place…very fond…but it doesn't possess quite the pizzazz of Berlin."

"Sacrifice is part of the job, Canning."

"I accept that, Sir Anthony."

"Your new responsibilities involves a similar role to that when you infiltrated the American International Yacht Club Berlin at Wannsee Lake. You brought over that old Communist sea-dog brilliantly. Textbook stuff! Well, we now need you to infiltrate another organisation."

He opened a drawer in his desk and removed a buff folder. Before opening it, he leaned into some elements of the 'slew of significant botherations' he'd referred to when first we were acquainted.

"D'you know, Canning, we still have a pretty shaky armistice over in Korea, President Eisenhower's administration is still recovering from Senator McCarthy's accusations of Communist infiltration into the American State Department. In consequence, the eyes of our closest partner in espionage are on Communism. Over here we've just had two of our brightest agents, Cambridge-educated Guy Burgess and Donald Maclean defect and resurface in Moscow. Our eyes should also be focussed strategically upon Communism but instead, I'm tasked with more domestic matters." He sighed loudly at the menial responsibilities he clearly felt were to be his lot and opened the folder. "MI5 have an interest in one Arthur William Donaldson. A sometime journalist from Forfar in Scotland who, in 1928, joined the National Party of Scotland as an overseas member while working in the United States."

"But we're MI6, Sir Anthony."

"You might be Canning, but this office straddles both and gives the state plausible deniability... an off-shoot of our Gower Street division. Effectively we're in the business of infiltrating entirely lawful organisations and would be in terrible trouble were this ever to be known. We deal with counter-subversive movements, home grown threats to the nation as well as certain of those from overseas. And this Donaldson chap worries us. He seems to be a man of no little talents, working his way up from a rather junior role in an engineering department in the American automotive industry to become the assistant secretary in the Chrysler Corporation's public procurement division, responsible for dealing with the United States Department of Defence. He's apparently very capable and our friends in the American Central Intelligence Agency also had an interest in him due to his nationalistic tendencies and his friendships within the Irish Fenian Brotherhood, the Irish Republican organisation in America. Just before the commencement of the Second World War, he returned to Scotland and in 1941, we arrested him and charged him with subversive activities following information that he actively supported the Scottish Neutrality League while we were at war with the *Boche*. He was interned under Defence Regulation 18B and sent to Barlinnie Prison in Glasgow where he was held for six weeks. We had to let him go for lack of evidence. We have just received information that not only is he back in Scottish politics but that he is standing in the October General Election for the new Scottish National Party - an offshoot of the National Party - in Kinross and Western Perthshire and that he is currently favourite to become the next leader of a political party avowedly determined to break the United Kingdom into its constituent nations. Our new young Queen Elizabeth is aghast at the notion as is our Prime Minister

Harold MacMillan who only recently reminded the good people of North Britain that they had never had it so good. It may be coincidence but as you know, there have been many successful attempts to destroy or deface Her Majesty's mail boxes during what the tabloid newspapers christened the 'Pillar Box War' and, much to my personal chagrin, they were equally successful in persuading politicians and the Post Office to replace them with the Crown of Scotland so as not to offend the sensibilities of the northern hordes." He caught my raised eyebrow.

"No offence."

A long sip of his whisky allowed the moment to pass. Placing his glass on the table, he became agitated.

"Before the war, due to the Irish diaspora, in Glasgow alone there were some thirty thousand registered members of *Sinn Fein* and they had a small arsenal of revolvers and rifles with lots of ammunition. We all know the despair caused by the Irish in Ireland as they attempted to secure their independence. We simply cannot allow that kind of movement to take hold here on these shores. They are fellow Celts and any kind of concatenation would be most troublesome. We have colleagues well versed in Irish affairs who are keeping an eye on that circumstance but we need eyes on this Scottish crusade, despite its relative incipience." The glass was raised again. "There has also been a recent attempt on the life of John Maclay, 1st Viscount Muirshiel, the Secretary of State for Scotland when he was sent poisoned vodka. Bombs have also been sent through the post to prominent members of the Conservative Party. Already there have been arson attempts on the site huts at Faslane, they burned down the bloody Holy Loch pier, they even had a go at our top-secret subterranean command centre at Troywood in Fife despite it appearing to all and sundry as an innocent farmhouse from above. Not, perhaps as 'top-secret' as we'd presumed, eh? We are curious at Donaldson's role in all this and require to nip this nascent Scottish Nationalism in the bud. It must *stop*, eh?"

118

A pencil he'd been holding in his right hand snapped as his temper peaked.

"So... your job is to catch the train up to North Britain and become Arthur Donaldson's best friend. You will be deployed using our 'Deep Entryism' approach. Once you have established a relationship we will determine how best to lay him low."

"And when might this new responsibility begin."

"No time like the present, Canning. You should return to Berlin and tie up any loose ends. No longer than a couple of weeks. Then you head for Glasgow and a new task. We will still meet each November or as necessary but your new operational boss will be a chap called Giles Collingham. He's as Scottish as you are. Comes from Gleneagles. Educated at Gordonstoun, Eton and Cambridge. Family owns half of Perthshire. You'll get along famously and you can determine your new persona, accommodation, that sort of thing." He selected a cigarette from his pack. "One thing, though, he's a bit of a lazy sod. You'll be doing much of the heavy lifting. Okay with you?"

I took a deep breath, remembering my political education at the feet of Wendy Wood, Hamish Henderson and Harry Selby whilst wondering at Caplan's casual presumption that I might share a measure of commonality with a privileged and entitled member of Vichy Scotland.

"Okay with me, Sir Anthony."

My fingers were crossed as I spoke the words.

Caplan placed the file he'd being using to one side. "One more thing. There are precisely thirty-six Chief Constables in Scotland; twenty-two in county forces and fourteen in city or burgh forces. It must be a bloody godsend for thieves and ne'er do wells. I've decided that your work cannot be shouted from the rooftops so only the Secretary of State for Scotland, a committed Unionist I must say, and his Permanent Secretary have been advised that three MI5 Intelligence Officers will be working to resist Scottish Nationalism. One of them...you... will work as a deep entryist within the ranks of the separatist movement. Your role will be camouflaged so completely that you could never be presumed to be other than what you claim to be...an enthusiastic nationalist and socialist. The Secretary of State for Scotland and his Permanent Secretary have each been advised to maintain complete confidentiality on the matter. That might give you some comfort. You won't be outed whether inadvertently or maliciously. On the down side, if you do fall foul of the law, you're largely on your own. One way or another we'd come to your aid but it may take some time."

I nodded. "I'll try not to drop any litter in front of a police officer!"

* * *

My next two weeks passed in an uncomfortable and confused miasma. I had become close to my colleagues in Berlin, had become used to their affirmation of my skills in my new profession and genuinely enjoyed the cut and thrust of espionage. On one occasion, Horst Janson and I marked my departure by painting Berlin a deep shade of red but most evenings during that fortnight were spent alone in a quiet German bar where I drank myself senseless while wrestling with my conscience. Commonly in those end of term days, I awoke the following morning with the apparent sound of a large Lambeg drum thumping rhythmically at the back of my head.

I found myself quite comfortable when instructed to act against those who were deemed to have the potential to imperil the United Kingdom - or indeed the West - but knew in my soul that I could not act against my country of Scotland. I decided I had three options; I could continue my work as an honest and upright agent of MI5, fulfilling the requirements of my superiors, I could resign my commission, or I could act as a double agent and attempt to protect the interests of my native Scotland while presenting as a committed agent of MI5. I'd had experience of double agents while in Berlin and was fully conversant not only with the complications of such a role but also of the likely penalties if and when my treachery were to be discovered. After much thought and many whiskies, I made my decision...I would become a double agent...but because I would not be working for a foreign power, I would only be answerable to myself for my actions and in consequence would avoid the trap of being exposed by another double agent transferring their loyalty to the British security services. Only I would be aware of my treachery. I could not be compromised as many double-agents undoubtedly were if only I kept my mouth shut.

As I organised my few belongings before flying back to Scotland, I began to feel quite heroic; me against the Westminster colonialists, and became more comfortable in my decision. I saw myself as a tartan Mata Hari...but without the exotic dancing. I also reminded myself that for her troubles, she had ended up being shot by a French firing squad!

Chapter Eighteen

SCULPTING A NEW ROLE

onaldson, as had been forecast, had become SNP leader and I stepped from the train from London St. Pancras, my duties in Berlin behind me. I'd received a message to advise that my new boss, Giles Collingham would meet me, not in the sequestered Glasgow offices of Brainchild and Carruthers but in the champagne bar of Glasgow's Central Station Hotel where only a few years earlier, American singing cowboy Roy Rogers and his horse Trigger had ascended the broad carpeted staircase, affording the hotel some significant publicity and, in respect of Trigger, the opportunity to defecate enthusiastically upon the stairwell's Axminster Moquette. I climbed those same stairs at eleven-thirty that morning marvelling as I did at the images of Gene Kelly, Charlie Chaplin, Frank Sinatra and Mae West on the walls, all of whom had earlier made use of the hotel's rather plush facilities.

Somewhat diffidently I entered the champagne bar, anticipating some hesitation in identifying Collingham. I needn't have worried. At that early time in the morning, the champagne bar accommodated only one person who sat in a leather chair, holding a cigar in his left hand and supporting a cocktail glass in his right. I approached him from behind. "Giles Collingham?"

Slowly he took a draw of his cigar and looked curiously at his interlocutor. Speaking in an languorous Edwardian drawl, he enquired, "And who might be asking this of me?"

"My name's Canning. I was told to meet you here at eleven-thirty. I'm a few minutes late. Train delay." Collingham laid his cigar on an ashtray and rose, transferring his cocktail glass to his left hand in order to shake my right.

"My dear boy, (we were approximately the same age) how delightful to meet you. Please have a seat and I'll organise a refreshment for you. You must be parched after your journey from London. Early start?"

"Very early. I'll have a whisky if you're buying."

Collingham grinned widely.

"You'll find that managed properly, Her Majesty's Government is usually the buyer of first resort, Canning. A whisky it is." He snapped his fingers, upsetting me with the arrogant entitlement it implied and a waiter wearing a crisp white apron approached. Collingham acknowledged his presence.

"Be a good chap... a large...eh.." He directed his question to me... "Have you a preference?"

"A Glenfiddich if you have one."

Collingham developed the order. "A Large Glenfiddich and another Martini, please."

I added to my request. "Some water on the side, please."

"Sir." He retreated.

We sat.

"So you are the man who kept Communism at bay in Berlin? I've been reading your file. Most impressive."

"I played a role but it was very much a team effort and now I'm here in our native Scotland. I gather that you and I together comprise the entire team."

"Not exactly. We have another man, retired airforce chap, Archie McKellar. Off sick just now. Bad back. Good man. Bit limited. Teetotal!"

I could see that this condemned him in the eyes of my new superior.

"I look forward to meeting him."

As we spoke I tried to take his measure. He was as thin as Ghandi and wore an outsized shirt and suit. Every time he glanced at me, his collar and Athenaeum club tie would stay still as his neck moved his head. A crisp white hanky protruded from his top pocket. An attempt at a moustache graced his upper lip. He seemed more of a practised diplomat, not untypical of many of my erstwhile MI6 colleagues, upper class snobs who'd sip at a gin and tonic and lie courteously to one another. As he spoke I came to understand more the notion of the 'Vichy Scot' that Wendy Wood had so inculpated and condemned in one of her speeches. He was Scottish only by dint of his place of birth. In all other ways he was the epitome of an English gentleman - accent included - with an Establishment condescension and *ex-cathedra* attitude that grated. I decided early on that I neither liked nor trusted him.

"Sir Anthony tells me you were based in London before your deployment up here?"

Collingham finished the Martini he'd been drinking before responding. He nodded his agreement to my assertion. His every supercilious gesture gave the impression of a man who was of the view that his station in life was such that he never really had had a boss.

"Don't know about you, Canning, but I can't say I'm overly enthusiastic about this latest wheeze of Caplan's. I mean for God's sake! Sent up here to quieten the northern hordes? I must have offended the bastard somehow. And for the life of me I can't understand why a chap of your pedigree was sent here when you'd quite obviously been such a stellar success in Berlin."

"I gather it was because we're both Scots and Sir Anthony thought we'd both understand and be able to infiltrate the dark underbelly of Scottish politics and its threat to the integrity of the United Kingdom."

Collingham leaned back and proffering his right arm theatrically to the ceiling, pronounced, "This royal throne of kings, this sceptred isle…"

I interjected. "Aye, and it goes on….'This blessed plot, this earth, this realm, this England'…it kind of ignores the northern hordes!"

Collingham ignored my intervention. "But it's so silly, Canning. Who in their right mind could imagine that there is any kind of threat to the Crown by some hairy, bekilted nonentities. The notion is completely rebarbative."

I demurred. "Their new leader, Arthur Donaldson headed up the Chrysler Corporation in America before returning to lead the Scottish National Party. He doesn't seem like an *complete* nonentity."

The waiter arrived to rescue Collingham who reduced his new Martini by half before venturing, "I must confess, Canning, the closest I've come to a Scottish person in the past ten years has been when I stepped over one of them in a doorway in the Strand. Beastly, drunken people. I simply cannot fathom why Caplan assesses any kind of threat by these exponents of such vagabondery. Our eyes should be firmly fixed upon Communism and the threat to the west…not a jumped up Scottish Lord Haw-Haw whose United Scotland Movement during World War Two was spreading confusion by false reports, minor acts of sabotage and by starting a whispering campaign to spread rumours of shipping losses."

"Well, he was arrested on those indictments and released without charge."

"Doesn't mean he was innocent, old chap. I can accept that he's a scoundrel, a cad and a bounder but the notion that he might lead a revolt against the mightiest empire in the world simply defeats me and convinces me that Caplan has decided I'm to be put out to grass at the tender age of thirty-nine, an age when my contemporaries are engaged in devil-may-care adventures fighting world Communism in Moscow, Berlin, Havana and Cairo. And I'm in fucking Glasgow!"

He pronounced the 'g' in 'fucking'. I decided to lie through my teeth.

"Well, in giving me this assignment, Sir Anthony praised you to the very heavens. He spoke very highly of you. Said you were a gifted strategist and that while you took care of the high level stuff that'd be beyond me, I'd be expected to get on with the day to day business of infiltration. Reporting to you as necessary."

Collingham paused his next sip of Martini. "Sir Anthony said that?"

I marvelled at his gullibility and truly shuddered at the idea that people of his wafer-thin abilities were charged with safeguarding the defence of the realm. I decided to press the point.

"I had the sense that Sir Anthony saw this as an opportunity to see if you could develop high level relationships and lead a small team to see off a threat before it developed into something more troubling."

Collingham became excited.

"His exact words?"

"Don't remember exactly, but something to the effect that you'd look after the Establishment in Edinburgh...diplomats,

126

politicians...business leaders and the like, with great aplomb and that I'd get on with the grubby end of the stick here in Glasgow."

Collingham positively glowed.

"The man has me to a tee! He sees my strengths for what they are."

He signalled to the waiter gesturing yet a further Martini. Thus far, I hadn't put my whisky glass to my lips, nor indeed offered it a splash of water.

Collingham continued, "I'll make early arrangements to find accommodation in Edinburgh. You, I'm afraid, should bed down in this city and begin efforts to worm your way into the affections of the Nationalist movement here in the west." He took a deep draught of his cigar. "I was at Cambridge with a few of the senior civil servants up here so I'll soon make progress in that regard." Increasingly animated, he warmed to his subject. "We must meet regularly so I can brief Sir Anthony...that'll probably require a trip up to London to update him in person...What d'you think, once a week?"

"Perhaps once a month in the first instance. That'll give me some elbow room and won't overmuch trouble Sir Anthony who has a lot on his plate. Actually until I become installed, perhaps once every two months..." I sensed a resistance. "But I could phone more regularly. You'll be pretty busy yourself, composing a list of dangerous cultural radicals. You'll need to keep me informed as well so I can follow them up."

"Ah, yes...dangerous cultural radicals...I'd hoped to discuss that, Canning. I was wondering...are you free this weekend? I'd hoped you might accept my invitation to join me for dinner at my family estate in Blairgowrie once my mother returns from Barbados. Stay over! You see, the thing is..." He looked embarrassed, hesitated and began again. "The thing is...my mother, one Margaret Collingham, a wealthy woman of means, the owner of vast swathes of Scotland, is an enthusiastic hostess. She simply loves giving garden parties, meeting new people and enjoying the occasional gin. However, my young sister Alison, the highly intelligent possessor of a degree in pharmacy will probably be there. She's well... what some might say, a dangerous cultural radical. She could have gone to Cambridge but chose instead to go to the University of Glasgow. God alone knows why. But she's a wild child. She's become quite heavily involved in this silly Scottish Independence movement, is very friendly with the wife of Margaret MacCormick, whose husband John was not uninvolved in the removal of the Stone of Destiny from Westminster Cathedral and I'm most anxious that she doesn't fall foul of the authorities as a consequence of your activities...of *our* activities," he corrected himself." He hesitated and took refuge in another substantial swig of his cocktail. "So what d'you say... d'you think she might be found to be missing from dispatches as it were when we're called upon to brief Sir Anthony?"

I smiled reassuringly, reminding myself how and why the upper classes remained the upper class.

"I'd love to accept your offer of a weekend in Blairgowrie and look forward to meeting both your mother and your young sister. She seems to me something of a character but not one who need trouble the authorities."

Collingham offered me his hand and I shook it vigorously.

Before I took time to visit Perth, I took to the Mitchell Library, also read the available MI5 files and had been able to glean some insight into the plethora of organisations dedicated to Scottish Independence, Socialism and Republicanism. There were the Scottish Citizens' Army of the Republic (SCAR), the Scottish National Movement, the Scottish Socialist Party, the Scottish Convention, the Scottish Reconstruction Committee, the Independent Labour Party, Scottish CND, United Scotland, the Scottish National Party and more. It was a bewildering superabundance of organisations, many populated by the same people and I'd to keep on my toes to understand them and their membership, something that Caplan would have expected of the most junior of his staff.

Chapter Nineteen

THE PORT O' LEITH

Angus Brodie sat nervously in the tiny Port O' Leith pub trying somehow to merge with the faded and torn wallpaper and thus render himself invisible. Two other customers sat at the small bar, ignoring him, each engaged in busy conversation with the barman about the fortunes of Hibernian Football Club. It was a quiet night. Nevertheless, Brodie had convinced himself that the next person to enter the pub would be someone who recognised him and who would wonder at his more casual attire than was usual and why he wasn't drinking in one of his more elegant and customary watering holes in central Edinburgh. Having taken time to dress down in anticipation of the tawdry pub with its gimcrack ornaments above the gantry, he still felt entirely conspicuous. The cravat instead of the tie hadn't allowed him sufficiently to blend with the lumpen proletariat, he decided.

At precisely the time he said he'd arrive, Dmitri Bozov walked into the bar, said two words, "Large vodka", and paying for it, sat in the corner table beside Brodie. He initiated a conversation before Brodie could commence the diatribe he'd been rehearsing about the unsatisfactory location.

"I said seven o'clock, Comrade Wembley. I have been outside for some time to monitor your approach. You arrived at six-fifty. Six-fifty is not seven o'clock. You must learn the lesson of precision… of punctuality…of complying with arrangements. I do not wish to have you feel more apprehensive than I'm sure you must feel but it can be a matter of some import. In all of our dealings you and

I must adhere very strictly to every aspect of the arrangement. You spent ten minutes in here worrying unnecessarily about being spotted but also ten minutes when something might have gone astray. Next time we meet it will be to the precise second of the arrangement. Am I clear?

Nonplused, Brodie could only muster an affirmative "Yeah, sure.

His tone changed. "And I have brought you a present, Angus. It is unrelated and additional to anything we have agreed but Mother Russia is pleased to provide you with two gifts." He reached below to his briefcase and after some tugging, released the straps and offered first a bottle of Zyr Vodka.

"This is an exceptional vodka, Angus. A Russian delicacy. Zyr is a very smooth and clean vodka with a creamy texture. You will love it." He reached then inside his coat pocket and withdrew an envelope. "And this is an envelope containing a further three thousand pounds in Sterling cash. It comes with no strings and is merely a gesture to advance our relationship and convince you that we have your interests at heart."

Brodie, accepting the envelope, thrust it hurriedly into his inside pocket, as he did so looking left and right, even given that right had him staring at a blank wall.

"Both appreciated, Dmitri. And I understand your comments re punctuality. I'm new to all of this and appreciate that you would choose a meeting place well outside my normal habitations but really...the Port O' Leith pub? I feel so conspicuous here. It's clearly more popular with Leith's brigandry. Surely we might find somewhere more in keeping with my...with our...status?"

"I will give the matter some thought, Comrade Angus."

"And I do wish you'd stop calling me 'Comrade Angus', Dmitri. I am only involved in this little escapade for the briefest moment until I can consider myself able to meet my short-term financial obligations and then, of course, we'll say our goodbyes and life will go on as if we'd never met."

"But my friend Angus, we have it in mind to make you a very important member of the British Civil Service with financial rewards that reflect that importance. You do wish to achieve seniority don't you? You do wish to become very wealthy?"

Brodie smiled. "Tempted as I am by the vision you offer, Dmitri, I find myself at a loss to imagine how you might realise those particular objectives."

Bozov Leaned over and placed his hands on each of Brodie's lower arms, kneading them.

"My dear, Angus. Surely you don't think we have friendships only with you? I must tell you, we have friendships with a host of people in the British Civil Service...many, many people, some in the very highest realms of your organisation. If we decide to see you achieve higher rank and greater reward, we have it in our power to make this materialise."

Brodie's first thought was of his conversation with Sir Edward Bland and of his presumption, however accurate, that being a man of homosexual proclivities, he was rendered unsuitable for seniority beyond his present role.

"You...you have the ability to...to..."

"Angus...you must believe me. I understand you. You seek no disadvantage to your United Kingdom. You are no traitor...but you are most certainly prejudiced against by your superiors and are being denied the ability to deploy your skills and knowledge to the greatest extent. And I will tell you one other thing. Your Western media presents Mother Russia as a military and political threat. Let me assure you, we have a particular wing of Embassy work, the area of my specialisation, which is focussed upon world peace, collaboration and the interchange of ideas. Trust me, there are many Russians like you who are assisting the United Kingdom and the West but because of media interference, much of this has to be undertaken surreptitiously. But I want to assure you that any assistance you provide my Directorate, will be known only to me. Only two people know that you and I are meeting tonight and each of us are sitting here. If you learn to trust my directions, you will remain anonymous, you will be known to no one within the Civil Service...but you will gain monetarily and in terms of seniority. Presently, you benefit financially but as we become closer, you will help me understand your professional ambitions and we will work to help you realise them."

"I...I had no idea that...!"

"Angus...you have worked diligently for many years, but your considerable talents have gone unrecognised. I must assure you, the world beyond your current pay grade is both expansive, exciting and will forever be denied you unless you accept the goodwill and philanthropy of Dmitri Bozov. We know that recently you were interviewed by Sir Edward Bland and that he denied you progress in the Civil Service because of your sexuality."

"But how..."

"Sir Edward Bland is a dinosaur. But he stands in the way of you realising your ambitions, Angus. I am what the French call an *éminence grise*...someone, as you know, who exercises power or influence without holding an official position. I have sufficient influence to steer your career in a very positive direction. We can help each other. Is that a bargain?"

"Well, I..."

"And next time we meet it must be in a more congenial location. Somewhere you feel more comfortable."

The conversation continued for a further half hour before Bozov eased into the next task asked of Brodie.

"My Angus, I would dearly love to understand better the capacity of the port of Faslane. How many submarines will it be able to accommodate, what will it have in terms of repair and maintenance and how many people will be required to be stationed there in order to service the submarine fleet."

"I suppose I could....but look, Dmitri, how does this information help world peace, collaboration and the interchange of ideas?"

"Alas, my dear Angus. I am not always privy to the reasoning behind my questions of you. I have superiors who deal with strategies and negotiations with the British Government and they feel, I suppose, that the more information they have to hand when sitting with senior British or NATO staff, the more likely the outcome will benefit everyone involved...so, perhaps we could meet two weeks from now, on Monday 3rd of May at 7.00pm sharp in the lounge bar of Prestonfield House Hotel in Edinburgh. They have a very fine selection of drinks and it is likely to be very quiet. It is also an establishment which more commonly you would frequent. Inside that envelope along with the cash is a phone number. If you have need to contact me, please use it. Identify yourself by introducing yourself as Mr. Wembley. Easy to remember and if I am unavailable, your call will be made known to me in minutes. Do you understand these arrangements?"

Still feeling rather out of his depth, Brodie nodded his agreement as Bozov stood. "Enjoy your vodka, Angus." He left the pub.

Waiting for a minute, Brodie lifted the bottle of vodka and feeling somewhat uncomfortable, drained his glass of Talisker and followed Bozov from the pub.

At the bar, the two topers continued their analysis of Hibernian's weekend's defeat by Kilmarnock, oblivious to the arrival, presence and departure of Bozov and Brodie.

Chapter Twenty

INFILTRATION

As suggested earlier by Giles Collingham, I took up the offer to meet with his mother and sister in their Perthshire estate. Introduced to Collingham's mother in a room the size of a billiards hall, she'd been sufficiently taken with me...or wanted to palm me off to someone younger... to urge me to meet her wild child, Alison who was sitting alone beside a roaring fire, her right leg draped over the arm of a bulbous sofa, her demeanour exuding overt boredom. Perhaps a few years younger than me and extremely pretty, she appeared mildly inebriated, a cigarette dangled from her left hand and she was dressed in the manner of the early sixties; a black and white pencil skirt worn with a cashmere black and white sweater. Initially almost rude and dismissive in response to her mother's introduction of me as a colleague of her brother in whose image she had presumed I was, she was gradually disabused as I described our relationship as friendly enough but, as her mother left us alone, that our politics were completely at odds. Now more interested, she asked for specifics.

"Well, I don't want to be unkind, but your brother is a bought and paid for Conservative who cherishes Queen and country. I, on the other hand, am a socialist who would see the Union broken up tomorrow as Scotland emerges as the world's newest republic!"

She sat upright on the sofa, swinging her leg demurely to the floor and looked at me with a new curiosity.

"All of Giles' friends...every single one of them...are complete idiots. They are all cast in the same image and bore me to distraction. They're all well-educated and can drone on in perfect Latin but they're ridiculous and pompous."

"Well, I wouldn't describe myself so much as a friend of your brother. We just work together and as I'm new to the job, he asked me to stay over this weekend. I'd nothing better to do, so accepted. I thought it was a kind gesture."

"God, that's so unlike Giles. He doesn't have a kind bone in his body...He's a man intent on keeping his Christmas card list nice and short." She looked at me with a new curiosity. "How old are you?"

"I'm thirty-seven."

"You look younger. Giles is thirty-nine and I'm twenty-nine."

"I was in the army during the war. They taught me to keep fit."

She eyed me. "You look fit! Are you a member of a political party?"

"It would be fatal to my career progression in the civil service, I'm afraid. Political affiliations are discouraged in those of us who are meant to serve without fear or favour."

"Unless you're a bloody Conservative like my brother," she opined. "Then you're promoted."

I smiled. "I couldn't disagree with you, Alison. Can I presume that you're not entirely cut from the same political cloth as Giles?"

"Not in a million years!..or my mother for that matter."

I decided to make my move. "If I had a free hand, I might be a member of the Scottish National Party."

"I'm a member..." She hesitated, calculating that she might be being set up. "Did Giles tell you I was a member?"

I shook my head. "Just that you were what he called a wild child and that he thought we'd get along!"

Smiling, she laced her arm through mine and walked with me to the dining room.

Over the weekend, always in company, we conversed, Alison now engaged and much brighter, although still with a enthusiastic penchant for her gin and tonic. She became sufficiently relaxed in my company to tease me over my job, calling me a 'fish monitor'. Her brother Giles found this highly amusing at dinner that night where I was seriously underdressed. I sported a decent suit, collar and tie while Collingham wore a white, double-breasted jacket to set off the new thin moustache he'd been cultivating so as to look like his hero, Errol Flynn. In conversation with Alison over the sweet course, we each agreed quietly that he looked quite ridiculous.

∗

Upon my return to Glasgow, the phone rang.

I'd rented a flat in Hyndland Road next to Byers Road in Glasgow's West End in an area more commonly associated with student living. It had but one living room, a small kitchen and a lavatory. The living room had a bed recess. It was perfect for my needs and suited my cover as a lowly civil servant. I had been found an artificial role by MI5 back in the world of ports and fisheries which would allow me to travel as I deemed necessary and importantly permitted me to talk knowledgeably about the work involved given my previous employment. I had an actual peripatetic role visiting ports, establishing opportunities for their improvement and reporting this to Edinburgh although I had no supervision and was able to make contact with many of the delightful individuals with whom I'd worked earlier. My erstwhile colleagues took the view that I'd fallen into the job of a lifetime but all wished me well. Given the long lead time between a civil servant's recommendation and the implementation of of any proposal, I could easily spend several years giving the impression of high activity whilst bemoaning the lack of action of my 'superiors'. My time spent in Germany was to be explained as similar work dealing with all sixteen ports on the North Sea from Emden to Husum but mostly Hamburg. I'd developed sufficient conversational German to impress those who asked about my time there.

I'd had a telephone installed in my flat and gave the number to a few people including those in the security services, never expecting much in the way of early communication. Following its installation, the first call I received was from someone to whom I hadn't yet given the number, Alison Collingham. She spoke in a clipped, posh Scottish accent, somewhat dissimilar to her brother, Giles who employed Received Pronunciation.

"Manus. It's Alison…Alison Collingham. I'm phoning to invite you to a talk in Glasgow University."

"Good to hear from you, Alison. But how did you get my number?"

"From Giles."

A second phone call, only minutes later came from her brother, Giles who wanted to congratulate me in having charmed his sister.

"She'll certainly open doors for you within the separatist movement," he gushed.

Not having reported to him that week, I was able to advise of my invitation to a meeting on the merits of Scottish Independence organised by John MacCormick and had been introduced to a number of other sympathisers, all due to his sister's indulgence.

Later, I walked the short distance to Glasgow University. MacCormick was very obviously in poor health and was to die a year later but he spoke passionately about the role he'd played in returning the Stone of Destiny from London when he'd been Rector of the University of Glasgow and of his legal case against the Crown when he argued (MacCormick v Lord Advocate), over the right of Queen Elizabeth using the  title Queen Elizabeth II, on grounds that there had been no previous Scottish Queen Elizabeth. He was both amusing and interesting and spoke fondly of his son, Neil, who was later to become Regis Professor of Public Law, Vice Principal of the University of Edinburgh... and a prominent SNP politician. The speech was erudite and academic, quite appropriate given the background of Mr. MacCormick.

In the aftermath of the meeting a number of those in attendance agreed a refreshment was called for and a man called Benji Henderson invited me and Alison, whom he knew, to come along. We entered the nearby portals of the unpretentious Arlington Bar in the city's Woodland Road and I offered to buy young Mr. Henderson a drink. Alison, who'd joined us, never left my side.

Benji played his gallus card. "Mine's a pint of Guinness if yer buyin', Manus."

We chatted and I was asked what had prompted my participation in the evening's meeting. "Ah've no' seen ye at any meetin's afore."

"I was invited by Alison here. She's friendly with the speaker's wife and she thought I'd find it interesting."

"And did ye?"

"Aye. Reminded me of a speech made by Wendy Wood a while back."

"Wendy's braw right enough. Here!" He reached out and grasped the elbow of a tall man near to us who was busily settling a bar bill, attempting an introduction.

"You'll need to meet this man," he said to me. "He's a clever clogs." Having completed his transaction, the man turned whilst sipping his pint, his eyebrows raised in question.

"Manus, this is Arnold Menzies. He's a lecturer up here at the University." He turned to Menzies. "Manus is here 'cos Alison brung 'im."

Menzies was obviously taken by the reference to Alison, shook my hand and kissed her on the cheek twice in that French way before, in the usual small change of conversation, each of us traded details. He spoke with authority and I decided to try out my practiced back story I'd decided might have me appeal to the movement in response to his questioning. Alison appeared to hang on my every word.

"So you're an islander, Manus?"

"I am, Arnold. I've never been much involved in politics formally. My job as a middle-ranking civil servant means I'm pretty much barred from political activity but that doesn't mean I don't have private views."

"And what are these, Manus…You can be assured that this is just two men talking in a pub. It'll go no further."

"Three men," interrupted Benji, smiling.

"Three men and a woman," interjected Alison.

I feigned reluctance but eased into the spiel I'd rehearsed. "Well, if you have the background my family has up in Lewis, you can't help but be a wee bit skewed towards independence for Scotland. Evenings were always spent round the fire in our small cottage and my parents routinely told us of the hardships their parents had had to endure. The great majority of the Lewis people were and remain crofters and fishermen. We are all deeply attached to the islands which gave us our birth. The Board of Education have done a fine job over the decades in helping the young of the islands learn not only the three 'R's' but also in understanding our background. It certainly left me with the feeling that the islands were being short-changed."

I sipped at my pint.

"However, back in the day, my grandfather, Donald Canning was arrested and charged with the assault of one James Mathewson, the factor and manager of land worked by fifty-six crofters. Regularly he would call upon his tenants and take the rents he was due. Each time he called he was paid in full, no matter the hardship that subsequently befell the family. Our community had a common grazing but it was being degraded by a parcel of deer and the factor said we could build a wall to resolve matters. We did so. It was a dry stane dyke and ran for three miles. The crofters built it over a period of two years after they'd finished their daily work. My grandfather told us it was gruelling times. Hard, hard work."

My audience was attentive.

"One year, not long after the wall had been finished, the factor informed a meeting of crofters he'd called that the owner, Lord Earshader had signed a stipulation that they all be removed from the land they'd tended for decades and that the same Lord Earshader had offered new crofting lands that were almost unworkable, or accept transport for everyone to Canada so he could introduce a new breed of sheep to the island. Well, not unreasonably, the crofters protested loudly and forcibly leading the factor to accuse them of rioting. The police became involved and my grandfather was identified as a ringleader. He faced many years in prison as back then, the word of a factor never mind a Lord, was worth many times the word of the people - no matter how many testified to the contrary. But to cut a long story short, my grandfather was possessed of an eloquence denied most men and managed to provide an execution of deforcement and thereby persuade the magistrate that not only had no riot taken place but that documents signed by Lord Earshader over the dry-stane dyke had given the tenants rights that allowed them to remain in their current workings. He became something of a folk-hero up by and what was passed down to me and mine was that power deployed by some form of allegiance to the King was very suspect and that politicians who earned their corn seven hundred miles away in London were even more suspect. I decided early on that politics should serve the people, not the rich, and that politics should be deployed as close to those who are affected as possible. When I added my school-learned and family reinforced passion for Bruce and Wallace, I knew that no matter the unpopularity of my positions, I couldn't vote for a Conservative, Liberal or Labour politician but was troubled by the absence of any political force proclaiming independence for Scotland. So I became a civil servant, a position in which I needn't be troubled by such matters."

"And you now supervise Scottish ports and assess their potential for improvements?"

"I've worked on Scottish ports my entire working life following my demob."

"Where did you serve?"

"I was proud to wear the khaki uniform and dark green, white and red kilt of the Highland Light Infantry and to serve in France and Germany with a wee dalliance in Italy."

"You've certainly got the gift of the gab, Manus. Were you a General or something?" asked Benji.

"A private for the most part, Benji but I received a field promotion to Sergeant aged twenty-one as a consequence of a few mentions in despatches."

"Very young for such a promotion...so you're a proud servant of the Crown, Manus?" quizzed Menzies.

"If, as you say, this is a conversation between two...or three...or four people," I said, acknowledging Benji and Alison, "But I'm a Republican. I'm a left-winger and I'm a supporter of Scottish Independence." I took another sip of my pint. "However, if you're a civil servant or a journalist or a member of the public I don't know, I'm above politics and have no views worth sharing."

"But you're not a member of any political party, Manus?"

"The SNP are a bit right wing for me...the papers say they're Tartan Tories, Arnold. I believe in nationalisation of all key industries, a National Health Service and decent pensions for the elderly. Any Scottish party that looks to settle on the status quo doesn't get my vote. The Labour Party started out well. They were both socialist and all for home rule but these days they've settled for careers in the House of Commons and the House of Lords. Home Rule has been made subservient to London control. So, I'm sorry if this upsets you but frankly, a Scottish revolution is what's called for, not more of the same."

"You and I should have a more private conversation," suggested Menzies. "There are wheels within wheels, Manus...wheels within wheels."

Alison looked at me as if I'd descended from the moon.

The discussion moved on to the news that the Russians had exploded two nuclear devices in the atmosphere and that as a consequence, Scotland's milk had been found to contain the highest levels of iodine 131 in the UK, putting Scottish weans at risk. Menzies was almost foaming at the mouth at this calumny denouncing the rampant British nuclear militarisation as was evident at Faslane. No one disagreed with his viewpoint. The Beeching Report which reduced the number of Scottish rail stations and halts from six-hundred and sixty-nine to two-hundred and thirty was also discussed and raised the temperature somewhat. St. Enoch's and Buchanan stations in Glasgow and Princes Street in Edinburgh were also to be closed and there would no longer be passenger trains north or west of Inverness. The more we drank, the more we fulminated.

Chapter Twenty-One

THE BOOK SHOP

Living with her mother in Blairgowrie, Alison didn't much stray from the estate so I didn't see a lot of her over the next month or so although she'd telephone me weekly when I was at home. These calls became increasingly lengthy, We'd talk for a couple of hours and at their conclusion it seemed that only five minutes had passed. I found myself hoping each night that the phone would ring. When it did, I was overjoyed.

I was able to travel freely and used the time to visit many of the ports I'd dealt with previously, and twice caught the MacBrayne's ferry from Ullapool to Stornoway to visit my sister, Jean and brother Seumas who now ran the croft, my father having passed away and my mother, now too frail to help. I confess I felt somewhat ashamed at effectively abandoning my family in their time of need but both siblings and my mother took great pains to disabuse me of any notion that I should do other than continue what they considered my 'important' work. My monthly postal order helped them considerably as the croft made little profit and they were vocal in their gratitude but in all honesty it was the least that I could do. It was also good fun visiting the odd pub in Stornoway with Seumas and meeting old friends.

Giles Collingham and I received an order to visit Sir Anthony Caplan in his London office and we both caught the train south; Collingham travelling First Class as I sat contentedly in Second, grateful that I didn't have to spend hours conversing with him. Additionally, while I took board in the small hotel next to the Brompton Oratory in Knightsbridge I'd stayed in previously, he stayed at Claridge's in Mayfair telling me that he'd contacts there and didn't want to have 'to explain me away.' I hoped that my delight at this news didn't convey itself overmuch as I murmured my understanding.

The following morning, Caplan called us both in to his office at nine o'clock. Even for him this was early for a snifter and although the tawny, half-empty bottles of whisky sat unobtrusively behind him, no refreshment was offered, nor even tea or coffee. He was more irascible than was usual.

"Sit!" he instructed as he shuffled his usual 'slew of significant botherations' whilst inhaling deeply from his Camel cigarette. "Smoke if you must," he allowed. Neither of us chose so to do.

"This world of ours is going to hell in a handcart," he intoned, more to himself than to us. "It transpires that we have Russian spies in British Intelligence, providing our Communist friends with who knows *what* information…and they've gone undetected for God knows how long. Khrushchev and East German leader Ulbricht have closed the border and are constructing a wall around West Berlin as we speak and I'm expected to organise what they're calling an 'interface' between MI5 and MI6 in order that certain questionable activities we undertake allows plausible deniability instead of permitting me to rout those traitorous bastards from behind the cowardly desks they hide behind. These imbeciles think they're better served by having me sit here worrying about Scottish separatism instead of the Communist threat. Well…I just won't! I'm going to have *you* two worry about our Northern friends instead of me."

He collected his paperwork and placed it in an already overburdened tray on his desk as he sat back in his chair, drawing deeply to inhale the last molecule of nicotine from his Camel as he did so.

"Collingham. Your report!"

The easy and practised charm utilised so naturally in the clubs of Whitehall deserted Collingham as he stammered a few words about Senior Civil Servants and major politicians he'd met with in Edinburgh.

"And you think that they'll provide you with insights that will end this separatist nonsense?"

I decided to rescue him.

"In addition, Sir Anthony, Mr. Collingham has already provided me with contacts that has led me to establish very good relationships with a number of well-placed, activist nationalists. In addition, on the train to London yesterday, we discussed a new approach that might bear fruit at little cost." Collingham looked at me askance wondering what I was about to share with Caplan. "My current role allows pretty free movement and permits an easily provable background but it occurred to me...to us...that the establishment of a radical bookshop run by me in Glasgow's west end might not only bring many on the left and on the extreme nationalist wing into our maw. If we chose premises with the capacity for, let's call it a 'reading room' which could be used of an evening as a meeting room, we might actually establish a headquarters for those we seek to track and monitor. It'd be low cost; a monthly rental and books could be secured on a sale or return basis. Because of this, my explanation of utilising my savings to finance this would be reasonable as I'm not known for extravagant personal expenditure. It would also cement my budding reputation locally as a left-wing nationalist and republican."

Caplan took a moment to withdraw another cigarette from his pack. He tapped it end-on against his desk a few times as he considered my suggestion.

"Sounds like a good idea, Canning." Collingham almost fainted with relief. "Although I'd like to discuss the acquisition of the books so we don't fall foul of the Lord Chamberlain. He's been busy in court recently banning books like there's no tomorrow. Lady Chatterley got through by the skin of its teeth last year and we're still awaiting the outcome of Ulysses. Last thing I want is to end up in court for selling books that offend the several Acts of Parliament designed to protect official information and national security." He lit his cigarette and lifted a single sheet of paper. "This letter informs me that the other intelligence officer allocated to the Scottish matter, one Archie McKellar has been discharged from hospital, has completed his rehabilitation and will be joining you up north shortly. Like you two, he's Scottish but he has limited mobility due to his back injury and is tee-total" Caplan obviously viewed both conditions as disabilities. "Collingham, I needn't detain you further. You may return to the watering holes of Mayfair. I'll discuss this book thing further with Canning."

Collingham half rose as if to argue his case for remaining but thought better of it and almost bowed in deference as he retreated to the outer office. The door closed.

Caplan turned and without leaving his chair, retrieved a bottle of Glenfidich from the cabinet behind him.

"You'll join me?"

I smiled at his insouciance.

"As long as I'm permitted a splash of water."

"Help yourself."

We settled in our chairs as Caplan poured two large whiskies, speaking as he served.

"I confess that man irritates me. I quite imagine he does you too."

"He does."

"You managed to conceal it well. He's precisely the type that populates MI6. Old Boys' Network. School tie and all that. Some of them are decent enough. Bright, dedicated...but he's a useless lump...a lazy sod who's just been sent here for me to babysit because MI6 don't like to sack one of their own. So he and you came up with this bookshop idea?"

"He heard about it much around the same time you did."

"Thought as much. And his efforts in dealing with politicians and senior people in Edinburgh?"

"My idea to get him out of the way. Actually told him you thought high level diplomacy was one of his great strengths."

"Out of harm's way", murmured Caplan acceptingly as he swallowed much of his glass, "The man's a danger to shipping." He rose. "Must go. This wall they're building in Berlin is causing chaos. The book shop has the green light. Write to me with a budget request. Keep it reasonable. I'll approve it." A further deep inhalation before stubbing his cigarette. "And if that idiot Collingham ever tests your patience, just let me know quietly. Don't want to offend his chaps in MI6 but I'll overrule him in a heartbeat. Now, away with you. I'm off to save the world from Communism."

We each disposed of the remainder of our whiskies in a single gulp.

* * *

I caught a taxi to Claridge's where I'd presumed Collingham would be holed up, contemplating his last hour. I was accurate in my presumption.

"Buy me a drink, Giles?"

"Canning!" He started rather as he beckoned the waiter's attention. "Why on earth did Sir Anthony ask me to leave whilst you remained?"

"It was a two minute directive on sending him a well-costed, but frugal budget. I almost caught the same taxi as you."

Somewhat mollified, Collingham ordered another of his cocktails and one of my whiskies.

"You may have got me out of a hole there, Canning. Caplan didn't seem that impressed by the wide range of senior contacts I'd made in Edinburgh."

"Och, he was fine. I know we hadn't discussed the book shop idea but he caught me a wee bit on the hop so I took a chance. It seemed to work. He's given it the green light."

"Actually, it was completely along the lines I'd been considering, Canning. It's just that I'd wished you'd mentioned it on the train up to London."

"*Down* to London", I corrected and emboldened by Sir Anthony's comments ventured, "And had we not been separated by our gulf in rail class, I'd have done so!"

My barb sailed completely over Collingham's head.

"I was handed a note by his secretary as I left, Canning. Apparently this chap Archie McKellar is joining us. Thought about it in the taxi and I intend that he should be completely oblivious to you and to your role in this. Caplan made it clear to me that you are to remain deep under cover and the fewer people who know about you the better. He will report directly to me."

"Sounds sensible." Inwardly I was relieved as I too, was anxious that my role be as subterranean as possible.

"I'm giving him the task of finding assets. Agents who will find their way into the various groups that concern us. Infiltrators, if you will. You will receive a monthly account of these individuals, the groups they've accessed and this, too must remain top secret. McKellar, quite obviously, will be unaware of the onward transmission of these names to you."

I left him to his cocktails and returned to Euston Station and the train north to Scotland.

Chapter Twenty-Two

ALISON

I loved the vibrancy of the West End of Glasgow; its university and hospitals, its pubs, cafes, antique shops and auction houses as well as its Bohemian atmosphere. For many years it had the reputation of being the most intelligent constituency in the United Kingdom, populated as it was by academics, their students, the administrative classes, successful businessmen, doctors and associated medics. And abutting the noisy flamboyance of Byers Road was the community of Partick where I lived; still red sandstone buildings but smaller, more crowded and rather more proletarian than the proudly elegant edifices of Kelvinside... although still partly responsible for the high average IQ.

I was enthused by the notion of finding a shopfront that I could convert into a bookshop. There were a number of empty premises but no indication of who might be responsible for renting them to me so I had to throw myself on the mercies of some of the innumerable estate agents in the area. As I'd earlier undertaken some personal research, a few of the shopfronts I'd identified were offered as options and I settled on an old and somewhat dilapidated jewellers near the intersection of Byers Road and University Avenue. It had the dual advantages of decent security and a large room at the rear previously used as a workshop. I signed a lease for three years and headed for Tennent's Bar across the road where I celebrated alone for some time whilst yet in the heartwarming company of John Barleycorn.

Upon returning to my nearby small flat, I could hear the phone ringing as I walked up the flight of stairs to the first floor.

Breathlessly I lifted the receiver and announced myself as 'Manus Canning, speaking'.

"*Someone's* been running upstairs!"

"Alison...it's good to hear from you. I was actually walking up the stairs to my flat when I heard the phone." I tucked the Bakelite phone receiver under my chin so as still to maintain the conversation, freeing my hands to remove my jacket. "I've had a few whiskies in Tennent's Bar. I'm not puggled but I wasn't taking the stairs two at a time."

"Puggled? There's you as ever with your rough Scottish parlance," she teased.

"Well...I was celebrating." I hesitated. I'd been practicing this announcement for a while. "I've just taken a lease out on a shop in Glasgow. I've decided to resign from the civil service."

The surprise in Alison's voice was evident.

"What...you...a shopkeeper?"

"Bit more nuanced, Alison. For some time I've felt constrained by my job. It's been like a political straight-jacket. Quite honestly, while I've loved my job and hold dear many of the people I worked with up and down the coasts of Scotland, I am driven more and more politically. I seek home rule for Scotland and a socialist administration when it achieves its destiny. I'd like to get rid of the trappings of Royalty as well. I can't do any of that just by improving our ports...so I'm using my savings and I've taken a lease in a shop in Byers Road here in Glasgow and I'm going to open a radical bookshop selling the kind of left-wing and nationalist publications people need to read in order to have an educated electorate. The movement won't achieve anything... Scotland won't achieve home rule, if people only read the right-wing, unionist Sunday Post or the Daily Express."

There was a silence at the other end of the line before Alison spoke. When she did, I sensed emotion.

"What time is it?"

I glanced at the hall clock. "Three o'clock."

"Do. Not. Move. An. Inch! I'm driving to Glasgow and when I get there I'm going to give you the biggest hug you've ever had. I'm so…so…proud of you. I feel…I feel…" She left her sentence unfinished and began afresh. "I'll be there around five and once I give you the promised hug we're going to get jolly drunk so prepare yourself, Manus Canning."

The line went dead and I found myself contemplating the earpiece on the telephone receiver as I processed the conversation. I'd anticipated her approval, if with certain reservations. I hadn't quite imagined her enthusiastic endorsement nor, indeed, the emotion that accompanied it.

* * *

At six-thirty (over time, I'd come to appreciate that punctuality wasn't one of Alison's strengths) three sharp knocks on my front door heralded the arrival of a whirling dervish. Alison launched herself at me, threw her arms around my neck and, as promised, hugged me tightly for some time.

"Manus…my Manus…you've not only liberated yourself…you've liberated me and I can't wait to hear your plans…and tell you mine! I've been thinking of this all the way down from Perth…but let's get out of here. Choose your pub!"

I was aware that Alison had studied pharmacy for four years at the University of Glasgow and that she'd know more of Glasgow's pub-land than me despite my enthusiastic apprenticeship but I suggested the Central Hotel, her brother's favourite, as I also knew her preference for gin and that my preferred haunts tended to major on beers and chasers, spit and sawdust.

We caught the subway to Buchanan Street and walked the short distance to the lounge bar at the Central Hotel. Fortunately, the ear-splitting noise of the Glasgow Underground train *en-route* had curtailed conversation and had allowed me further time to ruminate on what was going on.

Alison's gin and tonic and my Glenmorangie having been ordered, she leaned over and squeezed my hands.

"You're an absolute gem, Manus. The most perfect man. Now, I want to know everything about your idea."

I squeezed her hands back as a manoeuvre to remove them from mine and raised my glass in a toast, to which she responded, all smiles.

"Well, I'm confident that I can handle the rent of seven pounds, four shillings a month for a year or more, even if I don't sell a single book, and that I can stock most of it from publishers eager to sell their books on a sale or return basis. There's a generous back room and I'll use this either as a stock room although I don't really see a need for that, or for a reading room which might be used by my political friends as a meeting room free of charge."

"What are you going to call it?"

"Well, I want it to become known for politically radical scripts so I thought I'd call it 'Red Books'..."

"Red Books! Brilliant! You're so clever!" She paused, smiling. "And now you've given me an even better idea for my own plans which I've been formulating all afternoon since we spoke on the phone."

"And they are?"

"It shouldn't come as a complete shock to you that my begrudged presence at our family's estate is a complete anathema to me. I've spent the years since my graduation wondering how my life might shape up. My mother sees only marriage to the right sort and a brood of chinless wonders as the optimum outcome of all her distant mothering. To assist this end, she has bestowed on both myself and my well-read but idiot brother, Giles, a considerable annual sum from a trust fund that allows each of us to live the high life should we choose before we inherit the millions. Giles so chooses although, because my mother is nine parts Neanderthal, he has one third more than me on the basis that he's a man and I'm only a lowly woman fit at best for reproduction. I've used my trust fund to anaesthetise myself using gin mostly because I've never worked out what I want to do with my life but now…now due to the clever imagination of my dearest friend, Manus, it all becomes clear. First, I'm going to move back to Glasgow, a city I love. Second, I'm also going to open a bookshop…" Had Alison set out to see my eyebrows raise to somewhere north of my hairline, she'd have succeeded in spades.

"Third…and this is the clever bit, if I might say so myself, I'm going to call it not 'Red Books' but 'Med Books'. My principal objective is to sell first and second hand medical books to university students studying medicine, pharmacology, dentistry and even bloody veterinary medicine because I remember when I was a student, there was always a hassle trying to buy course text books for lectures. The professors always recommend their book which they'd use for year-end exams and it was exhausting trying to buy one from a student a year ahead of you. Also, doctors and nurses need to keep up to date with the latest research and this area is chock-full of doctors, nurses and students. I could see me make a decent business out of this and it'd allow me to spend as much time as is necessary to help you achieve your own political aims as I share each of them. So…what d'you think?"

I mumbled some platitudes but all the while I could do little more than gaze upon her face; her soft lips parting and issuing words largely unintelligible to my ears, her long black hair falling in a shiny blade over one eye She seemed unaware of her beauty while her excitement grew as she apprised me of her ambitions. Her eyes flashed as her exuberance became enhanced by her gin and tonics. Two hours must have passed in her company and I missed much of her conversation as I wrestled with my now undeniable affection towards her whilst considering the implications for an intelligence officer now in MI5 to be consorting with a target...and this notwithstanding the fact that she was sister to my boss, further compounded by the realisation that she was about to inherit what must be presumed to be in the millions of pounds along with 'half of Perthshire' as Sir Anthony Caplan had put it. Whilst Alison's consumption of alcohol made her more excitable, mine had the effect of persuading me that this was a potential relationship that was doomed before it even started.

As last orders were shouted, Alison, now quite drunk, leaned over, gazed into my eyes, coquettishly placed her hand on my arm and slurred "I've nowhere to sleep tonight, Manus. Have you room in your flat for a somewhat inebriated young lady?"

I withdrew my eyes from her gaze lest she could read them.

"My flat is tiny, Alison. Not sure that'd be a good idea. We're already in a hotel. I'm sure they'd have vacancies."

Slowly she released the fond grip she'd had on my right forearm and spoke, and attempted to enunciate her words very precisely as can be the case in someone under the influence of alcohol when they endeavour to present themselves as sober. She spoke theatrically.

"Do you find me ugly, Manus? Am I a hideous *grotesque*?"

I stumbled over a selection of platitudes expressing how lovely and intelligent she was but it made not one scintilla of difference to her new attitude towards me.

"I'll have you know that I've spent much of my adult life batting away regular advances from young men...and some older who should know better...because I've never met anyone remotely who interests me. And for your information, I've never even properly been with a man, even when I'm in the state I'm in this evening because I still have my wits about me and I'm not going to end up like my mother; in a loveless relationship characterised only by a sense of duty rather than passion. I'm not going to lead a life devoid of fire and intensity." Tears started slowly to roll down her cheek. "And now when I meet a fellow traveller...one who seems to me to possess all of the qualities I'm looking for...he tells me his flat is too small and that I should sleep in the hotel." Unhurriedly, she rose from the table. Lifting her coat from the rear of the chair, she swept the tears from her eyes with the back of her hand. "It took a lot for me to say these words, Manus Canning. Don't bother walking me down to hotel reception. I'll find my own way there."

Staggering only slightly, she made unsteadily for the long exit corridor leading to the broad stairwell. Instinctively, I rose to preclude her departure but slowly I regained my seat and settled for watching her retreating shapely form whilst ruminating broodingly upon my decision. No matter my next move, it could only end badly.

Chapter Twenty-Three

THE PHILOSOPHER

The following morning as I rose, I must have confronted my telephone for more than fifteen minutes without lifting the receiver and dialling, my mood as black as its Bakelite casing. Every impulse directed me simply to lift it, phone the hotel, apologise to Alison, confess my true feelings towards her and let the chips fall where they may. Further reflection suggested a walk to clear my head.

I dressed and walked down to Dumbarton Road where it joined Argyle Street and stopped for some minutes before Glasgow Art Galleries in Kelvingrove Park. Built in a grand Spanish Baroque style, it followed the Glaswegian tradition of using Locharbriggs red sandstone. I'd visited many times but today I merely observed the beauty of its external structure before walking thither to the Mitchell Library, certainly it's equal in functional beauty. The sky was leaden and bruised as I reminded myself how majestic Glasgow architecture is before my walk took me along glistening, rain-soaked cobbled streets down to the bustling port-side along the Clyde at the Broomielaw where buildings were a bit more prosaic. I stopped for a moment at the Broomielaw where the open doorways released the smell of countless whisky barrels that had been manhandled under its arches, a scent that fought for air superiority with the discordant but inviting aroma of a nearby bakery. Across the river over the George V Bridge where it links Oswald Street in the city centre to the south-side Tradeston area, I started to witness the dull Hogarthian poverty experienced by too many of the denizens of the great city of Glasgow. Small boys in the community of the Gorbals played football happily in the street, dodging the very occasional car. Their smaller sisters, equally happy, remained on the chalked pavements, a few of them wearing their mothers' cast-off high heeled shoes. Graffiti was prominent and Glasgow gangs, notably 'the Cumbie', whose territory this was, featured regularly. Shopfronts were boarded and those that remained open were tawdry and tatty. Inky black puddles were everywhere and I found myself anxious at the young who used them as play ponds, their shoes wet through as they splashed joyfully in the grime. Built using the same red and blond sandstone used in the west end of Glasgow, these tenements, more affected by the sooty discharges of local industry on the south side, were universally coloured black. Pubs became almost ubiquitous, each corner displaying weathered advertisements for McEwan's Pale Ale, Tennent's Lager or John Walker & Sons Kilmarnock Whisky.

I marvelled at the dilapidated back courts of the tenemental buildings of the Gorbals. Washing flapped in the damp wind, hung from lines strewn across the no-mans-land between buildings. Old prams, their wheels earlier removed to make wooden 'bogies' lay discarded, litter was everywhere and somehow, despite the squalor, children flourished, just as Glasgow's coat of arms promised they would. I saw no men in these dank back courts, only children and hard-faced women who were either shilpit or grossly overweight. Whatever their dimensions, the one characteristic they shared was that each looked simply worn out. They communicated with their weans not with words of a soothing and caring nature but rather barked at them in harsh tones.

Heading north, I crossed the Clyde once more using the St. Andrew's footbridge at Glasgow Green and was transported once more from Glasgow's poverty to Glasgow's greenery. The People's Palace stood strong as a rebuff to its more celebrated cousins in Glasgow's west end but still led on to further communities such as Calton, the Gallowgate and Bridgeton exemplifying deprivation, overcrowding, crime and disinterest.

The ancient Saracen's Head hostelry, known colloquially as the 'Sarry Heid', had by now opened for custom and I decided upon a modest libation to set myself up for the day given my excesses of the previous evening with Alison.

A light rain had hurried my last twenty yards and I found myself standing at the bar next to an elderly man wearing a Tam O'Shanter bunnet pulled down over his right ear unlike all the rest of the men in the pub who each sported a more traditional woollen bunnet worn almost ubiquitously by Glasgow male adults. He had a full white beard and resembled something out of the Book of Leviticus, had only the prophets in the Old Testament been prone to wearing woollen Tam O' Shanters.

"Gey dreich, the day!" I ventured as I waited for my Guinness to be poured.

He surveyed me slowly through the harsh smoke of a meditative cigarette as he turned his head towards his interlocutor.

"It's no' dreich in here, ma man. This early in the day, few things are dreich if ye can get a few glasses down ye. Mine's a Bells if you're buyin'."

I couldn't resist my grin at his brazen self-confidence. I looked at him squarely and decided that ill-advised as it might be, I'd buy the man a whisky.

"And a wee Bells, thanks." I said to the barman before addressing my neighbour, smiling openly. "And who might I might be buying this Bells for?"

"Well, thanks very much, pal. Appreciated! Ma name's William Wallace Mitchell Lennox...but everybody just calls me Wallace. This is ma local. Been drinkin' here in the Sarry Heid, man and boy since the war ended...the First World War, that is. Ah know ah could pass for seventy-seven but ah'm only sixty. Ah had a hard upbringin'."

"And what do you do, Wallace? Are you in work?"

"Ah'm a bar-room philosopher, son. Ah get a wee drink here every morning, recover what might be called ma composure in the afternoon, help people roon aboot until near six or seven then get drunk until the morn. Ah've a wee army pension. You've caught me just afore ah recover ma composure."

"*Slánte*!" I toasted his health. "Well, I'm drinking to make sense of a scary woman!"

Wallace laughed as he dropped a molecule of water into his whisky. "Well, a' the best wi' *that* yin!" he exclaimed. "Wummin?...*Wummin*?... Ah mean, as a bar-room philosopher, ah'm right up therr wi' Socrates, Plato and Aristotle. But wummin defeats the lot o' us. Wummin?" Shaking his head, he lifted the Bells to his lips and sipped.

"So you read Socrates, Plato and Aristotle?" I asked, rebuking myself for patronising him as the words fled my lips.

"Never underestimate a Glaswegian wi' a library card, son," he said disparagingly. "The world should speak of Socrates, Plato, Aristotle and one Wallace Lennox here."

"I'm impressed, Wallace. Is there a local library?"

"Aye, but oftentimes I'll take a walk to the Mitchell if there's something particular I want to check."

"I use the Mitchell for much the same purpose. It's excellent."

"It is...it is...and only last week, I was reading that Plato was open to the equality of men and women, whereas his student, Aristotle at the Academy in Athens, believed that women were fit only to be the subjects of male rule, so you'd pick your philosopher just like you'd pick a horse in the two-thirty at Hamilton."

"Jings, you're a philosopher right enough, Wallace."

"I am a wee bit, I suppose. I go by Socrates' view that the unexamined life is not worth living." He took another sip of his whisky. "Mind you, I'm more prone to examining the bottom of a glass."

"You impress me, Wallace."

His second sip having emptied the glass, he held it up to the light ostentatiously as if attempting to find a drop remaining. As with the mischief of his first request for a whisky, I found myself smiling again at his theatrics and nodded to the barman to fill his empty glass."

"That's my last one, Wallace. I'm not made of money and I don't want to be taken advantage of by a bar-room philosopher."

"That makes sense, son... that makes sense. Now tell me this... what's your lassie's name?"

"She's a girl called Alison. She's really lovely and clearly has feelings for me but she comes from a wealthy family and I don't really have a penny to my name. I also do work that she'd probably disapprove of if she found out..."

"So are you an axe murderer?"

I grinned. "No...not an axe murderer."

"Are you a cheat or a scoundrel?"

"No... I think I'm mostly honest and trustworthy."

"Aye, you come across that way." The barman placed the refilled whisky glass before Wallace. "And you're generous too...for a man that doesn't have a penny to his name."

He added a touch of water to his glass. "So you're worried that she won't like the real you? I take it she knows you're not as wealthy as her?"

"Aye."

"Well, is she one of they people that only eats vegetables but you work in an abattoir killin' coos?"

"No."

"Christ, it's like gettin' blood outae a stane, talkin' tae you. What in God's name d'you do that upsets her?"

"Might upset her,' I corrected. I hesitated. "I help the police from time to time. Back office stuff."

"Och, that'll no' upset her...unless of course, *she's* an axe murderer!"

"No. She's perfect...but she can get a little excitable when she's riled."

"Well, she'd be hard pushed to find fault wi' a man just because he's involved wi' the polis. He paused. "Ah was a polis masel'"

"Really?"

"Well, *Military* Polis. I signed on with the Met just afore World War One and ended up being one of the youngest Military Policemen in uniform. Got promoted to sergeant and stayed in the military until the drink found me out and I retired to grow ma beard an' spend more time wi' the bevy. Saw out the Second World War afore that, mind you."

I raised my glass in an informal toast. "I wore the green, white and red kilt of the Highland Light Infantry and ended up a sergeant as well."

Wallace looked at me with a new regard.

"Well, if ma daughter brought you hame, I'd take tae ye right away. You seem a good sort." He finished his whisky in one swallow. "Ah'm away up the road. Thanks for your generosity son. Listen, you and your lassie'll be fine. Just remember. Be kind, 'cos everyone ye meet is fightin' a hard battle. Even if you've got a' the money in the world, ye still have battles tae fight. But if you have feelings for her an' she's got feeling's for you...then that's no' half the battle...that's the *entire* battle. You look after yersel' son. Ah'm here every day at the same time so if there's another wee Bells in it, I'm your local philosopher for the day. Maybe see ye!"

He left the premises, his gait steady, his back ramrod straight and his friendly hands patting other topers on their shoulders as he bid farewell. I returned to my Guinness and thought more of how I'd deal with Alison. I hadn't mentioned the age difference, my boss being her brother, my overt role as an intelligence agent working against the values she and I shared...and only too aware that I couldn't explain without exposing myself as a double agent. I mulled over his parting comment.... 'If she has feelings for you, and you have feelings for her...' I sipped my Guinness and changed my mind several times over how I'd deal with this.

Chapter Twenty-four

MAJOR BOOTHBY

Over the next few months, Alison and I each opened our shops; hers only four doorways along from mine in Byres Road. Neither of us spoke of the hotel awkwardness and we remained on good terms, occasionally and usually through drink, teetering on the brink of sharing our feelings towards one another but never doing so. She also bought a flat in the West End although hers was a pretty substantial apartment in Highburgh Road in the adjacent community of Hyndland, big enough to have a drawing room and a few bedrooms. As far as I could make out, she wasn't having a romantic relationship with anyone else, and nor was I although it did occur to me from time to time that if she was to find someone special in her life, although depressing on one level, it might also serve to allow me to keep my mind on the job without my thoughts straying to her so regularly.

Her shop ticked over and seemed to satisfy her entrepreneurial ambitions but much of her time was spent in Red Books where I'd built up quite a circle of republican, left-wing and nationalist customers and groups in the meeting room. None of the groups were formally affiliated one with another but often the same individuals attended on different nights. Collingham's monthly list allowed me to identify the shills in the group - and on some nights they outnumbered the regular radicals. It was clear that the true believers had no idea that certain of their comrades were batting for the other side and were nothing more than fifth columnists used by the police to infiltrate these entirely lawful organisations. I was also amused by the appearance of my name atop these lists as a dangerous extremist but one, according to Archie McKellar, who had an ability to win the confidence of others by quiet and rational persuasion rather than table-thumping declarations. Clearly, Mr. McKellar remained completely oblivious to my role as his comrade-in-arms, and totally unaware that I spoke from the heart. He seemed a decent enough chap, slim, bespectacled and with a pronounced limp, doubtless due to the back injury that kept him sidelined for such a time. I sometimes thought of introducing myself to him even if only to have someone else with whom I could share the frustrations and troubles I experienced as an intelligence agent but thought better of it and allowed my hidden self to remain in the shadows.

Certainly those attending tended to be a disputational lot, arguing the toss at the drop of a bunnet. I was treated as something of an avuncular fellow-traveller by all participants due to my ownership of the radical bookshop and by making the room available freely to them. I'd attend all of the groups most of the time if only for a short spell and was usually in the company of Alison who was much more vocal than me in her denunciation of all things Establishment despite her membership of same. I was able to describe quite a collection of named insurgents, insurrectionists and anarchists to Collingham (using his terminology) secure in the knowledge that the individuals I named would already be recorded by McKellar as quasi-revolutionaries. Alison was never named by me despite the reality that she'd be on the books of one or other of the moles. However, her name never appeared on McKellar's list either so he, too must have been warned off by her brother. It became evident that the assets used by McKellar for this purpose were usually those in the group who found an issue that divided the room and argued for a split on the basis of ideological purity. The approach taken by London since the notion of colonisation had taken hold centuries earlier had been that divide and rule was the most effective way of drawing the teeth of an organisation or nation and securing benefits for God, gold and glory. On a global scale, Pakistan, India, Ireland, Hong Kong, the Arab Trucial Sheikhdoms, the Straits Settlements, Palestine and more all came to understand this tactic and more locally, workers' parties the length and breadth of Britain had seen their numbers ebb and flow as groups affiliated, disaffiliated and fought each other rather than those they'd sworn to oppose when first engaged.

I almost found it almost amusing to see this play out and had many a conversation in the pub afterwards as tempers flared and accommodations were found only for heated exchanges to resurface at the next meeting. Alison, it must be said, was one of the most vociferous in decrying people whom she accused of parting company with the group's dogma and world view and I sometimes reflected that were it not for my relationship with her and her open, admitted and obvious connections to the ruling class, she'd be one of those whom I'd suspect of agitation. But... surely not...surely not? She often cited her admiration of the entitled Countess Markievicz who was the only woman sentenced to death for her role in the Irish Rising of 1916 before it being commuted due to her gender.

My main achievement during this period was to be elected as Chairman of the Glasgow Branch of the SNP. In this capacity I began to meet in fora where Arthur Donaldson, the Leader of the Party presided. Over the course of several meetings I managed to charm my way into his confidence and found him bright, honest and hard working. It was easy to see why he'd worked his way up the corporate ladder in America. I also formed the opinion that while he was committed to achieving home rule for Scotland, he was no bomb thrower, no loose canon who would work outwith the legal framework of the United Kingdom to achieve his ends. I made known this assessment to Caplan.

* * *

One afternoon in Red Books, a man appeared, wearing a Colquhoun tartan kilt and browsed silently, picking up and reading books from my shelves that seemed to interest him. A tall man with a neatly trimmed white beard, he lingered at the section on Scottish Nationalism and after a while, approached the till with a few books in hand which he handed to me as he reached for his wallet. While not exactly slurring his words, he seemed well-lunched.

"Interesting selection of books you have here, young man. Everything from *'Das Kapital'* by Karl Marx, indeed all three volumes...the 1867, 1885, and 1894 editions... all the way to 'From a Highland Croft' by Wendy Wood. Even books in the Russian language. Although these Communist tomes are not to my particular taste, I confess I'm impressed."

I calculated the amount owed me.

"That'll be two pounds, two and sixpence, thanks."

As he handed over the precise amount of money due. He offered me his hand which I took out of politeness. His accent was cut-glass, Received Pronunciation, English.

"Allow me to introduce myself. My name is Fred Boothby, Major Frederick Alexander Colquhoun Boothby once of Hertfordshire, now resident in Broughton in the Scottish Borders. I edit and produce a newsletter called *Sgian Dubh* a mouthpiece for Scottish Independence. I am also a founder of the 1320 Club named after the date of the Declaration of Arbroath and I am aided in this venture by Hugh MacDiarmid, Oliver Brown and Wendy Wood."

"Your accent does suggest Hertfordshire rather than the Scottish Borders."

He laughed. "My accent is useful when engaging with the political elite. You may have heard of my cousin Bob Boothby. He was the member of Parliament up in Aberdeen and Kincardine East for over thirty years, Minister of Food during the war, before accepting a peerage. Now he's Baron Boothby and we all have to defer to him at Christmas parties."

"Then I suppose the accent is understandable. But you're now interested in Scottish Independence?"

"Interested?" he spluttered. "Interested? It's my life's work. My all-consuming passion. Don't let the accent fool you. I was born in Edinburgh. I've witnessed the English Establishment up close and it's not a pretty sight. I fought for the bastards in Poland during the war and I wouldn't trust our high command as far as I might throw them...and I include my esteemed cousin who's more interested in fraternising and smoking cigars with homosexual London gangsters than serving the needs of the Scottish people who trusted him with their vote for decades."

"Well, we seem to be similarly politically inclined although I might be a wee bit more to the left than you."

"That's as maybe," he responded, dismissing my caveat. "The first order of business is whether this marvellous bookshop of yours would sell my *Sgian Dubh* broadsheet. I charge fourpence. You get a penny on each copy sold and the movement gets the rest. If you don't sell a copy, return it and there's no charge." As I pursed my lips in hesitation, he countered. "You can't lose...and nor can the movement."

I scanned his broadsheet. It was effectively a typewritten version of Blind Harry's account of '*The Actes and Deidis of the Illustre and Vallyeant Campioun Schir William Wallace*'. I contrasted this with the much more professionally printed periodical I sold called 'The Patriot' written by Wendy Wood which addressed topical issues relating to independence for Scotland. I didn't see much interest in '*Sgian Dubh*' but it was sale or return.

"When and how might I receive them?"

"By post once a month."

I offered my hand again.

"Then if I can deduct any return postage costs, we have a bargain. I've a bookshop to run in order to make a living."

He agreed and suggested we go for a coffee to discuss matters further but I declined explaining the need for me to be available to customers. He then suggested drinks in the Doublet Bar in nearby Park Road that evening and I accepted. But before meeting him I called Sir Anthony Caplan who promised that someone would call me back before I left to meet him.

Just before I left to walk the twenty minutes to Park Road, my phone rang. It was Oliver Beamish, Caplan's duty officer in London that evening.

"Got what you were looking for, Manus. Boothby is something of a hot potato and is listed as a 'Person of Interest'. He's cousin to the Conservative politician, Baron Boothby as he told you. He left the Army in 1953, at the rank of Captain, but was granted the honorary rank of Major in the Army Reserve so I'd challenge his rank if it suited you. As you said in your earlier call, following the war, he moved to Hertfordshire where he became involved in a local folklore group. However, there were rumours about rituals taking place on his property involving naked youths and blood rites which received publicity in the national press. Immediately thereafter, he upped stakes and moved to Broughton in your Scottish Borders. As he told you, he launched his own newsletter, *Sgian Dubh*" (he pronounced it Skagin Dub) "and was a founder of the 1320 Club where he was appointed its secretary. However, Boothby is on record as calling for a Scottish Liberation Army and our military people and Special Branch are aware of his predisposition. We understand that the Scottish National Party are uncomfortable with this and our sources tell us they are posed to to prohibit its members from joining. He's also involved with Matt Lygate of the Workers' Party of Scotland...also a 'Person of Interest'. Sir Anthony says he seems worth the watching...actually, both of them. Having said all that, Manus, Boothby's file is only partially available. Certain elements seem to have been redacted...expunged...buried! Pages are missing. There may well be those who argue that he's a Scottish Republican terrorist in the making but there are equal numbers who see him as an MI5 plant...although I have nothing on file in that regard. Having said all that, it would appear that Special Branch have become anxious about the existence of an entity called the Scottish Army of the Provisional Government, an extremely secretive organisation which they've had no success in infiltrating. They know only that its commander hails from and is based in Aberdeen although they were aware that Boothby is involved due to his military experience. Something to go on maybe?"

"Thanks Oliver. Much appreciated. I'll keep an eye on him."

Chapter Twenty-Five

THE LION IN HIS DEN

Three years passed. Alison and I grew closer and closer without either of us ever acknowledging our very obvious feelings one for another. Eventually I decided. I loved this woman and resolved to have it out with her brother. I was fascinated by the world of espionage and had come to realise that over the preceding few years, my exposure to the arguments set out each evening in the back room of Red Books had convinced me with ever greater conviction of their certitude. I was fully resolved that the future of Scotland lay in its independence and in a left wing approach to its social and economic policies. I also felt I was in a uniquely privileged position to advance the cause but convinced myself that despite this, I would give it all up to formalise my love for Alison if she'd have me. If I could, I'd have my cake and eat it too. That would involve obtaining the blessing of her brother, and my boss, Giles but I acknowledged that this would also require me to reveal my role in Scotland to Alison and attempt to persuade her that I was a double agent...not an agent of the British Establishment. In doing so I'd require to reveal Giles as an MI5 agent...not a civil servant who dealt in passport matters and yet convince Giles that I was still a *bone fide* British Intelligence Officer. The more I thought about it, the more it seemed unlikely that any one of these might come to pass. Nevertheless, I came to the view that my backstop was to declare my love for a Alison, resign my commission with MI5 and run a couple of bookshops in Glasgow's west end with the love of my life.

Before saying a word of this to Alison, I decided to brave the lion in his den and made arrangements to meet Giles in the lounge bar of the North British Hotel in Edinburgh. When I arrived he was there as I'd predicted to myself, a contented glass in one hand a lit cigar in the other. When he saw me approach he placed his drink hurriedly on the table before him and stood up, almost embracing me with excitement.

"Canning, old chap. How delightful." He bid me take a seat whilst simultaneously beckoning a waiter. "A large Glenfiddich for this man. No ice but water on the side."

I was impressed that he'd remembered my tipple but sat before him somewhat more nervous than when I discussed matters of national security. Usually I treated him as something of a dilettante inferior who had to be indulged and endured if only so as not to place Sir Anthony in an awkward position. Today I required his dispensation in order to further my relationship with his sister. He was more excited than ever I had experienced him as the drinks arrived.

"Canning, old bean. Caplan was on the phone. He was delighted with our progress. When this little escapade originated we knew little or nothing about the threat from these separatists but Sir Anthony not only was impressed by the depth of knowledge we've amassed in regard to these Jock Nationalists and left-wingers but he confided that we're so on top of things that he's been able to focus his sole attention on what he sees as the real threat... Communism. He even suggested that you might be able to handle matters up here on your own and allow me to return to MI6."

I smiled widely. "That sounds like promotion for us both!"

"Absolutely." His demeanour changed as he buttressed his remark with the a further recollection. "That said, there was nothing concrete. In fact now that I think of it, he said the words, 'steady as you go' as he finished the call which kind of implies the opposite of what I've just stated."

He waved his hands before him as if wiping clean a blackboard.

"Anyway, I'm sure it'll work out as I've described but anyway...
anyway...you wanted to meet today. Said it was important."

I swallowed hard.

"Yeah...thing is Giles..the work's going well. No mention has
been made either by myself or McKellar of your sister Alison
despite the fact that she's been one of the most prominent activists
on the scene."

"Delighted dear boy. She's a lovely young lady but something
of a wild child. However, I've been most taken by the efforts
you've gone to to keep her under your wing...and conceal her in
the shadows."

I swallowed..this time twice as hard as I'd done earlier. No
retreating now.

"Look, Giles. I'll be straight with you...Alison is everything you
said she is. She is delightful as you mentioned...a wild child as
you've told me on several occasions... but the thing is...the thing
is..." I caught his gaze and understood instantly that he knew
where I was going with my stammerings.

"What?..." he interjected. "What are you saying, Canning?"

I found a new determination.

"Look, Giles. Over the years, I've fallen in love with Alison and I
want to ask her to marry me. I'm not stupid and I've thought
through the implications...all of them...If necessary, I'll resign
from MI5...if necessary I'll..."

"But you can't, Canning. If you do there'll be no chance of my
being returned to London. But having said that, there's most
certainly no prospect of you marrying my sister. She is going to be
responsible for producing the bloodline that will continue the

great heritage of the Collingham family and I'm afraid you just don't have the breeding...the education...the connections..."

I found a new steel.

"I could not care less about any single aspect of these matters, Giles. I care only for the feelings I have for Alison...feelings I'm sure she has for me..."

He interjected.

"So she knows nothing of our meeting today...nothing of our discussion?"

"I cannot share my feelings with her without explaining my professional responsibilities...and in doing so would have to reveal you as an Intelligence Officer with MI5 rather than a senior civil servant as she now believes. I would also have to explain my role here in Scotland and appreciate that that would not sit well with her."

"But surely you must appreciate that what you ask of me is impossible...no matter your feelings for my sister...it would compromise everything we worked for over the past years. You've signed the Official Secrets Act...It would..." He hesitated and fixed me with a glare. "Oh, I see it now. She's told you that I'm not particularly inclined towards marriage and that she's going to be responsible for producing heirs...All you can see is money...lots of it...you're a carpetbagger...a good-for- nothing rapscallion...a fraud..."

I angered.

"I'm none of these things Giles." Earlier I'd rehearsed several lines of rebuttal. My temper got the better of me as I dismissed these, raised my voice and spoke in a threatening manner most unlike me.

"Listen, Collingham. I won't be deterred from my objective. You will support me in this and life will go on. If you challenge my proposal to Alison, I will merely contact Caplan and explain that your sister is one of the greatest threats to the Union imaginable, that you are complicit and that in consequence you are protecting her. I'll also explain that you've sat on your fat entitled arse in Edinburgh doing nothing while I've been breaking my balls working with agents and supplying him with each and every piece of information in what is laughingly referred to as our regular reports - each one of which is supplied solely by me. I will resign my post immediately and would be surprised if you survived the episode."

Collingham recoiled slightly at this blast and regained his seat. His tone became more emollient.

"Canning...I...perhaps I was being too hasty. I'm no expert in affairs of the heart but we both can see the difficulties in your proposition, both for my family and for the important work we're doing here in Scotland. We're trying to protect the very integrity of the United Kingdom, man...the United *Kingdom*. This is a very precious assignment and we are privileged to have been asked to undertake it. We surely owe it to God and the Queen to see it through and we must not allow distractions like this to have us waver in our duty." He looked at me almost in appeal. "D'you see?"

I eyed him suspiciously.

"I remain firm in my endeavour, Giles."

"Listen, Canning. Allow me to do some thinking. I know I can be a bit brittle when it comes to Alison. And I do appreciate the heavy lifting you do in Glasgow." He took a sip from his glass. "Tell you what. If you might hold your horses for a brief period, let me ruminate on your suggestion and I'll give thought to how best this might be handled. There's no doubting the difficulties involved in squaring all of this within the department but I'm sure there's a solution somewhere. So...what do you say? If you keep this enterprise to yourself for the time being, don't say anything to my sister quite yet and I'll see what accommodation might be found."

I found myself nodding my agreement. I emptied my whisky glass in one gulp.

"Don't take too long!"

Chapter Twenty-Six

PERFIDIOUS ALBION

One group I was not allowed to attend in my back room was that convened by Arnold Menzies. Despite his being warm towards me and engaging me in friendly discussion before and after his meetings, I was still being excluded and couldn't help but wonder what topics of conversation were being discussed. I was also somewhat perplexed given the obvious erudition of university lecturer Menzies when compared with the almost child-like enthusiasm for Scottish Independence exhibited by Benji Henderson. No one, not even Alison, was permitted to join their group. When informally I asked their purpose of Menzies, I was fobbed off with talk of 'civil disobedience'.

I thought little of it until one week I was chatting with Menzies and Archie McKellar. Menzies' group was the only one which hadn't been infiltrated by one of McKellar's agents and he argued with Menzies that himself, me and one of his agents, Gus Aitchison should join. Menzies initially wasn't keen but relented as he Archie and Gus had become drinking buddies (Archie drinking only soft drink but happy to buy his round) and he clearly thought well of me. We were informed that the matter of expanding membership had been under active positive discussion but were told firmly by Menzies that all matters in the group were confidential and that the initial agenda would be entirely benign until the group were comfortable in our presence. I feigned detached interest but was pleased that I'd been admitted to the cliquey quartet. The first meeting had been scheduled for the coming Thursday evening, two days hence.

* * *

Alison joined me at the bar the next night as I was in the process of ordering drinks. Four others with whom we were drinking sat enjoying the dregs of their last pint.

"Have you spoken to Giles, recently, Manus?"

"A couple of days ago," I confessed. "Why?"

"He's acting strangely. Wants to buy me dinner in the Central Hotel tomorrow evening. He never buys me dinner. Never wants to see me where someone he knows might bump into him and he might have to explain our political differences."

My mind raced at the prospect of him speaking to Alison when I had not had an opportunity to raise the issue of our relationship as that had been Collingham's proposal. I'd met my side of the bargain even though it tested me considerably. Although an inner anguish beset me, I played it down."

"Probably just brotherly love," I smiled. "Unless he wants to introduce you to the new Mrs. Collingham."

Alison frowned. "We've never had the conversation but he seems more comfortable in the presence of young men than with young ladies. I mean heavens above, it's 1964...pirate radio is all the rave. This is the era of the Maharishi and spiritual enlightenment, LSD and cannabis. The Beatles have just released 'A Hard Day's Night', we've just abolished the death penalty and Malta has just obtained independence from the UK. Times are changing. Until recently people thought that Liberace was just camp and theatrical. The world is becoming more open these days but my brother is so conflicted about his sexuality. He's said more than once...the term he uses is that he's 'not the marrying kind'...as if he just wants to remain a bachelor when in fact he's a roaring homosexual."

"I did wonder!"

"I'm sure everybody does. I don't care one way or another but from time to time he, and my mother, put pressure on me to deliver progeny that will maintain the family bloodline."

"I'm sure it'll be nothing more than a pleasant meal, Alison. Here...help me lift these drinks over."

I exuded reassurance but internally I was both perplexed and anxious about Collingham's agenda.

* * *

I tried to put matters out of my mind but all day Thursday I fretted. Even in the evening when I was to be introduced to the one group that had been denied my participation, I still found myself wondering how Alison's meal was going.

We all convened in the bookshop before retreating to the back room and at seven forty-five when all but Archie McKellar had arrived, Arnold Menzies announced the start of the meeting. "We've waited long enough. Punctuality is important in this man's army!"

We all gathered around the table and Menzies made the obvious point that we all knew one another and that therefore introductions were unnecessary. "That said," he went on, "We must emphasise that this group, of all the groups that meet here, is disciplined. I need to point out at the start that we believe that civil disobedience will be important to bring home to the Scottish people just how crucial independence is to our country. The four original members have taken an oath to lay down their life if necessary to achieve our ends. It will be a requirement for any new members to take the same oath. Before we proceed we must establish that principal. And to ensure that it is an oath that is kept, I have made it clear to those already involved that any loose talk, any fraternising with the enemy, any departure from our shared mission and I will personally shoot dead the miscreant." He looked directly at Gus and myself. "I am deadly serious. What has been accomplished by the four original members will remain with them. It serves no purpose to widen the knowledge of earlier activity. We know that the British authorities will, at some point attempt an infiltration so we propose to expand our numbers only slowly when we are confident that those we admit could not be traitors. But if we are wrong and we discover treachery, I will take personal responsibility to remove that individual from God's green earth."

I smiled inwardly, acknowledging that he was about to admit two Intelligence Officers from MI5 and an agent recruited specifically to infiltrate groups, but said nothing. Indeed, I heard myself say, "Arnold, I am completely at one with you and the group. I have no problem agreeing those ideals and accept the sanctions that would be imposed should I fail to meet the standards you set."

Gus looked a bit green about the gills but also nodded his endorsement.

"Then let's make a start," said Menzies. "Benji here wants to discuss the stoning of the ministerial car ferrying Willie Ross, the new Secretary of State for Scotland when it passes underneath a flyover en route to the opening of the equally new Forth Road Bridge."

As all round the table looked to Benji for his proposal, the door opened and two men in dark suits entered followed by three uniformed police officers. I noticed with some small measure of alarm that the two suited men each held a pistol in their hand. The first man through the door spoke sardonically.

"So this is the Hole in the Wall Gang? Hands flat on the table everyone! And be quick about it. These guns are real. We are police officers and you are all under arrest." The taller of the two men struck Benji on the back of his head with his pistol as an encouragement for him to comply. Benji shouted in pain but the blow wasn't too vicious and no blood was drawn. As each of us complied, the uniformed officers placed handcuffs on the wrists of all seated. Menzies issued a series of protestations which were ignored by the police. At the rear of my reading room was a bookcase with reference books that weren't for sale. One of the suits started clearing the books and periodicals from the shelves allowing them to fall to the floor. In consequence I found myself adding to Menzies' furious denunciation of their actions. As he cleared the bottom shelve, he stood erect and said, "Found them, Inspector. Looks like two Glocks and a Walther P99."

Instantly there was silence in the room as each man took account of what had just been witnessed.

The plain-clothed police inspector turned to Menzies and spoke quietly in a deep, guttural Glasgow accent.

"Looks like we have you and your pals dead to rights, Mr Menzies. All of yous can consider yourselves huckled. Yous are under arrest for the possession of firearms without a licence and being in possession of a loaded firearm in a public place without a reasonable excuse. Your attempts to overthrow the legitimate government of the United Kingdom by acting in consort one with another to carry out a criminal purpose will also see a charge of conspiracy made against you. Never mind all the legal jargon, I'd suggest that you say fuck all."

He turned to a uniformed sergeant. "Kenny, get this lot in the van and tell forensics they can come in now."

As we were all manhandled from our seated position and taken from the room, I realised exactly why McKellar hadn't attended, why Alison had been removed from the scene by her brother and how easy it would have been for McKellar to place these weapons behind books on the bottom shelf. As an example of false incrimination, it was text book!...and all because my breeding, education and contacts weren't just as Giles Collingham wished to see in the continued ascendency of the family name.

Chapter Twenty-Seven

BALMAIN WOOL

A ngus Brodie stood in front of a full length mirror and admired the Balmain wool and cashmere coat he intended should become his latest purchase.

"What d'you think, Simon? Is it me?"

"Darling, it's gorgeous. It flatters you. Makes you look like a celebrity."

Brodie inspected the label affixed to one of the buttons.

"It's expensive."

"As my old mother used to say, 'to hell with poverty', Darling. It looks fabulous on you."

The shopping expedition continued for the rest of the afternoon until Brodie and Cavendish sat at a booth in the Cafe Royal with an assortment of bags, each one prominently declaring it's designer contents within.

Simon Cavendish raised his glass of Champagne.

"I know it's always sad to lose a family member but, let's face it Darling, you hardly knew her and as her only surviving family member and sole beneficiary you were entitled to your aunt's entire fortune. So…a toast to those who've left you…particularly as they've left you in the pink!"

Brodie nodded, only slightly abashed at his fictional account of his new found wealth. Bozov had been generous in supplying him not only with cash but with advice on when and how to spend it without drawing attention to his new affluence. He'd decided to ignore it that morning. One small shopping spree surely wasn't going to be noticeable, he told himself, particularly if he exhibited his new wardrobe only socially and amongst friends.

Two taxis dropped each shopper home separately as Brodie had a meeting that evening in his apartment in Linlithgow, Bozov having decided that his skill in moving silently in the shadows offered the encounter more security than making contact in bars and restaurants.

At precisely seven-thirty to the second, Brodie noticed, the doorbell rang. He answered it and Bozov entered.

"Punctual as ever, Dmitri."

"It must be this way in our line of work, my friend." Instantly he noticed the shopping bags lying on the settee. "These are yours, Comrade?"

"A few nick-knacks. Haven't had time to put them away yet."

Bozov inspected the contents, eyeing the receipts which still lay inside the bags. After a few moments he turned to Brodie.

"These are not items that would be worn by a civil servant. They are expensive and ostentatious. I will take them with me when I leave and you will not purchase such garments again. It would be obvious to the authorities that you have access to resources beyond your pay grade. I have spoken with you before about this. You must restrain yourself."

Brodie protested.

"Boris, what exactly is the benefit to me if I am to profit from our relationship but be denied realising those rewards?"

"I have been clear. The bags go with me when I leave. Now sit. I do not wish to remain long."

Still gesturing his protest, Brodie nevertheless did as he was bid, eyeing the bags that would soon leave a space on his sofa as Bozov took an envelope from his jacket pocket.

"Comrade, here is a further payment. I hesitate to give it to you. We have been very pleased with the information you have supplied but you must use this money wisely. Be discrete."

He handed the envelope to Brodie who resisted the temptation to open it and count the money. Bozov removed a cigarette lighter from his side pocket and placed it on his open palm.

"You can see that this is approximately the same size as my index finger. To an observer it is a lighter for one of your cigarettes. However, concealed within is a miniature film camera manufactured in Mother Russia by Kiev Vega. It is very easy to use and produces very clear images. I will show you."

Brodie interrupted. "Dmitri! This is a departure from our previous arrangements. It's one thing for me to provide you verbally with information as it is made known to me. Quite another if you expect me to photograph documents."

"It is simple and will not subject you to any peril. You told me last time we met that you have open access to drawings of a new maintenance shed that it being built at Faslane. All you need to do is work late one night and when you are not observed, you open the drawings, hold the camera above it, pull back the chamber of the lighter thus..." He demonstrated. "And that is all there is to it. You place the camera back in your pocket and I will collect it from you."

Brodie seemed agitated.

"It is simple, Comrade...and of course because we ask more of you, the incentive will be higher when next we meet."

"All very well as long as I only spend it on an extra portion of fish and chips!" replied Brodie, churlishly.

"We are also working on a promotion for you. I can guarantee that as I know it is important to you but if I am being honest, you must be patient as you are in a very valuable post right now... but be assured it is in both of our interests that your talents be displayed at the higher reaches of your civil service."

"I want to reach Permanent Secretary status, Boris. That is my objective."

"It is one we share, Comrade. Now, let us practice a few times with the camera before I leave with today's purchases."

After some rehearsal, they shook hands and Bozov left, clutching the several bags of garments purchased earlier that afternoon. Closing the door, Brodie headed directly to the envelope and opened it. He shuffled through the notes and his facial expression announced satisfaction as six thousand pounds lay in a pile before him. He turned his attention to the camera, lifted it and took a photograph of his feet, speaking to them both in a heartfelt tone.

"You two should be shod tonight in dark brown Artisanal Oxfords to match my lovely Balmain coat." He sighed. "One day you will!" Turning again to the pile of banknotes, he counted them once more.

Chapter Twenty-Eight

BEAMISH

I'd been in Barlinnie for exactly one week. No one had come to visit me, I shared a cell with a monosyllabic alcoholic who had beaten his wife sufficiently to warrant arrest and only glimpsed my fellow accused distantly during our time in the exercise yard. We were deliberately being kept apart. These were *travails* I had not expected when signing up as an Intelligence Officer.

One evening as 'lights out' was being called, the door of my cell opened and a prison officer (I was not yet sufficiently immersed in the prison culture to refer to him as a 'screw') entered.

"Gillespie, outside!"

My fellow cell mate grunted his displeasure but left obediently, encouraged all the way by another officer.

As the cell door slammed shut, a punch to my solar plexus dropped me involuntarily to the floor where a boot thumped into my ribs.

"I fought a fuckin' war against your type, Canning. Fuckin' Nazi!" He knelt beside me and spoke, his face only six inches from my ear and in a spittle-flecked stage-whisper growled, "You're the fucking scum of the earth yous Separatists. Tartan Tories! Well, let me explain. My name is Ronnie Irving. You get to call me Sir! I have a soft spot for the famous Glasgow Rangers, I have a portrait of Her Majesty Queen Elizabeth the Second above my bed and am a Unionist who has always voted Conservative. I am your worst nightmare. I am in charge of this fuckin' wing and every chance I have, I will enter your cell, dismiss any witnesses and kick your fuckin' head in"

I rolled on my side, grimacing at the pain in my ribs. Two of them might be broken, I decided. A bravado that may have been unwise overtook common sense. I spoke in spasms as I tried to catch my breath.

"Well, thanks for the warning, Mr. Irving, Sir." I eased myself into a leaning position against the cell wall. "But I'm no Nazi. I fought for Queen and Country too. Wore the uniform of the Highland Light Infantry. Was awarded a field promotion to Sergeant. I can handle myself when I'm not ambushed, so next time, come with another six prison officers. That way you might escape without a hiding."

Irving looked somewhat abashed as he took on board my admonition but he maintained his attitude.

"I've dealt with bigger shites than you, Canning. I'll be back, mark my words." Somewhat melodramatically, he raised his big right hand and drew the side of it across his neck in a slow, slitting motion.

He left and I slumped to the floor. A few minutes later, my cell mate, Gillespie returned and, ignoring my obvious impairment, merely stepped around me and levered himself up into the upper bunk where he went to sleep.

* * *

Two days later I had a visitor, Caplan's Duty Officer, young Oliver Beamish.

"I was the least prominent person they could send. Caplan doesn't know whether to be annoyed with you or outraged by your entrapment so he sent someone no one knows to find out which emotion should prevail as his head hits the pillow tonight."

"Tell him to be outraged," I rasped. "I've probably got a couple of broken ribs due to being ambushed by a prison officer who didn't approve of what he thought were my politics."

"I'll deal with that," responded Beamish confidently. He continued as if dismissing my complaint as trivial. "You are charged along with one Benjamin Henderson, Douglas Chalmers, Cameron McLaughlin, Christopher Aitchison and Arnold Menzies with various firearm offences and conspiracy. You also avoid sharing a wing in Barlinnie with one Major Frederick Boothby who has been held in Saughton Prison in Edinburgh. He was arrested around the same time as you down in the Scottish Borders. He'd been throwing bricks through windows under the influence of strong drink, proclaiming an independent Scotland and was also found with loaded weapons on his person. Anyway, how do you plead?"

"Well, Chris Aitchison is an agent working for Intelligence Officer Archie McKellar who in turn works for Giles Collingham as a Senior Intelligence Officer. He should be known to you. McKellar, according to Collingham, knows nothing of my role as an Intelligence Officer as Caplan wanted to ensure I remained under deep cover. The first four are *bona fide* nationalists but the weapons were planted, I suspect by McKellar. Boothby, you know, is an apparently committed nationalist but his file is worryingly short on detail. I had dinner with him recently and found him disingenuous."

"So MI5 set up one of its operatives?"

"I believe so."

"Then I will report this to Sir Anthony. I will first of all arrange that your prison guard...what was his name?"

"Ronald Irving."

"He will trouble you no more. And if you are correct in your assumption about the firm inadvertently setting you up, I will arrange for your release at an early date unless Sir Anthony believes that you serve the cause more effectively by remaining behind bars."

I was impressed by his confidence.

"I'm impressed by your confidence!"

"I'm new to MI5, I'm young...but if I say so myself, I know my business and I'll keep my word."

"I very much hope you do. Otherwise I might find myself up on a charge of assaulting a prison officer."

* * *

It was dark when the doorbell at number seventy-four Church Road rang. It was answered by prison officer Ronnie Irving. As the door opened, it revealed Oliver Beamish smiling beatifically.

"Mr. Irving?"

"Yeah."

"I gather you are an enthusiastic grower of Bathsheba Roses and that you have cultivated them with great care and attention over the last two decades."

"Yeah?"

"Well, I regret to inform you that over the next five days each and every one of them will die and that you will have to watch this sad event every day as they perish, no more to bloom."

"Eh?"

"Mr. Irving. Two days ago, you assaulted Manus Canning, a war hero. When you return to work tomorrow you will take the

191

opportunity to apologise to Mr Canning. Thereafter you will go out of your way personally and will also instruct your colleagues that Mr Canning is to be treated…"

"What the fuck!…"

Beamish continued undaunted. "…treated as if he were Lord God Almighty."

Smiling more widely, he pulled back his jacket revealing a holstered pistol.

"Shame about your roses. But you will follow my instructions to the letter. If you deviate from these, we are aware that your wife, Shona works in R.S. McColls in Central Station, your lovely wee girl, Annette, attends Thornliebank Primary School and your brother Sam, with whom you drink every Wednesday evening, shifts permitting, is a taxi driver who answers calls from many people he presumes are only interested in being transported from point A to point B. It'd be a shame if it was point A to point C for Cemetery." He closed his jacket, concealing his weapon. "I hope I'm making myself clear. You don't know who you're dealing with and will never discover with whom you are dealing unless you transgress. The first casualty will be your right knee. The second, your left knee…after that?"

Irving exploded in anger and grasped Beamish by his lapels. "You fuckin'…"

Unperturbed, Beamish merely removed the Glock from his holster and pressed it against Irving's groin.

"Sure about this? I specified your knee but will happily blow your balls to smithereens if that's your preference…so remember, first an apology. Tomorrow morning…first an apology."

Chapter Twenty-Nine

YOU'LL BE HEARING FROM MY LAWYERS

I had a number of apparently innocuous meetings with fellow prisoners whom I suspected immediately of being stooges but I had two meetings with fellow prisoners that would affect my future.

The first was when I was in the prison library. I was scanning the shelves for something to ease the tedium when I was tapped on the shoulder. As I turned in its direction I saw a man in prison garb, a big smile on his face and a huge, bushy white beard. There was no mistaking Wallace Lennox, my drinking companion and barroom philosopher from the Sarry Heid.

"Wallace, I smiled. I hardly recognised you without your Tam O'Shanter bunnet.

"Och, the inability and disinclination to pay a fine imposed a couple of years back. Thirty days for being poor. I'll be out next week and can renew my acquaintance wi' a glass of Bells. I've always enough for a wee dram." He took my arm and eased me round the corner to ensure privacy. "Here, listen, I thought you said you were wi' the polis? If that became known around here you could be in big trouble."

"A wee misunderstanding with the high heid yins of the polis, Wallace."

"Well, I was looking out for you in here. Your face was all over the papers. I recognised you."

"Did you mention to anyone that we'd met before?"

"I told you in the pub that I thought you were a good sort. I told no one. My silence wasn't because you bought me a couple of haufs but because you seemed to me to be an upright citizen and that whatever brought you in here seemed to be political in nature not rank badness like most of the people in here. I like to think I can keep a confidence so, no, your secret's safe with me." He smiled again. So you're Manus Canning?

"I am, and I appreciate your discretion."

"Well, Manus Canning. Enjoy your stay. Your name won't feature in my conversations other than to say I met you in the library and that you seemed a decent bloke."

Over the next several days, he and I met regularly in the library or in the yard. When I raised the issue of politics, he was quite specific. "It's not that I'm disinterested in politics, Manus, but over my life I've discovered that politics isn't much interested in *me*. I've always taken the view that a healthy society doesn't need politicians to tell us what do, it merely requires that we each live an honourable, respectful life, helping each other as much as we can. Politics, it seems to me, has been too concerned with right or left instead of right or wrong. So I decided to hide at the bottom of a whisky glass and spend afternoons helping people in the Calton where I live. I know that politics matter but I can't affect the economy although I can help auld Mrs. Hanlon do her stairs now she's getting on."

I enjoyed our conversations very much and removed from his favourite whisky, he was completely engaging, articulate and quite obviously highly intelligent.

My second memorable engagement took place when I stood alone in the exercise yard one day when I heard a match scratch against its box. I turned my head only slightly and saw a young man, slightly balding at the temples and with a moustachioed upper lip draw heavily on a rolled up cigarette. He didn't meet my gaze, focussed instead upon the middle distance.

"I hear you're a political prisoner like me."

I decided upon a disinterested demeanour to match his.

"So you're a political prisoner?"

His demeanour changed and he smiled.

"My name's Matt...Matt Lygate. I'm here because I robbed a bank. But I robbed that bank because I founded the Workers' Party of Scotland and the John MacLean Society and we needed funds. Our beliefs are based fundamentally upon the Communist Manifesto of Karl Marx and we support Scottish home-rule, just like you by all accounts."

I smiled. "I've heard a lot about you, Matt. You're an inspiration to many people."

He offered his hand and I took it.

"And I've heard a lot about you, Manus. We should have met before now."

"Aye, we should've. Sounds like we share the same political beliefs."

"I'm surprised they let us mix together in the yard."

"Me too, but they've become surprisingly polite recently. Still, they've kept apart the six of us who were arrested over the last two weeks."

"So you're still on remand?"

"Aye. Still to plead. There's another one of us who was lifted but I'm less sure of him. Major Frederick Boothby from the Borders but he's got a cut-glass English Establishment accent and he's in jail for throwing bricks through windows to advance Scottish Independence."

"I got twenty-four years. You expect something similar?"

"Like every single prisoner I've spoken to in here, I was innocent. We were stitched up. Guns were found in a meeting we were having. No idea how they got there but there was clear involvement by the security services.

Matt and I spoke for the hour we were allotted for exercise. In the papers that morning was the news that Lord Alec Douglas-Home had just been introduced to the electorate of Kinross and West Perthshire in order that he could replace the Prime Minister, Harold MacMillan who'd had to resign due to a liaison between John Profumo, his Secretary of State for War and Christine Keeler, a nineteen year old model who was also sleeping with Yevgeny Ivanov, a senior naval *attaché* at the Soviet Embassy. The matter took on a national-security dimension when Profumo lied in Parliament about the affair, eventually resulting in the elevation of his Lordship. Lygate was incandescent that Lord Home, having been asked if he'd now buy a house in the constituency, replied that he would not as he had 'too many houses to live in already!'

Our beliefs were completely in tandem and it was a session I looked forward to each day until one day three weeks after I'd been arrested, Irving came into my cell. His eyes were still afire with hatred but his words were considered, his voice low.

"Mr. Canning, the Governor would like to see you. Would you accompany me, please?"

I trudged behind him along corridors painted green and beige, the scent of antiseptic cleansing liquid permeating every nook and cranny, the segs on the heels of Irving's shoes acting like a metronome until we arrived at a glazed door emblazoned with the words, 'T.M. Mallory, Governor'. I entered and stood as Irving snapped to attention in front of his boss and announced, "Prisoner Manus Canning, Sir, as requested".

"Ah, Mr. Canning." He placed the pen with which he was writing on a stand. "I brought you up to tell you that all charges against you have been dropped. Apparently the weapons taken by the City of Glasgow Police Force were not found to be lethal barrelled weapons but were instead found to be designed never to fire a projectile. Replica guns, as it were. Once Forensics had examined the weapons, they reported to the Procurator Fiscal who has decided that you, and indeed each of those arrested with you, should be released without further blemish on your character. That said, it has been decided that these firearms will not be returned to you as they are deemed capable of being rendered functional." He stood. "You have spent three weeks in custody and this shouldn't have happened. I am instructed to apologise on behalf of the Crown and to acknowledge that this error might well result in litigation. If so, it would not be defended... at least, robustly."

I thought back to the confident assertions of Oliver Beamish and realised that Caplan's hand must have been behind this turn of events. Despite some part of me angered at my incarceration, I decided that it hadn't been such a torment and found myself impressed by the smooth intervention by Beamish. I smiled at the Governor.

"You'll be hearing from my lawyers."

I thought that this is what would have been expected to have been said by someone who had been wrongfully jailed but inwardly I had imagined that something of this ilk might transpire to set me free. That the others were also to be released was a bonus although I realised that me being set free and the others not would have had people asking why I'd been preferred.

Had my life been a movie, I'd have walked free with my five colleagues and would have been embraced by cheering crowds. As it was, I stepped from the austere gatehouse of Barlinnie on my own. No one was there to meet me. Fortunately I had three pounds ten shillings on my person when arrested and so was able to catch a couple of buses that took me back to my apartment in the West End.

After a bath and change of clothing, I did what I'd been dreaming about since I first lay back and stared at the ceiling of my jail cell; I phoned Alison. I let it ring for an age but it remained unanswered so I left and walked to Med Books which was closed. I opened the doors of my bookshop and went first to the back room where the damaged caused by the police still remained. All copies of 'The Patriot' and 'Sgian Dubh' had been removed. I started to tidy up and after half an hour had returned the books and remaining periodicals to the shelf, had wiped all surfaces and swept the floor. It looked back to normal although I took the time and trouble to search carefully for any listening devices that may have been planted. There appeared to be none. It was evident that the front store had also been inspected by the police but it was relatively untouched and took little attention to have the place look as it was some weeks previously. All the while I was thinking of Alison. She hadn't visited me in prison, she hadn't written, her phone was unanswered and her shop closed. What on earth might Collingham have told his sister to have her break off all communication with me. I decided to walk the short distance to her flat but the repeated pressing of her doorbell brought no response.

I spent the day absent-mindedly tending the till, selling a few books and drinking coffee. I was still there in the evening when slowly at first but increasingly as dusk descended, many of those who attended one or other of the many groups which met in my back room came in to greet me and welcome me back from prison. Four of my fellow prisoners also came in and received their fair share of back-slapping but of Aitchison and McKellar there was no sign. Some people had brought bottles of whisky and before long there was a full-blown party atmosphere although there was also an undercurrent of growls regarding the police raid and the certainty amongst everyone that the police had been up to serious mischief in planting weapons in order to see us arrested and removed as a threat to the State. All involved rather overstated their assessment of the threat we posed the Establishment but it was forgivable as the whisky enhanced our feelings of joy, relief and determination to press on. 'We have them on the run', was the *leitmotif* of the evening.

Chapter Thirty

A CLOSE SHAVE AND
A PHONE CALL

Brodie walked into his outer office, sat on the edge of a desk and lit a cigarette with his special lighter. He did so deliberately and in front of other colleagues so as to introduce his gadget to them as inconspicuously as possible. A long day of meetings had culminated in a session with some American naval personnel who sought reassurances over the capacity of the complex to administer to the needs of certain aspects of their submarine fleet if ever they required an urgent harbour.

Brodie was weary but had decided that this was the evening that he'd put his camera to use. He remained in his outer office as one by one his team members left.

"Working late tonight, Angus?" asked Jeanette, his secretary.

"Not too long, I hope. Just want to write up the notes on the meeting with the Yanks. See you in the morning."

"Night!"

Fifteen minutes passed and Brodie wandered round his office checking every room to ensure that he'd been left alone. Satisfied, he turned the lock on the front door and walked slowly back to his office where he pulled out seven charts which showed the plans, interior and exterior elevations, building and wall sections, interior and exterior wall sections, interior and exterior elevations, schedules and walls finishes, and framing and utility plans. Carefully he spread them on top of one another on his desk and switched on the green-hooded anglepoise lamp the better to illuminate them. He returned to his office door and looked out once more, listening for any footsteps. Nervous now, he returned to the desk and took the camera from his pocket. Positioning it above the plan of the maintenance shed, he slid the mechanism back and heard a double-click as the shutter opened and closed at speed to capture the image. Quickly he removed the chart to the side of his desk and focussed upon the interior and exterior elevations. Again the camera slid into action and photographed the chart. As he removed it and revealed the building and wall sections, a voice from outside his office said, "That you, Angus. Still here?"

A few seconds later, Bill Cook, a security officer with the MOD entered his office using his master key, his torch in hand but unlit. "Your door was locked. Expecting an invasion?"

Brodie turned around, his smile concealing his stunned perturbation. In his right hand was the camera, in his left was a hastily removed cigarette which he attempted to light to give himself a few seconds thinking time.

"Must have been Jeanette. She's just left."

"I saw her leave about twenty minutes ago, Angus." He laughed. "You got a woman in here?"

"No such luck, Bill. Just me and little Miss Administration. I'll be out of your hair in a few minutes." He drew heavily on his cigarette.

Cook rested his large rear end on the edge of a desk near the door of the office.

"I see the Yanks were here today. Are they allowed to carry guns on site, Angus? Last year they shot their President because everyone in America is armed it seems. Hope they're not allowed to carry them over here. I've only got a torch. They've got Carbines. Not a fair fight if things got ugly, eh?" He eased himself from the desk. "Anyway, I'd better let you get on. I'll see you at the gatehouse when you leave. Don't work too hard."

He left and Brodie watched as he walked away from his office block, every so often approaching a door and testing that it was secure. Returning to the front door, he locked it again and resumed his photography.

* * *

Collingham sat before Caplan in London.

"D'you see, Sir, we'd no idea that Canning would be in attendance. That group forbade any outside involvement. We had our suspicions that they were engaged in proselytising for civil unrest. Canning wouldn't permit listening devices in the room in case they were discovered and he was unveiled as an Intelligence Officer" His tone became more supplicatory. "Canning can be difficult, Sir Anthony. He's terribly assertive and often I'm unsure what he's about!"

Caplan sat impassively behind his desk and allowed a silence, causing Collingham to continue. "I mean, he's a fine officer and his experience in Berlin was exemplary. Indeed the relationship's he's developed in Glasgow has placed him at the heart of the Separatist movement. He's befriended the Chairman of the SNP. His management of his budget has been to the exact penny and..."

"And you caused weapons to be placed in his shop without telling him and causing his arrest to the consternation and complete embarrassment of us here in London? I've had the Minister on to me asking what the devil was going on. I've had the Permanent Secretary call me asking what the devil was going on. I've had Sir Roger Hollis, our Director General on telling me I'm a fucking idiot when all the while it's you who is the fucking idiot!" He placed the palms of his hands on the desk and rose slowly. "You will return to Edinburgh, Collingham. But there are to be changes. From now on, Canning is your superior. You are henceforth demoted. You'll take orders from him and if I were him, my first order would be to send you to fucking North Uist to determine if there are any fucking Communist sheep up there. You were a passenger in MI6. You were sent here because no one had the balls to fire you due to your connections. Well, I don't give a flying fuck about your connections. I have my own and they trump yours by a considerable margin. So go back to Edinburgh. I will explain my decision to Canning tonight and you will apologise profusely to him tomorrow. You will beg his forgiveness for being such a dolt and if he asks you of my mood during our conversation, you have my permission to say I was fucking incandescent! Am I clear?"

Collingham nodded and left in his usual manner, almost bowing and scraping.

* * *

Still unable to contact either of the Collingham siblings, I had taken refuge in the bottle and had spent a couple of hours in the Lismore Bar drinking whisky. As last orders were shouted I sank one more before heading back unsteadily to my flat. Fortunately it was nearby given my condition. My thirst had not been sated and I poured yet a further large measure of Johnnie Walker whisky and was about to show it a drop of water when the phone rang. It was Caplan.

"Canning, I've had Collingham in here today. I'll be brief, as I have an appointment with my favourite whisky at home. I have demoted the idiot and have decided to promote you to the Senior post he held until a few hours ago. Another field promotion for you if you like. As you may have appreciated we had to work quietly to see you released from your confinement. I now understand that

Collingham made an error of judgement in arranging to plant weapons without clearing it with you and in consequence was unaware of your presence when plod called."

"Sir Anthony," I slurred. "I've spent the evening drinking whisky."

"I approve, young man."

"Aye, but *in vino veritas, in aqua sanitas*. In wine the truth, in water there is health…which is why I add a wee drop." I paused, trying not to sound so drunk but the whisky decided that I would unload my troubles on a man who had made it clear to me on a number of occasions that he had an over-sufficient slew of botherations. I cared little.

"Sir Anthony. Thank you for the confidence you have shown in me. However, I must apprise you of the real situation as it applies up here. Now…" I took another swig of whisky." First of all, Giles Collingham is a chump…a dullard. His own sister describes him as a well-educated eejit…I mean idiot. I spend much of my time developing strategies to work around him."

"So far, we are in complete agreement, Canning."

"Aye..well there's more." I took a deep breath. "I happen to have fallen in love with his sister. His sister is an important player in the Independence movement in Scotland. When I spoke with him about my feelings, he exploded because my breeding was not what was required to continue his fucking posh family line. He asked me for time to think through a solution to this dilemma for him and the next thing guns were planted in my back room. You'll forgive my jumping to the obvious fucking conclusion."

"Mr. Canning, if you're saying what I think you're saying, Mr. Collingham has placed his personal interests before the professional interests of MI5. That's serious."

"I don't give a fuck about Collingham. I do give a fuck about living a lie and not being able to develop a relationship with someone because of the job I do and because my then boss betrayed our agreement to work out some solution, instead putting me in jail to remove me from civil society."

"Two problems here. First, Collingham. He's been demoted. If I find that he's behaved as you aver, then he's no future in the security services. I'll deal with that. Second problem. Your relationship. If it's any comfort, my wife knows exactly what I do for a living. I don't share the details of my work and she knows not to ask me. That is problematic for her as for many years she was an active member of the Communist Party. She no longer holds office in her local branch but her political beliefs remain as strong as ever they were. I've not kept this information from my superiors and I'm pleased that you have not kept your information from me. I can only wish you fair weather in both your important work in Scotland and in your affairs of the heart. Now...my own whisky awaits. I bid you goodnight." The phone was placed on the receiver and the call ended.

In something of a daze, I sat back in my chair. Over a period of a few minutes, I had been promoted, I'd unloaded my frustrations about Collingham, I'd been given tacit permission to reveal my love for Alison and my secretive but unwavering support for Scottish Independence had apparently remained concealed, at least at present, from Sir Anthony. In addition, my reputation as a bonnie fechter for the radical left and the independence movement had been given a major boost amongst the *aficionados*. I sipped my whisky slowly and, as the almost empty glass slipped gradually from my grip to the floor dampening the carpet, I fell asleep in the armchair, contented.

Chapter Thirty-One

AN INDUSTRIAL DISPUTE

Brodie rose and made himself an early breakfast of scrambled eggs and a rasher of bacon. He drank a coffee and counted the cash left by Bozov for the fifth time. He did some mental arithmetic. *I have the grand total of twenty-two thousand pounds in six separate bank accounts,* he thought. *I've no debt anymore and I've furnished my Linlithgow flat adequately. This camera in my pocket will bring me a further bounty...I'd say, perhaps eight thousand this time...so let's say this totals the guts of thirty thousand pounds. I could buy a mansion!..one of Simon's yachts, open a bistro somewhere...He thought further and his eyes lit up...A holiday! No one would witness my spendthrift nature if I holidayed somewhere exotic.* He considered his idea further. *Bozov would interfere if it were somewhere exotic.* He paced the room. *I'll consult him! I'll ask him for suggestions and pick the one with most sunshine, most delicious cocktails and most extravagant shops!*

Leaving and walking to a pay phone on the front at Helensburgh, he pushed coins in, his head almost swivelling lest there was danger in the vicinity and dialled the number he'd been given to arrange a meeting with Bozov.

***

At seven-thirty in the morning, Benji Henderson reported as usual for his job as a welder in the shipyards. As he walked between the red sandstone pillars and beneath the sizeable lintel proclaiming 'The Fairfield Shipbuilding and Engineering Company Limited',

206

a crowd of workers lining the alleyway entrance broke into spontaneous applause. As he progressed, the lines closed and he was enveloped in a swarm of back-slapping platers, welders, hauders-oan and electricians. Unused to anything remotely close to admiration, Benji initially was incredulous at the reception, then anxious as the crowd of smiling, boiler-suited men submerged him before realising that his standing in the informal shipyard politics had just risen exponentially. Gradually he was released from his adulation and made his way to the engine room where the working environment was akin to Dante's Inferno. The roaring noise was deafening and the air was a rich mix of violent expletives, welders' sparks, hot slag from the burners' torches and smoke from his colleagues' welding equipment.

Carelessly he threw the paper-wrapped sandwich he'd prepared for lunchtime beside his locker and opened it to remove the clothing and equipment he'd require for his duties.

A burly man in a bowler hat denoting his role in management (the workers wore bunnets) approached Benji, who was still glowing in memory of the adulation he'd received upon entering his place of work.

"Haw...Shite fur Brains! Henderson...Aye, you! What the fuck do you think you're doing walking into a shipyerd without permission?"

"Ah work here, Mister Frame an' well d'you know that! Have done for seven year!"

"Aye, well ye don't nae merr! This shipyerd disn'y employ terrorists nor people that don't turn up fur work fur three weeks!"

"Well, if ye read the papers this morning, Mister Frame, you'll see that there wiz a gross miscarriage of justice and that me an' ma co-accused were a' set free cause there wiz nae evidence."

"Aye, well ah huv ma orders, Henderson. Collect yer cards and fuck off. You don't work here nae merr."

Benji sat for a moment to collect his thoughts. Half an hour ago he was being celebrated by his workmates...possibly the most important several minutes in his lifetime. Not ten minutes later he'd been sacked by a bowler hat. Benji was well schooled in the politics of the shipyard. He well knew his next move.

 Jimmie Airlie was the son of a boilermaker. The yards were in his blood. Starting as a fitter in 1953 he had gradually worked his way up the Trades Union chain of command in the Clyde Shipyards until he was elected Convenor of the Shop Stewards although his friend and colleague Jimmy Reid stole most of the headlines. Airlie was an approachable man who could be stern at times but as a long-term Communist he was fully on the side of the workers and Benji expected a supportive ear. He got one!

"Well if it isn'y the man of the hour! Benjamin Henderson if my eyes don't deceive me."

"Naw, it's me right enough, Jimmy."

"Ye up here for more back-slapping, Benji?...C'mere!"

"Naw, Jimmy. Ah've been bagged...sacked!"

"Whit? How fur?"

"Auld Shields says ah'm a terrorist an' cause I got the jail fur three weeks, ah've tae pick up ma cards an' fuck off."

Airlie gestured to Benji to sit down. He did so.

"Benji, don't you worry. You don't leave here sacked, son. Haud on. I'll make a phone call.

The phone was dialled. Airlie asked to be put through to the Managing Director and was connected.

"Sir Iain...Jimmy Airlie. Happy with the laying of the keel on Atlantic City this morning?"

"Delighted, Jimmy. Work seems to be progressing very well."

"Well, I'm delighted about that, Sir Iain. But I regret to inform you that one hour from now, every man in this shipyard will be on the streets and will stay on the streets unless you right a wrong."

Sir Iain Maxwell Stewart had dealt with Jimmy Airlie many times before and was well aware of his ability to carry out his threat."

He sighed wearily, "Righting wrongs is what Managing Directors are put on this earth to do, Jimmy. Please explain the wrong."

"Well, one of your welders has become a national hero. He spent three weeks in Barlinnie on a trumped up charge. He was released without a single blemish on his character but your bowler hatted eegit, Raymond Shields has just seen fit to dismiss him for not being at work without a reasonable excuse. When the gates opened this morning he was carried shoulder high into the engineering shed. But as soon as his feet had hit the ground Shields tells him he's sacked. Well, we just had a meeting there of all the Shop Stewards. And it was agreed unanimously that if this decision isn't rescinded immediately, we're all out. This is a direct attack on the working class by a management that doesn't seem troubled by the fact that idiotic acts like this will put back the building of this ship by God knows how long."

Sir Iain calculated the cost of a workforce downing tools against the reinstatement of a welder. He was conciliatory.

"Jimmy, perhaps something was lost in translation. I'll speak with Mr. Shields and if it is as I suspect, Mr. Henderson will be back welding in no time at all. I'll phone you back shortly. If you'd be good enough to stay your hand on any industrial action until then, it'd be appreciated."

"Can't say fairer than that, Sir Iain. I await your call."

He turned to Benji. "Get the gist? He's going to speak with Shields and call me back to avoid a walk out. Think you'll get your job back?"

Benji was still pessimistic. Ah canny tell the future, Jimmy. Ah'm no' Houdini!"

Despite not being an escapologist, Benji was back at work thirty minutes later.

* * *

Bozov called the number of the phone box in Helensburgh and Brodie lifted the receiver at the first ring.

"Have you the photographs?

"I have. Can we meet?"

"Tomorrow evening. Seven thirty. Your apartment. Is okay?"

"That works beautifully. And when you arrive, be a darling and bring some travel brochures with you, will you?"

"I do not understand the Scottish sense of humour. I will see you tomorrow."

Chapter Thirty-Two

A SPY REVEALED

I had decided. The only place I hadn't tried to find Alison was her family's country pile up in Blairgowrie. The subway, a train and a taxi and I'd be there by late morning. I showered, shaved and dressed and was about to leave when the doorbell rang. I opened the door and there was Alison. I stuttered…

"I've been looking…."

"I've been hiding! May I come in?"

She shouldered her way past me and sat on a chair in my small kitchen.

"I thought we were close, you bastard! I thought there was perhaps something between us. Yet you…you…"

"Alison, I've looked everywhere for you. I was just about to leave for Perthshire to find you."

"Are you or are you not an MI5 spy sent by London to wreck any chance Scotland has of becoming independent from England?"

There have been few times in my life when I found myself at a loss for words but had there been one hundred, this would have topped the list. I stared rather open mouthed at what must only have been a few seconds but seemed to have been a few minutes. Eventually I found my tongue.

"What?" I mustered.

"You and my brother Giles. You both work for MI5 and for four years you've been lying, lying, lying. You've deceived me from the word go. I trusted you. I introduced you to key people in the movement. My reputation will now be in tatters. I actually moved to Glasgow to be next to you!"

Still I found it difficult to have my lips produce sounds that resembled intelligible words.

"These people were our friends, Manus! Benji, Dougie, Jamie, Gus and Arnold. Do they know of your treachery? They all spent time in Barlinnie because of you and my stupid brother!"

I pursed my lips and sat opposite her at the table. I made a decision...another decision, and started with the words which have failed to convince anyone, ever.

"I can explain..."

"Your boss...your boss...my *brother*...has already explained. He told me how you were both sent north from London to quiet the natives. How you were a spy in Berlin...and you are a spy up here. He told me your bookshop idea was deliberately conceived to bring all the worrisome warlords together so you could keep an eye on them and you only developed a relationship with me solely...solely to gain access to the higher reaches of the nationalist movement."

At last I found my voice.

"Your brother said all that?"

"That and more. He didn't paint a very attractive picture of you."

"I bet he didn't! But I'm afraid he had ulterior motives. Now, much as it wounds me to have to say this to you, your brother is a fucking dolt...a fucking no-talent, entitled buffoon. A clown without principles, a self-interested, inconsiderate laughing stock of an entitled...have I repeated entitled?...fucking eejit!"

"Well at least we can agree on something."

I swallowed hard.

"Look, I'm about to rip up a career. I'm about to breach the Official Secrets Act. I'm about to betray your brother and I'm about to speak to you honestly on this subject for the first time since we met. Now...much if what you accuse me of is true. *Much* of it. But what Giles doesn't know...what Giles *cannot* know...is that my passion for Scottish Independence and for socialist principles is real. I was schooled by Wendy Wood, Hamish Henderson and Harry Selby. When I was lured into MI6 initially, I became completely immersed in the need to protect the West from the murderous, sleekit Soviets. But when I was ordered up here to Scotland, I made a conscious decision...a decision I could not share with anyone else, that I would betray my oath and that I would strain every sinew to use my position to advance the cause I would willingly die for. Now no one knows this, and this is by design. In MI5...I was seconded from MI6 to MI5...it's common for double agents to find themselves compromised by others who are attracted to defect. They end up dead or in jail unless they're traded and I realised I wouldn't have that problem if I shared my venality with absolutely no one. So, no one it was. But the reason that Giles spoke to you the way he did and the reason I ended up in Barlinnie is that I sought his permission to tell you how I felt about you and all I got was, because he wasn't the marrying type, how I wasn't the right sort to continue the genetic line of Eton educated toffs of whom he approved and how I was only interested in inheriting the great assets of the Collingham estate. He asked for time to mull over the situation because I told him I would rather resign my post and spend the rest of my life running a radical bookshop with the woman I love rather that live a lie. He asked for time to consider but used it instead to plant weapons in my shop and see me and our friends incarcerated. Had it not been for the fact that my real boss in London had acted to see us released, I'd be in jail for God knows how long. What transpired however, has been that I've been promoted to Giles' role and he's been demoted...probably likely to be dismissed from the service. I'm now the top man in Scotland but I'll give it all up if you would...would consent...eh, consent...well, agree to be more...to be more... well, than just a friend to me," I finished weakly.

Alison was silenced. She took a moment to consider my soliloquy and rose from her chair.

"How am I expected to believe you? Fuck off, you fucking traitorous liar!"

She left, slamming the door on her way out.

* * *

Again to the precise second, Dmitri Bozov rang the doorbell of Angus Brodie and was admitted.

He scanned the living room as he entered checking for signs of expenditure that would offend him. He found none. Satisfied, he sat on the couch when invited to by Brodie. Bozov was all business.

"You have the camera? You took the photographs?"

"I told Control I did. Everything you asked for."

"Give me the camera."

"Give me my envelope."

Narrowing his eyes in displeasure, Bozov withdrew an envelope from his pocket and offered it to Brodie. Brodie reciprocated.

"You really must take care not to become too wedded to financial reward, Angus. It has seen the downfall of many good men."

Brodie smiled. "Is it my imagination or is this envelope somewhat thicker than previous envelopes?

"Substantially, Angus. We appreciate your efforts. Did you get all of the drawings?"

"I did and it was no little effort. I was nearly caught by a security guard."

"But no one knows of your work?"

"No. I was careful. Everyone had left." He changed the subject. "Dmitri, I fully understand your requirement that I'm not too ostentatious but I was wondering if my taking a holiday...a nice holiday...would be acceptable. Indeed I was wondering if you might have ideas of a destination that would allow my enthusiasm for the nicer things to go unnoticed."

Bozov bit his lower lip in thought and shrugged.

"Perhaps a week in London?"

"I was thinking of something more extravagant."

"Ten days?"

Brodie had given the matter some thought. "Paris...what about Paris?"

"Have you known any other of your colleagues to holiday in Paris?"

"Why yes! Two that I can think of immediately."

"Then Paris it is. You go with a friend?"

"My friend, Simon Cavendish."

"Then go…but do not bring back gifts or expensive purchases."

"Shame…I was going to bring you back an expensive Parisian silk scarf and tie."

"I have no need of these Western vanities. Thank you for the photographs. Let me know when you take your holiday and when you will be back."

The door had barely closed behind Bozov as Brodie ripped open the envelope and started counting.

Chapter Thirty-Three

MAN DOWN, MAN UP

Alison wasn't answering her phone but I had to have it out with my new underling, Giles and made arrangements to meet him in the Press Bar in Glasgow's Albion Street, taking some pleasure in convening in an ale house more suited to my tastes rather than one of his cocktail bars. Popular with journalists from nearby morning and evening papers, it merited its not too inaccurate *soubriquet*, 'a pub that produces a newspaper'.

Collingham was late.

I was half way through a pint and had almost finished my Glenfiddich when eventually he arrived and sat before me all smiles as if none of the recent past had transpired. My demeanour was grim.

"They don't do cocktails in here. What'll you have?"

"Perhaps a gin and splash?"

"That might work."

I returned and sat having taken the precaution of repeating my own drinks order. I placed the glasses on the table and faced him.

"I'll come straight to the point, Collingham. Your behaviour may well have seen an end to your career in MI5. Caplan is reviewing the matter as we speak...and that's before he hears from me of your conversation with Alison where you breached the Official Secrets

Act by revealing the identity of an Intelligence Officer and of providing a key member of the nationalist movement with chapter and verse of our mission up here. That you have dishonoured yourself professionally is one thing but having me and others jailed on a trumped up charge and attempting to ruin my relationship with your sister is quite another...and that is the reason I shall offer no quarter in our dealings. I await Caplan's instructions but in the meantime, you are henceforth on gardening leave. Return to your clubs and cocktail bars. You have no further business here. Caplan will be in touch."

Collingham didn't even wait to drink his gin but rose and left, his face fixed in a fury. I sat for a while musing over my new responsibilities and calculating whether my relationship with Alison had received a mortal blow. Certainly, the loss of Collingham was a reverse if only because my work in the book shop tied me largely to Glasgow and I would only be able to develop pretty thin intelligence across Scotland. I knew I'd have to confront McKellar whom I suspected would not have known of Collingham's deviousness when planting the guns. Perhaps he could look after the bookshop. Then I had a better idea.

* * *

I made my way to the nearby Saracen's Head Bar on Glasgow's Gallowgate. I wasn't certain that Wallace Lennox would have yet been released but calculated that if he'd continued his good behaviour, he'd have been escorted to the street outside Barlinnie by now and dispatched. He wasn't in his usual place when I arrived so I ordered a pint which was still being poured as the swing doors opened and Wallace walked in, still ramrod straight and bushy of beard. The black Tam O'Shanter had been returned to its usual place.

"Hi Wallace. A wee Bells?"

A wide smile broke over his face. "Manus...I confess I didn't expect to see your ugly face in here." He shook my hand warmly.

"I saw you'd got out. Well done, son. I read about it in the papers but it smelled a wee bit. All of a sudden the guns are found to be replicas? Gie's peace!"

"When did you get out?"

"You mentioned a wee Bells?"

I turned and ordered Wallace's pleasure.

"Two days ago, Manus. Time off for good behaviour and straight back to the Sarry Heid."

"How did you find the days in prison without your Bells and your bunnet?"

"Ach, I'd rather have had them but like most things, you deal with the realities. I couldn'y get drink so I just got on wi' things. Didn'y get the screamin' abdabs if that's what you meant. No heebie-jeebies for Wallace here."

His whisky arrived.

"*Slàinte Mhath!*" We clinked glasses and continued our conversation about our time in prison interrupted from time to time by well-wishers who seemed delighted to have Wallace back in their community.

Once alone again, I leaned into the subject I'd intended raising with Wallace.

"I've come to admire you, Wallace."

"And me, you, Manus...me you."

"Well...on a trial basis for both of us, how would you like a job?"

"A job? At my age? Mind, I'm sixty years old! My days of active duty are behind me, Manus. I've been in prison, I'm a wee bit too fond of the hard stuff and I've people here in the Calton that depend on me."

"Aye, but you're ex-military, ex-police, you can keep a confidence, the drink doesn't have complete control over you, you still walk erect, you're a barroom philosopher and you're well read. I need someone who understands books to help me run my bookshop in Byers Road. It's a wee walk then a subway ride for you from St. Enoch's to Hillhead, cross the road and you're there. You'd meet interesting people, have all the books you'd want to read and if we don't stock something, you just order it up. The pay's the same as any librarian in Glasgow."

"Time off for good behaviour?" he smiled.

"Aye. We're not too bureaucratic in Red Books. Don't get too pissed during the day, don't rob the till and use the evenings to enjoy a glass and help your people."

His face took on a new seriousness and he checked to make sure he wasn't being overheard.

"And what about all this stuff wi' the polis?"

"Well, I need to be honest with you as far as I can, Wallace. I do police work on the side but I can only promise you that while what I do is confidential, it's for good, not ill. No one knows of my police work and that'd have to remain completely...and I mean *completely* between you and me."

"I'd probably need my glass refilled to help me think this one over, Manus."

Grinning, I raised my arm, beckoning the barman towards us.

* * *

I knew I'd need to have a conversation with Archie McKellar but surmised it'd be easier for me than for him. I was unsure what Collingham might have told him but given my assessment of his character I imagined he'd merely have avoided him. I decided not to rush things and merely to await his arrival in the book shop. He arrived the next night, all bonhomie and backslapping as he greeted all of those who had endured jail time at his hand. The meeting dealt not with strategies to see Scotland become independent but interlaced with yet more whisky brought in by Menzies, the dark tone was one of conspiracy and lighter tales of prison life. I contributed and enjoyed the *craic*.

As people began to head for home, I put my arm round Archie McKellar and asked after his injured back. He responded positively, and conspiratorially I suggested that I'd a wee medicament that would aid his recovery. Producing a bottle of malt from behind the counter, I invited him into the back room, poured a glass for myself and offered him a soft drink.

He nodded approval. "Glenkinchie? Only the best for our Manus eh?"

"Well, I wanted a wee chat and thought a glass might ease our conversation."

It seemed to me that McKellar was still completely in the dark regarding my role so I decided to use both barrels.

"I am an Intelligence Officer with MI5, Archie as are you. I was seconded from MI6 and have been in this business for many years. Collingham is on Garden leave. He failed to tell me that weapons were to be planted in the room here. Sir Anthony Caplan, our boss in London, was somewhat upset at this breach of protocol and has promoted me to Senior Intelligence Officer. In my role as an Intelligence Officer here I was amused to view copies of your reports to Collingham with my name at the top of dangerous subversives. In order to maintain my cover you were not told of my role. No blame attaches itself to you for the debacle which saw an Intelligence Officer jailed.

To give McKellar his due, he remained completely unperturbed and shook his head as if bewildered.

"Manus, I've simply no idea what you're talking about."

"I don't like carrying this with me. It's usually in a secure box in our Glasgow offices but I brought it with me today." I flashed my MI5 identity card and returned it quickly to my pocket. "If you like I can show you your MI5 file or ask Sir Anthony Caplan to call you. I'm being serious, Archie. If necessary I can accompany you to the law offices of Brainchild and Carruthers in London and we can have a face to face with the boss. I gather that you met with him the week before you took up occupancy of your role here in Scotland."

He looked at me for a long moment and decided I was genuine in my approach.

"Collingham is gone?"

"I put him on gardening leave. Sir Anthony has to make a final decision but he's off the team here. That's final."

"So you spent three weeks in jail due to my efforts? Any hard feelings I should know about?"

"None whatsoever, Archie. You did your job professionally as tasked by your superior. Unfortunately, Collingham was attempting to cause me personal harm and allowed his particular animosity to eclipse his security role."

"Am I to be entrusted with the reason for his animosity?"

I decided to be open.

"Well, at the time I was enamoured of his sister, Alison whom you know. He disapproved of the relationship and took the action he did to thwart me."

"You and Alison? You'd make a nice couple. I must admit I did wonder about Collingham having a sister who was so immersed in Scottish politics. He instructed me to keep her name out of any and all communications."

"Aye, he told me the same." I changed the subject. "I'm also bringing in a new colleague. Name's Wallace Lennox. He's not vetted, doesn't know of your status and role and isn't to be advised of any aspect of our work but he's a good man with a background in the police and military. He takes a fierce drink but in comparison with those posh Cambridge boys who have been revealed as double-agents down in London, he's almost teetotal. However, Wallace knows he's to behave and I think he will. He'll look after the shop to free me up to take on Collingham's role as well as evening work here. Your role doesn't change."

He raised his glass.

"I look forward to working with you."

I smiled. "Me too...but you lose Brownie points for accepting me at face value without closely examining my ID card that says I am who I say I am....but, relax... I am who I say I am."

Chapter Thirty-Four

A SOMEWHAT MEMORABLE DINNER

I continued to fret about Alison when I received a phone call at the bookshop as I was engaged in explaining the cataloguing to Wallace.

"Hi, it's Alison. We need to talk. Dinner tonight?"

Embarrassed at dealing with a personal matter before Wallace, I turned my back, realising in doing so that it mattered not a jot and he could overhear every word I said.

"That would be wonderful. I'll book a table."

"No. Round at my place. I'll rustle something up. Seven-thirty?"

"Yeah. That'll be…"

The phone went dead. I turned and mustered an embarrassed explanation to Wallace.

"That was Alison."

"Short and sweet!"

I attempted humour. "Aye, but she's tall and crabbit right now."

We each turned to the shelves and continued discussing the categorisation of books.

* * *

At seven-thirty sharp I clasped tightly the bottle of red wine I'd brought and rang the downstairs doorbell. It was answered after a pause and I climbed the stairs admiring, as ever, the significantly more elegant tiles that lined the walls and the beautiful stained-glass windows that allowed coloured illumination on each landing compared with my own humble abode. The door was ajar when I arrived at the first-floor flat and I entered, knocking it as I did so.

Alison was in the kitchen and I noticed that the table in the dining room had been set formally.

She shouted from the vicinity of the Aga. "Have a seat and I'll bring this through"

I did as she asked noticing that a bottle of red had already been decanted, betraying her upbringing. I would never have thought of airing the wine.

I sat and shouted through. "Will I pour this red I've brought and let it breathe?"

Rather than responding, Alison came through with a plate in each hand. I caught myself staring at her exquisite beauty as she placed the plates before the two settings. She had obviously made an effort to dress in a pretty frock and while I found her most attractive without make-up, it had to be said, that when lipsticked and mascaraed, she looked absolutely stunning.

"I'll pour," she said, and did, before sitting opposite me. "It's baked Cheddar with roasted cherry tomatoes and honey. Hope you like it."

I struggled to find the words that I'd rehearsed a dozen times on the walk over.

"I'd have been happy with burned toast as long as you'd made it."

"Thanks! she said with an edge. "I put a lot of effort into that dish."

I didn't lift any cutlery.

"Alison, I don't think I can eat or drink until we clear the air. I just wanted to repeat my words of a few nights ago. I can only promise you that you mean everything to me. I'll willingly give up all I've been working for if only..."

She interrupted.

"Have you told this chap Caplan of my brother revealing your identity to me?"

"No. Not yet."

"Then I have a great favour to ask of you." She bit her lower lip as if calculating her next words. "Please don't."

I grimaced. "Alison, your brother is an elitist, arrogant, danger to himself and others. He..."

"He's all of these things, Manus. We both know that." She lifted her glass of wine and replaced it without troubling its contents, setting it before her. "He came to me last night. He was distraught. He actually cried. Most unlike him."

"Only himself to blame, Alison."

Alison's voice took on a firmer tone.

"Again...we both know that. What I'm asking is..."

It was my turn to interrupt.

"What are your feelings towards me?"

Her eyes moistened. She took a moment to compose herself.

"Until very recently I thought you were the most perfect man I'd ever met. I cherished the hope...without much in the way of encouragement from you, I might add, that perhaps someday... someday... Well, that we might..."

"And have these feelings changed?"

Weeping softly now, she shook her head. "But I'm confused."

"And you'd like me to do you a favour?"

This time she nodded.

I allowed a silence.

"Then perhaps you understand my own position. When last we spoke I asked you to believe that my feelings towards you were honest and true. I asked you to trust me. Instead you left my flat in something of a hurry because your doltish brother allowed you to think that I'd developed an instrumental relationship with you. Now you ask me to believe that your feelings towards me are honest and true and that you're not just saying that in order that I might grant a favour. D'you see?"

"But I *am* being honest. I've seen you as a desirable man since... almost since we first met up in Blairgowrie. That's years ago. I came to Glasgow because of you. I opened a book store because of you. I bought this apartment because of you. And when I made an approach that I never would to another man, you rebuffed me. It hurt but I tried to stay the course. My brother upset me hugely by revealing his own murky responsibilities. Then he compounded matters by telling me that you were in the same business of espionage. After everything we'd done together, you can understand how distressed I was."

"I can."

"Then you tell me that really, you're as passionate about Scotland and about socialism as ever you were and that it wasn't at all a sham."

"I can."

"So when you tell me that the position you now hold allows you to protect Scotland and that despite your formal role with the British Government, you're actually still in lockstep with everything you've told me you believe in?"

"I can."

Now I took a drink. Alison did so too. I continued.

"But we need to understand the implications of this conversation. No one...*No* one knows what I've just revealed to you. Were those in power to become aware, I'd spend a lot of time behind bars and there's no one out there that the Brits would see as worthy of trading for me. I'd be in for life *pour encourager les autres*. That's the power I'm giving you. That's the dominion over my life I'm offering you. You'd be complicit to some extent in my activities, although..." This time, in pursuit of false pluck, I almost finished the glass. My next words certainly hadn't been rehearsed. "A wife cannot be required to testify against her husband."

Alison's eyes moistened once again. "What are you saying, Manus Canning?"

My own eyes moistened. "I think I'm asking you to be my wife." I swallowed hard and paused, willing myself to say the words that had tested me now for some time. "Alison Collingham, will you do me the honour of upsetting your brother and of marrying me?"

Now weeping openly, she nodded and rose silently from the table. I reciprocated and we held one another in a long embrace before our first kiss. Again for the first time, I stayed the night.

* * *

Two months later, Alison and I were married in a civil ceremony in the magnificently ornate registrar's office in Glasgow's Park Circus. We'd had a discussion about the wisdom of this given my new status offering untold wealth to a committed socialist, how it might affect my role with MI5, the likely reaction of her brother Giles and whether just living together informally as partners might not be a more acceptable solution. What trumped my reservations was Alison's desire for children whom she wished to grow up in a normal family. I also suspected that the ongoing lineage of the estate might have featured in her calculations.

Wallace Lennox was my best man. He turned up dressed to the nines and looked very smart in a new suit paid for with his librarian's wage packet but still wore his Tam O'Shanter bunnet, as ever pulled down over his right ear. Alison brought a university friend as her bridesmaid. Giles Collingham wasn't advised of the union and wasn't invited. However, Alison contacted him and informed him that I would not reveal his breach in revealing the identity and mission of another Intelligence Officer.

Afterwards we had dinner in a nice restaurant in the West End, got gloriously drunk and observed Wallace work his way through an entire bottle of Bells Whisky but somehow seem more sober than any one of us in doing so. Impressive!

Chapter Thirty-five

HAMILTON

It took four months but Caplan called me to London and advised that powers above his pay grade had determined that his decision to demote Collingham and my promotion, while both justified, were deemed sufficient and that Collingham still had a role to play in Scotland if at a lower grade. I took the decision stoically.

"As long as you understand that the man's a balloon, Sir Anthony...a bibulous balloon!"

"A what? puzzled Caplan.

"A Scottish expression...a fool, an idiot."

"He's that and more. Tell me now. What's your assessment of things in Scotland? Everything quiet?"

"It's difficult to monitor everything we'd like to. Few people have telephones so electronic surveillance is problematic and there isn't the same hierarchical structures normally associated with other groups so it's not always easy to identify ringleaders. Plus, there's a lot of social change going on, Sir Anthony. In 1955, the Conservative Party in Scotland won fifty-five percent of the vote and the SNP won just over twelve thousand votes across the whole of Scotland. Fifty-eight per cent of Scots were church members compared with only twenty-two in England. Now, it may not be connected but ever since the USA secured nuclear basing rights on the Clyde, I detect that things are shifting. We're well into the sixties,1967 music is bringing change, stage shows promote nudity, new prosperity allows foreign holidays, television offers kitchen drama showing the realities of poverty, and the repatriation of the Stone of Destiny a few years back has seen a rising in Scottish sentiment."

"Repatriation? You mean theft?"

"It's not the view up in Scotland. These people who took the Stone were treated as heroes, especially when the Crown was too fearful of a reaction to prosecute. Prime Minister Atlee's view that conviction would merely set them up as martyrs, I fear, would have been proved right."

"Really?"

"I sense a new mood in Scottish politics. Folk clubs are springing up all over the place, songs reminding the audiences of Scottish folklore and history, of battles won and lost are presently having a minor impact."

"History is bunk, as Henry Ford insisted."

"Perhaps, Sir Henry but increasingly people are quoting stanzas from the Declaration of Arbroath."

"And what in the devil's name is *that*?"

"It's a text written in1320 which sought to assert Scotland's position as an independent kingdom. It states among other things, 'For, as long as but one hundred of us remain alive, never will we on any conditions be brought under English rule. It is in truth not for glory, nor riches, nor honours that we are fighting, but for freedom – for that alone, which no honest man gives up but with life itself.' It has increasing appeal."

"Historical bollocks!"

231

"And I see a tripwire just up ahead."

"And what's that?"

"The Labour Party, Unionist to its core these days, has called a by-election in the constituency of Hamilton just outside Glasgow following the resignation of their sitting MP Tom Fraser who wants to take up a more remunerative post as Head of the North of Scotland Hydro-Electric Board. It's a safe seat but they've a young lawyer standing for the SNP. My contacts in the movement suggest a possible upset. It'll take a huge swing but Labour are complacent and Conservatives and Liberals are nowhere. If it goes Nationalist, who knows the end point?"

Caplan sorted some paperwork before him betraying a measure of skittishness.

"It may be worse than you think." The papers were reshuffled. "This is ultra-secret," he growled.

"Then I'll keep my mouth ultra-shut!"

Caplan looked at me to ensure I was taking his briefing seriously. Satisfied, he continued. "Our man in the Netherlands has reported that oil and gas has been found by the Norwegians in the Groningen field of the North Sea. Our own geologists have briefed Cabinet that following the 1964 Convention on the Continental Shelve and the sovereignty this confers on Great Britain, it might well be that following discoveries in the Ekofisk Field in the Norway sector, a plenitude of oil and gas resources may lie untapped in the North Sea...but largely in waters that would technically be under the Scottish sea bed. The English sea bed, they say, might be barren. I needn't explain the potential political fallout if this comes to pass and is made known to the Scottish electorate."

"Not sure how conceivably you'd be able to hide it, Sir Anthony."

"Quite!"

Papers were transferred into a buff folder. Over the years I'd come to understand what I'd initially imagined was a short temper when Caplan spoke in staccato fashion was in fact more to do with his focus.

"Thanks for coming down. We're done here. Keep up the good work. Find something for Collingham to do. Congratulations on your recent nuptials. That'll be all."

I was shown the door armed with simply explosive information.

* * *

A few weeks later in the margins of a meeting with Arthur Donaldson, the SNP leader, I asked sociably about the prospects of an SNP victory in Hamilton. He spoke animatedly about polling returns which showed a substantial swing, but perhaps not one that would bring victory. I found myself asking him what he made of the oil discovery in the Norwegian sector and whether it made sense to engage geologists to assess the Scottish potential. Donaldson was a bright man; very bright, but also cautious and although he offered warm words, his eyes told me it wasn't high on his agenda. All he could focus upon was the short term vision of an electoral victory in Hamilton.

I reported Donaldson's polling results dutifully to Caplan and decided to bide my time on the oil and gas information.

At the beginning of November, Winnie Ewing won the by-election for the SNP with a stunning forty-eight per cent of the vote; a thirty-eight per cent swing. Alison and I were both in the cheering crowds that night. I didn't bother reporting it to Caplan as it made UK headlines in both the print and televisual media. Some reported it as a one-off, aberrant result but other more reflective writers sensed something was in the wind.

* * *

A week later, Alison, Wallace and I were in Red Books, each undertaking separate small tasks. The bell above the door rang to inform the shop of a customer entry...now Wallace's job to deal with. I was busily reordering books on a shelf when from behind, two hands covered my eyes and someone said, "Hi, Manus!"

I turned and was at once embraced in a hug and had a huge kiss planted on my cheek, dangerously close to my lips. Alison watched this open-mouthed.

"Pleased to see me?"

My eyes darted to meet those of Alison who had the beginnings of a frown emerge on her brow.

Taken somewhat aback I could first only muster her name.

"Emilia...how nice to see you." I turned to my wife... "Alison, this is Emilia Meyer. She's a German National I worked with when I was in Berlin."

"When Manus was looking after fishing ports," amplified Emilia.

Alison joined us with a completely fake smile on her lips as Emilia, still youthful, slim and very pretty, stood and looked round the shop.

"Horst told me you'd left the service and had set up a book shop. I'm in Scotland for a while and decided to surprise you."

"You certainly did that!" I smiled. I held out my arm welcoming Alison to my side.

"Emilia, this is Alison...my wife!"

The smile left Emilia's eyes for a moment but soon returned.

"How wonderful. Horst did not mention this."

"I haven't told him yet. We are only married a few weeks."
I beckoned Wallace over. "And this is Wallace. He's really the boss
of the shop."

Emilia offered her hand and Wallace shook it.

"You look exactly like I expected all Scotsmen to look, Wallace."

Alison couldn't restrain herself.

"And what did you do when Manus worked in Germany,
Emilia?"

"Oh, I was only a junior person in administration within the
commercial section of the British Consulate. I thought I'd nothing
better to do than surprise Manus and take him for a drink."

I realised that this visit could not be a social visit and decided to
remove her from the shop before anything awkward occurred.

"Best idea I've heard all day. This pair can man the barricades this
afternoon." I gave Alison a kiss on the cheek. "When you shut up
shop, we'll be in the Curlers Bar. You two should join us."

We left. Wallace looked straight ahead, his face devoid of emotion.
Alison, if anything opened her mouth even further in astonishment.

In the nearby Curlers Bar, I bought a couple of drinks and sat
before Emilia.

"I'm assuming your visit is no accident of social curiosity."

The stern face I so remembered returned.

"You have not appointed Giles Collingham to any work worthy of his station. I have been sent to deal with that along with another matter that troubles MI5."

"Can you share that?"

"Partly. The CIA is of the view that information is being passed by someone in the Faslane Naval Base up here to Soviet sources. My boss has complained to the Director General. They have decided that I am to report to you in Scotland and am to partner this man Giles Collingham to get to the bottom of the leak. I am to meet Collingham tonight."

"My wife, Alison is his sister. She knows nothing of our work. Sir Anthony Caplan is aware of the marriage and gives it his approval."

Emilia smiled. "I do not. I am experienced enough to understand. It will be difficult to maintain a second life quite apart from your wife. She will break your resolve and you will tell her things. So I do not approve."

"I'll try to live with your disapproval, Emilia. Do you need anything from me?"

"If I do I will let you know."

We reminisced fairly equitably. I was circumspect about Collingham, allowing her to make up her own mind about him. Only half an hour later we were joined by Alison.

"It was quiet so we shut early. Wallace will hang on for a bit. I thought I'd join the party".

I stood and made to buy Alison a drink knowing that she'd interrogate Emilia in my absence more thoroughly than any sceptical Soviet quizmaster.

Chapter Thirty-Six

THE SHORT LEET

I was subsequently asked many and persistent questions about the beautiful Emilia by Alison who showed considerable interest in what she called 'our relationship'. I was tested due to my chosen inability to discuss anything remotely to do with my espionage duties but tried manfully to persuade her that not only had Emilia been only tangentially involved with my work but that she was absolutely not to my taste and that...and here I used my most cod conspiratorial tone...that she was a very dangerous woman and that each of us should strive to stay out of her way as much as possible. When pressed by Alison and asked if Emilia was an espionage professional just like me, I surrendered.

"Look, Alison. She's in the same business as I am. The difference is she's one percent cloak and ninety-nine percent dagger. Keep your distance. I certainly will!"

The fact was that Emilia moved through to Edinburgh at Collingham's suggestion and I saw little of her. When I did it was in the presence of Collingham or Archie. The months passed and Alison and I were deliriously happy. Our relationship was out in the open although we kept relatively quiet about the Perthshire estate...indeed I asked that I be removed from any conversation dealing with it. It had eventually been passed equally to brother and sister against normal Establishment protocol as Mother Collingham apparently, was as dubious about her son's talents as was I. She favoured Alison, so one sibling could not make a move on estate matters without the consent of the other. Sensible as this was, running an estate requires a lot of administration and that was not Giles' strength. Alison appointed an Estate Manager who took on the burden of paying staff, crafting a development plan and maintaining the estate and also, God bless her, instructed that each of them should benefit from a wage rise plus confirmation that those who stayed in lodges distributed throughout the estate, be reconfirmed in their accommodation. She received a weekly report and was content that matters were being dealt with adequately. The fortune that each had been left allowed Giles to maintain his cocktail lifestyle but I left Alison under no illusion that I was not to be a beneficiary in any way.

That said, I now lived in a rather grand apartment in Hyndland, we bought a car and for the first time, we could afford a holiday which I used by taking my new wife up to Lewis to meet my siblings, cousins, aunties, uncles and friends. She adored the trip and insisted that we return regularly. I was also able to leave a few quid at the croft.

Friends just assumed that our comfortable existence was as a consequence of Alison's Med Books being somewhat more profitable than my Red Books - which it was, incidentally.

These were turbulent times in Scottish politics. The SNP won a council seat in Pollok in Glasgow and I informed Caplan that there had been a resurgence in the Scottish feel-good factor as Glasgow Celtic had won the European Cup and their rivals, Glasgow Rangers reached the final of the European Cup Winners' Cup, while in the previous month Scotland had beaten world champions England at Wembley – in football, at least, Scottish confidence was riding high, and I told him that this would inevitably feed into the national psyche allowing me to forecast further impetus for the SNP bandwagon...and the continuing need for me to stay in my role as MI5's most senior undercover man in Scotland.

In the meantime, Emilia had secured a *faux* post in the personnel division at Faslane and Giles was positioned as an external contractor who ostensibly took to do with health and safety, allowing him access to most areas of the site. I was provided with updates on progress, of which there seemed little when I met with Collingham. I confess I expected little more than that unless Emilia slept her way through the entire community of Faslane but as the most senior Intelligence Officer in Scotland I had to find a way to assist two colleagues, each of whom I held in some small measure of contempt.

Everything came through me and my meetings with Caplan could be fractious on occasion as the Nationalist movement gained impetus and the mole who was apparently passing on nuclear secrets to the Russians was no closer to being identified. The CIA groused at MI5 and Caplan groused at me. One advantage of this was that it permitted me to grouse at Collingham.

I became ever more impressed by Archie McKellar. Not only did he carry out his duties as an Intelligence Officer with great aplomb in Glasgow, he also groomed and placed a senior civil servant working within the office of the Secretary of State for Scotland, Labour's Willie Ross M.P. Ross was vitriolic in his disdain for Nationalists and was the person who first coined the term 'Tartan Tories' to describe the members of the SNP. The Labour-supporting media nicknamed him "the Hammer of the Nats" for his many attacks on them. But, to be fair, he was a vociferous supporter of all things Scottish and was for sure 'Scotland's man in the Cabinet' rather than 'the Cabinet's man in Scotland'.

Archie had been a Squadron Leader during the Battle of Britain and had been awarded the Distinguished Service Order and the Distinguished Flying Medal with Bar for his efforts. He'd been wounded and had had countless operations on his back and leg as a result leaving him with a limp. However, his injury probably allowed him to survive an air war that killed very many of his colleagues. I found him warm and enjoyed his pithy conversation other than his confession that while on sick leave it had allowed him time to indulge his hobbies of gardening, oil painting and freemasonry. In his guise as a fellow Nationalist, his colleagues found him humorous and wise but with me he was largely business. It was clear he was both an enthusiastic Royalist and

Unionist but appeared to find in me someone he not only respected and more than once congratulated me on my passionate presentation as a Republican and *Independentista*. He found it very convincing. If only he'd known.

I challenged him tepidly about the wisdom of placing an agent within the office of a known hater of the independence movement rather than within the Nationalist's emerging administration but he was unapologetic, largely because not only was he a committed Unionist, he was very much a supporter of the Conservative Party and viewed Churchill as almost a deity but Scottish Secretary of State, Willie Ross as an untrustworthy lefty. Despite his politics, I not only admired him, I became quite fond of him. He was curious about my marriage to Alison and, like Emilia, was concerned lest she either 'infected' my politics or discovered my real role as an Intelligence Officer. I had to reassure him several times that both concerns were without substance. Nevertheless, my admiration for his talents in the world of espionage was sufficiently high to ensure that I took modest steps to protect my household against any surveillance he might attempt to introduce. I also cautioned Alison as far as I could against loose talk. It was difficult finding a balance that reassured her that I was as committed a Nationalist and Republican as was she but without providing her with information that might render her vulnerable should the day ever came when one of my fellow officers interrogated her about her relationship with Manus Canning, the spy.

Upon my return from a crabbit meeting in London with Caplan, I decided that I'd need to take a keener interest in Faslane. A week later, I called a meeting with Collingham, Emilia and Archie to assess progress. We met in the offices of Brainchild and Carruthers in London, much to Collingham's delight at finding a reason to visit his watering holes. His suggestion of him organising the meeting at his Athenaeum club was peremptorily dismissed.

Emilia was as flighty as ever, delighting in the obvious embarrassment it caused me. I'd confided earlier in Archie in order that there were no misunderstandings and he was great at interjecting early on in her nonsense and steering matters back to the business in hand.

Collingham tried hard. He set out the steps they'd taken to assess every person who worked on the base, the bugs they'd planted, the interviews they'd conducted but all to no avail.

"Have you a shortened list of those whom you suspect?" I asked.

Emilia took over.

"We have five people. Tom Johnstone in engineering because he was until very recently a member of the Communist Party and still promotes their world view, Edward Stewart in maintenance who each year holidays in an Eastern European country, usually Kiev in Ukraine. Port Director, Angus Brodie whom we believe is somehow living beyond his means, Eleanor Boyd in Personnel who is married but who has a lover who is a senior Trades Unionist and has connections with counterparts in Cuba and Jack Pembroke who is a member of the Scottish National Party, wears the kilt at every opportunity and who protested the appearance of Her Majesty the Queen when she visited Glasgow last month."

"Of these, who might have access to information of interest to the Soviets?"

"All of them," responded Emilia. "Obviously Brodie, but also Boyd and Stewart. For that matter, also Johnstone and Pembroke."

I sighed allowing a pause. "What are you doing surveillance-wise," quizzed Archie.

Collingham answered. "We've had people place bugs in their office. In Johnstone's case and with Boyd and Stewart in their homes also. Nothing of interest beyond confirming our assessment of them being general security risks due to their beliefs."

"Nothing on Brodie?"

"Not really. We've tried and failed three times. He owns a flat in Linlithgow as well as one he rents locally in Helensburgh. We've a device in Helensburgh but he really just goes home, watches TV and goes to bed. Coffee in the morning and back to work. We've more interest in his main property in Linlithgow but haven't been able to install anything yet. We've followed all of them but nothing has emerged of interest."

"Seems to me he's our main suspect. Spending above his means?"

"He holidayed recently in Paris. Went with a friend. He's unmarried. Sexual partiality uncertain. Up-market hotel."

"Nothing ostentatious in the way of purchases? New car, clothes?"

Both Collingham and Meyer shook their heads. Meyer introduced an option.

"I will test whether he is homosexual or not. It might be important."

I looked at her, inwardly wondering how someone could be so matter-of-fact about using their body for purposes other than love or lust. Then I looked a second time. She was very obviously beautiful. Her face in repose was undeniably pretty, her figure slim and statuesque. No wonder she was a whiz at her chosen profession.

"Let's know how you get on. In the meantime, let's work at getting a bug in his Linlithgow apartment.

The meeting ended. Archie and I caught the next train north. Both Emilia and Collingham found pressing reasons to stay in London.

Chapter Thirty-Seven

NIRVANA

The months passed and little progress had been made in identifying the Russian agent in Faslane. None of the bugs planted had produced any information which suggested espionage. Emilia Meyer had attempted her seductress charms on both Brodie and on Johnstone. They succeeded with Johnstone but were spurned by Brodie. Neither produced anything evidential.

"Brodie is quite obviously a homosexual," she declared at a meeting I'd called as if there could be no other reason for her allure failing to elicit a sexually positive outcome.

"Perhaps!" I reasoned. "Caplan phoned this morning. He's sending up two of his 'best men' as he called them, to support our work. Don't think he's too enamoured of our progress and the Yanks are giving him a hard time. He blethered on about motivation inevitably being Money, Ideology, Coercion or Ego; MICE...a fact we all learned at spy school 101. The issue of Scottish Independence troubles him little at the moment. It's all about skewering this leak from Faslane.

Collingham spoke. "Perhaps I might have a word with Brodie, Manus. I've already explained that I'm not the marrying type and last month the Sexual Offences Act was passed which decriminalised private homosexual acts between men aged over 21. If I could persuade him that I was that way inclined...which I'm not incidentally..."

"It only applies in England, not Scotland. Here you'd still be hung by the bollocks."

"Worth a try, though?"

"Okay. See if Emilia's assessment of his sexuality is accurate. Frankly any activity is better than none once Caplan's men visit to show us how it's done."

* * *

Outside work, I was deliriously happy. Home life with Alison was perfect. My routines surrounding the bookshop allowed a relatively normal home life. Archie was super at his job and was forever soliciting more agents prepared to provide him with information regarding the workings of the Independence movement and the left-wing usurpers, as he called them, who infiltrated the Labour Party in Scotland and who began to occupy positions of importance. Some of those infiltrators were Archie's place men and some of them were agents provocateurs, placed within left-wing groups specifically to split them and render them less powerful.

As 1968 approached, things began to change, immeasurably for the better. First, I returned home one evening to be greeted by Alison and a Golden Labrador puppy we named Alba and with whom we fell in love immediately. Almost as we were coming to terms with this new acquisition, Alison told me over a glass of wine one weekend that she was pregnant. We were beside ourselves with happiness although that was the last glass of alcohol Alison consumed for many months. As the summer of 1968 drew near and Alison entered her third trimester we were informed that my dear wife was in the process of incubating twins. Suddenly everything became very real and plans had to be made.

Alison drew both on her maternal instincts and her gargantuan bank balance to announce that we were moving house. She'd employed a couple of staff to look after Med Books and now showed little interest in her business. Arguing not unreasonably that I couldn't expect her to lug a pram with two babies up a flight of stairs, she showed me the prospectus for a solid stone villa in neighbouring Partickhill. I had to confess it made sense but worried about how it might be perceived by friends.

I discovered that once Alison set her mind on something, it was hard to dissuade her. The villa was purchased and upon the birth of the twins, mum, dad, Fergus, Rory and Alba the Labrador moved into a home that even in the latter stages of her pregnancy, Alison had cleaned, designed and furnished. Nesting, I believe they called it.

I was madly in love with a wife who loved me, was now a proud father, a dog owner, had many genuine friends whose politics I supported, if covertly, and a job I found intellectually stimulating. Cash was never a problem. Alison had earlier insisted on making life easier for my kith and kin up in Lewis who now lived in the same properties as had their forefathers but where the roof didn't leak, modern appliances of every nature assisted their everyday life and their ability to earn money was assisted by her investments in their business. Life couldn't get any better.

Then Caplan phoned.

* * *

I was ordered to visit him next day at three o'clock in the afternoon and I entered the portals of Brainchild and Carruthers in London knowing that as I made my way up the stairs, he'd be unscrewing the top off a bottle of whisky - a recent innovation replacing the cork but one of which Caplan wholeheartedly approved. He launched into a panegyric. 'Saves time old chap. The only reason cork has been the traditional cap is because we didn't have the technology for a screw cap back in the day. Modern technology...but as I say...it saves time...and doesn't break or crumble quite as often.'

He was in ebullient mood and as per usual we sat facing each other separated only by a tower of files and two large glasses of whisky. For once, Caplan seemed affected by alcohol, which surprised me.

"Always liked you, Canning. You're a good sort. Salt of the earth and all that."

"Thank you, Sir Anthony. It's reciprocated."

He disappeared half of his glass.

"The bastards want to retire me!"

Confused by his up-beat persona and his disappointing news I was flustered and could only manage, "W..w..what?"

He leaned over conspiratorially and smiled.

"They haven't a fucking snowball's chance in hell to move me out. I know too much. The Yanks are giving the Director General grief and want a scalp over Faslane...but it won't be mine."

"No?"

He shook his head before continuing.

"Now...in retrieving my position, I might just have dropped you in it, young Canning." Another sip. "Y'see, I might have suggested to these boneheaded, crewcut, inarticulate, poorly-read, redneck cowpokes that the leak we're investigating suggests that *inter alia* and all that...well, that it might be one of their *own* who is supplying Mother Russia with nuclear secrets. D'you see my drift?"

I nodded. I'd learned enough Latin in the Nicolson Institute to understand that *inter alia* meant, 'among other things'.

"Sir Anthony, we're currently looking at five individuals we believe might be susceptible to one or more of the MICE incentives.

All British. It wouldn't take much to advance a case *sine causa* against one or two American nationals. They need never know of our interest, it need never interfere with their progress through the American ranks but it would allow you to tell them to shut their smug faces up!"

Caplan slapped the table in something approaching glee.

"You grew up in Lewis. You speak Gaelic and English yet you throw around Latin phrases like you were a centurion in Ancient Rome...even if you finish the odd sentence in a preposition."

"A broad Scottish education, Sir Anthony...and the preposition rule as you would have it is overwhelmingly rejected by modern style guides and language authorities and is based on the rules of Latin grammar, not English. Trying to avoid ending a sentence with a preposition often results in very unnatural phrasings. I could have mangled something along the lines of 'up shut their smug faces'...but really?"

"Canning, you are a fucking wonder of nature!" He finished his glass and reached again for the bottle. "Have I told you that I think you're a good sort?"

"You have, Sir Anthony...but the pace at which you're drinking whisky today makes me wonder if you'll remember anything of our conversation tomorrow."

Caplan allowed a silence as he poured himself another drink.

"Young Canning! You're not the first to draw to my attention that my fondness for the water of life might impair my judgement. Trust me. I can function perfectly well after destroying a bottle of malt."

"I believe you. I have an assistant, one Wallace Lennox who can make a bottle of Bells disappear and you'd never know it."

"I must meet this Colossus. I'd bet he's often operating in the same state of nirvana that I'm in."

I saw my opportunity.

"Never finish a sentence with a preposition!"

He had the good grace to laugh out loud.

* * *

Arnold Menzies stood at the gravesite of Scottish Republican and Red Clydesider John MacLean who was buried in a somewhat anonymous grave in Eastwood New Cemetery, just outside the City of Glasgow by a few yards. He stood erect, alone with his thoughts.

John Maclean MA. Died thirty November 1923. Buried along with his sister Margaret. That's it! No mention of Red Clydeside… no word of Home Rule for Scotland…just him and his sister…no flowers…just the roots of a fir tree trying to push over the gravestone…just like the British Establishment tried to push over our John. Say what you like about the Americans but at least they carve the images of their heroes sixty feet high into a bloody mountainside. Here, we just ignore them once they're planted!

Behind the gravestone, between it and its neighbour, a flat tile lay covered in weeds and fallen leaves. Checking to see that he was unobserved, Menzies bent down, removed the earthen detritus and, with some effort, lifted the slate. Concealed beneath it was a concrete container the size of a large shoe box. Within it, wrapped in an oily rag, were three British anti-personnel grenades.

These are the boys, thought Menzies. *We'll do a bit of damage with these.*

248

Chapter Thirty-Eight

THE SNIFTER

Giles Collingham knocked timidly at the door of Director Brodie's open office door, having being permitted to do so by his secretary, and introduced himself.

"Mr. Brodie? I'm Giles Collingham. I've been conducting an assessment for the MOD on our overall Health and Safety concerns of the site. I've done the rounds and wanted to discuss the broad findings of my team before reporting back to the Supreme Soviet...if that's not too facetious and unseemly a reference given your level of security."

"Mr. Collingham...I'd been told to expect you. Come and have a seat. Margaret will bring us a coffee...or would you prefer tea?"

"To be candid, I'd prefer a gin and splash but if that's all on offer, I'll have a coffee." He replied to Margaret who stood in the threshold he'd just crossed. "Black, no sugar." He continued, now speaking directly to Brodie. "Congratulations upon having what I must report as a site inspection that deserves the most meritorious assessment. My team have lifted every stone, peeled back every cover, read every file we're allowed to...and while there were a couple of extremely minor awkwardnesses, you've passed with flying colours."

Brodie clapped his hands in evident gratification.

"Tell me now. Were you serious about the gin and splash?" He consulted his watch. "It's now after four o'clock. I have all sorts of refreshments in this cabinet here and, frankly, I'd enjoy a strong snifter if you're game."

"A snifter would just be super, Mr Brodie. Good gin, good food, good friends and good times are my watchwords. I indulge whenever I can."

Brodie poured two rather generous gins, introduced some ice, added some tonic water and opened a small drawer within which were located three limes. One he cut, before placing a thin slice in each glass.

"Not a patch on the Ritz, I'm afraid but it'll have to do on a naval base, eh?"

"Superb...hadn't expected such a welcome, Mr. Brodie."

"Name's Angus...What's yours, Mr. Collingham?

"Giles." He reached out his right arm to shake Brodie's hand and crossed it with his left to accept the G&T.

The two spoke affably for a while, every so often leaning into the purpose of Collingham's health and safety audit but more often veering off onto other subjects during which Brodie was advised of his new friend's estate in Blairgowrie.

"But with these assets, why on earth are you scuffling around in a naval base with a torch and a notebook?"

"Well, Angus, I must confess I much prefer a life of leisure and the cocktail bars of London and Edinburgh but my late father instilled in me notions of service and insisted that after Cambridge, I occupy myself with work that would 'keep my feet on the ground'. However, I fear that this might be my last assignment. My father and mother are now deceased; mother most recently, and I am free to share the burden of running my estate with my sister, Alison and forsake the obvious pleasures of managing a team of worthy but otherwise extraordinarily boring colleagues who care about health and safety in a way that escapes me."

Brodie smiled widely.

"Another gin?"

The conversation, which had commenced around four o'clock that afternoon, continued until seven, interrupted only by Brodie's Secretary reminding him of the time at six and intimating her departure. It was concluded only when Brodie suggested a further refreshment in an establishment in Helensburgh.

"Look here, Giles. I'm having such a fun time, why don't we continue our chat elsewhere. There are only one or two establishments in the town sufficient to match your...dare I say...*our* tastes. But I have a car and a driver. If you have time we could enjoy a drink made by someone else's fair hand and not trouble the local constabulary with our over-consumption of alcohol behind a wheel. It's so delightful to meet someone who shares my outlook on life."

Collingham decided quickly that this suggestion not only fed into his remit of assessing this man as a potential agent of a foreign power but also permitted him to enjoy his company in more convivial surroundings.

"What a lovely idea. I have rooms in the Imperial Hotel and would be able to walk back...although if I have any more of your gin and tonics I may have to be carried."

"Super. I have a small apartment in the town but it'd be my pleasure to carry you home if the fates determine that outcome." Dinner was forsworn in favour of continued drinking. Brodie migrated to his favourite Talisker whisky and Collingham commenced his enjoyment of a series of improbably named cocktails.

Now both drunk, much giggling replaced earnest conversation until Brodie fashioned a furrowed brow.

"Shouldn't you be getting home to the little lady, Giles? She'll be fretting."

Collingham sipped at his Cosmopolitan shaking his head sadly.

"No little lady in my life, Angus. Not my cup of tea. I decided many years ago that I'm not the marrying type. Much prefer the company of chaps."

Brodie held his Talisker steady at his lip, eyeing his new friend.

"I find myself in a very similar position, Giles. I'm a chaps sort of chap myself."

"No *hausfrau* back at the ranch?"

"Never has been, Angus. Not my cup of cheer." He placed his cocktail on the table, leaned over and squeezed Collingham's arm. "I'm exclusively a chaps' chap."

Both men, having experienced this transaction with others many times before, understood the coded discourse very well. Collingham, mindful of the listening devices in Brodie's apartment, offered a suggestion.

"Suddenly I'm very tired, Angus. My hotel is closer than your apartment, perhaps we'd be more comfortable there. Would that be too much of an imposition?"

Brodie was inebriated but well understood Collingham's lubricious tone. Collingham understood the obvious awkwardness that might shortly materialise should he sleep with the enemy. He rationalised quickly. Pillow talk might offer information denied more usual enquiries.

The two men rose and left unsteadily.

* * *

As Brodie and Collingham made their way towards the Imperial Hotel, Arnold Menzies sat before a coal fire in his west end home smiling at Cammy McLaughlin and Benji Henderson.

"So what's the big surprise, Arnold?" asked McLaughlin

Menzies exhaled a plume of smoke, swept some ash from his cardigan and removed a sliver of tobacco from his tongue, taking his time before the big reveal. Still grinning, he reached into a briefcase beside his armchair and removed an object, which device he partially concealed, exhibiting only the back of his hand to his two colleagues.

"Catch!" he bawled, throwing one of his three grenades underhand to McLaughlin who caught it in his lap, appreciating its nature as it reached the top of its arc.

"Fuckin' hell, Arnold...a fuckin' grenade?"

Menzies laughed uproariously. "Och, you're fine unless you remove the pin!"

McLaughlin was in no mood to be mollified.

"Christ, Arnold! Ah've a good mind tae remove this pin and shove this grenade up yer arse! Ah nearly died a' fright there."

Benji intervened, ever curious. "How are ye gonnae use them, Arnold."

Menzies withdrew the remaining two anti-personnel devices and inspected them thoughtfully. "I've not decided yet, Benji. I took them from a hiding place to have them here and available in the flat on the basis that a bird in the hand is worth two in the bush."

McLaughlin continued his vexed attitude as he leaned forward and returned the grenade gingerly to Menzies.

"Sometimes a bird in the hand just shits oan yer wrist, Arnold!"

Chapter Thirty-Nine

AN UNANNOUNCED VISIT

I'd been through in Edinburgh having lunch with a friend of Fred Boothby who still languished in Saughton Prison and had arrived back at Queen Street Station around four. A subway from Buchanan Street took me to within a stone's throw of Red Books and I looked in to help Wallace close up shop and to invite him to join me, Alison and the twins for dinner. No meetings had been scheduled that evening.

Upon arrival, the till had been abandoned and raucous laughter could be heard emanating from the meeting room. Curious, I looked in and found, to my astonishment, Sir Anthony Caplan seated across from Wallace who was pouring each of them a glass of Bell's whisky. Judging by the reduced amount of whisky remaining in the bottle, it wasn't the first they'd enjoyed.

"Sir Anthony!"

"Young Canning! Come and join us. I've been introduced to blended whisky by your man Wallace, here. I confess I've never considered this blended stuff before. Felt it was beneath my refined palate. Always a single malt man but Wallace has educated me." He clinked glasses with Wallace. "I was just explaining that I used to be your boss when you worked in Fisheries and having found myself in Glasgow, I thought I'd look you up. And in your absence, Wallace here has been a simply wonderful host."

Wallace looked at me, curious to see my reaction to him drinking on the job. I smiled at both men. "Each of you is more incorrigible than the other. I'll join you." I took a glass from a bookshelf set aside for cups and glasses and poured myself a dram.

254

The conversation became more general in nature and remained so for a further half hour until Caplan intimated that he was to take his leave, shaking hands warmly with Wallace. I offered to walk him to the taxi rank. Outside, his cheerful disposition changed and instantly he seemed sober. He anticipated my questioning.

"The Yanks tried to push me out. They're furious that no progress has been made regarding the leak at Faslane and have persuaded the Director General that they should take over investigations. The Minister has been involved and has had to capitulate to these crew-cut buffoons on the basis that we need their warheads and can't really contest their insistence within the confines of the naval base at Faslane. Having said that he's expanded my duties slightly, I suppose in order to assuage my feelings. I retain Scotland but have other responsibilities and suspect I'm going to need your assistance furth of this place as these duties came with no additional personnel. MI5 have two people now in Faslane and the Yanks have three. I have no oversight. Between them they're interviewing everyone who might have a remote access to information of interest to the Communists. We'll see if they get any further than Collingham."

I couldn't help myself. "Wallace in there would get further than Collingham after he'd drained a couple of bottles of his Bells Whisky."

Caplan smiled. "I liked your man. He seems a solid citizen. Not had security clearance?"

"None needed. He's in the dark as to my role and is a man who knows how to keep his own counsel. A good man."

"Indeed, so." He nodded at the Curlers Bar on the other side of Byres Road. "Why don't we continue this conversation over there. I need to talk to you about Norway."

* * *

Having spent the night together, Brodie and Collingham had breakfasted and with some little affection, parted company; Brodie to Faslane and Collingham to his Blairgowrie estate. As he drove north, Collingham reviewed the night before. *Interesting chap, Angus. Similar background to me. Both of us are senior civil servants, both of us are in security-sensitive jobs and both of us are queer.* He made his mind up. *I like him.*

* * *

Brodie had spent an uneventful day in Faslane punctuated by a few phone calls from his secretary intimating the need to schedule meetings with two Americans who sought a conversation about site security. He placed no great importance on this and, having worked late, was driven home to his flat where outside his front door he deepened his pockets looking for his key. Behind a nearby bush, a man stepped forward sufficiently to make himself known to Brodie whilst yet maintaining cover. His accented voice was all business. "Tonight, nine o'clock in the bar of Central Hotel in Glasgow. You must attend. Ensure you are not followed." The man stepped back and disappeared into the shadows.

Realising that the message must have come from Bozov, Brodie pushed back his left sleeve and looked at his watch. Ten past seven. It'd take over an hour to drive to Glasgow and park. Time enough for a quick sandwich and a coffee.

Brodie's timing was excellent. Parking his car, he ascended the stairs to the cocktail bar of the Central Hotel. Seated in a booth caressing a half empty glass of vodka was Bozov. He nodded perfunctorily at Brodie who joined him after asking for a Bloody Mary as he passed the bar.

"You have learned the lesson of punctuality, Comrade. I believe you are becoming very good at your job."

"I've asked you before, Dmitri, please don't call me 'Comrade' in public. As you know better than I, the walls have ears."

"More than these walls, Angus…more than these walls."

"I don't get your meaning, Dmitri."

A Bloody Mary was placed in front of Brodie. Bozov remained silent until the waiter was out of earshot.

"Last night you spent the night in the arms of one Giles Collingham. In his hotel in Helensburgh."

"Wha…you…how might you know this?"

"We keep an eye on you, Comrade. It is for your own safety. You must believe we are not interested in any prurient matters but you are a very important asset to Mother Russia and we look after our assets."

Indignantly, Brodie bridled. "I don't know what to say. You have people spying on me? That is a gross invasion of my privacy. I have a good mind to…"

Bozov silenced him.

"The man you slept with is an Intelligence Officer working with MI5. Giles Collingham is tasked with unearthing the person who is passing information to us Soviets. Is this not information that might protect you?"

Now frozen in apprehension, Brodie remained speechless. Bozov continued.

"He is not regarded as a particularly effective officer. Something of a *dilettante*. But you like him?"

"I had no idea!"

"We need to check that you are not playing for both sides, Angus. If so, that would be very foolish. Shortly one of my men will interview you. If he is satisfied, we see great opportunities in your new relationship and rewards will follow. If not, a different outcome can be expected."

"Bbbut, I can assure you, Dmitri…"

"Of course you can. I don't doubt you for a second. But we are at a crossroads, Comrade. The Americans are very close to identifying the source in Faslane. You may soon be compromised. If you pass our interrogation, and if you maintain your relationship with Collingham, we intend that you should leave your current post and we will arrange promotion within the Civil Service to a post that would satisfy your ambitions whilst also permitting you to continue your relationship with the Union of Soviet Socialist Republics."

"Honestly, Dmitri…"

"I have complete faith in you, Angus. You will come through our questioning unscathed. Of that I am certain. In the meantime, you do absolutely nothing that might raise eyebrows. Continue to see Collingham. Deepen the relationship if you can but you will shortly be interviewed by Americans. They are not as subtle or effete as Collingham. They will test your unquestioned verisimilitude. Prepare well. They have no reason to identify you as the source but are working through a process of elimination. Be your usual charming self and you need only worry about your interview with my people. They will also test you!"

* * *

Caplan and I had commenced our bar conversation as dusk fell on Glasgow's west end. Now, deep into the evening, we remained at our station, me drinking whisky at half the rate of my boss who yet remained in apparent control of his sensibilities. The conversation had veered wildly from my domesticity through Scotland's political situation, the Berlin Wall, Vietnam, the assassination of America's President, John Fitzgerald Kennedy and Caplan's insistence that his demise was most certainly at the hand of his Vice President, Lyndon Baines Johnson.

"You mentioned Norway", I slurred, changing the subject.

"Ah, yes. I'm afraid I may have to disrupt your cosy life of dinner *en famille* at seven each night, walking your Labrador and selling anarchistic books during working hours."

"I'm all ears."

"These faceless bureaucrats...and thank your God you only have to deal with me, young Canning...these blasted faceless bureaucrats have removed me from the Faslane fiasco but have landed me with all other matters Scottish as well as European responsibilities which they get to pick and choose. Honestly, sometimes I feel that the only benefit I have in this role is an office chair that swivels."

I ignored his momentary gloom. "And one of these other benefits is Norway?"

"No! One of these is prisoner exchanges. These are somewhat tedious affairs. All the work is undertaken in committee rooms. One month hence, a low-key exchange will take place just outside Kirkenes in the far north of Norway where it meets the Russian border. It's not far from Murmansk where the Russian fleet is berthed. They have the better of the deal. We get a journalist who's been held on trumped-up charges. They get a full blown Soviet spy who's done great damage within our body politic."

"So why me? You need a babysitter?"

"Not so. While the Soviets are focussed upon the exchange at the border, you will nearby be instrumental in aiding the defection of one Arkady Nikolayevich Shevchenko, a Ukrainian and Soviet diplomat who would be the highest ranking Soviet official ever to defect to the west. He's an advisor to their Foreign Minister Andrei Gromyko. It's the biggest defection imaginable. Think you're up for it?

"What am I expected to accomplish?"

"Just his safe defection. I picked you because you're calm under fire...figuratively speaking", he hastened to add. "He speaks perfect English. You'll have back-up but you call the shots...again figuratively speaking."

Chapter Forty

FREEDOM OF THE PRESS

I was informed that I'd shortly fly to Oslo thence to Kirkenes in the Arctic Circle and was advised by telephone of the kind of clothing with which I'd be supplied. I was also instructed to call into MI5's offices of Brainchild and Carruthers in Glasgow and collect a Walther P99 in preference to the Webley revolver I'd rejected earlier following my argument that the Webley resembled something that Wyatt Earp might have used. I quizzed them about the need for weaponry as this was relatively unusual for MI5 officers.

"Just in case", I was told. I decided that further discussions with Caplan were necessary before I headed north.

I organised a meeting with Archie McKellar to advise him of Sir Anthony Caplan's new role, told him I was to be called away and that he should deputise in my absence. I had, if I'm honest, a grudging respect for Archie as he was very, very good at his job. I was fond of him as a person but couldn't help but be frustrated at just how effective he'd become. Every single group of note in Scotland; nationalist, trades union, anti-nuclear or left wing, had been infiltrated by one or more of his agents. Orchestrated by Archie, they had become very effective not only at providing a running commentary to the security services on all matters under discussion and the personalities articulating them but also at engendering disputes within the groups resulting in frequent disputes and splits. 'Divide and rule', he'd repeat *ad nauseam* in our meetings. Sometimes subsequently I could quietly suggest a manoeuvre to a leading figure in a group that allowed the membership to avoid splintering and could be relied upon to sprinkle some *eau de cologne* on fractious meetings but usually I was helpless as Archie's men did their stuff. I was still operating *incognito* as Archie was the man who faced the world and in consequence, my name still appeared at the top of most lists submitted to Archie recording those who posed a threat to the continued status quo of the United Kingdom. I wrestled with my role from time to time as I often felt out-manoeuvred but quelled my conscience on the basis that if someone else did my job there would be no constraints whatsoever.

We had a pretty substantial sum of money allocated to us for our various mischiefs and, admittedly with my consent, Archie controlled a large amount. He informed me that in pursuance of our objectives, he'd come to an agreement with the editors of the Scotsman, the Glasgow Herald, its stablemate the Evening Times, the Daily Record and the Aberdeen Press and Journal that he'd pay the salary costs of a senior reporter (and make available an additional small personal 'fee' to the editors in gratitude) if their paper took lines which were favourably disposed to the fundamental interests of the state. Of course, bland assurances were given of journalistic freedom and that if anything untoward were to be unearthed in respect of the ruling administration then it would go without saying that undoubtedly it must be pursued. This generosity was a gesture merely to support the free press, he'd argue. Only the Daily Record and Evening Times showed slight resistance given their support of the Labour Party and Trident but they agreed a hostile line when it came to nationalism. Archie also explained he didn't contact the Daily Mail, the Telegraph or the Express as they were already supportive.

While I pride myself on my ability to remain calm, my frustrations got the better of me in this instance. I recognised immediately that this move by Archie was a serious set-back; check, if not check-mate for the movements I supported and my irritation showed itself as I upbraided him for the amounts involved arguing he should have consulted me first as I'd have to answer for our spend.

Archie apologised profusely but argued that the powers-that-be would be delighted at this initiative and that we might both expect congratulations. I reclaimed my temper and agreed the likelihood of this. Archie then spent some time stroking my ego and telling me how impressed he was that I could play the role of a committed left-wing nationalist so convincingly. "You are completely believable", he concluded. I smiled, thanked him for his compliment and returned it, all the while wondering if he harboured suspicions as to my real attitudes.

I invited him round to the house for dinner in an attempt to persuade him that such a family man couldn't possibly be a double agent. This was a social invitation I made every three weeks or so and it wasn't therefore particularly remarkable. We enjoyed a lovely meal prepared by Alison who mid-soup, broke the news to both of us that she was considering returning to her first love and making use of her pharmacy degree by opening a chemist's shop next to our book shops. Archie was well aware of Alison's wealth and her academic background and spoke strongly in support. I found my irritation surface once more, believing this to be a matter more appropriately discussed between husband and wife but whilst two people as empathic as Archie and Alison would certainly have picked up my vexation, all three of us refrained from making an issue of it. Over the steak pie I decided that my petulance was more to do with the mission I'd been given by Caplan. It was one thing being a single man on the front line in Berlin, quite another when I had a wife and family to consider. As if reading my thoughts, Alba, our Golden Labrador snuggled against me and reminded me to include him in my affections.

The following morning to clear my head I visited the offices of the Scottish Secretariat bookshop and publishers of radical pamphlets in Elmbank Street. My friend Tom Spence and his wife served in the office and they were very supportive of me. From time to time I used to take a pile of leaflets which strained against their elastic bands and make them available in my shop. And every so often when time allowed I'd deliver them around a mapped area whose streets they'd helpfully outline in effulgent yellow, follow up replies from their office and recruit members. Their main task was to publish short books and pamphlets that were supportive of Scottish Independence. Titles such as '*Scotland Arise*' filled their shelves. A coffee in their company always cheered me and so it was today when I called round. They, like me, were on the left and we laughed at an exchange they'd had that weekend with Wendy Wood who'd sherricked them at a Bannockburn rally, saying that John Maclean, whom they revered, had taken his orders from Lenin. In fact, Tom insisted that Maclean was on record as saying that Scotland would not be dictated to by Lenin and that he'd come out for a Scottish Workers republic. On a more somber note, they shared their concerns that they'd heard that despite the Scottish Secretariat's offices being owned by Roland E Muirhead who was a wealthy Scottish Republican Socialist and a founder member of the SNP, he nevertheless intended to sell the premises and move the operation to Edinburgh. Regrettably, when Winnie Ewing won the Hamilton By-election, this transpired and Muirhead retired to Wemyss Bay where he owned a tanning company. I lost my regular contact with two great friends. Coming on the back of the advances made by Archie, and my trepidation regarding Norway, I wasn't in the best of moods when I turned the key in the lock of my home. Alison had taken the twins and Alba to Blairgowrie for the afternoon so, in reflective mood I poured myself a whisky and sat back in a chair looking out of the window.

I considered the depth of committed individuals who now spoke regularly at our evening meetings. The youthful Stuart Christie, a committed anarchist, was a popular and frequent visitor before he was arrested in Spain for attempting the assassination of General Franco and, upon release, becoming a member of the Angry Brigade. He was a highly intelligent man who had witty repartee and the room was always full when he was billed as speaking as he railed against pretty much everything and therefore inevitably touched on something to inspire all members of his audience on least at one point in the evening. He was involved in the Glasgow Federation of Anarchists and the anti-nuclear Committee of 100.

Tellingly, he spoke of how the British State in 1832 they installed agents within the National Political Union to act as agents provocateurs arguing that they had had to foil a pilot to blow up Queen Victoria during her Golden Jubilee. They were extremely successful and the practice grew and grew. He fulminated about how the state now routinely used agents to infiltrate frustrate and split legal organisations due *not* to their level of criminality but to the extent that they threatened the formal institutions of parliamentary democracy - and in turn, the Establishment and the Union.

Walter Morrison, an ex-Royal Fusilier who had served in India during Gandhi's demonstrations spoke once or twice about the absurdity of armed warfare and the need for peace. He took many a swipe at the ambitions of the British Army to become a world power backed by nuclear force. Morris Blythman, known better as 'Thurso Berwick' entertained us with his anti-nuclear song, '*Ding Dong Dollar*' popularised subsequently by singer Josh Macrae. Hamish Henderson came and spoke twice. Also on two occasions, Matt McGinn sang and recited funny poems, the second time not long before he died of smoke inhalation whilst sleeping having set his chair on fire via an unsmoked cigarette. He should have been celebrated by his likeness being represented in a marble statue in George Square.

My old inspiration, Harry Selby (subsequently revealed as an active Trotskyist and a member of the Revolutionary Socialist League) would attend but often just sat and listened as did my old jail pal Matt Lygate who'd decided following his release to focus upon educating the masses but the greatest attendances were reserved for a young man of searing intelligence called Tom Nairn (shown here in later years). Some speakers majored in misremembered facts, misty optimism and would repeat analogies

many of us knew to be semi-invented. However, Nairn had a mind like a steel trap. At that point he had been lecturing on political science at the University of Birmingham and was an articulate and compelling speaker on Scottish Independence and European Integration at a time when the left was largely against the notion...indeed, often both notions. Every night we had a meeting with a speaker, it could be presumed that seated in the front row would be Arnold Menzies, Cammy McLaughlin, Benji Henderson and Dougie Chalmers, Benji always seeking me out afterwards to tell me with a rueful smile that whoever the speaker was he was brilliant...but that, "Ah didn'y understand a fuckin' word he said!"

A stalwart in those days was Donald Anderson (also shown in later years) who campaigned tirelessly for socialism and republicanism within an independent Scotland. His efforts to introduce socialism to the SNP resulted in him and fellow travellers being scunnered and setting up a cross-party Scottish Republican Socialist Club. A history and modern studies teacher in the East End of the city, Donald campaigned for Scottish independence at a grassroots level and through cross-party organisations like Independence First, also organised regular events, including the annual 1320 Declaration of Arbroath Rally, the Glencoe Rally, and the John Maclean graveside commemoration in New Eastwood Cemetery. He was always a great attraction in Red Books as he was well informed, passionate but also very witty. Handy with his fists, he regaled us with stories of the times he spent on 'jankers' and in military prison during his two years' national service with the Cameronian Scottish Rifles (before serving a third year due to the higher pay) occasioned mostly by his spontaneous and unthinking reaction to Sassenach soldiers referring to him or his fellow Scottish squaddies as 'Jock-wogs' or 'Porridge-wogs'!

One of Donald's themes when speaking at Red Shop meetings was the traitorous behaviour of senior trades union figures who he believed had betrayed their memberships by accepting peerages and becoming members of the Establishment. "Lord Gormley, formerly President of the National Union of Mineworkers, became a Labour Peer and was ultimately found to have been in the pay of Special Branch," he thundered. "But you won't read much of these truths in the papers as no lie is too wee, too big or too dirty for the British State and its paid flunkies."

Possibly the hardest-working, Maryhill member of the SNP in Glasgow at that time was Hamish McQueen who was out in all weathers arguing the cause of independence. Postering Sauchiehall Street one afternoon when he argued 'it would be quieter than at night' ended up with him in court. Impersonating a friend who informally asked him to vote in his stead saw him spend a few weeks in Barlinnie. He was very popular around the place and a great source of funny stories.

Another teacher from Glasgow, geography this time, a Lanarkshire man from mining stock, was Robert Johnston Hutchison who was a great conversationalist and who was involved in the 1934 merging of the National Party of Scotland and the Scottish Party to form the Scottish National Party with the Duke of Montrose and Cunninghame Graham as its first joint presidents. He contributed articles and lines often to the Scots Independent publication and was no mean poet. He only addressed the occasional meeting but asked canny questions and was a popular individual within the movement. His passion was land reform and he'd regale the meeting with his insistence that land was in the ownership of the elite due to their forbearers being particularly successful rogues, murderers, pirates and vagabonds. Over centuries, Scotland's land had been stolen by fraud or by force, that the nobility in the House of Lords was far from noble and that the chamber was occupied by nothing more than an agglomeration of charlatans. I enjoyed our chats.

Dominic Behan, brother of Brendan, had decided to base himself in Glasgow from Dublin and not only spoke at meetings but was easily persuaded to lapse into song. Living with Scottish poet Hugh MacDiarmid (who never troubled the book shop) in the South-side of the city, he wrote over than four hundred songs. Many of his songs were sung in local pubs including *'The Patriot Game'*, *'McAlpine's Fusiliers'* and *'Liverpool Lou'*. He was a great playwright and entertainer.

Mulling over these stalwarts improved my mood and gave me confidence that perhaps all was not lost. However, I could see no way of countering Archie's cultivation of the Scottish media and took the view that even where there was cause for great celebration of Scottish ingenuity, progress or achievement, it would now be diminished or ignored by the media. My despondency returned.

Chapter Forty-One

A SIMPLE PRISONER EXCHANGE

Caplan himself briefed me on my task in Norway. He stressed that secret and careful planning had been undertaken over several months both in London and in Moscow. Internally, a defection was referred to by the rather twee term of an 'offer of service' which intimated formally to the agency that an important individual sought to come over to the West. Arkady Nikolayevich Shevchenko was one such person and he would be of inestimable value to NATO and to the western powers generally. In consequence, it was underlined to me that this was a 'exceptionally big deal'. It was to be a British initiative as Shevchenko had a higher estimation of the reliability of MI6 and the UK security services than the CIA. In addition, according to Caplan, due to initial feedback from Shevchenko himself, London had been put on alert and was now going through one of its regular periods of introspection as the organisation could not be entirely confident that there wasn't a mole infiltrated somewhere within. Ironically, to my complete astonishment, Caplan had persuaded the top brass that I was an ideal candidate for the job due to my military accomplishments, my record of service in Germany and that I was completely immune from suspicion of any treachery due to my recent role being confined entirely to Scotland. Had he but known!

However, they were half right and my initial reservations eased as young Oliver Beamish was wheeled in to deepen my knowledge of the mission. I hadn't had an opportunity to thank him for securing my release from Barlinnie and greeted him warmly. He spent an afternoon with me pouring over maps and explaining in detail what arrangements had been put in place. He was completely on top of his brief and I found myself forming the opinion that he was set for greater positions of seniority within the security services as time passed...and I surmised that not too much time would elapse, either.

I returned to Scotland and had to tell Alison that I'd been ordered to undertake a special mission abroad but that I could not share any of the details. She was relatively unconcerned, her sole question being whether 'that vamp' Emilia Meyer was to be involved. I smiled at her wariness of Emilia and confirmed that she was uninvolved. Her concerns then centred on the twins and domestic matters. I'd be away only for a week.

I was flown by scheduled airline first to Oslo then to Kirkenes in the Norwegian sector of the Arctic Circle where Norway borders Russia. I was collected from the small airport that serves the town and taken to a safe house close to the tiny Lilliputian high street which solely ministered to the commercial needs of the little town. It was February and the snow lay deep on the ground. The local authority had used snow ploughs to permit both driving on the roads and walking on paved areas but mother nature would not be denied and any kind of movement was seriously curtailed.

In my safe house, a wooden construction, I peered through the curtains noticing the extent to which locals made use of fairy lights to brighten up their otherwise dark lives, decided to brave the swirling snow and have a meal alone in one of only two restaurants in the small town.

My heart sank as upon entry, I sloughed off the snow from my boots and noticed that sitting with two men in a booth towards the rear of the small snack-bar was Emilia Meyer, the very woman I'd promised Alison would not be involved in this mission. I considered leaving immediately, realising that she must be part of the formal assignment tasked with collecting the journalist but too late, she recognised me and excusing herself, approached me at the door as the waiter offered me a table for one.

"Well, now, Manus. Fancy seeing you here! We weren't advised that the big guns were to be involved in our Nordic escapade."

"It's as much a surprise for me as it is for you, Emilia. I'm here with friends to do a spot of fishing. So there's something going on?"

"If I might paraphrase Humphrey Bogarde, 'Of all the gin joints in all the towns in all the world, you walk into mine…Now, neither of us believe in coincidence, so why are you here?"

"Just like I said. I'm fishing."

"I'm fishing too, Manus…for information."

"Gave it, asked you a question you didn't answer and now I don't feel hungry." I nodded my regretful thanks to a confused waiter. *"Å takke nei"* and then to Emilia, "Think I'll just head off."

I turned and left, acutely aware of Emilia's eyes boring into the back of my skull. Instead of the pizza I'd coveted, I bought a sandwich in a snowbound store and returned to my safe house, checking all the while that I wasn't being followed…my footprints in the deep snow making it rather easy should anyone have sought so to do. That said, I was satisfied that the constant and overwhelming snowstorm would within minutes obliterate my tracks.

No one appeared to be interested and I enjoyed my coffee and sandwich, spending more time than was necessary twitching the curtains to observe any external activity. There was none and somewhat surprisingly I slept well.

Rising the following morning, my attention was still on the street outside. I slightly inched opened the curtains at my eye level when I noticed a nondescript Volvo cruise slowly and silently in the snow past my location, Emilia in the passenger seat.

A man whom I didn't recognise drove and another sat in the rear. I watched as it turned a corner and disappeared down one of the very few streets in the town, avoiding the piles of snow at the junction deposited there by the town's snow-ploughs.

A car had been assigned to me and I decided to take the opportunity to drive around a bit and get used to driving both on the right and in the snow. The harbour in the town bustled for a while with some fishing boats depositing their catch and I drove a few miles out towards the airport where yesterday I'd arrived. It had been built by the Germans using Russian prisoners of war in order that the Allied convoys heading for Murmansk could be attacked by air and troops could be repositioned north rapidly. The town was of importance to the Germans because of the area's substantial deposit of iron ore which was exported to the Fatherland in furtherance of the war effort. Now adopted by the Norwegian Government, the airfield had experienced something of a small renaissance due to the emergence of ship-repair work for which the town was becoming well-known.

I made a decision and called Oliver Beamish from a phone box asking him to confirm that Emilia was part of the mission to govern the prison swap. He knew nothing and made the point that in our business, at an operational level, everything was compartmentalised. I realised this but still felt unnerved. He said he'd investigate further but confirmed that my particular mission was strictly on a need to know basis and should remain so. A lot was resting on my shoulders.

Nightfall in winter comes early in the Arctic Circle and around three o'clock in the afternoon I made my way to the Russian/Norwegian border post taking a left turn before arrival along a stretch of road signposted '*Jarfjordveien*' and pulled into a small wooded track where I turned off the lights and waited.

* * *

Arkady Shevchenko was known by his close support team as something of a womaniser when business took him away from Moscow and a childless wife he'd divorced six years previously but whom he still supported financially. Precisely because he had no familial ties to Mother Russia, he was watched slightly more closely than others who had kinship and obligations.

The city of Murmansk was a ninety-one mile, three hour drive from the Norwegian border and Shevchenko had prepared well. At his behest, a meeting was to be held in the military zone within the city to discuss the extent to which border security with Norway and Finland was sufficient to safeguard the secrets of Russia's Red Banner Northern Fleet. In previous months, a number of Russians had merely walked across the long, unguarded wooded border to Norway and had claimed asylum. Shevchenko made something of a song and dance about this and excoriated officials who insisted that all was well. In the evening, having announced with a grin to his security detail that he intended spending some off-duty time with a young lady, the three-man bodyguard team each shrugged their shoulders conspiratorially and jocularly asked whether he'd like company.

In anticipation of the possibility of being stopped, he had provided himself with an alibi that he was travelling unannounced to inspect the border post at the Storskog-Borisoglebsk crossing point specifically to avoid alerting the guards. His Kremlin ID, his faux fury and a believable story, he reckoned would be sufficient to have any inquisitors stand down should he be pulled over en route to the border.

He walked in darkness to nearby Novoye Plato where a car had been parked in the shadows, helpfully placed there by British Embassy staff who knew nothing of the purpose to which it would be put. Keys and documents, as ordered, had been placed in the glove compartment.

Turning the key in the ignition, Shevchenko set off on a journey that would determine a life or death future. Ensuring that he made no driving manoeuvres that might inspire police interest, he covered the distance in custom time. A mile from the border he drove onto a small track not dissimilar to the one used by the Volvo, took a deep breath, turned off the ignition and, in pitch blackness, opened the door.

* * *

The Storskog-Borisoglebsk border crossing was monitored closely but as something of a backwater, the guards on both sides had come to a series of accommodations that allowed life to be led a little easier. The barter of cigarettes, vodka and *aquavit* were exchanged regularly and shifts spoke each others' language. First names were often used. Little drama was ever experienced and a couple of times each year there was an evening gathering for border guards on both sides where food and drink were shared... but tonight was to be different.

One hour before the eight o'clock exchange, tensions were rising. New faces appeared on each side of the border and took command. Four grim-faced Russian members of *Komitet gosudarstvennoy bezopasnosti,* better known as the KGB, or Committee for State Security, sat in a huge Zil 4102, it's engine purring. Between two large men in the rear seat sat Turner McWhirr, a Times of London journalist arrested for espionage by the Russians solely to have him as a bargaining chip to secure the release of Colonel General Vitaly Vasilyevich Margelov, who had been working as a Soviet spy in London for several years. McWhirr was known widely as a decent man, completely unconnected to espionage and a thoroughly professional journalist whose reports fairly recorded the political to-ing and fro-ing of Kremlin *apparatchiks*. For three months on fabricated charges, he had sat alone in a cold, rat-infested jail cell in Lefortovo Prison, infamous for mass executions and interrogational torture. Urgent diplomatic efforts had at last secured his release and now a slow dance commenced as each side produced their prize and slowly closed on the political boundary.

On Norwegian soil, Frode Berg, the veteran head of the the Norwegian Border Commissariat stood before Soviet spy, Vitaly Margelov who was himself positioned behind him and between two members of MI6, one of whom was Emilia Meyer. Other than those who were to be exchanged, all carried concealed weapons.

Berg was well known to the regular border guards but all of the usual members of the fraternity had been replaced for the evening and trust was in small measure. Berg's main responsibility was to ensure that both parties complied with the Agreement between Norway and the Soviet Union concerning the regime of the Norwegian-Soviet frontier, however, the rule book was silent on the exchange of prisoners. Slowly, both parties converged on a demarcation line.

* * *

About a mile above the border crossing and sitting concealed in a hollow created by the roots of a large tree that had fallen, I consulted my watch. I'd been given very precise coordinates and had been ordered not to make a move before eight o'clock pm when the exchange was to be made and Russian attention would be elsewhere. I was also instructed than on *no* account was I to enter Soviet territory as any apprehension of someone from the West's security services would cause a major international incident and would also provide the Kremlin with a huge prize which would certainly involve the West having to negotiate the release of someone they'd prefer to keep under guard.

The Soviet/Norwegian border runs for one hundred and twenty-two miles. Compounding this is a further eight hundred and fifty mile Russian boundary with Finland. Due simply to the sheer length of the area to be controlled, a dilapidated reindeer fence similar to that used by farmers to confine cows, defined the entire frontier. Only where formal border crossings existed was security absolute. To the south of the Storskog-Borisoglebsk border crossing, a lake frozen solid and white with snow glimmered even in the darkness. On the hills above the buildings housing the guards, a pine forest stretched for many miles.

Shevchenko had been instructed to make his way from his car to my coordinates and arrive at precisely eight o'clock. By five past the hour there was no hint of his arrival. The sky had been leaden all day with flurries of heavy snow showers. In the absence of moonlight, only the white luminous snow on the ground allowed a silhouette of slim tree trunks of Scots Pine, native also to Norway, to be identified before they merged into a dense pine forest. It would be an uphill climb for Shevchenko but I'd been told he was fit and would manage the short distance of only five hundred yards easily.

My attention was captured when first I heard what I was sure was the muffled barks of dogs. The wind had dropped and silence reigned. As I listened, I thought I could hear a soft moan and rose to my feet. Some hundred yards through the trees I could see some movement and observed a man lying at the base of a tree. Ignoring my orders and hearing the rising level of snarling and barking dogs, I leapt the fence easily and made my way down the hill. My briefing had included an exchange that would allow each person to identify the other and in a rather modern style not normally associated with the security services, I'd been instructed to ask Shevchenko his favourite Beatles' song and he'd been required to answer, 'Norwegian Wood'. As I approached, it was evident that he'd been injured and at pace I slid down beside him and said, "Arkady Shevchenko?" He grasped my arm and answered, "Norwegian Wood!" Clearly he was more used to espionage routines than was I.

"My name is Manus. How are you hurt?"

"My ankle may be broken."

"Take my arm. I can hear dogs."

He did so willingly and after a few steps I realised I'd have to carry him so using a fireman's lift, I crouched, heaved him over my shoulders so his weight was evenly distributed and made my way up the hill towards the reindeer fence. Dogs were closing and I could now discern the shouts of men who had discovered his tracks. A sharp crack was followed instantly by a bullet which thwacked into the trunk of a nearby tree. Another screamed overhead. Although I felt I was a fit man, I was breathing heavily when we reached the fence. Unceremoniously I levered Shevchenko over and found a last measure of energy to leap the fence ignoring his screams of pain. Roughly collecting my defecting Russian diplomat, we made the protection of trees just as growling dogs collided with the fence.

"Men will not be far behind, Arkady. That fence will not stop bullets." Again I shouldered him and we moved deeper through thick snow into the forest.

* * *

At the Storskog-Borisoglebsk, Margelov and McWhirr had been exchanged and each was whisked away in opposite directions from the border. In the rear of the large SUV, Frode Berg offered McWhirr a hip flask with *aquavit* in it.

McWhirr smelled the open lid and asked with a smile, "Have you no whisky or brandy? I've been dreaming of this moment for three months."

The driver reached into his inside pocket and removed a larger flask. Grinning he passed it back without diverting his gaze from the road ahead.

"This is for my own personal use. It's cognac. Don't be greedy, now."

McWhirr sniffed again, took a large draught and his face lit up.

"Thanks, driver. Pure nectar."

* * *

Once we had removed ourselves from immediate danger, I lowered Shevchenko to the ground and supported his injured limb.

"Not far now. Limp there if you can. If it's too painful, I'll lift you again."

Shevchenko steadied himself and tested his ankle, grimacing at the pain.

"Sit down," I ordered.

He lowered himself to the snow. I kicked a few thick branches from a dead tree, stamped on them until they were some eighteen inches long and gathered some lighter pine branches. As Shevchenko watched, curious as to my actions, I removed my own scarf and undid the red one he sported against the cold.

"Lie back, Arkady. I'll immobilise your ankle until we can get you some medical attention. Keep your shoes on."

I placed the softer branches around his calf and placed two pieces of wood on each side with a further splint behind his calf. Stretching both scarfs, I tied each of them round his lower leg tightly before strapping my belt around his ankle, much to his discomfort.

As we readied ourself to hirple back to my car, Shevchenko steadied himself and placed his hand on my upper arm. Breathing heavily and wincing in pain, he squeezed my arm tightly.

"My friend. You have saved my life. I know that your orders would have been not to cross the border under any circumstances and I have to tell you that had circumstances been reversed, we Soviets would not have done as you did. We would simply not have crossed! Orders are orders! But you used initiative. Had you not entered Russian territory, the dogs would have caught me and I would be on my way to a firing squad. I want you to know how grateful I am to you. I hope to be of service to the West and they have much to be thankful to you."

"Aye, you can buy me a beer on the plane."

Some ten minutes later, Shevchenko was seated in the rear of the car and I drove carefully for twenty minutes to the small airport at Kirkenes. A private plane was waiting at the end of the runway, the airport having closed for the night. I abandoned the car as close to the plane as possible and burly men appeared who helped me carry Shevchenko up the stairway and onto the plane.

As I stooped to enter the cabin, I noticed perhaps a dozen other people already seated. One of them was Caplan. Another was Emilia Meyer. Caplan ignored me and embraced Shevchenko in a bear hug. Both men clearly had history and knew one another. Each enfolded the other and spoke in whispers. Broad smiles wreathed their faces.

"Medical kit?" I asked of a man standing with rows of braid around his uniformed wrist. He called to one of those seated at the rear of the plane.

"Doctor Evans?"

A man rose from his seat, came forward and began to attend to Shevchenko's ankle. Caplan approached me and embraced me much as he had done my new Russian friend.

"Manus...(he seldom used my given name). Arkady has told me of your bravery. I want you to know you can have anything this Kingdom has to offer. That man is the most senior asset we have

279

ever spirited across the border...ever! Not only is your reputation within the service now at an all-time high...so is mine! Let the bastards try to retire me now," he laughed. "Name your posting!"

I returned his smile.

"Glasgow!"

Chapter Forty-Two

BENJI'S WEE ACCIDENT

I stepped from the London train in Glasgow's Central Station, still feeling the warm glow of Caplan's palms patting me on the back. Waiting to greet me was Archie McKellar. I placed my case on the concourse as he shook my hand warmly.

"Glad you're back. Everything go well?"

"No comment, I'm afraid, Archie but the wide grin you see on my face might allow you to hazard a guess." I lifted my suitcase. "Didn't expect a welcoming committee."

"I was in the shop and Alison told me you'd be on this train."

"Anything amiss?"

"You could say. Wee Benji is in hospital refusing to say how his left foot was blown off."

"What?"

"He's being tight-lipped but the worrying thing is the possibility that Arnold and his gang of three disturbed acolytes have somehow got their hands on explosives. That would raise the stakes a wee bit, eh?"

"I'll say!" I thought further. "Have you spoken to Benji?"

"He's refusing visitors other than Arnold."

"And what's Arnold saying?"

"Nothing. He's not at university and not answering his door at home."

"Cammy McLaughlin and Dougie?"

"Same. They've gone to ground."

"Cops involved?"

"Not yet but I'd imagine they'd want to ask some questions. I've not been on the blower to them until we had a chat."

"And this happened when?"

"Last night according to the ambulance driver who dealt with him. Cost me a tenner but he was able to share the time, location and the extent of his injuries. According to him, Benji will probably lose his left foot. His right leg is also pretty beaten up. The call came in from caller unknown at five-forty last night. Benji was losing a lot of blood and was lying near the Botanic Gardens in Kelvingrove Park. The medic said that according to witnesses, an explosion was heard."

"Glasgow's finest will make their enquiries of their own volition. We needn't get involved. Is he in the Western Infirmary or the Southern General?"

"The Southern. Ward twenty-six as of this morning. Came out of surgery around dawn."

I placed my suitcase on the concourse once more.

"Listen, can you take this back to the shop? I'm going to attempt a visitation. Once you drop off my case perhaps you could have another go at Dougie, Cammy and Arnold."

We parted company. I caught a taxi in the rank at Gordon Street and headed for Govan.

* * *

Confidence is everything. I stepped from the taxi, paid the driver and strode purposefully into the hospital looking only for signage directing me to the ward. Now suited and dressed in my collar and tie following my debriefing in London, I climbed the stairs and walked with composure along a corridor where a nursing station was helpfully unoccupied. Ward twenty-six had a glass pane on its door which allowed me to identify within the somnolent figure of Benji Henderson abed. First checking the corridor left and right, I tested the door which opened, allowing me access. Seated in a corner previously removed from my gaze was Arnold Menzies. He sported a keeker that appeared to have been applied in instalments.

"Christ! I go away for a wee holiday and return to find you two in bits!" Both men looked at me shamefacedly. I turned to the patient. "Jesus, Benji, what happened?"

"Just a wee accident, Manus."

Menzies interjected. "Benji, we agreed you'd say nothing to no one...*no* one!"

"Manus is hardly no one, Arnold. He's one of our best pals."

I ignored the exchange.

"Looks like you had a wee accident yourself, Arnold. Walk into a door?"

Benji clarified matters. "Him and Cammy fell oot, Manus. Blows were exchanged. Arnold got banjoed by Cammy 'cos he did'y like the hale idea of grenades."

283

"Benji...!"

"Is that true, Arnold or just one of Benji's rumours?"

Benji interrupted using one of his usual malapropisms, encouraging Menzies to tell the truth.

"Tell him, Arnold..." Then to me, "It's no' jist Chinese whiskers, Manus. It's the truth."

I lost patience "Look, you two. I'm here to help. Now, what the fuck happened? We don't have much time."

Each man looked at one another apparently gauging how to respond. Arnold blinked first.

"I found a grenade and..."

"You found a fucking *grenade*?"

"Aye. Beneath a hedge up at the canal. Took it to show the guys. Met them in Kelvingrove Park when were meeting up to go to a CND thing. Gave it to Benji to hold and he larked about a wee bit and dropped it. We all dived for cover but Benji got hit."

"Really? Have the cops been up?"

"Not yet but I dare say they will."

"If you stick to that story they'll have nowhere to go...but you'll need to stick to that story. The cops'll know of your political activities even though it's all above the law. If they think that the explosion and the politics are linked...if *anyone* thinks that, it'll have huge ramifications legally and politically. So stick to your story no matter what. You might want to add that you were in the process of taking it to Partick Police Station when it was dropped." I looked again at Arnold's black eye. "So, Cammy hooked you?"

He nodded uncomfortably.

"Blamed me for Benji's injury...and in point of fact he wasn't wrong. I should have thrown the bloody thing in the canal."

Benji stirred. "Ah canny be doin' wi a' this...ah just want a quiet life. Manus, ah just want tae fade intae Bolivian."

"*Oblivion*, Benji", corrected Menzies, quietly.

"Well, the doc says I might only have the wan fit. If that's right I'll need tae think aboot ma future. Ah canny be weldin' in the yards wi' the wan leg. Couldn'y even be a hauder oan...Canny see me in the office..."

I made a possibly rash decision.

"We won't see you abandoned, Benji. If things go badly medically, we'll find you a job in the shops. Alison's thinking of opening a chemist's..."

"Christ, ah couldn'y be a chemist, Manus. Ah've no' got any 'O' Grades."

"I was thinking more on the janitorial side, Benji. Helping Wallace. He's not getting any younger and Alison has a lot on her plate. But we'll cross that bridge if we have to. In the meantime you focus on getting better. Get your story straight both of you."

I leaned over and squeezed Benji's shoulder affectionately before turning to Menzies.

"A word outside, Arnold?"

In the corridor outside, Menzies couldn't meet my eye.

"Arnold, you're an educated man and I'm no fool. Now, beyond Cammy, Dougie and Benji, I'm the one person you tell the truth to. I can help. I have resources. Now let's start again. Let's start with the bollocks about you finding the grenade up at the canal."

I placed full emphasis on the word 'bollocks'. Menzies maintained his gaze on the floor tiles. I allowed a silence. A long sigh presaged his decision to trust me.

"Look, Manus, I had three anti-personnel grenades. Bought them a couple of years back from a guy in Newcastle. No questions asked. He'd no idea who I am. Buried them behind the grave of John Maclean in Eastwood Cemetery. I dug them up a wee while ago and brought them to my flat." His tone changed. "What you need to understand, Manus is that no appeal to the moral authority of a colonising power ever brought a benevolent outcome. Ask Gandhi, George Washington, Menachem Begin, Eamon de Valera, William Wallace, James Connolly..."

Two nurses passed conversing one with another. Menzies allowed them to move from earshot before continuing.

"I am of the view that at some stage, violent revolution will be necessary. At this stage I'd rather see it happen without blood and so I decided...and I didn't tell the guys what I intended...to blow the power supply of the Unionist-supporting BBC in Queen Margaret Drive and leave a note declaring Scottish independence. You have to remember the word 'Parliament' derives from the French and signifies a talking shop, Manus. It's serves no practical purpose beyond keeping the Scots in their place! We need action."

My frustration erupted.

"Fuck me, Arnold, that's right up there with Benji throwing a bin through a Unionist's window. These things have to be thought through." I thought quickly. "First things first. Where are the other two grenades ? Still in your flat?"

He nodded.

"Okay, taxi for Menzies! You and I are going to collect them and deposit them in the canal. The police will be sniffing around and if they gain access to your apartment and find them, you'll be facing a long time inside. That won't help the cause."

"I'm prepared to die for the cause, Manus!"

"I'd far rather you *lived* for the cause, Arnold. You're highly intelligent but you need to be more of a team player. We need to think strategically. We work together and we keep our lips sealed. No one else gets to hear of this. We track down Cammy and Dougie, make peace and insist on *omertà*. Will they comply?"

"*Look*, Manus. Cammy, Dougie and Benji are as capable as the Keystone Cops. They're not the brightest but they're solid citizens. Great foot soldiers in this movement. If they're ordered to keep quiet. They'll do so."

I chose not to argue his assessment.

"Okay?"

A nod from Menzies and we headed for the taxi rank.

* * *

Later that afternoon I opened the door of Red Books to find Wallace and Archie in conversation at the till.

Archie acknowledged my entry.

"Any luck, Manus?"

287

"Aye. Tracked down Benji and Arnold in the hospital. Looks like an idiotic accident right enough. Essentially, Arnold found a grenade up at the canal. Before taking it to the police, he showed it to the boys in Kelvingrove while they were on their way to a CND meeting, Benji being Benji, dropped it. They all dived for cover but Benji got hit. Might lose his left foot. He's sedated and making as much sense as usual."

"And you believe that?"

"No evidence to the contrary, Archie. I dare say the cops will ask questions but Arnold seemed sincere and Benji's too daft to come up with a fairy story."

Archie pursed his lips.

"I hae ma doubts, Manus. I hae ma doubts."

Turning, he took his coffee cup to the sink to clean it. Wallace leaned over and spoke conspiratorially in a whisper.

"He had his doubts before you came in, boss. Don't think he likes Arnold's boys too much." He lowered his voice even further. "This may be beyond my pay grade but he spent a good while on the phone while you were out. I might be wrong but the conversations were not normal in that they were conducted in a low voice with his hand protecting the handset. Think he might have called the polis."

"Between you and me, Wallace...between you and me...and thanks."

Due to inevitable suspicions held by Special Branch, doubtless prompted by Archie, Menzies' apartment was searched and weapons found. He was tried and found guilty of being in possession of weapons that contravened the 1968 Firearms Act which governed the possession and use of firearms in Scotland.

He pleaded ignorance of the law, explained they were viewed by him as WW2 memorabilia and as there was no evidence that he'd used them in anger, was fined £50 and given a finger-wagging by the Sheriff. He returned to his lecturing duties at Glasgow University, his reputation unsullied by fellow academics and much enhanced in respect of members of *Siol nan Gaidheal*.

Benji was unconvinced.

"They framed a guilty man, Manus!"

Chapter Forty-Three

ALL CHANGE

In the following months, things settled down. Benji's foot was saved but he had a severe limp. "They've pit a steel plate in ma fit an' refused the bones in ma ankle so ah canny move it, Manus", he'd tell me. "A steel *plate*! Ah canny straighten ma fit noo."

Alison had acted promptly and had bought a small underperforming pharmacy across the road from the book shops. She enthusiastically agreed the appointment of Benji who thereafter left the yards on a pension and undertook waged light duties in each of the three shops, despite frequent visits to hospital as part of his rehabilitation. Other than his tortuous use of the English language he was reliable and affable and those in our circle were effusive in their praise of his engagement. As had been prophesied, the police took an interest in the explosion but couldn't break Arnold and, somewhat surprisingly, Benji's story. It made the papers as a minor story though and I suspected Archie's hand.

I decided upon a new strategy. Caplan had asked me down to London for talks and it was clear that I was still the golden boy. We chatted and I steered the conversation round to Shevchenko, asking after the health of his ankle, which had improved. As I anticipated, Caplan spoke in the most effusive terms in regard to my performance. I segued into his earlier offer of anything my heart desired.

"Sir Anthony. You mentioned your gratitude following the successful defection of Shevchenko."

"Indeed, Canning. You're in credit."

"I have no personal ambitions, Sir Anthony. I'm happy to perform my duties in Scotland as I feel I'm perfectly placed there and have now built up a substantial breadth of relationships that can only benefit the United Kingdom. However…"

Caplan leaned forward.

"Yes?"

"My colleague, Archie McKellar. He's absolutely excellent. He's first class, but his potential is not being realised. In my opinion he might better serve this nation in another role. Our nation faces great difficulty at present in Northern Ireland. Archie is an enthusiastic Protestant, well established as a long-standing and genuine Glasgow Rangers fan and has good relationships with individuals within the Orange and Masonic Orders. He would be perfectly placed to engage with those entities such as the Ulster Defence Force as we come to terms with terrorism in Northern Ireland - particularly as it affects Scotland. Trust me, I know enough about Scotland's relationship with sectarianism to realise that this will become of crucial importance to the integrity of the United Kingdom."

"Persuasive. And how would you replace him?"

"I've given some thought to that and worry that I've been a bit harsh on Collingham."

"My God, *Collingham*? D'you know…the most exercise I get these days is shaking my head in disbelief!"

"You must remember that he's my wife's brother. For that reason alone he should be disqualified but on the other hand as I've got to know him, he's bright, well connected in Edinburgh and, on a short leash, could be of great assistance. I've covered the ground in terms of all of the political groupings in the west but someone who could assist in the higher reaches of Edinburgh power is something that neither Archie nor I have been able to penetrate. I've given this a lot of thought and have decided that I must disregard my minor personal antipathy towards the man and put the mission first. He's not blundered outrageously in my view and is presently at a bit of a loose end within the organisation."

Caplan made as if praying and placed his outstretched fingers over his mouth. He paused.

"You make a compelling case, Canning...but *Collingham*? I'll give it some further thought and give you a decision within the week."

Just a few days later, Caplan phoned and agreed my proposals. I asked him to suggest to Archie that it was his idea and not mine. He agreed and Archie subsequently concurred on the basis that he was a military man and understood orders. In one stroke I'd removed a real threat to the movement and had had him replaced by an incompetent. As a bonus, Alison was delighted that I'd 'looked after' her brother. He phoned the house one evening and seemed delighted that I'd recommended him for a role given that he'd reconciled himself to a mission in Scotland rather than London and that I'd placed him in Edinburgh. That said, he was bold enough to suggest that one day...*one* day, he might be permitted to be returned to his watering holes in London. Unstated was his new infatuation with Angus Brodie...a relationship of which I was as yet unaware.

For some time I'd suspected that Archie McKellar had suspected my loyalty to his cause. I had been careful and now that he'd been replaced by Collingham and, as no one knew of my treachery other than Alison, I felt safer. Quietly, through Collingham who now became the face of the agency in Scotland and was the handler of a raft of agents, I began to adjust their roles through him. I remained as shadowy as ever. It was a firm rule that each placed agent knew nothing of any other agent so gradually I removed some individuals from important groups and covered them myself relocating them to groups where they were over-represented, taking some little pleasure from each agents' contribution and in the attention they gave to my own high-level involvement and those of their colleague agents amongst the ranks of *independentistas*. In one group active on nuclear disarmament, about a third of those attending were my agents. I had to force the pace rather with Collingham but he soon agreed when I fed him guff about CND being by a distance the most troubling group which needed extra attention. In others, to ensure no infiltration, there were none - except me. Collingham also arranged that Ivan Jones, a Welshman and one of our agents speak with the editors to explain to them that due to budgetary pressures we'd had to end our subsidies but that we hoped they'd nevertheless continue to push the interests of our nation. Collingham again exhibited discomfort at what was quite obviously an effective tactic but accepted my explanation about budgetary considerations. To my dismay, but to Collingham's delight, while they all expressed disappointment at the loss of income they nevertheless all agreed to continue the propaganda.

* * *

Brodie had followed the advice given him by Bozov and welcomed advice it had been too. He had genuine feelings for Collingham and had taken to visiting him each weekend in his family estate in Perthshire where he found himself in seventh heaven. Simon, his erstwhile friend with benefits had been reduced in the ranks and was now a friend but without benefits. He took his relegation stoically and before a week had passed was involved with another man. This time a leather-clad motorcyclist with a droopy black moustache.

The Americans had made no further progress in detecting the leak at Faslane and could not be sure that the flow of information had eased or had, indeed, accelerated. They continued their probe. True to his word, Bozov used his influence within the British

Civil Service and Brodie was interviewed for a role as a Grade Two Deputy Secretary, remit unknown. It took a few weeks but when advised he was to be appointed to the second most senior job in the Scottish Office, the Champagne flowed. Both he and Collingham were now working in a similar geography. Brodie believed that Collingham was an officer working with the civil service's Health and Safety people but Collingham had no idea that the man he bedded at weekends, whilst quiescent and resting during the period he changed jobs, was steeped in espionage and was shortly to become a very effective conduit for information passed to the Soviets.

Bozov continued to meet with a grateful Brodie, pointing out that now he would have regular weekly contact with the most senior civil servants in Whitehall and that his breadth of information would be of utmost importance. He reassured him that further and enhanced remunerative rewards would fall to him once a period of reorientation had elapsed and encouraged him to relax and enjoy himself unobtrusively until his new posting became active.

* * *

Despite the media being universally opposed to the notion of independence, the next seven years saw the rise and rise of the SNP. Caplan had been retained as Scotland's man although I sensed when we met that he couldn't handle his appetite for whisky as once he had. In this regard, neither could Wallace. However, he coped by reducing the amount he drank, an approach that hadn't seemed to occur to Caplan. He made use of me from time to time in matters outwith my main brief. Important sojourns in Cairo, a brief return to Berlin and a short spell in Cuba offered salt to my porridge and not only did I enjoy these ventures, they were all successful and yet further enhanced my reputation within the security services. Caplan imbued me with powers and abilities usually wielded by Superman. I was both flattered and not unaware that it protected my traitorous role in Scotland.

Increasingly, Wallace had become my informal *consiglieri* but I only spoke to him in general terms and in hypotheticals. However, with his keen mind, I was pretty sure he'd have a reasonably accurate understanding of the kind of role I was playing. He was fastidious in his neutrality on all matters political and seldom offered an opinion one way or another but he was excellent at gauging character and was a great listener. I trusted him absolutely.

Chapter Forty-four

THE RISE AND RISE
AND FALL (1973)

The next several years were ones of contrasting circumstance. Alison, the twins, Alba and I had become a very happy, contented family. We'd settled into complacent middle age, the twins were doing well at school (both Alison and I were perfectly content to have them educated locally in a state school despite wider family pressure to have them dispatched to Gordonstoun or some such hideous education establishment) and although our dog Alba was beginning to show some small signs of middle-age, he was still a much-loved and well-exercised family pet. The pharmacy was doing well under Alison's management and both book shops held their own. Wallace had become adopted as a virtual member and *ersatz* grandfather of the family. His drinking continued apace and age was beginning to tell on him but he was as reliable and wise as ever. Alison had persuaded him to attend the doctor's periodically and his blood tests showed amongst other things that he appeared to be the proud owner of a somewhat remarkable liver. His doctor, a friend of ours, would shake his head at Wallace's alcoholic appetite over dinner and Wallace would invite him to tell those gathered how robust was his constitution.

"There's none of us gets out of this life alive, Wallace," he'd counsel.

"Aye...but I'm working on it, Doctor Robertson...I'm working on it."

Alison's brother Giles had managed to perform reasonably well in his Edinburgh role, staying out of my way and wining and dining with the city's upper crust. Every so often he'd mention his desire to return to London but his work in Edinburgh, I'd tell him, was respected, he enjoyed his weekends in Blairgowrie and his relationships outwith work seemed to be stable and mutual.

Caplan, however was coming under pressure to have his Scottish team perform better. In the 1970 general election, the SNP scored a dramatic win in the Western Isles when avuncular Donald Stewart became the first candidate from the SNP to win a seat in a general election. It had become general knowledge that oilfields off the coast of Scotland were boosting Westminster's pocketbook and the cry, 'It's Scotland's Oil' began to carry some weight.

 In 1973, a young teacher, Margo MacDonald won the Govan seat from veteran Harry Selby and the following February in a general election, although Margo lost her seat to Labour, the SNP racked up seven MPs. The Red Book Shop *aficionados* were ecstatic and most evenings, small groups of canvassers would appear after leafleting their local constituency, yellow fabric rosettes the size of small dinner plates pinned to their lapels.

Harold Wilson had won the election for Labour but was seventeen short of an overall majority. In consequence, a second general election was scheduled in October of that year and the SNP won thirty percent of the Scottish popular vote and eleven of Scotland's seventy-one seats in the party's then most successful general election result.

All were confident that an Independent Scotland was just round the corner. Caplan was of a similar view although he did not welcome it as much as our Red Books' customers. The Labour Government had had to concede a demand for Scottish Devolution.

Matters began to become somewhat frenetic around this time. A majority (51.6%) of voters supported the proposal, but a Labour amendment to the Act instituted by Dunfermline-born George Cunningham, the Labour MP for Islington South and Finsbury, stipulated that it would be repealed if less than 40% of the total electorate voted in favour. As there was a turnout of 64% the "Yes" vote represented only 32.9% of the registered electorate, and the act was subsequently repealed. Scots screamed about how this was a rigged vote as that test was never applied to UK elections. The Conservative's best ever win percentage was 49.7% in 1955. The highest share of the vote received by Labour in a general election was 48.8% in 1951. Nevertheless, 51% was deemed insufficient by the Unionist parties.

The SNP were not unreasonably, pretty angry at this and promptly withdrew its support for the minority Labour government ushering in a new Prime Minister, one Margaret Thatcher and losing nine MP in the process.

Well, as they say, 'beware the law of unintended consequences'! She had the gall to stand on the step of Downing Street and begin her Premiership with the Franciscan pledge 'to bring harmony where there was discord, truth for error, faith for doubt and hope for despair'. Had we but known then that her reign would be known by the left as bringing nothing but discord, error, doubt and despair...and war and poverty and unemployment and the enrichment of London at the expense of the Scots who'd have to watch their oil siphoned off to benefit the rich and the powerful. I was convinced some time later that not only did she take some considerable enjoyment in closing the coal mines across the UK but that she'd have preferred to have seen them shut with the miners still down the pits!

* * *

Scottish politics was gripped by internal debate with some within the party arguing for civil disobedience and stronger measures to be adopted in view of this calumny. One reaction to this in Scotland was the expulsion of the socialist '79 Group from the SNP and the proscription of *Siol nan Gàidheal*, Seed of the Gael. Although many of the '79 Group were subsequently readmitted and indeed, stood for elections, the proscribed *Siol nan Gàidheal* remained outlawed.

 Two of *Siol nan Gàidheal* members were both interesting and troublesome. Adam Busby and David Dinsmore began to frequent the book shop, their closest confreres being Menzies and his pals. Whilst they purportedly met to advance the traditions of Scotland, paying homage to folk music, traditional dress and Scottish history, I began to hear talk of their instigation of a shadowy organisation called the Scottish National Liberation Army. They spoke openly of the "Englishing" of the country,  and insisted to me in conversation that in order to prove the point of what they considered the disproportionate number of English people in positions of influence in Scotland, I need only phone up hotels, businesses, or key Scottish organisations and hear the accents of the heid bummers for myself! They argued that these people were not there on merit but through a kind of mutual conspiracy to promote and reward their own kind. I had no real argument with their analysis other than to make the point that there might be an equal proportion of Scottish accents around the Cabinet table and boardrooms in London.

I was always leery at the thought of armed rebellion that went beyond civil disobedience as I could see it playing into the arms of the Unionist Establishment who'd like nothing more than to send the troops onto the streets, glens and housing estates of a recalcitrant Scotland should push come to shove. I decided to inveigle myself into the confidence of *Siol nan Gaidheal* and used my relationship with Menzies, McLaughlin, Henderson and Chalmers to cultivate them.

It became clear that a Machiavellian influence behind the scenes might just be the Vice Chairman of the Scottish National Party, one Willie McRae. I'd never met him at that point but he was something of a folk hero within the independence movement and, much to the chagrin of the leadership of the SNP, could hold controversial sway in party conferences such were his oratorical gifts. He was witty, popular and was a successful lawyer in Glasgow. A sociable and gregarious man, he was also no fool and it took me a while to reconcile his professional demeanour with the notion that he might be behind some of the suggestions made in the back room of Red Books. He'd just had had substantial publicity by defeating almost single-handedly, the UK Atomic Energy Authority which sought to bury nuclear waste beneath the Mullwhacher Hills above the douce and largely Conservative seaside town of Ayr.

He was to the fore when a bye-election in Garscadden in Glasgow was called in 1978 due to the untimely death of the little-known MP William Watson Small. The SNP were entirely confident of a victory and many of us campaigned long and hard for that result but Labour's lawyer Donald Dewar scraped home requiring the cancellation of the Nationalists' party booked that evening for Partick Burgh Hall. The media took the result as a final nail in the coffin of the Nationalist movement as their percentage share of the vote rose by less than 2% but all it did was to inspire regular members to greater effort and persuade those in the SNLA and *Siol nan Gaidheal* of the need for a more underhand response. Back at Red Books I confess I noticed little difference in the amounts of whisky consumed in defeat as in victory. We were a thirsty group of revolutionaries!

While I was trusted in the main by Menzies, Busby and Dinsmore, I sensed that I was removed from certain of their plans.

One evening after dinner, Alison was putting the twins to bed and Wallace and I had retired to the comfortable chairs in front of our coal fire. Now and again we'd pay for a taxi to take him home to his flat in the east end but increasingly frequently we'd just put him up in the spare room. Initially he'd protest at this extravagance but slowly his reluctance became only for show. He'd love staying over as much as we'd love having him. Alison, in particular was exceptionally fond of him. The twins loved him completely. He was, as I say, their *ersatz* grandfather.

We poured ourselves a whisky and for a while stared contemplatively at the fire. Wallace broke the silence.

It's an interesting life you lead, Manus."

"How so?"

"Well, of course I'm only an observer but some of the people who come around the shop of an evening are a funny bunch are they not?"

"S'pose."

"You were good enough to let me know confidentially that you were not uninvolved with the polis and that you were in the business of doing good."

"I'm sure the police would argue that they were *all* in the business of doing good."

"Aye, maybe so, maybe so." He took a long sip of his whisky. "The other night I heard tell...I mean I wasn't eavesdropping...I was just listening for want of something better to do...and Arnold was talking quietly with thon new fellah David Dinsmore about two organisations they said must remain secret...one called the Scottish National Liberation Army and one called the Dark Harvest Commandos as far as I could make out." He took another sip. "Probably nothing, but I thought it better to tell you in case you needed to know what they were blethering about."

I held his knowing gaze. "That's helpful, Wallace. I know about the first but not the second. Perhaps tomorrow evening when we meet to discuss the leafleting of Govan, I'll have a word."

Wallace nodded his assent. "Aye…that might clarify matters." He finished his drink. "My heavens, this whisky seems to have evaporated wi' the heat from that fire."

Chapter Forty-Five

THE DARK HARVEST COMMANDOS (1981)

I cornered Menzies the following evening and browbeat him into clarifying comments I told him I'd overheard concerning the Dark Harvest Commandos. He relented only sufficiently to agree that I should speak with David Dinsmore when he arrived.

Explaining to him the breach in security, Menzies grimaced his reluctant approval suggesting that Dinsmore should spill the beans. Glowering at him, Dinsmore turned his attention to me.

"I would much rather you'd become involved due to our assessment that you'd be of use rather than because you've got big ears..." He sighed, hesitating before yielding. "Okay. We're planning to visit Gruinard Island. It's been contaminated by the MOD since 1942. They sewed anthrax into its soil to see how it affected the local sheep and their environment. Their test was conducted as part of Operation Vegetarian, which was a plan to disperse tablets spiked with anthrax across the German countryside to bring about long-lasting contamination of their soil by anthrax spores. They sent a fifty-man team to conduct the trial caring not at all for the population of Scotland. The island is located in Gruinard Bay, about halfway between Gairloch and Ullapool. At its closest point to the mainland, it's roughly half-a-mile offshore. We intend to remove some of the soil and deposit it in Blackpool Tower when the Conservative Party are having their annual conference in a couple of weeks."

"First of all, who's we?"

"An off-shoot of mainstream nationalism."

"Is this the Dark Harvest Commandos I heard you speak of?"

"The same."

"But isn't it insane to dig up contaminated soil that might kill or poison those involved?"

"Aye...maybe...but we've a plan to deal with that."

I'd made my mind up earlier.

"Well, if you say it's safe, that sounds like a wee escapade I'd be happy to be involved with. I've a vehicle, petrol money, a strong back and sealed lips. I'd love to give Westminster one in the chops!"

"Well, according to Arnold, we don't appear to have much choice in involving you. It's crucial that this doesn't go beyond the six people, now including you, that know about this in order that it works. There's another twist I've not revealed. There's no risk involved but it'll scale up the temperature substantially. All will be revealed."

* * *

Two nights later I found myself driving two men, purportedly microbiologists from Glasgow University. They sat in the rear seat and neither of them spoke much, although I could hear them discussing their shared intention to purchase their council house following Margaret Thatcher's Right-to-Buy legislation earlier in the year. In another car following behind, Menzies, Dinsmore and Busby were doubtless having a whale of a time.

Around midnight we pulled up just off the A832 at Gruinard Bay near Ullapool. We convened outside the cars, each of us stretching and stamping to return circulation to our legs after our five hour journey. A small rowing boat lay conveniently pre-arranged at rest on the beach before us. The microbiologists were donning shielded outerwear.

"Okay. Jonathan and Sam. Over to you. We need a couple of hundred pounds of earth. Get yourself fixed up. Manus here will row you and bring you back. He doesn't have a protected suit so keep the stuff away from him."

To say I was somewhat shocked would have been something of an understatement. I took the man I now understood to be Sam aside.

"This is all news to me. Rowing a boat, no problem. Contracting anthrax? Not even in the small print of the agreement."

"You'll be okay," he reassured me. We have containers that'll... well...contain everything we bring back."

Dinsmore interrupted.

"You said you have a strong back, Manus. Prove it. Half a mile there. Wait for Jonathan and Sam then bring them back here."

"Just keep that stuff away from me!"

* * *

Fortunately the weather was benign but half-a-mile in a rowing boat in the Northern Minch would have tested many. To be fair to my two new microbiologist pals, they took little time before announcing that they had scooped up something in the order of two hundred pounds of contaminated soil making the return journey that much more difficult.

Now weary, I beached the boat, helped by pairs of hands who hauled it further up the shingle shore.

Hastily the sealed plastic buckets were placed in Menzies' capacious car boot and with a few smiled handshakes, the occupants of the two cars left the bay and headed south, my car returning to the west end of Glasgow where the two scientists thanked me monosyllabically before leaving as the sun rose.

* * *

The following day was uneventful but the next evening Dinsmore and Busby came to the shop wreathed in smiles.

"Hi David."

"Read tomorrow's papers!" he instructed.

"Really?"

"It worked like fucking clockwork. We managed to place two buckets of the poisoned soil in Blackpool tower and announced both to the local plods and to the media that the Tory conference will have to be cancelled if they don't want to suffer the same deadly poisoning that Scots have had to endure for decades."

"Excellent," I exclaimed, meaning it.

"Aye, but there's a kicker. A good one. Maybe a couple of days hence. Until then, my lips are sealed."

Next morning, I couldn't wait to buy a selection of national newspapers and sure enough it made headlines throughout the United Kingdom. Credit was given ubiquitously to this new organisation, the Dark Harvest Commandos. My first act was to pick up the phone and contact Caplan.

"I'm on the case, sir. Indeed, I was part of the group which took the soil samples," I explained while lying that I'd no idea about the placement in Blackpool Tower and advised that there appeared to be further developments of which I was currently unaware but that I was working on it. "A report will be on your desk this afternoon."Caplan was surprisingly relaxed. I couldn't decide whether it was because of his complete trust in me, because he was rather more phlegmatic in his recent years or because he was unperturbed about the ruling political administration getting a bloody nose.

"Let me know as things develop." His phone was placed on the receiver.

* * *

Willie McRae visited the shop the following evening and was welcomed like the returning hero. Everyone seemed to know him. He was a squat figure with a crumpled suit and carried a leather briefcase. He held the position of the legal adviser to the SNP and was their Vice Chairman. I rebuked myself for not getting to know him better earlier. He  was clearly a central figure in the independence movement. He'd taken the trouble to bring three of bottles of his favourite tipple, Islay Mist and poured it generously.

Wallace was particularly impressed.

"It's a blend, you see, Manus. Not every whisky has to be a single malt. Your Mister McRae has a fine palate. This is the very nectar...the very dab!"

After a while McRae was introduced to me by Dinsmore, explaining to me that he was the only person outside the six of us who knew of the visit to Gruinard.

"Manus is the owner of this fine establishment, Willie. He was also the muscle that took the boys over to Gruinard in the rowing boat the other night."

"We are considerably in your debt, Manus. Will you have another wee Islay Mist?"

"I will, aye!"

McRae poured a generous glass.

"Tomorrow, there will be something of a stooshie in Her Majesty's drawing room, he announced." Both he and Dinsmore chuckled. "We've just informed the Unionist media that the soil they tested and had found to have been contaminated was taken not from Gruinard but from the mainland at a site as yet unannounced."

"Jesus," I exclaimed, grinning. "That'll set the cat among the pigeons. It'll mean they have to test the mainland and they'll have to try to reassure the natives who feel nauseous or who have diarrhoea that they're not about to keel over due to Government thoughtlessness in poisoning a Scottish island with anthrax and allowing the spores to travel on the wind to pollute our foodstuffs."

McRae laughed. "You're well informed about the initial symptoms of anthrax poisoning, Manus."

I grinned back. "If you'd been sitting on top of a dozen boxes of contaminated soil while you sweated your way back in a rowing boat to the mainland, the first thing you'd do would be to research the odds of surviving and what might be the signs that you may not."

McRae placed his whisky glass carefully on a nearby mantelpiece and placed his hands on each of my shoulders. He squeezed hard.

"You are a good man, Manus Canning. I'm a lawyer, so I measure people. I've heard much about you, all of it good. This book establishment of yours is a crucible. It's fundamental to the cause of Scottish independence and I'm proud that you are a subscriber to that cause. Many among us are cautious...careful. They don't want to scare the horses. I seek a stampede. Can I count on your assistance on whipping the Scottish Clydesdale stallions into a frenzy?"

Despite my natural reticence and my long-standing practice of never volunteering, never putting my head above the parapet unless it was necessary, I found myself responding emotionally to his request.

"I am yours to command, Mr. McRae," I said.

"It's Willie, Manus...Willie. We're comrades-in-arms now. Together with others of a similar bent we'll see the end of the English domination of our nation. Are we agreed?"

I summoned up Burns. "'Till the rocks melt wi' the sun!"

Dinsmore seemed impressed.

Adam Busby had been causing problems, not only for Special Branch but within the various organisations of which he was a member. Archie's source informed him that although Busby could be witty and funny, he was mercurial. He'd once turned up uninvited to a meeting of the SNLA and proclaimed himself 'Commander', (he was no stranger to strong drink) and on one occasion, in a fit of pique, took arms and explosives obtained from Ireland and dumped them in the Clyde. He was such a loose cannon that the organisation 'folded' informally and recast itself as the Scottish Citizen's Army of the Republic ensuring that he'd nothing to do with them. Our source suggested that Busby was lucky not to pay for his 'rifles in the Clyde' delinquency with a more serious sanction.

Chapter Forty-Six

CALTROPS

Despite his behaviour, Busby and fellow-traveller Dinsmore had been welcomed into Menzies' small group almost without demur. I was being tolerated, even after my heroics in rowing to and fro from Gruinard Island and having been enfolded in the welcoming arms of Willie McRae in the presence of Dinsmore. My assessment was that I was not sufficiently full-throated in my anti-English sentiments, arguing that it was Westminster that was our enemy, not the people of England. Busby, in particular, was dismissive of what he referred to as my naivety.

"Can't you see, Manus? They come up here, buy our properties, take our land and bairn our women. It's the typical colonial strategy. They ken fine they can't win Scotland unless there's a goodly number of Vichy Scots who support them from within the ranks. They well appreciate that while they have a preponderance of Unionists sapping the will of the Scottish people here at home, we'll never wake up to the potential of self-governance. They know that politicians of both main parties serve the interests of the Crown and the British State and by doing so, ensure that they themselves are personally well-rewarded for their obeisance. The ordinary people of Scotland have little to celebrate. The English control business, they control our culture, they control the political options available to Scots and they control the media. Unless and until we follow the lessons learned by our comrades in Ireland and take up arms against the body politic, we will never cut ourselves free from the straightjacket that is Sassenach domination. An armed resurrection is our only hope."

I found myself unable to criticise the thrust of his argument but counselled against actions that would see armed forces on the streets of Alloa or Ayr. "It would be playing right into their hands, David. They happen to have more tanks than us...more soldiers... more weaponry."

"Aye, well that was the case in Ireland in 1916 but these days, the boys over there are putting up a good show, eh? They're giving the British Army a bloody nose and pause for thought."

The weak point in their small group was undoubtedly Benji. He was immensely grateful to Alison and me for employing him after his self-inflicted accident and could be counted on to offer reservations and ideas offered by me, qualified by his imperfect command of the English language in private conversation when within the group.

Knowing that they styled themselves the nascent Scottish National Liberation Army, I understood the militaristic notions underpinning this and attempted to encourage more of a civil disobedience approach. Leaning on Benji's trade as a welder, I asked him innocuously one evening if it was possible to weld three steel nails together. He looked at me incredulously, realising that for once, he was on stronger ground than me.

"See, Manus. It'd be easy. These days we use a thingwy so's a slag bath is no' needed. We use electrode wires wi' gas shielding because this lets us weld thinner materials than we used tae huv tae dae wi' thon electroslag process."

I nodded my appreciation of his mastery of the welding process.

"So you could weld four inch nails?"

"Easy-peasy, Manus. A wee problem roon the hoose? Ah've still got ma welding gear."

"Not quite, Benji. I was thinking more how we could disrupt the opening of Parliament down in London. Remember Bannockburn?"

"Who disn'y?"

"Well, Bruce used a thing called caltrops to drop English horses. There were three steel pins brought together by a blacksmith so that whatever way they fell, there had to be one sharp pin pointing up. The English horses stood on them and were maimed, throwing their riders and allowing the Scots to put them to the sword."

"You want to kill horses, Manus?"

"No, Benji. I want to blow tyres. In a couple of weeks the Opening of Parliament takes place. It's a pretty important event in the calendar of the British Establishment and it's also a bit of a pain in the arse for Londoners going about their business as roads have to be closed. It occurred to me that if you could weld a lot of nails... caltrops, just like Robert the Bruce...we could drop them around the centre of London just before the roads close. They'd puncture the tyres of cars, lorries and buses and would bring the entire centre of the capital city of England to a complete halt."

Benji took a moment as the idea took form in his head.

"By the way, Manus...that's a great idea. All ah'd need wid be the nails."

My wide smile equalled that of Benji.

"I'm pretty sure that that could be arranged, Benji. Why don't you and me talk with the boys tonight and see if they've got the bottle to travel to London and drop some caltrops on some of the main roads in Londinium."

Benji eyed me.

"Wherr?"

I surrendered to Benji's poor Latin. "London, Benji. I mispronounced."

* * *

That night as Menzies conferred with his people in the back room, I was asked to join them following Benji's account of my proposition.

"It doesn't actually blow up Big Ben or the Houses of Parliament, Manus...but we've agreed it's not a bad idea."

"It's also easy to pull off, no one gets hurt but everyone gets inconvenienced. It'll make the TV and print media and, if we claim responsibility, it'd raise the matter to a political challenge to Parliament."

"Aye, it would that," agreed Menzies.

"It's two weeks away. We'd need Benji to create maybe a hundred caltrops and we head to London with holes in our pockets. We walk between vehicles stopped at traffic lights and drop a few caltrops down the inside of our trousers in front of each of the two front wheels so the vehicle is completely disabled, and step away. When the lights turn green we'd soon see a solid block of traffic. Side roads would be blocked, commuters wouldn't get to work, trains would be overwhelmed as people flocked to stations and the city would descend into chaos." I turned my gaze to Benji, building the importance of his role. "But it all depends on you, Benji. Can you supply a hundred spot-welded caltrops in, let's say, a week?"

Benji nodded enthusiastically. "If Robert the Bruce can spot-weld caltrops, so can Benji Henderson!"

Dougie Chalmers stifled a laugh.

"He didn'y actually spot-weld them, Benji."

Benji glowered at him. "Aye, well, we *will*, Cammy. See, that's progress!"

* * *

Two weeks later, six of us stepped from the early morning train at Euston Station and mingled with the horde of commuters all heading towards the exit. We'd earlier agreed to work in pairs. I was with Benji and we had been allocated the five roads leading to Trafalgar Square. Menzies and Chalmers were to deal with the tributaries of Piccadilly Circus and Busby and Dinsmore were sent to the roads around Victoria Station.

Benji saw it as a bit of a caper but I was testy and insisted he treat the matter seriously. I wanted to see the disruption but didn't want to see police intervention. Our plan was to claim responsibility when safely about to board the train - not to Scotland - but to Cardiff. We'd learned from those who'd repatriated the Stone of Destiny from Westminster Abbey that the obvious move north should be avoided.

Benji and I had thirty caltrops between us and we stood obediently in line as traffic pulled up at a red light on Whitehall indicating their intention to turn left onto Pall Mall. Allowing other pedestrians to go before us, we stepped between the second and third cars in front of a large lorry which appeared to originate from France.

So much for the Auld Alliance, I thought as I dropped a couple of caltrops in front of each stationary wheel. We crossed the road and moved on in the direction of Northumberland Avenue. Benji couldn't hide his excitement and almost walked backwards as he awaited the green light. The caltrops worked like a charm. Each wheel exploded followed by a long hissing noise as the driver applied his air brakes before investigating.

Benji was up next and we repeated the exercise in front of a painter's van with similar results. Opportunistically, I successfully dropped a couple in front of a bus going in the opposite direction thereby blocking both sides of the road.

It must have taken only some fifteen minutes for each of us to walk around the breadth of Trafalgar Square. Upon returning to our starting point we could already hear the squeal of police sirens and honking of horns as we witnessed the chaos I'd predicted. The other two sets had had equal successes and we met up in an Irish pub, the Tipperary in Fleet Street. We'd all empty pockets, the caltrops having been dropped and we laughed long as we witnessed journalists emerging from the UK centre of print media to write about the mayhem we'd visited upon the streets of London.

After we'd gathered, had compared notes and had satisfied ourselves that our initiative had produced exactly the results we'd sought, Dinsmore stood, an almost empty glass of Guinness in hand.

"With your permission, gentlemen, I'd like to phone and announce to our friends on the other side of the road that the SNLA have just brought London to a standstill. I'll also call the police as I want to give them a code word so, in future, they'll know it was us who're warning them."

The general mood of jollity...to which I subscribed...allowed no challenge. He made the call. I accompanied him to the door.

"I'm going to buy some fags."

I left and phoned Caplan from a call box round the corner, making sure I bought cigarettes to establish my alibi before I returned.

Chapter Forty-Seven

SHAKEN BUT NOT STIRRED

Georgy Nikolayevich Zarubin, Ambassador Extraordinary and Plenipotentiary of the Russian Federation to the United Kingdom of Great Britain and Northern Ireland wearily lifted a file and opened it, smoothing the first page flat to read it. As he did so, his most senior intelligence officer, Dmitri Bozov entered his office without knocking, a behaviour that riled the Ambassador but one he never challenged. Bozov was well-connected back in Russia and although Zarubin was the senior officer it was never good politics to upset those who had favourable relationships with the leadership. Bozov was troubled.

"Comrade Zarubin! We appear to have a problem."

Zarubin closed the file and placed it to one side from whence it came and gave Bozov his attention.

"Our people are telling us that officers of MI5 are following 'Wembley'. They have been seen taking photographs as he goes about his business. We have to assume he is being bugged. If he has been compromised it means that we have to treat any information he provides with extreme caution. He may well have been turned and persuaded to provide harmful intelligence."

Zarubin removed his spectacles and rubbed his eyes. It had been a long day. He shrugged.

"Comrade 'Wembley' was important when he was overseeing the naval base at Faslane. His role now is important but not quite as crucial as his previous one. Were it not for his relationship with the MI5 officer Collingham, I'd be much less interested in him."

"We are fairly sure that he is not a double agent, Comrade. We monitor him very closely ever since he provided such valued information on the nuclear base. We could take no chances. He is essentially an amateur who wants to conceal his homosexuality, seeks promotion to a level commensurate with what he sees as his abilities and who is eager to live a lifestyle that is predicated upon wealth. We have thus far seen to it that all three of his objectives have been realised."

"What is your recommendation?"

"That we interview him, assess whether he's been compromised and, if necessary, alert him to the interest of his employer. It may well be that if he has not been turned that he could still supply us with the occasional nugget of information that could be of use. If not he should be abandoned."

"I agree."

* * *

Caplan looked from his window onto the traffic on Brompton Road as Canning entered his office. He turned and greeted his guest with little more than a grunt.

"Sit!"

He took his place behind his desk but made no offer of whisky.

"Manus Canning...Manus Canning... our war hero, Manus Canning...I have thus far been so proud of what you've achieved in the time you've been in the service. Your role in Scotland, your efforts in Norway, Cairo, Havana and Berlin have been exceptional...simply exceptional. I viewed you as perhaps my most effective appointment. But now....but now..."

I interrupted his musings.

"At this point in our meetings, Sir Anthony, we're usually exchanging views on malt whiskies. Your opening comments trouble me."

"Forgive me piecing together a raft of facts that permit the merest hint of concern, Canning. Let me say from the off that I am persuaded that you will have a defence that will scupper the accusations made by other colleagues but as you'll understand, I have to address them."

I shifted uncomfortably in my seat.

"Of course!"

"We now have pretty conclusive evidence that your brother-in-law Giles Collingham is in a carnal relationship with one Angus Brodie, Under-Secretary at the Scottish Office and that the aforementioned Brodie is a Russian spy." He leaned back and lifted a bottle of Glenkinchie from a shelf. Pulling the cork top, he produced two glasses from a desk drawer and poured two large measures. "Further, I am guided that as you recently encouraged me to promote Collingham...a man we both agree is something of a dunce... from the wasteland of nowhere to the leading intelligence officer in Scotland's capital city, he is now in a most advantageous position to advise his *Russkiye* lover of the ambitions of the Scottish independence movement and that, should Russia decide to intervene in Scottish politics in order to rent asunder the unity of the United Kingdom, they would benefit considerably from his insights."

A silence reigned for some moments as I digested Caplan's comments. I regained my composure.

"Well, first of all, I am completely in the dark as to your determination of Angus Brodie as a Russian spy. I've met him twice at events in my wife's ancestral home. Shook his hand. Decided he was an uninteresting civil servant and returned to my bottle of Glenmorangie with a few well-chosen forgive-me's. He seemed to me to be a perfect partner for Collingham. Although he was introduced as merely his friend, I had little doubt as to his proclivities." I accepted Caplan's glass and took a sip. "Secondly, I perform as I do out of a sense of duty. I'd hope that my accomplishments furth of Scotland might persuade even the most dubious colleague of that. I sent Collingham to Edinburgh to a place where he does most good...dealing with other eejits like himself. I am well aware of his limitations and of his assets. He is of no use dealing with the broad sweep of nationalism in Scotland but every so often, he provides insights into the Edinburgh Establishment that is useful. In the meantime, I'm up to my elbows in mainstream nationalist politics as well as the dark underbelly that currently gives us most cause for concern." My dysphoria got the better of me. "Look, Sir Anthony, I'm an able and dedicated member of the security services. I've served where I've been asked and I believe that few in the organisation would believe I've been other than very successful in serving it. Now, that said, it must also be well known that I've a beautiful and very wealthy wife who...along with her dimwit brother...owns an estate in Scotland the size of Cornwall. I'm now of an age whereby I could easily say goodbye to all of this drama and retire to a life of bucolic ease. I'm inclined to say to those colleagues who question my loyalty to the cause, okay...I've committed no crime...you keep on working in the shadows...I'm just away to enjoy my life in Perthshire." I calmed down, but not much. "Over to you!"

Caplan had the good grace to smile.

"Manus, I love your passion. And accept without qualification your explanation of your defence." A deep swallow of whisky followed his comment. "Now, you have another mission. Our people are currently interrogating Brodie. On the face of it, he's as guilty as sin. We've managed to record conversations he's had with the most senior Russian intelligence officer in the UK, one Dmitri Bozov. You have a familial relationship with Collingham. They will want to have a conversation with you...let's not call it an interrogation. I want you to go through that process without punching anyone and after that I want you to keep a wary eye on this proposition that Russia might have an interest in Scotland breaking away from the United Kingdom." He poured himself another glass without troubling mine. "Collingham is a different matter. He's a dolt, a dupe, a traitor or all of these. Our people will certainly interrogate him within an inch of his life. Brodie will be quietly apprehended and his fate will be determined by the revelations which result from what will be a rather long-winded and uncomfortable chat, I'm afraid."

I took my first sip of whisky and regained my composure. I allowed a silence between us.

"Then I'm content, Sir Anthony. I'll speak to those you deem it worthwhile and I'll give them both barrels. But if I decide I'm working with a group of complete buffoons...yourself excluded, of course...then I'm off to Perthshire to become an artisan beekeeper or something and you and your clever colleagues can work out how to contain the increasing desire up north for Scottish independence."

We chatted further; the conversation being lighter, whereafter I took my leave and ordered a double espresso in a small Greek cafe across the road. I sat and mulled over the exchange with Caplan.

So my brother-in-law is sleeping with a Russian spy whom they have dead to rights? They are concerned at possible foreign interest in encouraging Scottish independence and worry that my posting of Collingham to Edinburgh is a convoluted way of presenting them with insights. I slowly stirred my coffee. *They'll doubtless investigate my use of agents and will realise that I've filleted all of them from key groups and tasked more that are necessary to keep an eye on CND. I'll need to work on my explanations.* Still thoughtful, I sipped absent-mindedly at the coffee until realising that it was scalding hot. I withdrew it painfully from my lips and returned to my reverie. *No hint of them worrying about my nationalism. They will worry about Alison's support for the cause vis-a-vis my role in subduing Scottish independence. Given Caplan's wife being a life-long supporter of Communism, I suspect I can fix that.*

Stirring the coffee once more in a forlorn hope of having it cool more quickly, I decided that my position was strong but shook my head at the knowledge of Collingham being bedded by a Russian agent. I'd need to give further thought to the prospect of Russian interests in my role and whether or not Collingham whether wittingly or not had revealed my undercover function. I let the coffee cool to the approximate temperature of molten magma, drank it quickly, grimacing as I did so and headed for Euston Station and Scotland.

Chapter Forty-Eight

ONE LESS BOTHERATION

That weekend, my interview with the internal spooks from the sixth floor of MI5 took a full day but wasn't unpleasant and left me feeling quite comfortable that they hadn't laid a glove on me. Indeed, at closure they were comfortable enough to reveal that they'd now obtained a full confession from Brodie and that the higher ups were now discussing how best to deal with him. Apparently, a public trial was not being recommended as it'd give the media a field day. Consideration was also being given to the future of Giles Collingham.

Given that I was already in London, much to my astonishment, I was ordered to accompany Brodie back to Scotland on the mid-day train. He wasn't to leave my sight but I was to dispatch him at Central Station where he would face further interrogation. I was given a pistol lest he attempted not to comply and was ordered to shoot him if he did so. To assist me in this venture, two burly MI5 field operatives sat apart, each a few seats away keeping an eye on things.

I confess I found it unusual that Brodie hadn't further been detained in the bowels of MI5 but thought little of it as we faced one another in the quiet first class compartment heading north. I was also aware that I'd be revealing myself as a member of the Security Services, married to the sister of his lover, Giles Collingham. It bothered me that my undercover role so deep it was almost subterranean must have been revealed to Brodie. *Caplan must know what he's doing,* I mused. But still, it bothered me.

322

I informed him of my instruction to shoot him should he even go to the bathroom without my permission. In consequence, small talk was awkward and uncomfortable at first but we eased into a decent chat once I'd reassured him that I wasn't recording our conversation. I decided to play the daft laddie.

"So what happens now, Angus?"

"Not sure. They've formally charged me with a host of offences. It's all a bit of a whirl."

"And you'll plead guilty?"

"No option, really. I've already signed a confession. They've recordings of conversations and photographic evidence. There was some talk about me working as a double agent but to be honest, I'm not cut out for all this. I was seduced by my own greed and hubris."

"And now I find myself involved personally because your lover is my brother-in-law, Giles Collingham."

"Quite...and Mr. Canning, I must assure you...and I appreciate that you have no reason to believe me, but I knew nothing of your role. My feelings towards him were real. He's a lovely man of whom I was very fond but I'm now somewhat stunned by the news that he too is an officer of the Security Services. He told me he was involved in health and safety innovations across the entire civil service. I had no reason to doubt him." He looked dolefully at his cardboard cup of coffee. "I must now take the obvious view that my affections were not being returned and that my relationship with Giles was nothing more than an instrumental one...one where he lured me into a loving embrace just so he might further his enquiries into Russian espionage."

My first reaction was that this might be a reasonable defence should Collingham pursue it but the absence of any line reporting over the period of their relationship would doubtless mark it as the fiction it was. Somehow, Brodie found a capacity for sleep. I remained awake until he resurfaced as the train approached Motherwell.

"Soon be there, Angus."

"What is to become of me in Glasgow?"

"The two men seated behind me will escort you to a place of safety. I've not been advised of any further detail. I imagine you'll find yourself interrogated quite a lot over the next wee while."

"I imagine so."

The hills around Glasgow were gradually changing colour from russet to green and a sunny day permitted the Dear Green Place ostentatiously to flaunt its wares as the train pulled in to the vast cast-iron Victorian canopy that is Central Station. Even the ubiquitous and garish graffiti on the sandstone approaches seemed to sparkle in the sunshine. I had had confidence that no handcuffs would be needed and had earlier instructed as such which permitted me to shake Brodie civilly by the hand and step back as my two silent colleagues ushered him on to the platform. I stood on the station concourse as the train emptied and watched as the three men disappeared into crowds of fellow travellers.

As I headed towards the exit and nearby Buchanan Subway station I caught a final glimpse of Brodie and his two minders entering the station entrance of Central Hotel. I may have been mistaken, but for all the world it looked like they were being greeted at the doorway by my fellow intelligence officer, Emilia Meyer!

* * *

"You must be tired after your journey, Mr. Brodie. Shall we enjoy a drink while we discuss your future?"

Brodie nervously held out his hand in greeting, a politeness ingrained in him over many years in the civil service.

"We haven't been introduced. Can I assume that you're a colleague of Mr. Canning?"

Meyer offered a brief rictus smile. "My name is Emilia Meyer. As you imagined, I am indeed a colleague of Manus Canning. He and I have worked together many times. I trust your journey north was not unpleasant."

Meyer and Brodie walked up the broad staircase to the hotel lounge, the two minders following a few steps behind them. Entering the lounge, Meyer indicated a comfortable-looking table in an alcove and bid Brodie take a seat. She joined him as her two colleagues each sat at the bar and ordered a soft drink. A waiter took Meyer's order, a gin and a somewhat mystified Brodie allowed himself his favourite whisky, a Talisker.

"Mr. Brodie, you have confessed to some very serious offences."

Brodie nodded his agreement.

"You have been questioned very intensively in London and have been sent back here to Scotland where I and others will question you more. We will have an enjoyable drink here then we will go together on a long car journey at the end of which you will be questioned further. Am I clear in my description of the next few steps?"

Brodie sipped his whisky and nodded. For the next half hour he repeated much of what he'd told London until, looking at her watch, Meyer turned and caught the attention of her two colleagues before returning to Brodie.

"We have far to travel. We will not stop. I recommend we make ourselves comfortable before we travel. My men will stand outside the door while you relieve yourself." So saying, she gathered up her bag and stood, awaiting Brodie's emptying of his whisky glass.

The group of four walked silently from the lounge along a wide carpeted corridor to where both the gents' and ladies' cloakrooms were situated.

"No more than five minutes, Mr. Brodie." She pushed at the door to the ladies' toilet as Brodie entered the gents'.

Mid-pee, Brodie heard the door behind him open but concentrated on his micturition. He let out a yelp as his right arm was grasped roughly, removing it from his member allowing his even flow to be interrupted. As he turned, confused, a long-bladed knife was thrust into his midriff. Severing his abdominal aorta, the knife was manoeuvred to ensure that it also laid open both his inferior and anterior vena cava thereby destroying his renal arteries. He died before the knife was removed from his abdomen.

Withdrawing the blade, Meyer, wiped it with a hand towel and replaced it in her bag. Stooping, she undid Brodie's belt and opened his trousers revealing his exposed member to a wider audience before removing a condom from her bag and tearing it half open. Throwing it on the ground beside the now still body, she removed the thin rubber gloves from her hands and placed them in her bag prior to rising, opening the door and joining her two companions in the corridor. She consulted her watch.

"We have ten minutes to catch our train to London."

The trio moved quietly along the deserted hallway and left the hotel.

Chapter Forty-Nine

AFTERMATH

That night I sat at home with Alison watching television. I hadn't been home for a few days and I treasured time with her, the twins who were now abed and our sleeping dog, Alba. Our phone rang. Alison answered it and not without warmth in her voice, greeted the caller before passing the phone to me.

"It's Sir Anthony."

I acknowledged him equally affably but he was all business.

"Some regrettable news I'm afraid. Our Russian spy, Angus Brodie has been found dead in the gents' toilet in Central Hotel Glasgow. He'd been stabbed. As you know he was an ostentatious homosexual and was found with an opened condom next to him. By all accounts the revenge of a spurned lover."

My face reddened. "I last saw him entering that hotel with Emilia Meyer and two others...each of whom pick up a salary from MI5."

"Indeed so. All most unfortunate. An official 'D' Notice has been issued by the British government advising the press not to publish any information about this murder beyond what I've just informed you because it would harm the country if it were to be made public.

I railed at this. "'DSMA' stands for 'Defence and Security Media Advisory'...how a murdered civil servant merits a 'D' Notice and has to do with defence and security escapes me!"

"As well it might, Manus but it does...but we face down the reality of media intrusion into an affair best left alone, we send a signal to Moscow that their customary approach of interrogating then garrotting their own traitors will at least be emulated here from time to time, it allows us quietly to rid ourselves of one Dmitri Bozov and his boss Georgy Nikolayevich Zarubin who will quietly be sent back to Mother Russia, it allows us to advise our American partners that we have cleaned up the Faslane mess and it puts the fear of God into your brother-in-law, Giles Collingham."

"Jesus...is he in any danger?"

"We are persuaded that when considering the options that he is a dolt, a dupe or a traitor, that he is probably not a traitor. We do not intend that he be removed from the service. We'd rather keep him under observation. In that regard, he remains under your stewardship but to answer your question, and I'm being honest, he is under no threat to his person. That said, he is incontrovertibly a fucking idiot!"

"I'm relieved but I warned you."

"You also promoted him."

"Into a dead-end job."

"See that that continues. And watch out for Russian interference in matters Scottish."

I replaced the phone on the receiver and turned to see Alison pallid and with a questioning look on her face. Her hand was placed over her mouth, exuding anxiety.

"What's happened?"

I sat beside her, took her hand and thought quickly.

"It's Angus Brodie. Giles' boyfriend…friend…he's been found dead. He'd been stabbed. The police are viewing it as a homosexual affair."

Alison removed her hand and replaced it over her mouth in disbelief.

"What? This is terrible. Is Giles involved? Is this woman Emilia Meyer involved?"

"No. Not at all. That was just a misunderstanding. But I'm just about to phone Giles. Might actually drive up to Perth and talk with him."

"I'll come too…"

I pursed my lips in challenge. "The twins are sleeping. I'll drive up, check his reaction and if all is well, I'll be back just after midnight. I'll keep you informed."

We agreed but before I headed north I sat for some minutes behind the wheel and considered matters. There was no doubt in my mind that Caplan had authorised Meyer, his favourite hit-woman, to rid himself of a problem. Another approach might have been to charge him, hold the case in camera and bury him deep in some secure prison never again to see the light of day. But Caplan had evidently favoured execution. I'd recently been made aware of the murder of a woman called Hilda Murrell, a rose grower from Shrewsbury who'd written a paper entitled What Price Nuclear Power? in which she challenged the economics of the civil nuclear industry. In 1982, after the Department of the Environment published a white paper on the British Government's policy on radioactive waste management. Murrell, wrote a critique of the Sizewell B Pressurised Water Reactor in Suffolk and became something of a thorn in the flesh of both the Government and of the nuclear industry. Inside the organisation there was talk of her being silenced by MI5 at the behest of Ministers. Having experienced the work of Emilia Meyer twice now I was open to that suggestion. MI5 could be deadly when it chose.

I put the car in gear and drove on.

* * *

Approaching the estate, I pulled off the A9 near Birnam, drove along the long, single-tracked road and pulled into the magnificent edifice that accommodated Giles Collingham, his butler, chef, and secretary. Twenty-eight bedrooms for a staff of three, two of whom did nothing but watch television and eat elegantly while the boss was away. Christine, his secretary, lived in the village while two groundsmen lived in estate houses some distance from the main building. *En route* I gave thought to my earlier question regarding Caplan's insouciance over my subterranean Scottish role being revealed to Brodie. He'd obviously known his fate in advance but had chosen not to tell me. He trusts me…but not that much, I mused. I could not rid myself of the thought that the British security services were quite adept at murder and mayhem should it serve the purposes of the Crown. I cautioned myself to insist that Collingham be more careful.

The front door wasn't locked and I entered, eventually finding Giles in front of a television in one of the many public rooms. Baxter, his butler flounced after me embarrassed that I'd been admitted without some fanfare.

Collingham was all hail-fellow-well-met as I entered the drawing room. I accepted the butler's offer of a glass and soon reduced Collingham's wide grin to a sob prior to Baxter's return with a whisky.

After I'd revealed most of that which had transpired, Collingham was curled in a tear-stained foetal position on his couch mouthing the words, 'why, why, why?'

I urged a brandy upon him and growled sufficiently to bring him to his senses.

"Your lover was a traitor. He was killed in the line of duty to Mother Russia. You are exposed as a fucking deluded fool for forming a relationship within which it appears that you were unaware that he was a Russian spy and he was, in turn, unaware that you were a British Intelligence Officer. You must see that this beggars belief! Presently the top brass merely think you a complete fool...not a traitor. I happen *also* to think you're a fucking eejit... but not a traitor. That could change. I am your guardian. Caplan has tasked me with your stewardship. This organisation can accommodate fools...God knows it has enough of them...but traitors will receive little quarter as Brodie found out to his cost. Going forward you will say nothing of this to Alison. You will continue your role in Edinburgh and report to me on anything of note. You will watch your back at all times and will be careful not to expose yourself to harm as I don't want your sister upset. If this has taught us anything it is that our organisation can by absolutely ruthless in disposing of problems simply by killing a threat. You will not make a move that has not been agreed with me in advance. You can forget any notions of returning to the gin palaces of London. Them's the realities...them's the futures. If you choose, you can retire with dignity and return here to your country pile and in many ways that'd be my advice...I need to know that you understand every single fucking syllable of these constraints on your behaviour. You need to know that given the sad *dénouement* of Angus Brodie, you choose here and now not to go down that road. I propose to tell your sister that you were very upset but that you take the view that life goes on...you're philosophical...Angus could be promiscuous. Am I understood?"

Collingham's staring eyes settled upon me for a long moment before his head nodded, almost imperceptibly.

"I agree everything!"

Chapter Fifty

A HOMOSEXUAL TRYST

It was now 1984 and matters had begun to settle. Brodie's death had been a one day wonder and had been attributed to a homosexual tryst gone wrong. Alison was settled, the twins were doing well in the local school and had developed a nice group of well-behaved friends who found themselves often round at our house for meals. Games in the back garden had been replaced by study groups as they prepared for their final exams prior to going on to study at university. Alba was bearing up although our walks had become much shorter and she more frequently asked to be lifted. Wallace was also slowing as he aged and spent more time in our house as we cared for him. He still insisted upon putting in a daily shift at work. I loved that man!

Red Books was as popular as ever as a meeting place and the various groups who used it were all pretty much under my eye other than Menzies' band of brothers who, whilst still very affable to my face, deliberately excluded me from many of their meetings many of which were now taking place in pubs instead of our meeting room. A year previously, I privately took steps to bug the meeting room as I didn't want any other intelligence officer to have access to conversations I'd rather be solely privy to. It wasn't used when most groups met but I'd quietly flick the switch when members of *Siol nan Gaidheal* or the Scottish National Liberation Army met in my absence. I didn't get much in the way of useful information.

We'd had to become used to an interloper when Roy Jenkins MP, formerly a Labour heavyweight, won the constituency of Hillhead for the Social Democratic Party. He loved to make the point that due to the preponderance of doctors, surgeons, students, lecturers and educationalists who inhabited the west end of the city, it was regarded as the most intelligent constituency in the UK - and by extension that it deserved to be represented by someone of his calibre. That said, he had such regard for his local Glaswegian constituents that he held his celebratory election dinner in the North British Hotel in Edinburgh. He had *gravitas*, an Oxford education, a posh English accent, was something of a gastronome, was a political heavyweight and he decided to avoid the accusation of being a carpetbagger by taking a small flat in Hillhead. He was not well regarded by those in my circle.

Unknown to me at the time, Dinsmore and Busby, with the connivance of Menzies, began to use Busby's flat to manufacture and send crude explosive devices to such as Margaret Thatcher, Home Secretary Leon Brittan and to Glasgow's Lord Provost, Michael Kelly although it had been timed to ignite in the presence of Lady Diana Spencer, then the Princess of Wales who was visiting that day. None were successful but as news appeared in the daily papers I tried my best to inveigle myself further into their confidence. Benji was always my best bet for information. He'd been schooled well enough not to provide any information but I thought I could read him like a book and was pretty certain that SNLA notions of civil disobedience were being replaced by violent opposition. My suspicions were aided by a drunken evening in the Curlers bar when I overheard Dinsmore and Busby toasting one another with the expression, "Every nite is gelignite."

Around this time I noticed a new face in their ranks and got to know a young lady from Dublin called Brigit Lynch, known to all as Bridie. I decided to check her out via Oliver Beamish and found that she was an enthusiastic member of the IRA who was known for her explosives knowledge. I was duty bound to provide this information to my superiors and was subsequently asked to keep tabs on her; MI5's concerns over Russian influence in Scottish affairs was being subordinated to Irish republicanism on the mainland. In the pub one evening she sat with a fellow Irishman who took pains to ensure that his name, identity and opinions beyond football and Dublin lodgings were not revealed. All I remembered of that encounter was the somewhat unusual characteristic that he spoke with a soft but very obvious English accent.

Only three weeks later my world changed. The Provisional IRA had attempted to assassinate Margaret Thatcher and members of her Cabinet during the Conservative Party Conference in Brighton. The IRA had correctly assumed, first that Thatcher and her entourage would reside in the Grand Hotel, Brighton's finest, and secondly that she'd be allocated a room with a sea view. Both assumptions proved accurate. A bomb with a long-delay fuse had been planted within the shell of a bathtub some weeks earlier. At the appointed hour when it was presumed that Thatcher would be abed (she was in another part of the hotel with aides working on the following day's speech) the hotel frontage was blown to smithereens. Five people were killed, including the Conservative MP and Deputy Chief Whip, Sir Anthony Berry. Thirty-one more people were injured including Thatcher's putative replacement should she ever have had the misfortune (to some) to have been hit by a bus, Norman Tebbit MP, her Secretary of State for Trade and Industry, whose wife Margaret fell four floors and was reduced to a wheelchair for the rest of her life. Thatcher escaped.

As the dust settled, a man-hunt, the like of which had never before been experienced within the UK was instigated. Weeks went by with no clues as to the perpetrator other than a statement by the IRA which read, 'Mrs. Thatcher will now realise that Britain cannot occupy our country and torture our prisoners and shoot our people in their own streets and get away with it. Today we were unlucky, but remember we only have to be lucky once. You will have to be lucky always. Give Ireland peace and there will be no more war.'

The immediate impact upon me was that a man called George Thomson, a Scot from Aberdeen, was introduced as Collingham's replacement as the face of MI5 in Scotland. Collingham was informed that I had special duties lined up for him but other than allocating him duties as a gay gigolo in an establishment frequented by effete Scottish Nationalists, I feared I'd struggle.

Thompson, who was a most affable chap, and who made a point of underscoring the esteem in which I was held by the service, nevertheless, took control of MI5 in Scotland. He reintroduced Archie McKellar to the Scottish portfolio and gave him additional duties related to Irish Republican surveillance...a role over which as an enthusiastic Loyalist, he almost slavered... he reinstated the 'inducements' made available to Scottish newspaper titles to promote the Unionist/anti-nationalist/anti-republican line (and even persuaded a couple of newspapers to hire journalists who might present as tepid supporters of Scottish Independence only to secure a guarantee that when he made the call, they'd find a reason to produce a *volte-face* and denounce the movement). I had to be impressed by his actions. Had I been an enthusiastic Unionist, I'd have made the same moves. Now I was both being flattered as to my pedigree and accomplishments within the agency whilst being comprehensively outmanoeuvred in my covert objectives. Ministry of Intelligence Section 5 was nothing if not intelligent. It was apparent that I was indeed well regarded but that in times of need, a less subtle approach was necessary.

Additional intelligence officers reported to him and in many cases I knew nothing of their role or location. Caplan reassured me that I shouldn't be troubled. He apologised for not informing me in advance, explaining that it had been decided by those at the top to beef up things in Scotland. This was a national emergency. The potential assassination of the Premier trumped all other considerations. I remained free to maintain my undercover role vis-a-vis Scottish Independence but, for the moment, the organisation needed to beef up to meet new challenges. Compounding all of this was the new relationship Thompson struck up with Special Branch in Strathclyde. They had a unit of some eighty staff on the second floor of Police Headquarters in Pitt Street in Glasgow and while Collingham had been on nodding terms with them, Thompson took it up several notches. Over the years they'd developed considerable expertise in matters to do with Ulster Loyalists who tended to use Glasgow as a safer arsenal than Belfast but were at that point less familiar with IRA activities and were almost completely blind to the Scottish National Liberation Army which sought to emulate the IRA. Thompson corrected that.

Helping him in this task was a newcomer called Chivers who'd been an Assistant Commissioner in the Met. Sent north by Metropolitan Police Commissioner Sir John Waldron, Caplan fretted rather about this appointment.

"He's a reputation for ruthlessness, spent some time in Northern Ireland and is comfortable having his people use weapons. MI5 domestically don't have easy access to guns but Special Branch do and I'd expect to see Scotland become something akin to the Wild West once Buffalo Bill Chivers rides into town."

As I engaged more with those involved with both Scottish independence and Irish reunification, one issue that was brought quietly to my attention was the covert visit of a group of senior and shadowy Scottish Independence supporters to Dublin to meet with Ruairi Ó Brádaigh, Chief of Staff of the Irish Republican Army. Their request was that the IRA avoid action on Scottish and Welsh soil as these countries were as exploited and oppressed by England as was Ireland. Ó Brádaigh not only agreed to this request but insisted that the Scottish contingent be feted and celebrated due to the past involvement of the Scottish Brigade who fought with the IRA against the British Army during the Easter Rising. Ó Brádaigh headed the delegation and visited the graves of many who died in the cause of Irish independence and who were buried along with the one and a half million people who are faithfully remembered at Glasnevin National Cemetery, Ireland's largest burial place. As a consequence of their visit, and quite unknown to the Westminster elite, was that peace had been preserved on Scottish and Welsh soil. That said, two pub bombings took place, the first in the Auld Burnt Barns in Calton and fifteen minutes later in the Clelland bar in the Gorbals, each at the hand of the Ulster Volunteer Force who argued that IRA fundraising was taking place therein. The UVF's top commander in Scotland, 'Big Bill' Campbell and eight others were convicted with Campbell being sentenced to sixteen years in prison. Underscoring the agreement reached with Ruairi Ó Brádaigh, the IRA did not retaliate.

I decided to share this information with Caplan on the basis that it might improve the attitude of MI5 towards the independence movement. I was wrong. They took the view that if they had this kind of influence it should have been used to protect England as well.

Weeks passed with no progress advised. Then Beamish called me. He wanted me to know that the suspect involved in Thatcher's attempted assassination was one Patrick Magee who was a very secretive and harboured member of the IRA who appeared to have been schooled in bomb manufacturing and, due to his early upbringing in the English Midlands, had a pronounced English accent. He was a member of what the IRA termed 'The England Department', deeply undercover operatives who might pass for innocent English persons. They were highly regarded and specially protected by the IRA. My thoughts turned immediately to the man I'd met only a few weeks earlier when introduced by Bridie Lynch. I was further nonplussed when Beamish informed me of an operation at that moment underway to apprehend him and some other members of the IRA at an address...I could hear him consulting a piece of paper he held close to the phone...at 236 Langside Road, in Glasgow, a four-storey sandstone tenement. I was stunned. I knew that area. It was Langside, a douce neighbourhood a few miles from the city centre and populated by a blended and diverse ethnic minority community, of which a certain contingent would be of Irish heritage but was comprised of generally a law-abiding working-class. The community was more known for the occasional incidences of shoplifting from its many fruit shops, sporadic argumentative neighbours and high-spirited students but not for subversives.

The man suspected of trying to assassinate Prime Minister Margaret Thatcher in Brighton lived just off Victoria Road, right under my nose.

Whilst the eyes of the agency were on Irish Republicanism and Patrick Magee, my attention turned immediately to Bridie Lynch, Dinsmore and Busby. Beamish had also advised me that huge quantities of Semtex explosive had been delivered over a lengthy period to the IRA by Muammar al-Gaddafi, the 'Brotherly Leader, Guide of the Revolution and Chairman of the Revolutionary Command Council of Libya'. British Intelligence were convinced that despite several large seizures and apprehensions, substantial quantities had been smuggled across the Irish Sea to Scotland to be used in attacks on English soil. The Brighton hotel bombing had been but the first deployment. If even a small proportion of these explosives had been obtained by Dinsmore and Busby, the impact upon the approach to Scottish independence as defined by the SNLA could be considerable. My anxieties increased when following upon the arrest of Magee, a huge arsenal of bombs and weapons were discovered by Special Branch under the flooring at 17 James Gray Street in Shawlands, another of the IRA's safe houses.

Chapter Fifty-One

THE CONFLAGRATION
AND THE FLIGHT

"**C**areful, Adam!"

"Ah'm *urr* bein' careful, David!"

It was three o'clock in the morning. David Dinsmore and Adam Busby crept soundlessly up the stairs of a quiet tenemental close-mouth in Glasgow's West End. Approaching the first floor, Dinsmore placed his forefinger to his mouth, gesturing silence. Whispering a short instruction, he gestured to Busby that he hand the container to him. Removing the cap, he poured the petroleum contents over the external mat and the bottom of the solid beech door. Satisfying himself that there was no alert evident within the close, Dinsmore waved Busby back and leaving the half-filled container in the doorway, struck a match. Instantly the threshold was enveloped in flames.

"Quick, let's get the fuck away frae here," he counselled.

Again as quietly as possible given the roar of the flames above them, Dinsmore and Busby descended and entered the deserted street. Having earlier agreed that they'd each walk as slowly and as unobtrusively as possible from the scene of the crime, it took but four strides before each man broke into a trot which became a sprint. In seconds they were beside their car and minutes later they were driving down Dumbarton Road, Dinsmore behind the wheel and Busby in a constant half-turn to check if there were any followers. There were none.

* * *

Police arrived shortly after the fire service had attended and extinguished the flames...flames which had awakened insomniac Sam Hardy who had been reading a book as a prelude to a sleep attempt and who had only hours before come off a shift as a fireman based in Springburn in Glasgow. Being a professional, he'd promptly extinguished the flames, evacuated his young family and called the emergency services. Questioned subsequently by the police, he could offer no explanation for the arson attack. He hadn't an enemy in the world. One floor up, Roy Jenkins MP slept the untroubled sleep of the just, earlier awakened only by the increasing decibel count of the blare of the fire engine's siren as it turned the corner.

* * *

Arriving in Menzies' apartment, Dinsmore and Busby were excited.

"Mission accomplished, Arnold. That door was ablaze. There's no way Jenkins could have escaped. No one followed us...we're sure of that. This is big. It'll be headlines in all tomorrow's newspapers. Roy Jenkins killed in arson attack. Scottish independence supporters say 'enough is enough'."

"Have you phoned the newspapers yet?"

"Not yet..."

"Well, my suggestion is to wait until the radio confirms his death before we claim responsibility. You two need to leave and find a bolt hole. I'll be raided any time now and you two'll be collared."

"Agreed! Just wanted to let you know. We're staying at Cammy McLaughlin' house tonight and tomorrow we've a meeting with Willie McRae. He knows nothing of tonight's escapade but we're certain he'll help us hide from the authorities."

* * *

Next morning, no newspaper mentioned the arson attack on the young family save the Daily Record whose reporter had been listening in to police radio. A two inch column sufficed.

At ten o'clock, Busby and Dinsmore arrived at lawyer McRae's office in Bath Street.

"You did what?"

"We were misinformed, Willie. We were told that Jenkins lived on the first floor but it seems he lived on the second."

"Was anyone injured on the first floor?"

Dinsmore shook his head. "Not according to the papers. The only damage was to the boy's door."

"Well, thank heavens for small mercies."

McRae sat behind a substantial desk cluttered with piles of paper. A small space had been left clear to permit him the opportunity to write. He placed his hands together as if praying and gave the matter thought.

"This sounds like an almighty mess, boys. Special Branch and MI5 will be after you. It doesn't take a genius to work out that the actual target lived above the victim. You need to disappear."

"That's what we thought, Willie. But we've no money and no idea how to disappear."

341

Further thought was given.

"Look…there's only really one solution. You need to get yourselves to the Republic of Ireland. They refuse to extradite anyone accused of political crimes to England or Scotland. I think I can get you there but once you're on Irish soil you're on your own. You'll need to explain your politics to the Irish *An Garda Síochána*. They might jail you for a few days while they work out the politics but they will release you and then you have to work out how to survive with no income. You might find comfort and support from *Sinn Fein* but it's over to you. Are you game?"

Both men nodded enthusiastically.

"Here's a tenner. Get your passports and spend the day reading in the cafe of the Mitchell Library. Do not spend it on drink unless it's coffee! Come back here at six o'clock after we close. Phone me from a call box and I'll let you in. Be ready to depart Scotland tonight."

The men left. McRae picked up the phone and booked two seats on the last flight to Dublin that evening, aware that Special Branch concluded their surveillance of Glasgow Airport at nine o'clock in the evening when their officer went off-duty. He used the names of two genuine members of the public gleaned from the phone book.

When Busby and Dinsmore arrived at the appointed hour, he contacted the airport once more and cancelled the two seats he'd booked then asked Busby to phone and rebook the two cancelled seats in his and Dinsmore's real name. The ruse worked and both men turned up with two hundred pounds given them by McRae just in time to take their seats on the busy flight to Dublin. 'We were so pleased, we forgot to pick up our duty-free', said Busby afterwards.

As they left, McRae turned from the window and sat once more on his comfortable leather chair, a desk-lamp illuminating his working surface. From his over-stuffed briefcase He removed a sheaf of papers and set them out before him. Rubbing his hand across his jaw in thought, he began to write. As he did, he allowed himself a self-congratulatory thought. *I've got them this time. I've evidence here of paedophelia within the political elite and the Scottish judiciary, further evidence that it extends to the security services via the Paedophile Information Exchange, new information about the secret proposals of the UK Atomic Energy Authority to pour untreated nuclear waste into the Pentland Firth at Dounreay.* He wrote hurriedly. *I'll finish this next weekend up in my wee but-and-ben in Dornie and when I announce it to the public, it'll likely bring down the Thatcher Government...and it won't take a bombing campaign to do it.*

Chapter Fifty-Two

THE BORDER

With Busby and Dinsmore in Ireland, my attention turned to Menzies and to Bridie Lynch each of whom had disappeared. My knock on Menzies' door went unanswered as did my phone calls. Lynch had been staying with Benji and once I'd ensured he was at work in Red Books, I visited his small flat hoping to find her. Again there was no answer but this time I determined to force an entry. My lock-picking skills hadn't been used since I worked in Berlin but after a few unsuccessful attempts, the door surrendered to my ministrations.

The flat was empty and showed signs of each small bedroom being occupied, the beds being unmade. There didn't appear to be any obvious romantic relationship between Benji and Lynch, although, knowing Benji, I couldn't imagine him in an amorous liaison. Putting on thin latex gloves, I searched the apartment pretty thoroughly using all of the techniques I'd been taught in Berlin. My first act was to ensure that no obvious attempt had been made to test whether the place had been searched but my careful observation revealed no hair or tape pressed against any door openings and I was diligent and vigilant in my movements to ensure that anything I moved was replaced exactly as I found it. I removed drawers and checked beneath them, cautiously lifted frames from the wall, checked their rear and went through the various garments Lynch had left hanging in a wardrobe. Nothing was found until I prized a skirting board from the wall in Lynch's bedroom. There I found three batons of gelignite rolled as if thick sticks of Blackpool rock; the distinctive smell of almonds identifying the explosives. Next to them was a roll of paper which

I spread before me and consulted. It was a section cut from an Ordinance Survey map and showed the Scottish and English border with an inked cross at the dual-carriageway A74 border crossing near Gretna, another at Carter Bar on the A86 and a third at the Coldstream Bridge over the River Tweed. No other information was evident. It didn't take much thought to imagine a bombing campaign using explosives to close the three main routes into Scotland from England. These three sticks of gelignite, if exploded within a vehicle filled with petrol would certainly close these arteries for a time and may or may not have caused casualties. I couldn't be sure that these three sticks were designed for that purpose or that other explosives hadn't already been placed.

As gelignite cannot explode without a detonator, I continued my search and prizing the next skirting board from the wall found three detonators and three timers. I knew the professional thing to do was to leave everything undisturbed and organise a watch on the flat to see if Lynch led us to bigger fish or an additional cache of weaponry or explosives held elsewhere. Still with only half a plan in my head, I removed the map, detonators and explosives and returned the skirting boards to the wall. My attempts at ensuring I left no trace of my being there were now thrown into utter disarray and I knew it would put Lynch on total alert but I stuffed the plastic explosives and the other devices into my jacket. Folding the map and placing it in my inside pocket, I left the flat.

Outside, I drove my car a few streets away and pulled in to a quiet cul-de-sac. I sat for some moments trying to determine my next moves. Whilst I understood completely the motivations that lay behind the Irish Republican movement, I was acutely aware that the Irish Republican Army's efforts to rid themselves of British imperialism and their determination to reunite the entire island of Ireland through bombings and shootings had, by 1984, resulted in the death of more than 2,500 people. I was determined not to allow that to happen in Scotland whilst at the same time being equally resolved in my dedication to see Scotland independent of England.

I was confident that political activity, supported by civil disobedience, education and bolstered by a more pugilistic approach would bring better dividends. Certainly, for all the woundings and deaths in Ireland and on the British mainland it was difficult to see any progress towards Irish unification through violence. I couldn't let Scotland be lured into that bloodletting. Lynch, Menzies and their fellow travellers were a problem.

Eventually, having marinated an idea in my head, I fashioned the bones of a plan and phoned Oliver Beamish.

* * *

I returned to Red Books to grab a sandwich and a coffee before heading off to Perthshire and bumped into Willie McRae who had been looking for me. Wallace had stalled him briefly, figuring I'd want to see him. He was in the back room reading a book from the shelve he'd picked up on the oil industry. When he saw me he was in hugging mode.

"Manus…it's great to see you. I was hoping to bump into you."

I returned his tight embrace. "It's always a pleasure, Willie. Is there anything I can do to help you?"

"Have we time for a wee dram across the road?"

"Alas no, Willie. I must drive up to Perthshire. Need to keep a clear head."

"Very wise, Manus. On two occasions in the recent past, Her Majesty's constabulary have decided that I've been too enthusiastic with the Islay Mist before taking the wheel. But have you a quick moment then for a wee chat?"

We repaired to the back room where Willie explained his actions regarding Busby and Dinsmore.

"I'm up to my legal neck in actions dedicated to bringing about the independence of our nation, Manus and having taken stock of our many fellow travellers, I find you unusually level-headed and equitable in these matters. I enjoy the patronage of many, the support of countless well-wishers and the abject fury of orthodox establishmentarians, but, here's the thing...both Dinsmore and Busby now languish in an Irish jail. They'll be released soon and won't be extradited to Scotland but they're living on thin air. I know that you and Alison are not short of a few bob and wondered if on this once-ever occasion you'd be prepared to siphon off a small amount of your funds to allow them to eat whilst in Dublin."

I smiled. "Happy to help, Willie but I'd rather do it quietly. How much are we talking about?"

"Could you handle maybe five hundred pounds?"

"Let's call it five hundred each. I'll have Alison forward that sum to you if you send me a bill for legal fees and you take care of the rest."

McRae leaned over and given his bulk, only managed a half-hug.

"Manus, you're a man among men! I'll make sure it's made available to them only in small regular amounts and then, only if they behave themselves. I promise I will not seek further funds from you."

I stood, shook his hand and offered a smiling farewell toast common to islanders.

"Never before you, never behind you...always beside you!"

Another tight hug. As he left he spoke of the importance of his work over the next wee while.

"I've got them this time, Manus...Thatcher's Government...I've got them this time!"

* * *

I phoned Beamish again before heading to Perthshire. On the way there I refined my plan.

Arriving at the Manor House, I headed for the drawing room where again I was followed by an excitable Baxter who, as a last gasp, managed to introduce me to Giles Collingham who appeared to be attempting the Times crossword.

"It's beyond you, Giles", I smiled.

"Manus...how delightful!" He seemed genuinely pleased to see me.

"Baxter, would you bring Mr. Canning one of our finest single malts and mix me a G&T?"

Baxter scurried away. I took a seat in one of Collingham's ancient horsehair sofas and faced him.

"Giles, I have a plan for your rehabilitation within the organisation...but you must follow my instructions to the letter. No deviation whatsoever. It all starts with you having received an anonymous phone call which you suspect was from someone in Special Branch..."

* * *

Bridie Lynch scurried to a nearby phone box and dialled a number, all the while looking over each shoulder lest she spot danger. She spoke in code.

"Seamus, the salmon you sent me has been stolen. I came back to the flat this afternoon and it was gone. Somebody's made off with it. I can't make dinner now. They took the asparagus and mushrooms as well."

The voice in the other end was devoid of emotion.

"And are you well, yourself, Mary? Any visitors recently?"

"No. It's been very quiet but someone stole the dinner."

"Your flatmate, maybe?"

"No. He's too stupid. A nice man but he's as much use as feckin' algebra!"

"Och, maybe Scotland's too rough and tumble for a fair maiden such as yourself. Why don't you come home to mammy? She'd love to see you."

"I'll do that immediately, Seamus. I have the funds. Should be home tomorrow depending on circumstances."

* * *

Collingham phoned Vincent Chivers in Strathclyde's Special Branch and established, as Beamish had informed me, that they'd finished the forensic examination of the flat at 17 James Gray Street in Shawlands. Initially suspicious of a colleague organisation renewing interest in a crime scene they'd already dealt with, Chivers was hesitant but agreed due to Collingham's artificially effusive charm that he could collect the keys that afternoon.

As suspicions between Special Branch and MI5 were always in evidence, Collingham was accompanied by a key-holding Branch officer the approximate size of a polar bear. He opened the front door and both stepped inside. After some twenty minutes of fruitless searching, Collingham could hear the officer relieve himself in the apartment's toilet. Taking his chance, he used the chisel he'd brought with him to lever four skirting boards from the wall and deposited the map, three bars of explosive, the timers and detonators on the floor beside the wall. Standing, he allowed his colleague to finish his ablutions and beckoned him from the hallway.

"Looks like my tip-off was solid. I can tell from the smell of almonds that we're looking at three bombs, gelignite Nobel 808, their timers and detonators. We should phone it in and have the bomb squad over. I want fingerprints and analysis."

The polar bear was nonplussed.

"I've been over this place a dozen times…easy a dozen times." He looked uneasy.

"You say you had a tip-off?"

"Anonymous," I lied. "Someone who obviously knew my role. Said your people weren't taking him seriously and that maybe MI5 could follow things up. Said his own investigations suggested a plan to blow three routes on the Scottish border and that the means of detonation were somewhere to be found in this flat, but hadn't been found. Looks like one of your people is frustrated! You'll probably be able to work out the informant."

Thoughtfully, the bear murmured to himself, "It'll be that bastard McPherson!"

Chapter Fifty-Three

A MONTH IN HELL!

April of 1985 was perhaps the worst month of my life. It started well. Collingham was commended for his discovery of the plot to blow up access routes to and from England and although Bridie Lynch had managed to reach Ireland and was therefore immune from prosecution, fingerprints allowed her identification. Further Special Branch enquiries saw Menzies, Benji, McLaughlin and Chalmers arrested but eventually released for want of any evidence. I met them in the absence of Menzies, gave them the mother and father of a bollocking and attempted to bring them back into the mainline fold of independence by peaceful means. Benji seemed contrite and apologetic but I couldn't be sure of the other two.

Alison phoned me when I was in the North British Hotel in Edinburgh to meet her brother where he'd taken a room. He handed me the phone saying, "It's Alison. She's upset."

I found myself frozen in grief as she told me that Wallace had had a heart attack whilst in Red Books and that it had not been possible to revive him. He'd died behind the till. Alison had been called from nearby Med Books and had witnessed his passing. Both she and I were bereft. I left for home immediately and was in something of a trance all the way to Glasgow.

Wallace had a daughter who lived in Australia. She was married and her only contact with her father in recent years had been by telephone and by an exchange of Christmas cards. Alison phoned her but she declined to travel to the northern hemisphere to see her father laid to rest. It was evident that she'd loved him and was distressed at his passing. It was just the sheer impracticality and timing of the journey. Alison assured her that we'd see him off in style.

As it happened, his funeral was a simply huge event. His two constituencies of thankful Calton neighbours and respectful nationalists and socialists turned out in number and he was sent to the great beyond in some style, funded completely by Alison who was even more loving towards him than me, were that ever possible. I loved that man. Our kids had never experienced death in the family before and were inconsolable.

After he was laid to rest in Cathcart Cemetery, we returned home to discover our wonderful dog, Alba lying on her rug, cold and stiff. She'd died that morning. This was more than we as a family could bear and we went into a period of genuine, tearful mourning that lasted weeks but grief is the price of love and it has to be paid. Compounding the felony was the death of Hugh MacDiarmid, a hugely important commentator on matters Scottish. Trying to boost the spirits of the family I nevertheless could not escape one fact. In private, I felt very low.

Just some time later as we were emerging from our grieving, I was behind the counter on a Saturday bookended by Good Friday and Easter Sunday when the radio announced the death of one Willie McRae who'd been in a car accident in a quiet Highland glen. It was announced in a matter-of-fact way that suggested that 'these things happen'. No mention of his Vice-Chairmanship of the SNP or his success in stopping the nuclear dumping of waste on the hills above Ayr. I was stunned and lifted the phone to Oliver Beamish.

"Oliver, tell me we weren't involved with this!"

I explained and he spluttered believable innocence which I trusted. Beamish was one of the good guys in my book. He appeared to know nothing of the circumstances and I had to rely on news items until a stream of people began to enter the shop telling me that they'd heard on the news that he'd been found with a bullet lodged in his brain. I could not but recall the last words he'd said to me, 'I've got them this time...the Thatcher Government...I've got them this time and recalled the words of Caplan who predicted the impact of 'Buffalo Bill Chivers'. I kept this comment to myself but thinking on my feet, phoned Alison. "Alison, have you sent that cheque for a thousand pounds to Willie McRae yet?"

"Just about to."

"Don't send it. I don't want a cheque from us lying on his desk when CID search his office for evidence of foul play. I'll try to find another way to keep my word to Willie and offer support."

Willie McRae's funeral was a private affair. I attended the ceremony at Camelon near Falkirk but kept a respectful difference. It was evident that the family sought no flowers, no politics, no hoopla. I waited until the mourners had left and visited the grave. I was appalled. One of Scotland's greatest heroes and his family tomb was to show recognition by inscribing on its side, 'Also their son William McRae'. McRae was a family afterthought.

I scanned newspapers for a couple of weeks afterwards but found few comments about the bullet. A couple of papers quoted the Procurator Fiscal from Inverness who announced a verdict of suicide on the Monday following Willie's demise on the Saturday. He'd been transferred to Aberdeen where the life-support machine had been switched off. I phoned Beamish who informed me that against all common sense, the Fiscal had announced a verdict of suicide before the gun had been found and tested.

"Were there powder burns found on his arm or clothing?"

"Wasn't tested, Manus."

"Powder burns at the site of the wound"

353

"Wasn't tested, Manus."

"Fingerprints?

"Eventually tested, but none found." He hesitated. "It does look rather odd…the four people who found him say he was wearing a tight seat belt. He was found upright and fixed in his driver's seat, his hands on his lap although the Crown insist that he wasn't wearing a seatbelt despite the car obviously having rolled down the hill towards the loch and overturned. They say his papers were left on a rock next to the car whilst he was pinned and in a coma in his seat. The police say the gun was found beneath the driver's door but I checked the individual police notes and it was only the commanding officer who stated that he *assumed* the gun had been found there as the car had been removed before the gun had been found. Individually, the attending officers' notes say variously that the gun was found behind the car, on the passenger's side and some distance from the vehicle. The police statement was that he was stinking of whisky. A half bottle of Grouse was found unbroken despite the car rolling down the hill and overturning once. When they checked his blood, there was no alcohol in it. Importantly, the police say the bullet wound was in his right temple but the nurse who discovered the entry wound and his brother who's an experienced GP, and who saw the body before turning off the life support machine, each stated that the point of entry was the nape of the neck."

"He never drank Grouse, Oliver. He only drank Islay Mist. It wasn't just Willie McRae that stinks to high heaven."

The evidence was all over the shop.

We finished the conversation as Beamish told me that Caplan was inclined to forgive Collingham his earlier follies and offer perhaps… "He said 'perhaps…Manus," more responsibility.

Beamish also told me that a local police officer had caused something of an internal stooshie (I'm paraphrasing) by insisting that he'd seen McRae leave Glasgow for his Hielan' hame and that he'd been followed by two cars belonging to Special Branch. I decided to speak with this officer. Beamish cautioned me that while he was not a drinker. Constable Donald Morrison was a man from the Western Isles as was I, a champion police wrestler and an enthusiastic bowler. I decided to fashion a meeting at his local bowling club.

After a successful competition against police opponents from GA sub-division in Newton Mearns, players changed into their street clothes and retired to the bar where Morrison, one of the players, ordered a soft drink. I shouldered my way next to him and introduced myself as a freelance journalist who was interested in what I called 'The McRae  Murder'. Morrison eyed me suspiciously and spoke in his mellifluous island accent.

"And how do I know you are who you say you are? Am I going to find myself on the front page of some newspaper saying things that'll get me fired from the polis?"

I held his gaze. "I believe that Willie McRae was murdered. I'm quietly bringing together as much evidence as I can muster. You've already made your views known internally to your police force…"

"Aye, and effectively ended my career in the process! But the truth is the truth!

"Listen, Donald…I was a friend of Willie's. His death grieved me. I'm trying to piece together information that might lead to a Fatal Accident Inquiry. I know already that there were no powder burns on his sleeve, that despite the Fiscal's nonsense, a blood test showed that there was no alcohol in his blood, despite him apparently 'stinking of whisky' from a half-empty bottle of a brand of whisky he never touched, and the gun most certainly was not found at the driver's door. I have testimony from his brother, who's a GP, to the effect that that the entry wound was in the nape of the neck not the temple as the Crown would have us believe. He was murdered, Donald and I can guarantee you anonymity if you help me. I promise you that."

I'd also been told by Beamish that as a consequence of a Western Isles upbringing in Uist, Donald Morrison was a believer. I decided to take a chance and emphasising my Western Isles accent, raised my right arm.

"*Mo làmh do Dhia*. My hand to God!"

Morrison seemed convinced. He did as all of we teuchters do when confronted with our accent and our language. We look for connections.

"Are you a Lewis man?"

"Man and boy."

That was sufficient for Morrison.

"I'm a Uist man. I watched Willie going into an off-licence in West Nile Street and noticed two men observing him. Glasgow city centre has been my beat for years. I know everyone including Willie. Willie came out of the shop with two bottles of Islay Mist and a carton of fags. He told me he was going up to his wee second home in Dornie to write up his notes and that 'he'd got them this time'…whatever that meant. He patted his heavy briefcase and repeated that he'd got them…the Thatcher Government…he'd got them this time."

"He told me that too!"

Morrison nodded his agreement. "He told a few people, Manus. Anyway, his car was on the downward slope on West Nile Street and he'd placed the whisky bottles on the roof of his Volvo as he prepared to leave. I intervened and removed the bottles saying they'd slide and fall and encouraged him to put them in the footwell of the passenger's seat. I held them until he got into the car. He was travelling north to his wee but-and-ben in Kyle of Lochalsh and in an act of typical polis kindness, I held up the traffic to allow him to do a U-turn up the hill and head north. It obviously wrong-footed these two guys who jumped into two double-manned cars and followed him, going through red lights to do so. I noted their numbers and later on it became evident that these cars belonged to Strathclyde Police Special Branch."

"You've testified to all of this?"

"And more! I was involved in a Special Branch raid in his law offices one night in which all his files were taken to Stewart Street police station and photocopied. I'd been told to stand in the wee stairwell leading down to McCormack's Music Shop where I watched them. McRae arrived at Stewart Street and went ballistic. Our explanation that we'd observed a break-in and were merely protecting his belongings was just so much keech...forgive my language...but it really was. McRae knew this." He sipped his coffee. "I've made a statement to the police which they've attacked as not being consistent with their truth. I've made a signed affidavit. I can do no more."

"Other than to help me put this to rights!"

A wide grin enveloped his face.

"Well, Manus Canning from Lewis, if anyone can, I'm sure you can!" He paused. "One more thing...when an inventory of his belongings was released, there was no mention of the two bottles of whisky. Why is this important? Because they had my fingerprints on them. It'd have confirmed my evidence and put Special Branch on the spot for his murder. Also, when the briefcase was returned to his brother, he said that there was nothing untoward inside it. Now either you believe that Willie was lying when he told several people repeatedly that he'd evidence that would bring down Thatcher's Government or you imagine that Willie had some pretty damning evidence which was removed by Special Branch to protect that same government before the briefcase was returned to his brother."

"I know what I believe, Donald."

"And I suspect that I agree with you, Manus."

Chapter Fifty-Four

A BUSY TIME FOR RED BOOKS

Donald Morrison became my firm friend and he pointed me in the direction of Iain Fraser, an ex-cop who had retired and had become a private investigator. I spoke with him and he told me that he'd been given a contract to follow McRae two days before his demise. He'd done so and had reported that his movements in Edinburgh were all to do with SNP politics and that there was nothing untoward. Fraser had cashed the cheque but had by then forgotten its originator. He only remembered that it had been someone from Newcastle.

In 1986, our shop was going great guns and the meeting room was full to standing most nights as nationalists and socialists found common cause in protesting the greed, duplicity and malevolent behaviour of capitalists using the market to further their ends and to disadvantage the working class.

The Red Books' meeting room was booked solid and was in regular uproar over this period as the millionth council house to be sold under the right to buy scheme was sold to tenants in Scotland some seven years after the scheme was launched in the United Kingdom. It was a sore point amongst the faithful even though that million house sales figure suggested a popular Tory policy amongst the electorate.

We'd a great night when Celtic and Scotland legend Jackie McNamara came along to say a few words. His father, Jackie Senior had been a member of the Communist Party, a Clyde shipyard shop steward and close friend of the shipyard leader Jimmy Reid. Jackie when younger, had sold the Soviet Weekly and the Morning Star on the street and was an articulate and humorous speaker. The line of questioning taken by our usual attendees was forgiven when many of the questions centred around goals scored from midfield.

Having been nominated as the Executor of Wallace's will, I attended the reading and was quite taken aback when I realised that while he'd been living on a soldier's pension for many years, he'd continued to do that while he'd worked in Red Books and had largely banked his librarian's salary leaving a tidy sum. He donated almost all of it to a Calton charity asking merely that they continue to do good works in the community. I was touched when the lawyer read out a paragraph in which he expressed his love for me, Alison and the twins and while noting that they'd want for little in their young lives, nevertheless made over one hundred pounds to each of them for use the first time they wanted to do something reckless that their parents frowned on. I loved that man. I loved the way he pronounced 'whisky' as 'whusky', the way he wore his Tam O'Shanter bunnet, as ever pulled down over his right ear..I sometimes wondered if he slept that way. I loved his wit and his wisdom. I loved his friendship. I loved that man.

In 1986 while I was beavering away trying to find out more about the McRae murder, events began to overtake me. Arguably Scotland's most prestigious firm, 'Distillers' which majored in alcoholic products as the name might suggest, had run into difficulties and had been bought by well-known Establishment rogue, Earnest Saunders, a reprobate fraudster nicknamed for good reason, 'Deadly Earnest', who promised as a formal and binding element of the deal that the company base would not be moved from Edinburgh. To pacify investors who knew of his reputation, he proposed as Chairman, Sir Thomas Risk, the Governor of the Bank of Scotland, a hugely respected individual. Key institutional investors were brought round and were persuaded that Saunders could be trusted. Once the ink was dry on the contract, Saunders moved the company headquarters to London, disposed of Sir Thomas as Chairman, took the position himself and closed the Johnnie Walker plant in Kilmarnock to outrage across the political spectrum. Even Edinburgh Tory Secretary of State for Foreign, Commonwealth and Development Affairs, Malcolm Rifkind mouthed tepid criticism in an attempt not to fall out with his champion of capitalism, Margaret Thatcher. Our Red Books people were motivated as never before and following protests, much celebration took place a wee while later when Saunders was charged with conspiracy to defraud, false accounting and theft and served ten months of a five years' sentence. The Johnnie Walker plant was never reopened and Kilmarnock continued its downward social and economic spiral. Not that this troubled the ruling Conservative Party. During this period I began to see the benefits of my brother-in-law, Giles. He was perfectly placed to acquire information from the Establishment and I was able on a few occasions to brief journalists anonymously on the duplicity of Guinness and of the strength of feeling among the left and the nationalist communities. Giles was delighted at my complements and was particularly elated at my encouragement to spend more time in London in furtherance of his duties.

Following a mighty controversy when Glaswegian Duncan Campbell presented a series of six commissioned programmes to the BBC called 'The Secret Society', MI5 crawled over it as one of the series provided information on a top-secret GCHQ spy satellite system called Zircon which was able to intercept signals not only from the USSR but from friendly western nations as well. Campbell, a noted academic and journalist was also a member of the Labour Party's National Executive Committee. He spoke to a well-attended meeting in Red Books and shortly thereafter I was called to London by Caplan who was at his most sociable. The whisky flowed as it had done in the past and he told me he'd been 'instructed' to interview me by the 'top of tree' encouraged by an ex-MI5 Intelligence Officer called Daphne Park. She knew of my association with Campbell, and as a consequence of her role as a Board Member of the BBC and used her previous contacts when it suited her. I had the complete sense that Caplan had little time for her so I only shared information that was available in newspapers.

Caplan was completely satisfied and leaned into the prospective General Election.

"What's your take, Manus?"

"The SNP are plateauing at the moment with a vote share of around 14%. Somewhat disingenuously I suggested that Caplan's own initiatives might have played a role in keeping their gas at a peep. I went on…

"The Tories look like they'll win big in England but I predict that they'll do poorly up north. Scotland hasn't voted for a Tory majority since 1955 back in the days when Rosa Parks, was arrested for refusing to yield her bus seat to a white man. That's how long ago it's been since Tories were popular in Scotland and it'll be the same again this time round, I'd expect Labour will win heavily in Scotland but lose in England."

"And no Nationalist threat?"

"Not at this election. Mind you, if you look at long-term data, you can see that the notion of Independence is edging ever upwards. Not spectacular, and attitudes ebb and flow, but left to its own devices the movement could easily gain momentum. Also, *Siol nan Gaidheal* have some more wind in their sails. They've said they've denounced the behaviour of Dinsmore and Busby but I hae ma doots."

"Pardon?"

"Have my doubts!"

He grinned. "Is that your way of suggesting that you continue in your role, Mr. Canning?"

I grinned as he topped up our glasses.

"And what of these Irish bombers in Scotland? Collingham did well."

"He did. He's subsequently been doing some work for me in London so he's a happy bunny."

"Getting along with our George Thomson?"

"He's an Aberdonian so his accent is almost impenetrable. Seems a decent enough cove. He doesn't interfere with my work and Collingham still reports to me as Establishment Liaison in Scotland. Thomson's getting on with Chivers in Special Branch and has revolutionised our relationship with them. Good appointment," I lied.

"Chivers, as you know, is up from the Met to look after Special Branch. Appointed to keep the Jocks in place by making sure London knows everything that's going on. As I've said, a bit of a bruiser."

Haven't met him but I know that's his reputation. I did wonder if he'd been involved in the shooting of Willie McRae."

"Suicide, I gather but if it *was* a hit by Special Branch, you can bet your bottom dollar that Chivers would be pulling all the strings." He pursed his lips, calculating the essence of our conversation, "So you are happy in your current role? You don't hanker after the bright lights of Berlin or Prague?"

"I am and I don't, Sir Anthony."

"Then we are agreed. Keep looking after Scotland. There's a General Election in the wind and this will show whether we are on the right track.

Chapter Fifty-Five

SHINY BOB

In 1987 Thatcher won the general election, her third with a landslide majority, trouncing Labour leader Neil Kinnock's Labour Party. However, in Scotland there was a seven per cent swing against her. The SNP gained one seat on a swing to them of two percent, still leaving them still with only fourteen percent of the Scottish vote. Unemployment in places like Cumnock and Doon Valley were at critical levels...some thirty-one percent of adults there were on the dole. Opinion polls showed that there was an increasing appetite for some form of assembly in Scotland to deal with domestic matters, including tax raising powers...even a majority of Tory voters supported this but when Thatcher came north she unequivocally denied the prospect of any form of devolution, 'No one ever asks me about this other than members of the media', she proclaimed, underscoring this by insisting, 'Scotland is part of the United Kingdom and wishes to remain so!'.

In furtherance of her tin-ear attitude to Scotland, she not only ignored the much poorer performance of the Scottish economy but had her government pass a bill proposing the abolition of domestic rates in Scotland and replacing it by the 'Community Charge', instantly and popularly referred to as the 'Poll Tax'.

The Red Books meeting room was in constant uproar as meeting after meeting, speaker after speaker insisted the tax would be unfair as it levied tax on houses rather than people... a flat-rate per capita tax that saw every adult pay a fixed rate amount set by their local authority and was based on the number of occupants living in a house, rather than on the estimated market value of the house. It meant that a Laird in his castle paid the same as his servant. Speakers argued for a mass campaign of non-payment of the poll tax. Tommy Sheridan of the Militant Tendency picked up the cudgel and chaired the All Britain Anti-Poll Tax Federation. Leader writers began to state openly that Thatcher should beware of 'unintended consequences' that might usher in the break-up of the United Kingdom.

Caplan had me visit his office more regularly during this period. A member of the Scottish National Liberation Army, one Andrew McIntosh was arrested and charged with 'furthering the aims of the SNLA by criminal means to coerce the government to set up a separate government in Scotland'. He was sentenced to twelve years, prompting the SNLA to issue a statement promising to escalate their efforts and calling for a campaign to free Andy McIntosh. I was able to rise above these controversies by advising Caplan that not only was it seen as a massively unfair tax on the poor, but that the decision to introduce the tax in Scotland one full year before England and Wales caused Scotland to be referred to as Thatcher's guinea pig and brought the 'spectre' of Scottish Independence much closer. MI5, I suggested, was pretty powerless when a Government was so out of touch with popular opinion. Caplan could only reach for the whisky bottle and agree.

"However, my dear boy, your job is to ensure that whatever policies are enacted, Scotland remains part of this United Kingdom."

For a long moment, the only sound in the room was of my breathing. I searched for *les mots justes*.

"Goes without saying, Sir Anthony!"

I was becoming a practised liar!

But did I convince him? I asked myself

***

I'd been speaking with a number of Willie's friends about his death and one or two had suggested I speak with a young student from the islands who'd been Willie's driver when not studying. His name was Donnie Blair and I caught up with him in the Students' Union. He was clearly set out for a glittering career (he ended up a world expert on Scotch whisky and all manner of alcoholic beverages working for monolithic global enterprises) and over a glass he expounded his theory of Willie's demise.

"I drove Willie all over Scotland. He stood in both of the 1974 and 1979 General Elections as the SNP candidate for Ross and Cromarty. In the October vote in seventy-four he only lost to the Tory, Hamish Gray by 633 votes. By God, what an impact he'd have made in Parliament had he won! He was a simply *brilliant* orator," he said, putting the emphasis on his adjective.

"He used to write, then practice his speeches in the car when we were heading to a hustings. His eyes would be staring straight ahead and he'd be not saying...but acting out the speech in the car. Every so often, cautiously, I'd offer an adjustment. He always took it in good humour and sometimes he'd agree the amendment but mostly he'd plough on, sure of his message."

I asked Donnie if he thought Willie's shooting was because of his impassioned belief in Scottish Independence.

"Maybe partly...but remember, SNP polling at that time was hovering around the fourteen per cent mark. It might have raised the eyebrows of some political academics but it wouldn't particularly have troubled Thatcher. His work in skewering the Atomic Energy mob would have made him a serious pain in the arse to the Establishment but of all the issues he was dealing with, it was the evidence he'd accumulated that put the Scottish judicial system and the Westminster political elite under threat...and that cooked his goose. Of that I'm certain. He was genuinely offended by the information he possessed on the sinful and degenerate behaviour of Edinburgh and Westminster sexual abusers of young children"

"And can you share this evidence?"

"Not in a way that'd convince a jury. I found it remarkable that he'd announce to several people that he'd evidence that would bring down Thatcher's government...and when I heard this, I assumed it was his evidence on paedophelia in the higher reaches of the Scottish and Westminster Establishments...but when his briefcase was returned, his brother Fergie said there was nothing other than some legal papers. I had to assume that the stuff he had on the pederasts in the Scottish judiciary and these toe-rags in London had been removed by Special Branch...they just had to be."

We had another couple of drinks as Donnie spoke more about Willie and the esteem in which he held him. I left determined to find out more about his comments about the missing papers. It wasn't difficult to uncover the troubling gist of his remarks.

I phoned Beamish.

* * *

That evening I suggested to Alison that we travel to the estate and dine with her brother, Giles. She was delighted to visit her sibling and, for the first time we agreed to leave our two teenage sons in charge of the house without Wallace as guardian. I warned them within an inch of their lives that there was to be no funny business, that we were putting them on honour and that we expected everything to be as we left it once we returned the following day. We'd both discussed our first departure knowing in our hearts that they'd have friends round, both male and female, once we'd turned the corner. They were both capable cooks and were guaranteed a square meal the following day in the school dinner hall they insisted on referring to as 'the dinshie'. So we were content they wouldn't starve and Alison became somewhat phlegmatic when discussing leaving them on their own. However, as we drove north, my mind was less on my anticipated conversation with my fellow intelligence officer and more on the mayhem that might descend upon the Canning household.

Our chat was edgier than normal but we pulled into the driveway of the estate acknowledging the fact that our twin sons were growing up, they were intelligent and socially responsible so we could expect nothing other than them keeping their word and our house not being reduced to ashes. At least that was Alison's view.

Baxter was at the main door of the Manor House and we allowed him to undertake his duties without demur. He took us through to the lounge where Giles was apparently enjoying one of several gins and tonic. He rose and greeted us graciously. It was obvious that he was genuinely fond of his sister as she was of him. After a whisky poured me by Baxter we withdrew to the dining room where again Baxter had excelled himself. The food was delicious and after we'd eaten, Alison excused herself as I'd asked her to do, leaving Giles and I alone with the whisky decanter.

"Well, Manus, I'm delighted you both visited me here but I assume there's some business you intend to conduct?"

"Exactly that, Giles. But it's a bit off-piste...and I'm afraid the main advantage you bring to the table is your sexual proclivities."

Collingham smiled. "I'm sure I haven't a clue about what you're talking."

"You're homosexual...and I have no problem with that, but we have a serious situation I'm keen to explore and it involves two aspects of society with which you're familiar...the homosexual community and the Edinburgh Establishment."

"Fair enough."

"For this mission you report to me and me alone! I don't care if Caplan or Thomson have one hand on your bollocks with a blowtorch in their other hand. You speak only to me. Are we okay with that?"

Collingham placed his glass with some precision upon the table. "Look, Manus, we're related...I genuinely respect you, you're the husband of my dear sister, professionally you're my superior and you rescued me from near fatal obscurity following the sad demise of my dear friend Angus. I owe you and I'm not completely without honour. If you ask me to perform a task, as long as it doesn't involve outrageous illegality...it doesn't involve outrageous illegality, does it?"

I smiled and shook my head. "No."

"Then I will do everything you ask of me...From the rumours I've already heard in the shadows, might I take it that you're taking an interest in Shiny Bob, one Bob Henderson QC?"

"I don't know anything yet about Shiny Bob but it might just involve being slightly underhand with our friends in Special Branch."

"No problem, Manus. How might I help?"

Chapter Fifty-Six

GOVAN

The following day we returned to Glasgow and inspected the house. It was immaculate. The boys had invited round two pals and they'd watched television and had consumed nothing but soft drinks. There was no apparent evidence that they were being untruthful. Ashamedly…I checked! Part of me was relieved and part of me wondered whether they were going to grow into adulthood without kicking over the traces. Then I remembered my own upbringing…a long walk to school, dedicated study, another long walk home, household chores, reading by an open fire, then bed. I hadn't exactly been a juvenile delinquent.

Back at Red Books, Beamish phoned.

"Looks like a bit of a can of worms, Manus. There are stories… rumours mostly…that there exists a group of senior lawyers, judges, police officers and politicians based in Edinburgh who behave appallingly towards young boys. They are being referred to as the 'Untouchables'. Others refer to them as comprising 'The Magic Circle'."

"Thanks, Oliver. Is there evidence that might see charges being brought?"

"My source suggests that the main character in this frankly outrageous tale, if it holds up, is a Scottish Queen's Counsel called Robert Henderson. He's known to the fraternity both as 'Magic Bob' and 'Shiny Bob'. His reputation is one of being a very successful QC but also of having a very dark interest in pederasty.

The rumour is that he holds a dossier on others in the fraternity... all these senior people...judges, cops, politicians, who protect one another so it's hardly surprising that nothing has broken the surface as yet. Any allegations that have emerged have seemed to have vanished from the justice system. Can I ask your interest in this matter?"

I'd anticipated the question and so as not to raise further issues about the death of Willie McRae, offered the best reason I could come up with.

"My concern is that if the Edinburgh Establishment comes into bad repute it could undermine confidence in the Crown and might be a godsend to those who seek to break away from England, particularly if any politicians are involved, they'll either be Labour or Tory, I'd imagine. The SNP politicians haven't been in office long enough to behave badly. Doubtless their day will come but in the meantime it's yet a further reason to vote for the Nationalists." I hesitated. "I've not yet approached Sir Anthony and won't do until I have more of a handle on matters. Perhaps you'd be good enough to keep this to yourself. I'll keep you up to speed."

"Can do, Manus. Unless he asks me a direct question."

"Couldn't ask more, Oliver. I'm in your debt."

I returned the phone to its receiver and, after a moment's thought, lifted it again and called Collingham. He seemed quite excited to have been allocated what I clearly viewed as an important task.

"I've made a few subtle enquiries and I'm going along to 'The Chaps Club' in Edinburgh tonight with a friend who's in the dark about my purpose. I've heard about it, of course but have never attended. It's a private club for those of my proclivities and I'd assumed it was something of a sleazy dive but I'm reliably informed that it's attended by many holding office such as you've described to me. The windows are all blacked out and apparently there's a bouncer on the door who asks if you're aware of the nature of the club. If you pass his test you're allowed in. D'you know, Manus, you must understand that there's a thriving homosexual scene in Edinburgh. Although this in itself is legal, sex, as you know, between or with men aged under twenty-one is illegal. In consequence, given the teenage appetite of many of my peers, the spectre of blackmail hangs over many of them...and frankly if they hold high office, it would ruin them professionally so you can see why it operates in the shadows."

"So you're on the case?"

"Indeed! I'm frankly intensely concerned that there might exist in the homosexual community, those who would prey on young children...and one of the people I've arranged to bump into this evening is Sir Nicolas Fairbairn MP. As you'll know, he has a reputation as a notorious adulterer, who has clocked up two wives and scores of mistresses. He was forced to resign as Thatcher's Solicitor General for Scotland in 1982, following a scandal stemming from his decision not to press charges against a group of men accused of attacking a Glasgow prostitute with razor blades during a gang rape."

"He's not homosexual, surely? He's married to some aristocrat is he not?"

"Many gay and bisexual men are supposedly happily married. He has a reputation within the community of being firmly in the closet but is promiscuously bisexual, a bit dubious in his choice of bedfellows and is a raging alcoholic. I intend to bump into him this evening. I'll call when I know more."

My mind was racing. If this was the information Willie McRae intended forcing into the daylight, little wonder the Establishment wanted it kept quiet. But would they stoop to murder...and if so, if

I were to be the custodian of the same information, might not I be in the crosshairs of the security services?

* * *

Back at Red Books the mood was optimistic. District council elections had put the SNP vote at twenty per cent - up six per cent just at a time when Labour MP Bruce Milan was appointed as a European Commissioner by Neil Kinnock, leaving the Govan Parliamentary Constituency vacant. In the previous year's general election, Labour won a record victory in Scotland, returning fifty MPs. Millan took more than five times the vote of his nearest challenger in Govan. Scottish Nationalists finished a distant fourth. It was considered an unlosable seat by psephologists.

The SNP selected Jim Sillars, a formidable politician whilst the incumbent Labour Party nominated the hapless Bob Gillespie (whose son, also called Bobby, would go on to greater acclaim as the lead singer of the rock band, Primal Scream). The energy put into winning the seat for the Nationalists was considerable while Gillespie was denied much opportunity to speak for himself, his two 'minders', ex-brain surgeon, Sam Galbraith MP and Michael Martin MP (who would become Speaker of the House of Commons and who would thereafter be referred to dismissively by a generation of Tory MPs as 'Gorbals Mick') answering all questions on his behalf.

At the same time, *Siol nan Gaidheal* was increasing its membership and was even establishing a woman's section. Alison had taken up the slack in Red Books following the sad demise of Wallace and had done so enthusiastically, leaving her staff to run the pharmacy and Med Books. She was heavily involved in Tommy Sheridan's *'Can't Pay; Won't Pay'* Campaign against the Poll Tax and was as often in Govan as she was in the West End. She and I had become, to a small coterie of West End Nationalists, almost beloved - to the extent of Archie McKellar congratulating me once again on how completely believable was my cover. I accepted his compliment, still undecided if he was subtly expressing his suspicion that I was too good to be true. He'd refer to Alison in my presence as the Scottish Countess Constance Markievicz, the moneyed Irish politician, revolutionary, nationalist, suffragist and socialist deeply involved in the Easter Rising of 1916. I never rose to the bait as he characterised her quite accurately and she'd earlier won the hearts of her fellow nationalists just as had the Countess back in the day.

It took until the eve of Jim Sillar's victory in Govan with a huge 36.9% swing that saw him win with 48.8% of the vote to Gillespie's 36.9% before Collingham came back to me with the information I was looking for. We met, at his request, in Glasgow's Central Hotel somewhat removed from the high-spirited victory celebrations taking place at Red Books. Alison had made sure that there would be an eloquent sufficiency of the hard stuff and part of me wished I was there but I was more focused upon the missing documents from Willie McRae's briefcase and what they might have revealed to an unsuspecting electorate.

Collingham was excited...as much as by his new-found role as a competent intelligence officer as by the *entrée* his homosexuality gave him to a new and open world of fellow-travellers.

"Think I'm getting somewhere, Manus. It's quite evident to me that the existence of the 'Untouchables' is real and is perverting the course of justice in Edinburgh. From what I can gather...and as yet I have no proof...there are indeed many judges, QCs, police officers and politicians who are either homosexual and  having sex with underage rent boys, having sex with small children - raping them...or are involved with incest. The man at the middle of the web seems to be Robert Henderson. He's a wonderfully eloquent and successful Queen's Counsel...well named in my view. He has a terrible reputation...all gossip among the *habitués* of the Chaps Club but everything's hush-hush as it's also rumoured that he has a dossier on all of the...what you would call, the 'High

Heid Yins'...the judges, police officers, politicians, etcetera. As a consequence no one will speak out against him. Frankly, he's depraved if only a tenth of what is said is true."

We talked more, Collingham left to return he told me, to the Chaps' Club (worryingly I did wonder if I hadn't sparked a somewhat unwholesome interest in their goings-on by my brother-in-law) and called Beamish who had also been active.

"Robert Henderson is one of a golden generation of lawyers who studied law at Glasgow University including Donald Dewar, Menzies Campbell, John Smith and Lord Derry Irvine...all senior politicians. He's of Orcadian extraction and is reputedly so gifted in court that other lawyers will attend to hear the master at work. Apparently, he has a compelling fluency of speech and is a charismatic court performer of the highest calibre."

"Aye, but is he a pederast?"

"At the moment, the jury's out, if you'll pardon the expression, but there are many fingers pointing in his direction. One theory is that 'Shiny Bob' as he's known for some reason, or Henderson, seeks to give the impression that he possesses incriminating information on others. It's presumed to be a calculated move as an insurance policy against charges relating to any serious irregularities in his private life which, should they ever be levelled against him, would ensure that they are dropped lest the entire Edinburgh pederastic ring be indicted."

"Really? Can there be any truth in the rumour that this is likely to be some kind of Establishment paedophile ring?"

"Look, Manus, in these Thatcherite times, Scotland is effectively being run by a small handful of Tories. *Per capita,* most of your judges hail from a minuscule number of private schools, live within a few hundred yards of each other in Edinburgh's New Town and socialise together. They are each of them older, white and men. Fairbairn and Henderson not only move in the same circles, but tried to enter parliament at the same time. In 1974, the year Fairbairn was elected MP for Kinross and Western Perthshire, Henderson was the unsuccessful Tory candidate for Inverness-shire. Apparently, he likes to boast about his voracious sexual appetite, albeit with women over the legal age limit and lists his hobbies as "making love, ends meet and people laugh."

We finished the call and I returned to Red Books where Jim Sillars and his wife Margo MacDonald made a brief appearance to great acclaim. I drank more than was sensible and had no memory of being escorted home that night by Alison.

Chapter Fifty-Seven

THE MAGIC CIRCLE

As Collingham amassed more and more information about the behaviours of judges and senior lawyers protecting those who carried out their harrowing depravities on young children, his attitude became more fixed that something had to be done to bring these miscreants to justice. He was personally horrified that those who might in other ways be his social contemporaries could act in such a debauched and dissolute way. Essentially, he was unearthing the foothills of a scandal that suggested that there was a collection of secretly homosexual judges and lawyers who were arranging that prosecutions against those in their licentious circle of peers would be made to disappear. I was ever more convinced that these were the people responsible for ending Willie McRae's life!

He caught a break when Colin Tucker, a homosexual lawyer was charged with embezzlement and gave his lawyers a list of powerful men within the legal establishment who were also homosexual. He was a junior partner in the legal firm Burnett Walker, and had been accused of embezzling thousands of pounds of clients' money. He was defended both by Robert Henderson QC and John Watt QC - each suspected at that time of being homosexual members of the Magic Circle.

Using senior police contacts he decided he could trust, Collingham discovered that Henderson, having persuaded Tucker to write a statement in his defence admitting to diverting client money, also asked that he compose a fulsome account of the nature of the blackmail he insisted was alleged. Taking possession of this list of homosexuals, many of whom were on the bench, Henderson used the document to protect himself from these self-same accusations.

Despite his open admission of guilt and as a consequence of being represented with great aplomb by Magic Circle members Watt and Henderson, Tucker was cleared by the judge. His ruling was evidently perverse given Tucker's confession and rumours continued to grow apace. As a result of the existence of Henderson's list and having been advised by his friend the Lord Justice General, Lord Hope,  that a newspaper intended publishing a story that Judge Lord Dervaird 'had used a certain house for certain purposes', Dervaird understood the code and resigned from the Court of Session following an enigmatic admission to having being 'indiscreet'. This prompted inquiries by Crown investigators who, in a remarkable case of the judiciary marking its own homework, found *no evidence whatsoever* that a 'so-called magic circle' of judges, sheriffs and advocates was conspiring to ensure that homosexual criminals were given soft-touch treatment by the courts. Talk of senior judges in the magic circle being blackmailed by 'rent boys' was dismissed by the investigators as fanciful and claims of corruption and collusion in the judiciary rejected as the ravings of conspiracy theorists.

Collingham wouldn't be deterred. At a social meeting he'd arranged with others, he 'chanced' upon invited guest, Lothian and Borders Chief Constable Sir William Sutherland whom, over two subsequent dinners he persuaded to open an investigation. His promptings coincided with Sutherland's shared frustrations being experienced by his police officers that cases they'd viewed as 'open and shut' were not producing convictions and so Sutherland appointed respected senior detective, Detective Inspector Roger Orr, who after an investigation, concluded there *was* evidence to support claims that justice was being seriously subverted by "a well-established circle of homosexuals", including judges, sheriffs and lawyers. Significantly, the report named names.

I was by now certain that Willie McRae had been murdered due to his intention to reveal these details, promised myself to leave no stone unturned to ensure that these individuals be brought to justice and was quietly certain that Collingham's new appetite for detective work would bear fruit.

One evening, Alison and I sat in front of the fire, each holding a glass of red wine, chatting amiably about the kids who were each beginning to consider university. Our phone rang and Alison handed it to me after a few minutes of social chit-chat with her brother Giles.

Given the evident lack of urgency evinced by Alison, I expected a similar conversation. Giles was all business.

"You know that the report commissioned by Bill Sutherland...the one written by Roger Orr and was for the Chief Constable's eyes only..."

"Aye?"

"Well, it was held under lock and key in the Police HQ in Fettes."

"Aye?"

"Well, last night someone broke into the building and with what was an obvious attempt to divert blame, scrawled Animal Liberation graffiti on the walls..."

"And no one stopped them?"

"No one!"

"Jesus!"

"They stole a range of deeply confidential police files...and one *huge* folder assembled by Roger Orr which contained all the evidence of the existence of a Magic Circle in Edinburgh."

"Jesus Christ!"

"Well, as you'd imagine, the forces of law and order are going ballistic. I'm told it has reached the desk of Prime Minister John Major who is equally incandescent."

"But the Orr Report was the basis for the potential collapse of public faith in the Scottish judicial system!" I left my other thoughts unspoken but it validated everything Willie McRae had argued with Donnie Blair... "And now, like the very magic ascribed to the Magic Circle, it's all disappeared?"

"I've spoken to one of Major's Special Advisers..."

"D'you know, Giles, I am constantly astonished at your ability to use your collection of right-wing contacts to a good end."

"Not so solid with your lefty friends, Manus! I'm more comfortable when the cocktails are potent and the napkins are as stiff as a card. Anyway, Major is in a purple rage. He's talking about the appointment of an independent judge to investigate what's going on."

"Well, I hope he's Norwegian or Canadian or something. We can't have the people who are accused of this calumny investigating themselves."

Well, it took a couple of years, but Lord William Nimmo Smith, a former Senator of the College of Justice, who was a Judge of the Supreme Court of Scotland and who sat on the High Court of Judiciary, was appointed by John Major to conduct 'an investigation into allegations of corruption amongst a so-called *Magic Circle* in the Scottish justice system, comprising homosexual members of the judiciary, legal profession and police. The allegations included liability to blackmail and giving preferential treatment, including unusually lenient sentences, to homosexual criminals.'

His Lordship's *Report on an Inquiry into an Allegation of a Conspiracy to Pervert the Course of Justice in Scotland* was presented to the House of Lords in 1993 by Lord Earlsferry, not only found no evidence of the existence of such a *Magic Circle*, but strongly criticised some police officers, who it said had treated rumours as fact or had been motivated by homophobia.

Hard on the heels of this verdict came the news that the Fettesgate thief was a criminal and police informant called Derek Donaldson, who subsequently fed stories from his stolen haul of police files to national newspaper journalists. Controversially and belatedly, Donaldson was assured immunity from prosecution in return for handing back the files.

Though Lord Nimmo Smith found *no* evidence of any such conspiracy, he was scathing about Henderson's behaviour, criticising the way he passed on Tucker's statement to a wider audience and had deliberately fuelled gossip. As a result, Henderson was fined £10,000 by the Law Faculty's disciplinary tribunal…but not prosecuted by the judiciary for rape, incest or sexual molestation. Controversially, the report also dismissed the young people involved – many of whom were children in care – as 'rent boys' and said they were not being abused because they were receiving payment!

In another contemporary trial against ten people in Edinburgh, fifty-seven charges were made and stories began to emerge suggesting that one of the witnesses, a young boy under the age of eighteen, would point to the trial judge as being actively complicit in the offences committed against him. The judge was removed quietly from the case and was replaced by Lord Clyde. At a preliminary pre-trial hearing all but ten charges were dropped, plea deals were accepted, five were allowed to walk free and others had pleas of 'not guilty' accepted by the Crown. In consequence, none of the evidence laid against the accused ever saw the light of day.

I was depressed by the somewhat sub-optimal ability of the judicial profession to assess criminality within its own ranks and spent a considerable number of evenings drinking a melancholy whisky and contemplating the ability of my country to rid itself of the elite Unionist Establishment which ruled us from London... and Edinburgh.

However, to set the records straight, and I know I'm getting a wee bit ahead of myself but just to tidy things up, a few years later, Henderson's daughter, Susie took out an injunction claiming she was sexually abused "from an early age" by her father, the late Robert Henderson QC. His legal partner, John Watt was one of many friends he allowed to abuse her, she claimed. She also waived her anonymity to shed light on the harrowing case, saying of her father, 'He would come home drunk and say, 'I'm taking Susie for a nap'.' Susie explained that aged from around seven or eight, she'd be taken to 'parties' to be abused by her father's friends and fellow lawyers. One day, he took her to John Watt's home in Leith and was told her to do as she was told. She told the court, 'Then he raped me.'

Subsequently, Watt was extradited from America, charged and was sentenced to ten years in prison. In addition, Susie Henderson told the court of how the then deceased Conservative MP Sir Nicholas Fairbairn first abused her at one of her father's parties at his Edinburgh home. She said: 'We were in the kitchen. I was maybe four years old, I could have been younger. Miss Henderson also claimed she suffered years of sexual assaults by her late father, prominent Scottish QC Robert Henderson, who was a friend of the MP. 'I had a skirt on and Nicholas and my dad had been drinking, and my dad told me to sit on Nicholas's knee. I sat on his knee and he put his hand up my skirt and abused me. My dad just stood there laughing. 'Recalling another incident, Miss Henderson claimed Sir Nicholas raped her when she was in bed with him and 'another guy' in a guest room on the top floor of her five-storey family home. She says she was aged just four or five years old at the time, and remembers the pungent smell of his feet. Sobbing, she said she was not sure how many times Sir Nicholas abused her but says it was 'a lot,' adding: 'Even once is too much.'

Over a brandy that evening, I mulled the significance of what had gone on and reflected on the points of view expressed so eloquently by Robert Johnston Hutchison in many of our Red Books meetings about how those who owned land and who had become the Establishment were just the offspring of successful murderers, thieves and fraudsters. *How had it come to this?* Now the Scottish judiciary - the self-same elite, were being accused of being a law unto themselves. Willie McRae was murdered by Special Branch in a futile attempt to have this politically criminal and iniquitous information concealed from the Scottish public... of that I was certain.

Chapter Fifty-Eight

SALMOND

Alexander Elliot Anderson Salmond, known to all as Alex, had deposed the outgoing leader of the SNP, Gordon Wilson in 1990, defeating Margaret Ewing in a subsequent election by winning seventy-two percent of the vote. He seemed to me like he'd be a far more aggressive  proposition. Articulate, witty and a highly intelligent economist, he seemed like someone who might shake things up and began the conversion of the party from a somewhat effete, rural and conservative (with a small 'c') party, to one which was left-of-centre and social democratic. I was impressed with him and reported so to Caplan.

Around the same time, Labour MP for Dunfermline West, Dick Douglas also defected to the SNP, citing his dissatisfaction with the way Labour had handled the Poll Tax, boosting the nationalist's number in Westminster to five. Still not earth-shattering but our people in Red Books took it as a very promising sign. This was underscored not by an increase in votes for Westminster but in the return of two SNP Members of the European Parliament, Winnie Ewing and Allan McCartney. They also came very close to winning the Monklands seat caused by the premature death of Labour Leader John Smith, generally regarded as the 'best Prime Minister we never had'. Salmond also introduced the slogan 'Independence in Europe'. The party was now polling some twenty-four percent - up from fourteen percent, they won overall control of three unitary authorities and Labour's new leader, urged on by

John Smith's friends and political allies, Gordon Brown and Donald Dewar, began to speak of the need for some kind of Scottish Assembly in order to 'head the Nationalists off at the pass'. Caplan asked me down to London, concerned at this increased popularity.

I was by now quite comfortable challenging Caplan up to the point of being just south of insubordination. It appeared that he respected my forthrightness and each of us spoke directly but often warmly to one another. He was aware, as was I, that I was sufficiently well-off to resign at any point but he seemed quite blind to my concern that any departure from my role would only see someone take office who would completely undermine much of what I'd worked for since I opened Red Books. In consequence, I never gave him reason to question my continuance in the role of Scotland's main undercover intelligence officer - but I did warn him that the rise in Scottish nationalism over the years was probably inexorable.

"The Scottish people...many of them...are on the outskirts of hope."

"Then we'd better come up with some ingenious and, if necessary, underhand measures that makes it less so, eh?"

* * *

As the *zeitgeist* in Scotland began to shift gradually towards greater degrees of devolution and independence, *Siol nan Gaidheal* began to scrutinise policy papers and articles brought forward by the Labour Party more thoroughly than the Zapruder footage of the Kennedy assassination. Their decision was that the ingrained Unionist Labour Party couldn't be trusted and that they had to organise to meet the challenge of a first step towards independence in whatever emerged. This saw an increase of meetings and of many new faces gathering in Red Books. Menzies was to the fore as both Dinsmore and Busby, members of the Scottish National

Liberation Army, at that point were still at large. Dinsmore handed himself into police in Rio de Janeiro after ten years on the run and when extradited and having shown contrition, was given the relatively lenient sentence of two hundred and forty hours community service. Hardly the sentence imposed upon a previous Scottish freedom fighter, William Wallace who'd been hung drawn and quartered.

The remnants of the Scottish National Liberation Army had gone underground but was still sending the occasional letter bomb and was vandalising and painting graffiti on the homes of 'English Colonialists' who'd had the effrontery to own second homes in Scotland. Perhaps their most dangerous device was called '*Icarus*' and was a parcel designed to ignite while the postal plane from Ireland to Scotland was in flight. Although Busby, in Dublin, had been free from extradition for over ten years, the Irish *Garda Siochána,* living up to their name as 'Guardians of the Peace', had had enough and arrested him. Ironically for someone who saw himself as a Scottish Ernesto 'Che' Guevara, his original crime was stealing cheese and ham from Dunnes store in Dublin. Further investigations allowed more serious charges and in 1997 he was sentenced to two years in an Irish jail on terrorism convictions.

Donald Anderson of the Scottish Socialist and Republican Movement was not persuaded that Busby was other than a British Government plant. At a meeting in Red Books one evening over a whisky, he told me, "I canny say if Busby was a Branch plant but he's certainly been responsible for an enormous amount of damage to the broader cause of Scottish Nationalism. He has been very, very useful to the British State in their quest to keep the Union intact."

Anderson was certainly very critical of the letter bombs allegedly being sent by such as Busby as he argued that they were more likely to injure or kill an innocent secretary than a key military target. He much favoured disruption of pipelines, rail lines and other disruptive measures. In this regard, he and I were as one in our concerns.

Certainly Busby had managed to remain at liberty for ten years while all of his associates in the SNLA had been arrested. It would have made sense for a central terrorist target to have been allowed to remain at large in order to surveil them and any others who came into his orbit. That was pretty standard practice for both MI5 and Special Branch.

Scottish MP George Robertson spared no effort in his attempts to link the SNLA with the SNP. Alex Salmond called this a 'cheap political smear' prompting Robertson to increase his attacks. SNP chief Executive Michael Russell spat back that, 'Democracy is very precious and democratic parties should be making common cause against extremists instead of making cheap political points against a party which has never endorsed racism. The SNP have always expelled people if they had any connection with extremist anti-English groups." Robertson merely argued that the SNP 'propaganda' inspired many naive individuals on their political fringes to take up arms. I thought immediately of Benji who had cooled his jets somewhat but was still inspired to mischief. That said, since he'd nearly blown off his foot and joined us in Red Books, he'd subsequently pretty well remained aloof from behaviours which might have seen him arrested.

The early to mid-nineties were turbulent years for the SNLA and the fact that many of their members had been arrested and jailed for their membership was not entirely due to their incompetency but entirely due to the fact that my colleague, Archie McKellar had his agents successfully infiltrate the organisation which was subsequently wide open to his decisions about who, when, and where to arrest participants. I thought immediately of the IRA, whose organising structure was to establish small, tightly-knit cells of between four and six volunteers under a central leadership, precisely to inhibit infiltration.

Donald Anderson, now a much respected activist within the socialist, republican and Scottish independence movements, was followed everywhere as he was so well connected. Not only was he being followed by Special Branch, he had to keep his wits about him when out and about due to recurring threats he'd receive from Ulster and Scottish Loyalists who didn't take kindly to his views. As well as all of the upright, legal political entities which many members were part of, there was the very undercover Scottish Republican Army which, due to operating in small cells, Archie had had no success in infiltrating. Donald knew everyone but was very selective in discussing anything to do with the movement.

As the decade moved past its mid-point, frustrations grew as those who opposed any relaxation in London's dominion held fast. Many on the left agreed with Margaret Thatcher that her most successful achievement had been Tony Blair's Labour Party however, in 1997, Donald Dewar steered the newly elected Labour Party to advance a Scottish Devolution Referendum. It was designed as a pre-legislative referendum for Scots to decide whether there was support for the creation of a Scottish Parliament with tax-varying powers.

Red Books was alight with optimism and fast became the base for political activity north of the Clyde in Glasgow. A frustrated Archie McKellar was inclined to show his true political colours now and again and once or twice I had to caution him and remind him that we were undercover Intelligence Officers not politicians. Every Scottish political party other than the Conservatives supported the proposals so it was perhaps unsurprising that on the day, electors in every single local authority voted 'Yes' to the proposal for a Scottish Parliament and all but Dumfries and Galloway Council and Orkney Council voted for tax-varying powers. Overall, a shade under 75% of Scottish electors voted for a Parliament and 63% voted positively for its powers. Worryingly, reports emerged that Dewar was finding it difficult to require the Whitehall civil service to fully deploy the powers that Parliament had granted but eventually, the bulk of powers were transferred to Edinburgh.,

We were ecstatic and the devolved Parliament convened for the first time in May 1999, following a first election which was fought poorly by Scottish Tories which had rubbished the idea of the body in the first place. Labour won 56 first-past-the-post seats, the SNP won 35 and the Tories won none, thereby having them secure all of their 18 seats via a list system devised to ensure proportional representation - although *Siol nan Gaidheal* insisted this was a device merely to ensure that the SNP could never have a parliamentary majority.

Chapter Fifty-Nine

THROUGH A GLASS DARKLY

A few days of unbridled joy saw many of us in one or more of our local pubs from early afternoon until closing time. Food was for wimps. There was a core of amateur dipsomaniacs who lasted the pace while others popped in and out dependent upon their other duties, their other halves, or their capacity for strong drink. Donald Anderson matched Wallace in his taste for whisky, eschewing all brands other than those owned by Scots. He was particularly against those whiskies owned by Pernod, the French company until I witnessed him later in the evening throwing back a glass of Chivas Regal. Whisky tends to dilute one's principles and sensibilities!

I fancied myself as one of the stronger runners. Alison forgave me and handled both shop and domestic duties with a heart that was as glad as mine but which was less giddy with elation and rather less enthusiastic about some of the tawdry pubs we inhabited which fortunately had less spit and more sawdust on the floor…at least when we came in. Some members of Glasgow's Cleansing Department who played in the Council pipe band which sported the Hunting McRae tartan (and which was referred to immediately as Clan Midden) turned up and regaled us with their presence. Benji perhaps summed it up best when he declared drunkenly, "Manus, it's like Glasgow Ferr Friday when it actually *isn'y* Glasgow Ferr Friday!"

It took me a few days to recover my composure. I met for a *post-mortem* with Archie McKellar who was evidently disgruntled and somewhat displeased with the result of the referendum. He and

I had had many chats about the political direction being taken by the Labour Party in pursuing the notion of a Scottish Assembly. I, of course, nodded along to his various denunciations and agreed his assessment that this could only be a bad thing for the unity of the United Kingdom.

"I have friends in Ulster who believe there'll be blood on the streets if ever the Nationalists use this as a platform to pursue independence. First, Scotland becoming independent, then *Sinn Fein* pursuing a United Ireland...that's everyone's great fear."

"Well, Archie, maybe not *everyone*...and that's kind of their *raison d'etre!*" I smiled, hoping to convey both general agreement and mild challenge.

"If it's not the bloody Commies, Lefties or wet Liberals, it's the bloody Nationalists. One way or another it seems that there's a bloody conspiracy to bring this country to its knees. Mark my words, Manus, there'll be a bloody revolution. You and I didn't fight a bloody war so ungodly and unscrupulous ne'er-do-wells could run the asylum."

The conversation continued in this vein. I figured Archie would calm down but he didn't so I found an excuse and returned to Red Books where I took a call from Caplan.

After pleasantries, "How quickly can you come up to London?"

"I've mentioned before, Sir Anthony, it's *down* to London...and if I catch the overnight train I can make it for nine tomorrow morning. That suit?"

"It'll have to." He seemed irascible. "Nine o'clock!"

* * *

As ever, the Caledonian Sleeper lulled me to sleep and I awoke refreshed in Euston. A quick electric shave in a less than spotless

Euston Station bathroom nevertheless had me feeling more civilised as I caught a black cab to the law offices of Brainchild and Carruthers at the junction of Brompton Road and Thurloe Place.

"You may sit," was the rather peremptory greeting from Caplan as I was ushered into his office. He took a moment to compose himself before continuing.

"You and I are both retiring!"

"Come again?" I asked, surprised at his statement.

"You and I are both retiring. And lest there be any doubt, we are each *being* retired!"

I attempted a measure of *sangfroid*. Over the years I'd tried to master the ability to establish a measure of self-possessed imperturbability when placed under pressure and this seemed an appropriate approach in these circumstances. I disguised my feelings by opening my packet of Capstan Full Strengths and withdrawing one. I searched for a comment.

"Well, we're both now of an age when there might be considerable advantages in taking our feet off the accelerator. I suppose I'm a bit surprised at its immediacy and don't quite understand the reasoning behind it."

Caplan seemed to unwind slightly.

"Even for me, it's a bit early for a drink". He seemed to be speaking to himself. "Look, Canning, I confess that ever since you darkened my door all those years ago, you've grown in my esteem and I've come to regard you as one of my favourite and most effective Intelligence Officers. The work you did in Berlin, Cuba, Egypt and Norway was textbook stuff. We still use your experience in securing the defection of Arkady Nikolayevich

Shevchenko as a key element in our training manual. But more than that I enjoyed your presence. You're a man's man. You understand the importance of a civilised single malt and you can be direct when speaking truth to power...not that I ever had much in the way of power within this bloody organisation." He hesitated. "Bugger this! I'm having a whisky. Will you join me in a Glenfiddich?"

"Bit early, as you say...but a Western Islander would deem it amiss to have you drink alone. I'll just have a wee snifter."

Each of us sipped at our whisky. Caplan had ignored my request for a small drop and had equalled his own measure. My timid sip was somewhat eclipsed by Caplan subsequently downing his entire measure in one endeavour.

"It will come as no comfort to you but you are to be retired without the benefit of the pension you have worked so hard to earn during your time with the organisation."

My self-possessed imperturbability deserted me. "Jesus, I really must have upset someone. What on earth has brought this about?"

"I'm afraid that for the past two years, your friend and colleague Archie McKellar has had a listening device placed in your home, one at the till in Red Books and another in its meeting room. Our analysts have had something of a field day. They have established discussions between many of the groupings that were almost treasonable and certainly should have been reported. When they compared your reports to the *transcripts* we recorded, it seemed evident that you had soft-peddled or simply avoided mentioning anything of note. You intervened quite unnecessarily in the circumstances surrounding the Bench in Edinburgh and took a lively interest in the suicide of that chap McRae. None of this was reported to London, At home, the conversations with your wife suggested that you both held very dearly to the vision of Scottish Self-determination and..."

"But my wife knows nothing of my role. She merely knows that I serve as an Intelligence Officer."

"Perhaps...but she must either believe that we have placed you there to encourage Scottish Independence or to thwart it. She's an educated woman. She will well understand that you would hardly have been tasked with ushering in independence so you must have been sent to stop it and to report on its condition. During the two years of surveillance, in private conversation, not *one* word of criticism fell from her lips. Never did she hint at a disagreement with your methods. Our analysts decided that there was, in their view and on the balance of probabilities, compelling circumstantial evidence that you were actually and personally completely supportive of the independence cause and reached the ineluctable conclusion that you were actively working against the Crown."

Another whisky was poured. I placed my hand over my glass.

"When you took office in Scotland, the independence movement was in the doldrums. Since then, even allowing for the ups and downs of politics, there has been a steady overall rise in the popularity of Scottish Independence and now we see the introduction of a new Scottish Assembly, which I am certain they will soon announce should be referred to as a Scottish Parliament. The public vote in these matters saw a 74% win for the principle of a Scottish Assembly and a further 63% agreeing that it should have tax-raising powers. Further, because its members will be elected by proportional representation, it almost guarantees a preponderance of nationalists and socialists in the new chamber."

Caplan's second whisky disappeared in one swallow.

"In addition, it was observed by McKellar that you had undone his work with compliant newspaper editors, removed funding he'd put in place and that you had redeployed all of his agents into a CND grouping where they easily outnumbered the fucking *members!* Only *you* had access to the multifarious groupings which would see harm befall the United Kingdom and in consequence was the sole arbiter of what information was to be relayed to London. For God's sake man, if we'd sent you to Scotland to make sure that Scottish Independence was rendered inevitable, you couldn't have done a better job!"

"You'll understand, Sir Anthony that I refute each and every allegation you've just made."

"Of course you do. And our superiors knew you would. In consequence, there can be no likelihood of this case appearing before a judge *in camera* never mind in open court. Because you do not work for a foreign power and we have no hard evidence, we have nothing that would convict you. We also happen to believe that *politically*, were you to be arraigned you would merely become something of a national hero and that this would only serve both to further the cause of Scottish Independence and to advertise the fact that MI5 has been active in attempting to intervene in an entirely legal Scottish democratic process, so our only option is to send you packing which we now do. I am to suffer a similar fate for not keeping a closer eye on your efforts."

"And can this decision be appealed?"

His lips pulled into a tight, grim line, the corners turned down in a hint of a snarl.

"This is MI5, Canning, not fucking *Woolworths*. If you're out, you're out...and you're *out*!

"Well..." I reached for words. "I don't even have a desk to clear."

Caplan stood.

"I must say I very much regret that it has come to this, Canning. I've enjoyed our chats."

We shook hands and I left.

395

A clear blue sky suggested that it was going to be a warm, hazy day in London and I decided to walk the few miles back to Euston Station, slowly threading my way through the hordes of pedestrians heading for a humid desk somewhere.

As I walked through Kensington I mulled over my situation. Caplan had been accurate in all he'd said. Scotland had won the right to its first elected parliament since May 1st, 1707 and the SNP were bullish. But I was now an aging man with greying hair, a beautiful wife and two clever and sociable sons, each now preparing to study medicine at Glasgow University. I enjoyed good health, had no financial problems and had cultivated a circle of true friends within the movement. Those relationships could now continue and I could express my views openly and sincerely. I decided I should be grateful and that my one regret was that Caplan had not been able to see out his remaining days with the organisation without something of a cloud over his head.

As I crossed Wilton Place, I looked into the drapers' window across the road and, as had become second nature since commencing my tuition in espionage under Horst Janson in Berlin, I looked not at the goods in the window but at my reflection in the glass lest I was being followed.

There, a few steps behind me, slightly older but immediately recognisable, and with a burly man at each shoulder, quite unmistakably, was Emilia Meyer.

My blood ran cold.

Ah! I thought.

NOTES

1. Frederick Boothby was a founder of the 1320 Club in 1967, not 1960 as portrayed in the narrative.
2. 'The Doublet' was opened in 1962 not 1960 as portrayed in the narrative.
3. Matt Lygate and MacLean's sister, Nan Milton founded the John MacLean Society and Lygate established the Workers Party of Scotland in 1967 not 1960.
4. Convicted of bank robbery in 1972, Matt Lygate served the longest ever sentence in Scottish legal history for robbery despite not committing bodily harm, serving 11 years of a 24-year sentence in HM Prison Edinburgh..not 1964 in Barlinnie.
5. The ship, M.V. Atlantic City was not launched until 1967, not 1964. Renamed Orient Coral it was broken up in Dalian, China in 1985, lasting only some twenty-one years.
6. Sir Iain Maxwell Stewart wasn't knighted until 1968.
7. In the Glasgow Pollok constituency, eight months *before – not after* the Hamilton by election, the SNP took nearly 30% of the vote in a seat Labour lost to the Tories. It was a harbinger of Hamilton, not a consequence of it.
8. Earnest.E. Clutterbuck, Wallace Lennox, Archie McKellar, Alison Collingham, Cammy McLaughlin, Manus Canning and others were all real people but lived lives far removed from those portrayed in this book. All now sadly deceased, I hope they won't protest their new fictitious role in life as presented in these pages.
9. Whilst the financial support by government of Unionist-supporting Scottish newspapers is a matter of record, the suggestion that personal financial inducements were made to editors is, for legal reasons, a complete fiction.
10. The small village of Faslane was sparsely populated until a naval base was constructed during World War Two although

Garelochhead was already a thriving village served by Clyde Steamers and a railway station. During the 1960s, the UK Government began negotiating the Polaris Sales Agreement with the United States regarding the purchase of a Polaris Missile system to fire British-built nuclear weapons from five specially constructed submarines. Faslane was chosen to host these vessels because of its geographic position on the relatively secluded but deep and easily navigable Gare Loch and Firth of Clyde on the west coast of Scotland.

11. Donald Anderson didn't establish The Scottish Republican Socialist Clubs until 1973. At the time of writing, in 2024, both they and he still go strong! Also, Donald Anderson is a simply wonderful man. Scotland could do with more of his stamp.

12. Matt Lygate wasn't released from prison until 1983 and so couldn't have spoken at Red Books.

13. Arkady Nikolayevich Shevchenko attended a meeting in the headquarters of the United Nations in New York in 1978 when he slipped out and defected to the USA, not as described in the narrative. His wife, Leongina was immediately summoned back to Moscow from New York where she died, allegedly of suicide, two months later.

14. Glasgow anarchist, Stuart Christie from Partick attempted the assassination of Spain's General Franco and faced the death penalty. He was sentenced to 20-years in prison but was eventually released after less than four years, only to find himself in prison several years later in Britain after being accused of being a member of the Angry Brigade, a group responsible for a series of explosions in London in the early 1970s. He was acquitted and went on to become a leading writer and publisher of anarchist literature. He died from cancer in 2020.

15. Colonel General Vitaly Vasilyevich Margelov served as a Soviet spy in Western Europe but was not involved in a prisoner exchange deal.

16. Frode Berg was a 24-year veteran of the Office of the Norwegian Border Commissioner, responsible for enforcing

and monitoring bilateral compliance with the Soviet/ Norwegian Border Agreement of 1949. Berg retired from the Office in 2014. He was not involved in prisoner exchanges.

17. Harry Selby, a veteran activist in Glasgow and a former Trotskyist did not become a candidate for the Labour Party until 1973.

18. Before his Usher Hall concert, Paul Robeson visited a pit just outside Edinburgh and both dined and sang with the miners.

19. The planning application to Kyle and Carrick District Council by the UKAEA to test drill on Mullwharchar for the purpose of dumping nuclear waste was not made until January 1978. On 24 October 1978, the Council rejected the application after considerable local protest, which included a petition with 100,000 signatures being sent to the Queen. Willie McRae was the leading light of the opposition.

20. The Scottish National Liberation Army was formed in December 1980.

21. The Dark Harvest Commandos - a proto-SNLA grouping - acquired Anthrax from the mainland near the Scottish island of Gruinard in 1981, and dumped it at Porton Down biological research station and at Blackpool where the ruling Conservative party conference was being held. They subsequently claimed it had been taken from an undisclosed site on the Scottish mainland.

22. Sir Alec Douglas Home was elected for the constituency of Kinross and West Perthshire in 1963.

23. Celtic became the first British Team to win the European Cup (using only local players, all born within a few miles from the stadium, let it be said) in 1967.

24. Thatcher's Right-to-Buy legislation was introduced in 1980, not 1981 as stated.

25. On 12 October 1984, the Provisional Irish Republican Army attempted to assassinate members of the British government at the Grand Hotel in Brighton, England. A long-delay time bomb was planted in the hotel by Patrick Magee before Prime Minister Margaret Thatcher and her cabinet arrived for the Conservative Party conference. Thatcher survived.

26. Witness statements from some involved testify to the role played by senior Scottish Nationalists in persuading the IRA not to carry out operations on Scottish or Welsh soil. Instead it was suggested that Scotland could be better used as an armoury and for finance (as it was by both Irish Republicans and Unionists).

27. The IRA's England Department was headquartered at 17 James Gray Street in Shawlands, Glasgow. It was used to store explosives and weapons and in another of the IRA's safe houses round the corner at 236 Langside Road, Brighton bomber Patrick Magee lived before and after the event. Bridie Lynch is a fictional character.

28. The SNLA campaign of disruption, letter bombs and arson began officially on March 1st 1982, the third anniversary of the referendum on Devolution, not in 1984.

29. David Dinsmore was arrested and charged with SNLA activities in May 1983. Adam Busby and David Dinsmore absconded to Ireland in September of that year to avoid prosecution for conspiracy. Extradition to the UK was refused by the Irish Government. While out on bail in Ireland, Dinsmore escaped to Spain and then to Brazil.

30. The Paedophile Information Exchange, a British pro-paedophile activist group, that campaigned for the abolition of the age of consent, included several Members of Parliament, members of the judiciary and Sir Peter Hayman, the Head of MI6. In 1984, evidence emerged that the Paedophile Information Exchange had received grants totalling £70,000 from the Home Office. In 1984, in his capacity as Home Secretary, Leon Brittan MP was handed a forty page dossier by Geoffrey Dickens MP which detailed alleged paedophile activity in the 1980s, including, according to Dickens, allegations concerning 'people in positions of power, influence and responsibility'. The whereabouts of the dossier is currently unknown. It was alleged that Brittan himself was one of those named. This was refuted by Brittan's wife, Diana Clemetson.

31. Distillers PLC was bought illegally by Guinness and Saunders was jailed for his part in the takeover. In 1997 Guinness

merged in turn with Grand Metropolitan which formed a new brand called 'Diageo'. It was this conglomerate that closed the Johnnie Walker plant in Kilmarnock - and in 1997, not 1986.

32. The Community Charge (or poll tax) was introduced into Scotland in April 1989, and in England and Wales one year later. Although replaced by council tax in 1993, the unique Scottish collection system meant that community charge arrears were still being collected up to 18 years later.

33. Thatcher was guest of honour at the 1988 Scottish Cup final between Celtic and Dundee Utd when the entirety of those attending showed her red cards and chanted against her and the poll tax.

34. The Scottish Government has determined that previous inquiries in 2007 and 2009 explored institutional abuse, addressed the particular challenges faced by the care system in Scotland and delivered major improvements. But no heads rolled.

35. John Watt QC, a criminal defence lawyer based in Edinburgh, preyed on three young girls and a boy over a 14-year period. In 2019, the 72-year-old was extradited from the United States to stand trial at whose conclusion, Judge Lord Braid told Watt he (Watt) had committed 'vile' crimes of the 'utmost seriousness and depravity' and sentenced him to ten years imprisonment.

36. Whilst the key details of members of The Magic Circle are accurate, the incidents referred to took place over a longer period than is set out in the narrative and have been truncated in the interests of the narrative. Indeed, the Edinburgh Establishment dined out on the behaviour of their colleagues for over a decade. Giles Collingham is a fictional character.

37. Dick Douglas defected to the SNP in 1992, two years after Alex Salmond was elected leader.

38. Margaret Thatcher didn't make her Tony Blair comment until twelve years after she left office, in 2002. left office, saying, "We forced our opponents to change their minds." Tony Blair himself seemed to agree, saying, "She was immensely kind and generous to me when I was Prime Minister... Politicly, certain

reforms she made, for example in Trade Union Law, we kept the basic legal framework. We didn't renationalise many of state industries that she privatised. I always thought my job was to build on some of the things she had done rather than reverse them."

39. In 2002, the BBC uncovered that Lord Joe Gormley, previously President of the National Union of Mineworkers, had worked for Special Branch by passing on information on extremism within his own mineworkers' union. A former Special Branch officer made this allegation and said that Gormley was a patriot and was very wary and worried about the growth of militancy within his own union. The BBC also claimed that Special Branch was talking to more than twenty senior trades union leaders during the early 1970s.

40. Number 22 Park Circus was Glasgow's Registry Office from1994. After the Second World War, it was used as a regional Italian consulate before being used for weddings. It would have been being used as a consulate at the time period described in this book.

41. The 'Caltrops' story is fiction.

42. The attempted assassination of Roy Jenkins MP in his west end flat is true.

43. The material allegations against those involved in Edinburgh's 'Magic Circle have, in the main, been proved to be true.

44. The Ulster Volunteer Force detonated explosive devices in the two pubs in 1979 as described. The investigation which saw 'Big Bill' Campbell imprisoned along with eight others wiped out the UVF's Scotland cell.

45. The author interviewed a member of the SNLA who was part of the delegation to Ireland whose task was to persuade Ruairi Ó Brádaigh, Chief of Staff of the Irish Republican Army not to engage in acts of violence in Scotland. The reporting of these events in the book are accurate. Later in the 'Troubles', hard men in the IRA attempted to persuade Martin McGuinness to allow attacks to take place on Scottish soil but McGuinness held fast to Ruairi Ó Brádaigh's ruling.

46. MI5 maintained a file on Harold Wilson under the name of Henry Worthington. It repeatedly investigated him over the course of several decades, before officially concluding that Wilson had had no relationship with the KGB. Nor did it ever find evidence of Soviet penetration of the Labour Party. A well documented coup to remove Wilson and have him replaced by a Government of National Unity, was instigated by Cecil King, the head of the International Publishing Corporation and involving Lord Mountbatten of Burma - then Prince Charles' great uncle and mentor. The meeting took place on 8 May 1968. Attending were Mountbatten, King, Hugh Cudlipp, Chairman of the Mirror Group, and Sir Solly Zuckerman, the Chief Scientific Adviser to the British government.

47. A Government inquiry by Sir John Mitting in July 2023 reported that 139 undercover police officers had infiltrated more than one thousand left-wing groups over four decades and that the spying was unjustified. However, the inquiry only covered England and Wales. Presumably there were no such infractions in Scotland, although there is incontrovertible evidence of the Scottish CND being infiltrated as well as trades unions, left-wing organisations, teachers' bodies and even that bastion of revolutionary fervour, the Scottish Young Liberals.

48. Despite the rather dramatic ending to my tale, as is now somewhat self-evident, Emilia Meyer did not kill me. I was merely asked to return to Caplan's office and hand in my ID. I was able to go back to my family and live the life I'd anticipated when compulsorily retired by MI5. *Alba gu bràth!*

SOURCES

1. *Granny Made Me An Anarchist:* Stuart Christie
2. *Yours Sincerely for Scotland:* Wendy Wood
3. *Scotland Arise:* Duncan Ferguson
4. *Patriot Broadsheets:* Wendy Wood (courtesy of Iain. S. Johnston)
5. *Sgian Dubh Broadsheet:* Frederick Boothby (courtesy of Iain.S.Johnston)
6. *The Last Scottish Rebel.* Donald Anderson
7. *The Bootlace Saga.* George Cuthbert
8. *The Break-up of Britain.* Tom Nairn
9. *When the Clyde Ran Red:* Maggie Craig
10. *The So Called Evictions:* Patrick Cooper
11. *The Trial of the Berners Rioters 1874:* Donald MacCormick
12. *The Defence of the Realm.* Christopher Andrew
13. *Scotland and the Easter Rising.* Kirsty Lusk *et al*
14. *The Dirty War.* Martin Dillon
15. *The Broken Journey.* Kenneth Roy
16. *The Invisible Spirit: Post-War Scotland 1945–75.* Kenneth Roy
17. *Acid Attack.* Russell Findlay
18. *A Case Study of the Scottish National Liberation Army.* Lara van Dijken.
19. *Scotland – Nation or Desert.* Oliver Brown
20. *A Short History of the Scottish National Party.* Hamish McQueen
21. *Labour in Scotland.* W.H. Marwick
22. *Homage to Catalonia.* George Orwell
23. *Thatcher's Spy.* Willie Carlin
24. *The Poor Had No Lawyers.* Andy Wightman
25. *Killing Thatcher.* Rory Carroll
26. *Firebrand.* Ron Culley

27. *Stone of Destiny.* Ian Hamilton
28. *Hamish Henderson.* Timothy Neat
29. *Our Duty in this Crisis.* James Connolly
30. *The Infiltrator and the Movement.* Connor Woodman
31. *Thatcher's Spy.* Willie Carlin

www.ingramcontent.com/pod-product-compliance
Lightning Source LLC
Chambersburg PA
CBHW020927020726
47495CB00002B/383